FLIGHT OF PASSION

"Yes, yes . . ." purred Micheline, long lashes fluttering over her violet eyes. She commenced to unbutton young Nat Mather's shirt.

The *Union*, the observation balloon that was carrying the girl aeronaut and the tall naval lieutenant, had traveled westward at five hundred feet to the Confederate side of the James River, and now was riding a strong breeze back to Fort Monroe.

The euphoria of flight had stirred their passions. Far above the agony of war and the misery of mud, one kiss led to another. Together, they slipped down to the floor of the gondola, azure sky and bright clouds above them. Micheline giggled and said something about 'love in the sky.'

"Then it's war you want . . ." Nat undid her blouse and she drew him down upon her.

To a seaman far below, on the frigate *U.S.S. St. Lawrence*, the balloon's wicker gondola seemed to be buffeted by unusual updrafts for a short period, before regaining its stability and descending toward Fort Monroe.

The Making of America Series

THE WILDERNESS SEEKERS
THE MOUNTAIN BREED
THE CONESTOGA PEOPLE
THE FORTY-NINERS
HEARTS DIVIDED
THE BUILDERS
THE LAND RUSHERS
THE WILD AND THE WAYWARD
THE TEXANS
THE ALASKANS
THE GOLDEN STATERS
THE RIVER PEOPLE
THE LANDGRABBERS
THE RANCHERS
THE HOMESTEADERS
THE FRONTIER HEALERS
THE BUFFALO PEOPLE
THE BORDER BREED
THE FAR ISLANDERS
THE BOOMERS
THE WILDCATTERS
THE GUNFIGHTERS
THE CAJUNS
THE DONNER PEOPLE
THE CREOLES
THE NIGHTRIDERS
THE SOONERS
THE EXPRESS RIDERS
THE VIGILANTES
THE SOLDIERS OF FORTUNE
THE WRANGLERS
THE BAJA PEOPLE
THE YUKON BREED
THE SMUGGLERS
THE VOYAGEURS
THE BARBARY COASTERS
THE WHALERS
THE CANADIANS
THE PROPHET'S PEOPLE
THE LAWMEN
THE COPPER KINGS
THE CARIBBEANS
THE TRAIL BLAZERS
THE GAMBLERS
THE ROBBER BARONS
THE ASSASSINS
THE BOUNTY HUNTERS
THE TEXAS RANGERS
THE OUTLAWS
THE FUGITIVES

THE FUGITIVES

Lee Davis Willoughby

A DELL/JAMES A. BRYANS BOOK

Published by
Dell Publishing Co., Inc.
1 Dag Hammarskjold Plaza
New York, New York 10017

Dell TM 681510, Dell Publishing Co., Inc.

ISBN: 0-440-02770-5

Printed in the United States of America

First printing—May 1984

"The first man I killed, I saw but twenty seconds; but I shall remember him forever. I was standing by my gun when a rebel soldier rushed up and lunged with his bayonet. I whipped out my revolver, and took him through the breast. He tossed up his arms, gave me the strangest look in the world, and fell forward on his face. He had blue eyes, brown, curling hair, a dark mustache, and a handsome face. I thought, the instant I shot, that I should have loved that man had I known him . . ."

—Anonymous Union Artilleryman, 1864

ONE

Jubilant cheers rose from the emerald banks of Lake Quinsigamond as the six-oared rowing shell, manned by blue-shirted stalwarts, spurted forward to within a length of the adversary from Cambridge. A third entrant in the annual intercollegiate event, Brown University's boat, was a half-mile behind.

Eager young ladies in billowing triangular white crinolines, flowered straw hats with trailing ribbons, and buffeted glacé parasols, strained for glimpses of their brothers and beaus. Glum round-hatted fathers in dark sack coats and dundreary whiskers maintained puritanical miens, befitting their stations in the clergy and respected professions. Here and there a woman—a mother—betrayed by emotion, waved the color of her son's school. Tutor's children, little girls in flat hats and zouave jackets giggled as their brass-buttoned brothers pulled toy boats and rolled hoops into the choppy water.

Clumps of undergraduates, holding onto their Panama

hats, urged on their midsummer heroes while boisterous townies from Worcester screeched from the elm trees.

"Stroke . . . stroke . . . stroke," cox'n Howell Swann Clyburn shouted in cadence as he gripped the rudder lines firmly, correcting for crosswind gusts. Nathaniel Mather, on stroke oar, looked up breathlessly as the count increased from forty to forty-five per minute. He wanted a sign—a glint in the cox'n's eye that would say "We're catching up." The Yale crew, backs pitching in unison toward the rapier bow, were as blind men, seeing only Brown's entrant hopelessly outdistanced astern, and *hearing* the whoosh of Harvard's oars ahead. With the stroke increased, Yale's six-oared cedar shell spurted ahead, raising a cheer from the shore.

One by one, the crew glanced sideways and saw the crimson adversary slide aft until the shells were parallel, long sweeps a scant yard from touching tips. Now the Harvard cox'n increased his stroke, and once more regained the lead. Howell, undaunted, called for forty-eight. Again the Yale boat clawed forward and was about to prevail when a sharp snap sounded. A starboard thole pin had sheared off, 'crabbing' its oar in the water. Yale's momentum was not enough and Harvard streaked by seconds before the gun.

Bess Mather tingled with proud feelings as the crews rowed briskly to the pier. It was like a victory even if her brother's boat lost, since the year before, Harvard had won by a full minute. She primped her auburn hair, lifted her skirts slightly and hurried down toward the landing, stopping for a moment to admire the quick sketching of the event by a *Harper's Weekly* artist. Waving her petite parasol, Bess took a short cut through a grove of elms as exuberant shouts were heard. . . . "You fellows were lucky" . . . "Just wait till next year; we'll show you."

"Bess," a well-dressed businessman startled her, stepping from behind a tree. "Howell is a right good-looking young man, but what you need is a well-to-do gentleman, like myself."

"Mister Whitlock," she chided, "now what would people say if they saw me with a married man, especially the brother-in-law of the man I am promised to."

Drawing in his vested paunch, Cyrus Whitlock took her gloved wrist and pulled her behind a large elm. "Bess, girl—this is the nineteenth century. Engagements and marriages are to be endured, yes; but that doesn't mean you can't have a little fun now and then." He tried to kiss her, but she resisted.

"Mister Whitlock," her eyes flashed in disbelief.

After furtively looking about, the businessman smiled contentedly. "We wouldn't want your father to find out about your indiscretion with Swanny, would we?"

At that, Bess slumped against the tree and Whitlock released her, then lit a cigarette. "Have one, my child? All the rage in Europe. Support your friendly southern states."

Bess declined with a shrug. "Just what are you talking about, Mister Whitlock. What about me and Howell?"

He leaned closer with one raised eyebrow. "The boathouse at Tomlinson's bridge on the Fourth of July. Everyone was at the clambake, except for three people. I'd gone inside to look at the *Atlanta*—beautiful boat built in Brooklyn. Then a young lady entered, leading a member of the Yale crew. They were carrying on so, that—well, I didn't want to intrude, so I climbed into the loft, while below me, the aforementioned couple got into the boat. Bess, you've got a right pretty birthmark."

Bess felt faint, almost swooning, and Whitlock tried

to assist her, but she pushed him away, dropping her parasol. "As I said, Bess—nobody wants any trouble, eh? So why don't ya stop on by the mill next time you pass and I'll give you a little tour. I'm putting on an addition that'll make me the richest man in the fair city of Stamford, Connecticut."

Bess snapped the parasol from his gloved hand. "Just what is it you're after, Mister Whitlock?"

Before he could answer, she'd run almost to the dock.

"And verily I say unto thee . . ." Gideon Mather boomed from the pulpit of the new Fourth Congregational Church of Stamford, "our brethren from New Haven who have opened up the wilderness in the territory of Kansas are yet in dire need of funds. The committee has informed me that twenty-two picked men have need of arms to protect our brave brethren from their vicious enemies, the slavers and the wolves, and to provide sustenance from the land. The territory of Kansas must enter the Union as a free state. As my colleague, the Honorable Mister Beecher has put forth so eloquently: 'it is the Constitution itself which is the cause of every division that this vexed question of slavery has occasioned in this country. The veins of the land are large, but they cannot hold the double blood of liberty and slavery.' "

Reverend Mather snapped his fingers and a robed elder came forth brandishing a rifle. "We Easterners don't know much about game rifles, so brother Ezra will demonstrate—with blank cartridges of course. The struggle in Kansas is but one bud on the tree of liberty. Each of our "protectors" in the territory will have pistols and shotguns, but each will want, and ought to have, a Sharps rifle or a carbine. Brother Ezra; if you please."

The church elder pointed the rifle upward, fired,

snapped down the breechblock, loaded and fired in quick succession, getting off six reverberating rounds in less than twenty seconds. The congregation, those who didn't duck in their pews, emitted sounds of awe as the smoke curled up toward the lofty ceiling, picking up stained glass colors from the morning sun.

"Again, in the words of Reverend Beecher: 'There is more moral power in one of these instruments as far as slave-holders are concerned than in one hundred bibles,' " continued Gideon Mather with dramatic gestures. "It is time that you opened your purses as well as your hearts. We need, in concert with the New Haven Congregational Church, to raise money for the purchase of twenty-two rifles. Let us show Kansas that the North is more than just one city. I shall start by contributing twenty-five dollars for the purchase of one rifle."

Gideon Mather held up a purse as if it were an offering to God, then drew out two gold coins. At a beckon, a choirboy holding a large pewter plate climbed up the pulpit stairs. With a beam of sunlight from a window high above the altar dancing on his white hair and poised hand, Mather dropped first the twenty-dollar piece on the plate, shattering the silence and then the smaller coin, prompting a murmur of approval.

"The boy shall pass amongst you, my friends. Open your hearts against vile slavery and for the free State of Kansas," extolled the Reverend, "For those who wish to give substantially, there will be a separate get-together after the service. Come join me for coffee in the meeting-room. All generous contributions will be recorded."

While the collection plate was being passed, Bess Mather, in the choir loft, caught Howell Clyburn's eye, but quickly looked down at her hymnal as Cyrus Whitlock, sitting beside the South Carolinian, smiled at her. The factory owner conspicuously dropped a silver dollar into the plate. Howell, not a one to hide his leanings, held up a penny before dropping it, to the embarrassment of his elder sister, Dinah, wife of Cyrus Whitlock.

The collection over, the choir rose and sang a hymn of Thanksgiving:

Come ye thankful people, come;
Raise the song of Harvest-home.
All is safely gathered in
Ere the winter storms begin . . .

TWO

Richmond, Friday,
December 10, 1859

Dear Nathaniel:

How I envy you, ensconced in the cozy embrace of Academe in pursuit of the secrets of chemistry and mechanics. What I would give to sojourn once more in old South College . . . to chat on *The Fence* . . . to have an ale at Moriarty's! (which didn't exist when I graduated with the class of '51).

Trusting that you are in as good health as you were on that delightful day of the regatta where I met your charming family, I must inform you that I am in a melancholy mood brought on by the rejection of my last Harper's assignment. No doubt you've read by now, several versions of John Brown's execution. Mine was returned to me, I suspect, because I was not vehement enough in deriding Mr. Brown as a madman for our Southern readers, and not elevating him to sainthood as the Northerners would have it. A stalemate! At least they may run the drawings. I suggested a solution to my editor: Publish two editions . . . Harper's Southern and Northern Weeklies.

One fact that you may not read in others' accounts was that Mr. Brown was shot and wounded *after* his surrender to Colonel Lee's Company of stalwart Marines. Incidentally, the abolitionists are loath to know that the raid on Harper's Ferry was facilitated by Sharps carbines originally sent to Kansas Territory by certain groups of citizens in New England. Is it true that our alma mater is also buying bullets for the pioneers? Ah, I am truly a man without a country. I believe in the status quo, therefore I am both against and for slavery. What would you expect from a Mason-Dixon liner?

However, all was not in vain. The celebrated Lydia Child had published that she wanted a good likeness of John Brown to hang in her Bay State chateau, so after the hanging, I removed Mr. Brown's hood and sketched a dynamic portrait which I hope she will purchase.

While I have your attention, may I be so bold as to tell you I shall be in Boston after the holidays, and the multiple abilities of "Porte Pencil" will be available for functions and portraits on the return trip. I shall send you particulars shortly.

With my sincerest remembrances to the Reverend and Mrs. Mather, and your lovely sister, Bess, I am,

Very respectfully and truly yours,
David Robarts, (alias P.P.)

Nat Mather folded the letter neatly and slipped it into his inner coat pocket. ''David Robarts may stop by after the holidays. You remember—the correspondent who drew sketches at Quinsigamond last summer . . .''

''Yes, of course . . . the socialite from the Potomac who has Southern connections and Yankee bosses,'' Howell Swann Clyburn stoked the fire, then took one of his toy cast-iron penny banks down from the white marble mantelpiece. ''Curious, my friend,'' he blew dust from the toy, ''that in this very room, labored a student, class of 1792. Shortly after matriculation he invented a machine which allowed me to enroll here as well—seventy years later. And he was a Yankee to boot.'' Howell set the penny bank down on his writing-table.

''Eli Whitney didn't do it for the *South,*'' Nat chuckled as he leaned down toward the fire and lit his tobacco pipe with a flaming taper. ''The cotton mills of Massachusetts and Connecticut owe their success to him as well. . . .''

''Then,'' Howell balanced a penny on the cast-iron hand of one of three miniature figures atop the toy bank with an engraved title on its rectangular flat base: DARKTOWN BATTERY, ''then. Yale's most illustrious graduate is responsible for slavery. The cotton gin has made it necessary to bring in more field hands, and without the sweat and toil in the fields, your abolitionists would have nothing to crow about. They never allow that personal servants live as well as some whites . . . and what about the Irish immigrants in New York and Boston? I hear they don't live as well as South Carolina's field hands . . .''

''But the Irish are *free.*'' Firelight flickered on Nat's dark brown hair. ''What the country needs now is a machine that will *pick* cotton. That will end the worst part of slavery.''

"Well, Yankee, you're the mechanical genius here. You invent a pickin' gin an' we'll send all the niggers back to Africa."

"Swanny, most of them were born *here*."

"Then you kin have 'em in Connecticut; I hear they make good shoemakers," laughed Howell as he pressed a lever on the penny bank, tripping a spring that flung the coin from the pitcher's hand past the batter's futile swing. Caught in the catcher's glove, it fell through a slot into the bank. Howell Clyburn laughed and repeated the action. "Lookee heah, friend," he drawled, "these niggahs cain't ever do anything right."

"I wouldn't say that, Swanny. The pitcher and catcher are doing all right—and they are iron negroes in the bargain. . . ."

"Nathan," Howell set the penny bank back on the mantelpiece, "do you know what the townsfolk are calling abolitionists?"

"In Charleston, unprintable."

"No; in New Haven . . . Connecticut in general. Nothing derogatory, suh. They are called *Gideons*."

"After my father, no doubt."

"Or after a biblical conqueror."

Nat reached into a satchel by the side of his chair and drew out a book. "Swanny, I'll never be like my father. He was so furious when I didn't apply for divinity school and continue the Mather Congregational dynasty. I told him there were many other Mathers in the business who could do better than I. Besides, I could never reconcile religion with science. Look what I bought in town today." He held up the volume proudly. "It came in from London hardly a week ago. I was lucky to get the last copy." Nat handed it to the southerner who held the title page up to the whale-oil lamp and drawled slowly:

"On the Origin of Species by Means of Natural Selection, or, the Preservation of Favored Races in the Struggle for Life. . . . by Charles Robert Darwin. . . ." He thumbed through the pages. "Very heavy reading and no pictures."

"It's going to become the Bible of the natural sciences, ultimately leading to proof that man himself has evolved through processes no different from those of the lowliest animals. The book will be damned by the clergy as a contradiction of the canon of divine creation. . . ."

"A jolly Christmas present for the Reverend," quipped Howell. "What does it say about niggers? Surely they came from monkeys. . . ."

"Swanny, Darwin is English and England doesn't have the problem of slavery that we have here."

"Then they just keep their slaves in other countries, as in India and the Caribbean. I see little difference." Howell got up and rummaged in his chest of drawers. Taking out a flat, leather-covered case, he sat before the fire again and opened it, revealing an unusual pocket revolver and an assortment of cartridges and accessories. The polished brass-trimmed weapon glinted, evil-hued, as Howell admired it in the firelight. "Jes' got this—sent all the way from New Orleans. Invented and made by one Doctor Jean Francois Le Mat of that city. General Beauregard speaks highly of it, and recommends that it be used by the military services, especially for use against Indians and other savages. Nine balls in the cylinder," Howell turned it, "and from here—this center barrel, a load of grapeshot. . . ."

"For a medical student, you have some strange interests."

"Well, one never knows. Ah could be riding 'tween

callin' on ailin' planters, and run smack up agin' a pack of Nat Turner's kind, armed to their white teeth . . ."

"Or Nat *Mather's* kind—"

"Gideon Mather, maybe . . . or John Brown. Hell, Nat, you damn well know I jes' like to rile you Yankees. What say we go on out for some of Marm Dean's coffee an' waffles?"

THREE

The tiny, green speckled swamp frog struggled in vain—pierced through its neck by a fishhook and being dangled on the olive surface of slow-moving Flat Rock Creek. At the other end of the fifteen-foot oak sapling, a pair of strong, ebony-hued hands worked the bait under ponderous flowering magnolia branches.

"C'mon now, fish . . . bite," Josiah Holladay entreated the unseen quarry that he knew would be heading downstream after a spawning summer, thence into the Wateree branch of the bounteous Santee River and on to the sea, a hundred miles away. A paradise, the Santee valley, from the primeval Blue Ridge Mountains to its Atlantic delta, abounding with lush vegetation and teaming with wing, claw and fin—a paradise for the free.

On occasion, Josiah's brown eyes would wander, watching the snowy egrets wading the marsh shallows, and he'd listen for the resonant sweet call of the Carolina wren in the vine-draped cottonwoods. Suddenly, a tremor in his long sapling and the bait was pulled under, dipping the end deep underwater, gut leader and all. A silver flash darted to the surface and broke clear in a froth of white, dancing on its tail before falling back and under—unable to shake the hook loose.

Playing the fish, letting it dive and run, Josiah steadily pulled in the long sapling, hand over hand. The fish, now exhausted, leapt once more in defiance, spitting out the frog and fell on its side, bold, iridescent black stripes from gill to tail marking it as a rock bass. "Tenny, ah got it—come quick," Josiah excitedly pulled the two-foot-long fish up over the muddy bank and into the grass.

A sixteen-year-old girl of light coffee color, delicate pink zephyr lily in her hair, sprang from a bay of fragrant myrtle, lithe body rippling under a short turquoise blue shift. "Josie," she squealed with delight. "Now we can celebrate; that beautiful rockfish ain't ever gonna see Marse's fancy table."

"No siree." Josiah's glistening bare shoulders tensed with pride as he held the weakly flapping fish down and raised his arm clenching a stone.

"Josiah." Tenah turned away.

"Then don' look—this is the way it has to be."

Tenah looked up at a clearing among the high cypresses and cottonwoods. A buzzard kited in the bright sky while a red-headed woodpecker hammered on a dead branch. From downstream came the low whistle of a steamboat on the parent Wateree, bound for Charleston, hull-down with a load of baled cotton.

"Tell me agin, Josie; it sounds so good." Tenah opened a basket and set out two tin plates on a worn patchwork quilt.

Wrapping the hot frying-pan handle in leaves, Josiah slid a piece of bacon back and forth then set it sizzling back on the stone-rimmed fire. Sharpening his bowie knife on a flat rock, he deftly cut filets from the bass, trimmed them and dropped them into the pan. "We eat only th' best pieces." He flung the remains into the creek as Tenah portioned out bread and a candied yam salad that she had prepared in Oak Hill's kitchen for the evening's supper.

Josiah stood up squarely to his full six feet. "Tell you agin what, honey girl?"

"What you tol' me las' night."

He smiled and swaggered proudly. "Tenah ain't gonna be Tenah nothing any mo'. She's to be Mrs. Josiah Holladay, otherwise known as Tenah Holladay . . ."

"Ain't never had a proper last name." She fluttered her long lashes as Josiah tended to the sizzling fish. "When you gonna tell the Marse about us?"

"By an' by, there's time."

Tenah didn't continue the subject, saying not a word other than nodding for a helping of rock bass

"How come yer so quiet? Ain't like you a'tall."

She stared blankly at him. "Thas because—because, maybe, I think—mind you I ain't said nothin' about . . ."

"C'mon girl," Josiah's eyes rolled.

Tenah smiled sheepishly, then patted her stomach. "Our baby will have a good name too. . . ."

"Damn, little honey—you sure?" Josiah burned his hand on the frying pan in his astonishment.

She looked deep into his eyes and nodded seriously, then he sidled over to her and took her in his arms. "I'll talk to Marse Clyburn tomorrow in the mornin' before he's had 'is dinner."

"Or his likker," added Tenah, "an' I won't let on to my folks til we're sure."

"Sure about what?" Josiah was perplexed.

"Jes' everything, that's all. When we're sure, then you can even write a proper letter like white folks do when they get married, an' send it by mail down to Moultrieville. My folks—they're gonna be so happy for their little girl."

"This is not the Maxwell plantation." Whitemarsh Clyburn shuffled some papers on his leather-inlaid cherry desk. "I don't run my place like they used to so you might as well forget you ever worked there. Josiah, you take my advice. It would not be in the girl's best interests if I said yes. Tenah is too young to get married even if she says she wants to."

Standing hat in hand before Clyburn and wearing his Sunday clothes, Josiah hid the rage that was welling within him. "But Marse Clyburn, I promise to work very hard for you. Ah'll do the work of two men if you jes let me marry Tenah. . . ."

Clyburn pulled at his greying sidewhiskers, appearing to revaluate his decision. Leaning back in his upholstered chair, he hummed and grunted, and toyed with his black string tie. "Josiah," his voice softened, "perhaps I've been a trifle hasty. Tell you what. I'll talk to Mrs. Clyburn and see what she thinks. Give me a few days and I'll have an answer." The planter waved his visitor off then reached for his writing-paper.

Low mackerel clouds, edge-lit orange over the swamp fog and sun not yet risen; a figure sat on the stacked cordwood behind the smokehouse reading by the light of a squat candle:

> "Ye see what ye'd get" said Legree, caressing the dogs with grim satisfaction, and turning to Tom and his companions. "ye see what ye'd get, if ye tried to run off. These yer dogs has been raised to track niggers; and they'd jest as soon chaw one on ye

up as to eat their supper. So mind yerself! How now Sambo!'' he said, to a ragged fellow, without any brim to his hat, who was—*officious* in his attentions . . .

Josiah recited the word out loud, but it made no sense to him. He scribbled the page number on a scrap of paper folded and tucked inside the back cover. How fortunate he'd been to have Missis Maxwell teach him to read and write. When the good Marse and the boy died of the fever, the missis said she would have to sell one of the fieldhands to pay for new seed and tools. He volunteered, knowing that he'd be sold to the Clyburns downriver. One of the reasons he volunteered was that he'd often seen Tenah in Camden doing the marketing with Missis Clyburn. How pretty she was, all decked out in fancy maid's duds . . .

''Josiah, where in all hades—'' Gregory's shout startled him and he slipped the forbidden *Uncle Tom's Cabin* into its oilskin envelope and slid it into a crevice under the smokehouse. The elder white-haired slave, seeing Josiah, threw his hands up. ''Now what you settin' out hyar fer, boy. Ye sposed to be in de shack. Massa want to see ye quick now, befo dere's hell to pay.''

''Jes watchin' the sunrise; ain't no law agin that.''

One of Josiah's weekly tasks was to deliver the plantation's mail to the Camden Post Office and return with the incoming. For this trip Clyburn had given him an extra errand—to deliver a letter to Mr. Pierce Jeter, owner of the Camden livery, and wait for a written reply.

While galloping along the river road, Josiah's horse shied at a fallen branch and threw him, scattering the mail pouch contents. Satisfied that no bones were broken and rubbing his bruised knee, he picked up the envelopes. One of them, having a loose flap, had disgorged its note. As Josiah was about to insert the letter, something caught his eye. His own name! Heart thumping, he slowly read it:

Oak Hill, Friday, July 13, 1860

Dear Pierce,

The bearer of this letter, Josiah Holladay, is about 23 years old and in the best of health. Aside from being an industrious field hand, he is a good carpenter and mechanic.

For certain reasons I am offering him up for sale to buyers outside of this county, preferably outside of this state. I will pay for his transport in addition to your commission. There will also be a bonus if the transaction is completed within two weeks. The price is firm at $1500. If you agree to these terms, send me a sealed note by the same bearer and keep this as binding.

Your Affec. Friend,
Whitemarsh S. Clyburn

Nervously replacing the letter, Josiah spit on his hand and moistened the gummed envelope flap. He then pressed it firmly against the leather mail pouch. Nervousness mounted to rage and only the thought of Tenah stopped him from ripping the letter to shreds. He remounted his horse and continued on to Camden. So this was Marse's plan. How humorous and degrading . . . to send the slave with his own announcement. But Clyburn would never laugh with the other planters at their grogshops. Now the laugh would be on Clyburn. He would play a dumb nigger and go along with the scheme, while forming his own plan. There was no choice . . . his child, Tenah's child—their child, would be freeborn.

Louisa Clyburn, propped up with pillows, sat motionless in her bed on the second floor of Oak Hill Mansion, looking out over the plantation's cotton fields that stretched to the western horizon. Not that she was sick, but Doctor Guerard had advised that she rest a good part of the day until his next call. Her constant headaches were a result of overwork and anxiety, especially since Dinah had gone north and gotten married to Cyrus Whitlock, a man old enough to be her father. It was easier, having Dinah to help manage after Howell had gone off to school. And her husband's drinking—it was a wonder there was any profit at all. Louisa stared at the daguerreotypes, standing like so many gravestones on her bedside table. Howell; blond and light-complexioned, as is Marsh—the Scotch strain, Dinah; dark and brooding, five years older than her brother—the Huguenot strain, spiced with Marions, Porchers, Prioleaus, and Galliards. Galliards. Louisa reached out and turned her father's picture toward her.

A quarter century earlier she had left the Galliard plantation—ruined after a hurricane changed the Santee from a river into a raging sea, all the way from the Delta to St. Stephens. A thirty-mile inland sea where once there had been homes and farms. She had left the lower Santee, as did many of her neighbors, for the safer upcountry—and for Marsh Clyburn. Now her husband was a stranger, a cussin', drinkin' planter. And her room was all that was left of the safe, old upcountry. Louisa looked at her hands. Puffy and wrinkled, just like the face she didn't want to see. She twirled her long, black hair about a finger and imagined that she was young again . . .

"Missis Clyburn, ma'am, can I bring your dinner in?" Tenah waited beyond the closed door, but Louisa didn't answer.

"Tenah," a hushed whisper startled her. "Go on down to Marse's rooms. He wants you to tidy up. Heah, you give me the tray now." Gregory frowned and pointed to the stairway. Abruptly, Tenah hiked up her skirts and scampered down.

Goody, she thought as she dusted the library shelves. Marse ain't here. Hate to work down here when he is. All these books, she marvelled. Nobody ever reads them . . . can tell by the dust. Wish I could read; then I could pick out a book for Josie. He's gonna teach me, by and by, an' I'll teach the little one. She stopped before the floor globe, dusted a little then tucked the duster under her arm. Next, she touched the globe and it moved; turned slowly inside its polished, fancy wood frame. There were pictures of animals on a ring about the globe: fish, a lion, a cow. She pushed harder and the "world" spun around, stopping with a landform before her that she recognized as Africa. Once more, Tenah surveyed the room, looking into the Marse's private study to make sure he wasn't around.

She examined the coastline of Africa, wondering from which place her great-grandparents had come. How she wished she could read. She might remember a name. A river or a city that the old slaves had talked or sung about. Tenah recalled what old Lemuel said just before he died. He spoke of a Governor of South Carolina . . . a Mr. Hammond and what he said many years ago: "Allow our slaves to read the writings of the abolitionists, and they'll cut our throats. That's why it is a crime to teach slaves to read."

She traced her finger from the coastline of Africa to

the interior where there was no writin' at all. Suddenly she was aware of a strong smell behind her. Whiskey! Before she could move, a brawny hand from behind grabbed her by her shoulder, and another, by her waist. She struggled and looked down. The hand was white, ruddy and freckled. There was a ruffled silk cuff and a gold ring in the shape of a snake, with green jewels for eyes. The snake and its attendant fingers moved up to her breast. Tenah knew better than to scream. This had happened once before and the hand had let go. And she'd run away and it was forgotten. But now it seemed different. She felt ashamed, for now she was promised—and the child. . . .

"Please, Marse Clyburn." She felt the raspy, wet whiskers on her neck, the panting, like an animal.

"Now, now, my little darky doll," Clyburn rumbled in her ear, groping about with his free hand. "Now ye wouldn't want to make things worsen they are fer a certain nigger who's out to Camden today, would ye?"

Tenah stopped struggling at the threat and Clyburn took advantage, his hand slipping under her skirts. "Ye didn't think I was about to let ye get married without first givin' me a little o' what I paid good money for." Squirming to get out of his violating grip, she saw his boot below her skirt. Measuring her heel against his toe behind her, she raised her knee and stomped down with all her might. With a shriek the planter let go, and clawing at his toe, danced and hopped in pain back to his lair. "Oh my dear, Marse Clyburn," cried out Tenah. "I'm so sorry I stepped on yer toe, suh. I'll get Gregory to see to it right away, suh. . . ."

FOUR

"Good afternoon, gentlemen," a clean-shaven, sandy-haired young man dressed in backwoods Indian attire save for expensive riding boots, sprang lithely out of the brush bordering one of Oak Hill's cotton fields. From his neck hung a strange contraption: two short spyglasses attached together. Following him came a Negro servant leading a pack mule laden with a folded tent and a profusion of sacks, boxes and valises.

Josiah shaded his eyes with a sweat-covered arm, then set down his bag of cotton. The sun was high and it was almost time to rest and enjoy some shade and the midday grits. Following Josiah's example the other dozen hands, including several women laid down their pickings and gathered under a large oak nearby.

"I am Alexander Ross, professor of ornithology—that means the study of birds. This is my freeman, Jesse. We've come from Canada." Ross joined the others under the oak as Jesse tethered the mule. "I've come to the Santee country in search of some rare birds that were described by a Mister Audubon who journeyed here a few years ago. Perhaps you can help me,'' he addressed Josiah in particular since the others seemed more interested in their food and drink than in the subject of birds. Ross gestured to his man: ''The *Audubon,* please.'' Jesse dug into a saddle bag, drew out a large book and handed it to Ross.

''Here,'' he opened the book and displayed a color print. ''This is the ivory-billed woodpecker. Do you know where I might find one?'' Some of the field hands, sitting on the oak roots and adjacent ground nodded in recognition. Josiah, interested, got up and examined the color print closely.

''They are in the deep forest and hard to catch,'' exclaimed the young slave. ''The Cherokees hunt them for their beaks and trade them in the mountains. One bird for three deerskins.''

''My, my, they are valuable. Since I have no deerskins and would never shoot a deer, I must either catch the bird myself or buy some deerskins and trade with the Cherokees. But that is my concern and I shall solve it.'' The professor looked around nervously as if he was expecting someone. ''Tell me,'' he confided to Josiah, ''do you know of any blackbirds who might want to fly north?''

Josiah grinned. ''I might, but where is north?''

''Canada, where all birds are free.''

''Is it possible to go north to Connecticut?''

''Why Connecticut?''

''My mother is a free woman in Stamford of that state. I would like to go to her and bring my wife. That is, we would be married when we get there. A proper marriage.''

''I'm afraid the migration route for blackbirds into

Canada is by way of Ohio or Pennsylvania, but I'll see what I can do.'' Ross took a pencil and notepad from his shirt pocket. ''Your name and that of the plantation and its owner. . . .''

''Josiah Holladay— Oak Hill, Marse Clyburn.''

''Very well, Mister Holladay . . .'' Ross turned to the others. ''Perhaps some of your friends?''

The ornithologist had taken down the names of several hands who voiced interest in going to Canada when a cloud of dust heralded the approach of a rider across the field. The fieldhands scattered and resumed picking as the horseman galloped to a stop before the professor, who was preparing to leave.

''What you'all want heah, man? Ah seen you talkin' to the niggahs. You aint rilin' em up now. . . .''

''I'm Doctor Alexander Ross—ornithologist.''

''Don' care much whut ye are—yer trespassin'. Ah'm the foreman on this heah plantation an' ah got my orders.'' Willie Joe Grubb snapped his long, black whip menacingly into the ground before Ross, causing his mount to rear up.

''I was merely asking for information. . . .''

''Then you ask me; those dumb niggers don' know nothin.''

''As you wish,'' Ross smiled shrewdly. ''I am looking for a certain bird. It's called *P. Principalis*.''

Grubb's jaw dropped and he scratched his head under the sweat-stained brim of his hat.

''Sorry, my good man. Of course I should not use the Latin. I need a specimen of your ivory-billed woodpecker for my collection, and I'm willing to pay well.''

''Fer fi' dollars a piece, Ahl git ye a bushel.''

"Alive?"

"Hell, no. Ah catch 'em with rat pison on th' trees. All ye want is th' beak anyway."

"I'll think about it, Mister—"

"Grubb. Willie Joe Grubb."

FIVE

It was almost dawn when Josiah, leading Tenah by a quivering hand, pushed open the wrought-iron gate of the Quaker cemetery on Wateree Street in the town of Camden. They had walked for hours, leaving Oak Hill in the small hours of Sunday morning, comforted in that the evening's revelry had rendered both Grubb and Clyburn tipsy enough to sleep til noon. Time enough to get out of Kershaw County before being missed. The Underground Railroad agent that Doctor Ross had put in touch with Josiah was confident that the coastline route north would further aid the runaways since the usual route from the Camden area was through Cherokee County and over the Blue Ridge Mountains. Grubb's hounds would be pointed up the Congaree valley.

Josiah opened his satchel and took out a candle. The agent had been very specific: "Go to the far end of the burial ground and find a stone marked *Agnes of Glasgow*. At this place, a conductor will arive at dawn and ask for the password. . . ."

Shielding the candle flame with his hand, Josiah went from stone to stone. What would have been the plan if he were not able to read? Thanks again to Missis Maxwell, bless her. The gravestones were all of simple appearance—ordinary bricks arched and cemented around small stone plaques. The Quakers observed simplicity in death as well as life.

"Here she be," Josiah proudly whispered. "Agnes of Glasgow . . . born 1761 . . . died 1780. . . ."

"She was so young," Tenah touched the stone.

"Probably the fever."

"And she had no real last name. I wonder if she was a slave too. Do Quakers have servants?"

"Not from Glasgow," Josiah blew out the candle, "that's a city across the ocean—in Scotland."

"I'm so proud of you, Josie. You know so much. I will learn too; so will our child. . . ."

"What is the password?" A woman's voice behind them. For a moment, Josiah was unable to answer, to remember the word. Such was the effect of being startled in a graveyard.

The woman, in dark silhouette, repeated the question.

"Denmark," blurted Josiah. It was a reference to Denmark Vesey, a free mulatto from Haiti who incited a slave rebellion in Charleston a generation earlier.

"Well, then," the woman's voice became softer, "Come along now, we've a lot to do." Shawl hiding her face from the brightening eastern sky, she beckoned the runaways to follow. Passing by the Meeting House, they went into a stable behind it and descended a stair into a provisions cellar. The woman walked over to a wall oil lamp, turned it up, then knocked twice with her hand on the paneling. Presently a vertical section of the wall moved aside, sliding on the baseboard, revealing a large, well-stocked storeroom and workshop with a cadre of busy Quakers.

"Welcome." A deep, resonant voice dominated the scene as a tall, ascetic-looking man wiht white side-whiskers and piercing eyes stepped forward with a hand extended. "Welcome, friends, to the Kershaw County station of the celebrated and despised Underground Railroad." Looking as if he'd stepped down from a Gilbert Stuart portrait, thumbs propped behind his coat lapels, he continued: "I am Silas Coffin, your stationmaster. I take you to be—," the Quaker adjusted his wire-rimmed glasses to a small book he drew from his pocket—"Mister Josiah Holladay . . . and the young lady is Miss Tenah. Come into our station and make yourself comfortable while we look at our timetables and prepare for the trip." The wall panel slid mysteriously back into position, cutting off the station from the stable. Tenah was bewildered as the woman who brought them had disappeared. Noticing her surprise, Coffin explained: "Certain of our agents have to remain unknown for obvious reasons. That woman's territory ends in the stable and mine begins here. You will notice that everyone in this room has a definite function. A person for the clothing stores, another attending the food, another the hardware, and so on. In this way and only in this way can an organization such as ours succeed, especially this deep in the south. . . ."

Josiah and Tenah were ushered to a table where they sat and were given a breakfast that would have made the plantation owner envious. Bacon, eggs, ham, grits and melon. "If runnin' away is like this," Josiah grinned, "I'm gonna run away more often."

Sipping hot coffee, Coffin went on: "Our organization depends on secrecy, on trust, and on each other.

There will be times when, on your journey, the agent or stationmaster will tell you to do something and not say why or with whom. Trust him, for he has good reasons, reasons learned and passed on since the Railroad's tracks were first laid down, and even before that—when our predecessors knew only the carriage. During this period people have not changed; they will be honest, they will lie, they will steal, they will give. Trust us to know, or you will never get to your destination. What you see here is not to be divulged to anyone, even upon reaching your promised land, for the enemy has agents also—even, I fear, where we least expect.

"I caution you especially, should you have any ideas of who inserted the notice of the cemetery meeting in your copy of *Uncle Tom's Cabin,* to be silent—lest that person be destroyed, and in turn, the freedom of many more enslaved souls.

"Now, may I introduce you to your new 'master', Mister Benjamin Fairfield, a poultry breeder of some renown, as well as one of the Railroad's most illustrious conductors. Mister Fairfield has guided more than fifty souls toward the drinking gourd, home of the north star, in violation of the state codes of Kentucky and the Carolinas. He's piloted them through forests and swamps by night and storm. Fair girls dressed as fancy ladies, men and boys as gentlemen or servants, men in women's clothing, girls dressed as boys. . . . On foot, horseback and buggies. In wagons under loads of hay, straw and furniture. In boxes and bags. Crossing the River Jordan of the slave by swimming or wading chin-deep; in boats, skiffs, dugouts, rafts, and often on a pine log. And he's never suffered one to be recaptured!

"Mister Fairfield and his charming wife are about to travel to Wilmington, North Carolina, as regards his business in selling poultry and provisions. You, Mister Holladay, will be his personal servant, and you, Miss Tenah, will serve Mrs. Fairfield."

Benjamin Fairfield was outwardly the epitome of a successful planter or businessman. His clothes were the latest tailored fashions from London, he was quick with a story and a kiss for the nearest lady. First to buy a round of drinks, he was also first to volunteer in civic and church functions. A southerner by birth, he detested slavery, but while among planters he upheld it. His wife, Eliza, quite the opposite, was quiet and introspective—given to reading the latest novels and inwardly lamenting the children that she couldn't have. All in all they made good parents for their charges.

"I'm looking forward to this trip," exclaimed Ben. "We haven't been to Wilmington in months." He studied the couple intently for a moment, then snapped his fingers. "We've got to get you all dressed up. We're goin' to a funeral!"

"Steady, now." The driver coaxed his brace of black horses as the tassled hearse rumbled around the bend on the road approaching the Scape River bridge, leading to Mayesville Station. Clattering over the wood slats the driver reigned in short as a swarthy woodsman stepped onto the bridge brandishing a long rifle.

"Pardon," the rifleman addressed the hearse driver, "but rules is rules, even on a Sunday mornin' " He walked over to the somber vehicle and peeked through one of the bevel-cut glass windows. Tipping his hat, he backed away, muzzle down and motioned the driver on toward Mayesville.

Inside the hearse, black mourning bands on their sleeves, the Fairfields sat at the heads of twin coffins which were covered with floral bouquets. Ben drew the curtains. First waiting for his wife to clear away the flowers, then he opened the coffin lids. "We've made it; you can get out now."

Josiah and Tenah rose as one, blinked incredulously at each other and climbed out. Eliza then replaced the bouquets.

"We'll get off at the station," Ben shifted a suitcase away from the rear door. "I'll send the rig up to Lynchburg's underground agent to wait a few days before going back to Camden." Ben sighed with relief and, to Eliza's consternation, drew out of his pocket an enormous Havana. "It's just phenomenal," he commented upon striking a match, "what the safety match has done for the cigar business."

Tiger emblazoned on a bronze plaque, the locomotive spewed white steam through its red wheels and snorted black smoke from its huge, conical funnel. Like a metal animal, it seemed to paw to a stop. Engineer waving from the green cab, the noon sun glinted on polished brass trim, whistle shrieking and bell clanging. An admiring crowd gathered to look at exquisite decorative panels, one, on the cab, featuring a crouching tiger with an exotic background of desert sands and palm trees. Over the green cowcatcher a cast-iron negro boy held a lantern outstretched. A warning for stray animals on the tracks.

"Marvelous machine," remarked Ben Fairfield as he helped Eliza up the stair into a passenger car. "It was built by a Pennsylvanian who had been a prominent jeweler. One might call the locomotive a diamond stickpin with wheels."

Asking to have the seats pivoted to face one-another, Ben and Eliza sat by the window, while their "servants" occupied the aisle seats. "Curious," observed Ben, "that in the north, Negroes, that is *free* Negroes, are often segregated on public transport, whereas here it is customary for servants to sit adjacent to their masters." Eliza looked up from her Harper's Magazine and whispered, "I think it amusing that the Underground Railroad is using the visible railroad." The three-car Wilmington and Manchester Line train chugged along a swamp's edge studded with a mute army of cypress stumps. Unfolding his copy of *The Charleston Courier,* Ben read the headline:

DOUGLAS SAYS LINCOLN VICTORY
NO JUSTIFICATION FOR SECESSION

The conductor, taking tickets, eyed the two young Negro servants for a moment, then looked at Ben's newspaper and chuckled. Ben slapped it sharply with his hand. "Now we know Yankee politicians are all damn fools, eh?"

"That's fer sure," the conductor went on his way.

Josiah strained to read the headline without being too obvious, so Ben turned the *Courier* around. "Mistah Douglas, he's a northerner," explained Josiah to Tenah, "and he run fo' president agin Mistah Lincoln. He said that if Lincoln gets elected, th' southern states, they should stay in th' Union."

Tenah put her knitting down, slipped her hand under it and touched Josiah's knee. "What will happen if they—*we* don't stay in the Union?"

"My child," Ben interjected as he watched a steamboat puffing down the Great Pee Dee River, "it will be up to the good Lord to influence the minds of the fanatical leaders on both sides and avert a calamity."

Approaching the town of Mullins, near the North Carolina state line, Eliza complained of dizzy spells. Shortly after Ben notified the conductor, a brusque, heavy-set man, dressed in a white linen coat and tawdry plaid trousers appeared, carrying a black leather bag upon which was lettered in flourished gold: *Rufus J. Bratton, M.D.* His perfunctory examination of Eliza was peppered with anecdotes about himself, and he gave voluminous information of the sights and conveniences of Wilmington, where he was going to attend a medical convention. Shaking his clinical thermometer down, he hesitated for maximum dramatic effect before delivering his diagnosis. "I don't think it's the fever, but just to be sure, her temperature should be taken again this evening and I'll be happy to oblige should you be staying in the vicinity of the Hanover House."

"We shall make a point of staying there," Ben drew out his money purse.

"Later," Bratton waved Ben off, then rubbed his chin, and added "Well, make it two dollars for now." Putting his instruments back in his bag, he hefted a pint bottle of bourbon. "Fairfield, ye said?" Ben nodded. "Where ye from?"

"Just east of Camden. We're new there. Moved up from Charleston a few months ago."

"That makes us practically neighbors. I'm from York County—north o' Kershaw. Say, Ben, if yer of a mind, leave yer wife rest a bit and we can, er, talk back where I'm at." Bratton showed Ben the bottle in his bag.

"Go on Ben," joshed Eliza. "The doctor's right. I'm tired and you can smoke a cigar in the next car. That'll cure me immediately. She motioned for Josiah and Tenah to come back and sit down. Tenah was strangely reluctant, and waited in the aisle until the doctor had left with Ben.

* * *

"Them's good-lookin' servants you got, Ben." Rufus Bratton poured Kentucky bourbon into both cups. "I could of sworn I'd seen that nigger girl before somewhere. How long she been your servant?"

"Hired her out from a planter down by James Island. She's got kin there," Ben lied. "Name's Mary."

"Reckon that wouldn't be the name o' the nigger gal I was tryin' to remember. She had a queer name. Gettin' so I can't tell 'em apart anymore. Hound dogs are easier—at least they got spots," guffawed the doctor.

"I guess you're right," Ben had become suspicious of Bratton's motives. The doctors' overture fit a pattern that Ben had experienced several times as an agent for the Underground Railroad. It was best to play along, especially in the 'enemy's' camp. "You're so knowledgeable, Doc. Are you also a planter?"

"I've got a few acres, you might say—and more than a few to work the place. One thing niggers respect is toughness—and being kept in their proper places. They feel a damn sight better when things are run with no hitches . . . when they know that they can't fool their masters." Bratton's thick, gray brows arched and he gritted his browning teeth. "But those crazy ones—the ones who get riled up by the abolitionists and all those book writers—sitting by cozy fires up north and writing about a life they no nothing about. We don't tell *them* how to live, so they shouldn't tell us. There aint gonna happen down here what happened up in Virginia when white women and children were axed to death by Nat Turner's gang. I aint gonna wait around an' have my throat slit in bed by an aborigine. We've got a bunch of boys up in York County that are organizing like an army just in case the niggers get too riled up by those northern Gideons. They all will have to reckon with our Clover Creek Clan."

"Do you belong to this . . . *clan*?"

"I kind of started it, but now I just help out when I can. Politics and business mostly."

"Has there been any need for this army so far?"

"One nigger family, free they were, got uppity so one of our boys rode over to their place wearin' a bedsheet with holes for 'is eyes an' mouth. He stood in front of their shack and drank a five-gallon bottle of water. All of it went into a rubber bag he wore under the sheet, but th' niggers got so scared they all ran away and we aint seen 'em since."

"Africans are very superstitious, I hear," Ben prodded on.

"Let me show you somethin'." Bratton stood up and swung a sack off the luggage rack. He undid the drawstring and reached it, bringing out a bleached human skull. "I got this hanging in my house," he held it by a hook bolted on its top. "It's a complete skeleton; you just hook the pieces together," he shook the sack, rattling the bones. "You'd die laughing at how the nigger kids and servants are afraid of it."

"Do you always travel with it?"

"I'm bringing it to Wilmington to exchange it because somebody played a fool joke on me. Look at this skull—it ain't no white man's skull. Jaw's too big. And you should see the arm bones—longer'n blazes. Nigger arm bones. That's what I get for buying something an' having it sent out in a box." Bratton pulled down the skull's jaw, tensing the spring and let it snap back with such impact that several teeth were knocked out and clattered into the aisle. But all the while Bratton was discoursing, he was also ransacking his memory about Fairfield's servant girl. As a practicer of physiognomy, he rarely forgot a face, or a body, especially a woman's. The servant's *café au lait* complexion, her slim, lithe figure, and the dimple on her chin. . . .

Ben, upon returning to Eliza, quickly briefed the runaways about the potential danger of recognition and "rechristened" them Mary and Dick for the duration of the trip.

As the train chugged past Waccamaw Lake in the Green Swamp approaching Wilmington, Doctor Bratton entered the car and abruptly spoke to Tenah.

"And what is your name, my dear?"

Taken aback, she hesitated, then answered "Mary." Bratton pondered a moment, then went on with his examination of Eliza as the servants again rose and stood in the aisle. "Mister Fairfield," the doctor concluded, "her temperature has not risen. That's a good sign. Unless Mrs. Fairfield feels worse this evening, there is no need for further concern. Should there be a change in her condition, just notify the desk at Hanover House and I'll stop by."

Leaving Eliza and his charges in their locked rooms, Ben spent the next two days contacting the Wilmington area UGRR and arranging the next leg of the journey north. The confrontations with Bratton indicated a need for inconspicuous operation. Clearly the doctor was suspicious, and to move to another hotel would only aggravate the predicament. It was also important that Eliza get as much rest as possible. Ben had food sent to the rooms or brought some up himself when advantageous. On Wednesday at noon he was called on the voice tube. It was Doctor Bratton.

"I have something of great urgency to discuss with you. May I order you a drink? I'm in the saloon."

Ben agreed to come down, but sensing a trap, first made his own plans with Eliza. He had never lost a slave and was not about to spoil his record.

When Ben arrived at the bar, lined with merchants, planters and professional people, Rufus Bratton offered him a cigar and set a glass of bourbon on a page of an open copy of the *Charleston Courier* next to a woodcut of a Negro running barefoot and carrying his belongings in a kerchief tied to a stick over his shoulder. The doctor's smug silence was a signal that Ben should read the advertisement. . . .

> HEAVY REWARD. Ran away on Saturday night, October 13, 1860, from the subscriber, my negro man Josiah Holladay and my female servant Tenah. The man, aged about 23, is 5 feet, eleven inches high, dark copper color, full suit of bushy hair, broad face, square shoulders, stands and walks very erect. Though industrious, he can be sluggish in action, except in a dance at which he is hard to beat. He is good at mechanics. He wore away a black coat & brown pantaloons. Also ran away at the same time, my girl, about 18 years old, of light brown color, round-featured, good looking and of ordinary size. She had on when she left a tan colored silk bonnet, dark plaid silk dress, a light muslin delaine and a watered silk cape. For the man I will give $1200 and for the girl $700 if taken and secured in jail so I can get them.
>
> W.S. Clyburn
> Oak Hill, S.C.

"I'll be . . ." exclaimed Ben, "a man could get rich in the slave-catching business."

"Or lose a fortune by aiding them to escape," added Bratton, swatting at a bothersome fly. "Who'd ye say hired out yer two niggers to ye?"

"You don't think that I—"

"Of course not, Ben. No sane man would, especially in your position. A businessman in the south. I do hope that Mrs. Fairfield gets well soon. . . ."

Ben slapped some coin on the bar. "My turn, Rufus. I think I'll go on up and see to Eliza." Once reaching the mezzanine, Ben went down a service stairway in the rear and out into the street where a hired carriage was waiting.

That afternoon, Rufus Bratton waited with an armed sheriff in the hotel lobby, expecting to intercept Fairfield's group in the act of leaving. After a time, they went up to Ben's rooms and used a desk key for access.

The rooms were empty.

SIX

As Ben's carriage careened down Market Street, a crowd was gathering in front of a building, queuing up before a ticket window. A playbill was posted:

McLean's Theatre
Saturday Evening, October 20, 1860
J. Wilkes Booth
Pride of the American People
Youngest Tragedian in the World
A STAR OF THE FIRST MAGNITUDE
Son of the great Junius Brutus Booth
Brother and artistic rival of Edwin Booth
is engaged to commence on that evening
in THE APOSTATE as PESCARA
and will remain
ONLY SEVEN NIGHTS

Inside the theater, stagehands were working on the scenery and various actors and managers of the newly-arrived troupe were milling around and watching as a local performer was demonstrating his act in the previous production. It was not often that a North Carolina boy could show his talent to a troupe from New York City. In a purple and rose zouave costume, complete with fez and tassle, the performer leveled a flintlock carbine at a padded target onstage to which was tacked a life-size portrait of Abraham Lincoln. After lighting a match he applied the flame to his exhaling lips, producing a flash of fire which he directed at the powder pan of his weapon, discharging a half-inch lead ball that buried itself in the presidential candidate's likeness.

A mixture of bravos and boos greeted his bow, with one of the troupe, in a dove-gray coat with an astrakhan collar, continuing his raucous applause alone.

An old Virginia pilot schooner, with dark green hull and peeling white masts and deckhouse, lay at a ramshackle pier in a creek off Middle Sound, five miles east of Wilmington.

Gabriel Pigot, stocky and of Mediterranean ancestry, had all he could do to keep his *Kathrine* afloat. Built at Norfolk in 1820, she'd brought her share of vessels over the banks. Cotton, turpentine, tobacco and landed gentry, she'd escorted out through fickle Ocracoke Inlet and past stormy Nag's Head. And she'd brought in tea from the Orient, hardware from Connecticut, woolens from Scotland—and slaves from the Congo . . . until the great hurricane of 1837, *Racer's Storm,* drove her up on Core Banks and near wrecked her.

Among the many boats lost and seafarers drowned was a sloop and its captain, Claude Pigot, father of Gabriel. Gabriel's uncles, in a futile search for Claude, came upon the wreck of *Kathrine*. Unmanned and unclaimed, the schooner came under salvage law and the brothers patched it up and towed it south to Beaufort and rebuilt it in their yards with an eye toward porpoise fishing off Shackleford Banks. After some initial successes, the *Kathrine* was rigged for mullet, and later, for oyster and terrapin work inside the banks.

Diamondback terrapin soup and stew was in great demand throughout the eastern seaboard and no area had better breeding grounds than the Carolina banks. Gourmet tastes were such that, when scarce, seven-inch long female terrapins, called "counts" sold for a dollar a piece. This incentive prompted a Mr. Midgett of the banks to invent a "terrapin drag", which he used during the winter, when the animals were dormant, buried in the mud. Such dredges decimated the breeding population, catching several thousands on one foray. For some years the schooner, *Kathrine*, working with two skiffs equipped with drags, vanquished the competition by sailing the transferred catch swiftly to Wilmington or Morehead City, assuring a freshness that brought high prices.

But, by the 1850's, the terrapin beds were depleted and those who made their living from the sea were forced to seek new methods. Gabriel Pigot, like others of his trade, resorted to carrying cargoes other than seafood. One of the most lucrative of these were runaway slaves—but only when forwarded by certain "respectable" citizens who paid well for such transport. Eventually, the boatsmen found themselves so enmeshed in the business that a code of secrecy was upheld to avoid being liable to the Fugitive Slave Law which drastically penalized complicity in the escape of slaves. The Underground Railroad, managed by astute northern businessmen in part, had perfected a seacoast spur to augment its many river and overland routes.

* * *

Gabriel, after counting out the gold coin given him by Ben Fairfield, called for his two-man Negro crew to slip the cables and catch the outgoing tide. As the jib was being shook out and the first mate was putting the helm over, Josiah called out to the Fairfields. "We thank you for all you've done . . . and when we have a baby we will call it Benjamin. . . ."

"Only if it's a boy," answered Eliza, waving a kerchief.

Tenah felt a strange, cold fear take hold as the boat's mainsail filled above her, and the shore slipped away. They were with people whose ways were different from any she'd ever known. They had left the state she was born in—had left her kin without so much as a word to them. And there was such a long way to go. She tucked her light brown hand into Josiah's palm. His strong hand closed tight around hers and she felt safe once more.

"You sure you wouldn't want to work for me?" Gabriel was impressed by Josiah's ability with the terrapin drag.

"I just want to do my part on this trip and show you that I am grateful for what you do for us." Josiah heaved a basket of diamondbacks up from the skiff. It took both Cato and old Tom to carry it to the schooner's hatch. "I think your men do not go deep enough with the dredge. The creatures have learned to go deep in the mud to escape." The mate, Willis Sickles, looked down at the other skiff with envy. Sickles and Cato had returned with a meager catch, hardly a third of what Josiah and old Tom had brought back.

Sickles, a gaunt man in his mid-twenties with a touch of albino in his pale coloring, tugged at Gabriel's shirtsleeve.

"Next thing yer gonna give that nigger m' job . . . well, ye better had not or I'll. . . ."

"Or you'll what, bonehead?"

"Don't call me that."

"Well, you are one. Like the nigger said, you don't drag deep enough . . . bonehead." Pigot turned away from his first mate and went below to supervise the loading. He didn't notice Sickle's clenched fists.

A brisk southerly blew up in Topsail Sound and *Kathrine,* recalling her pilot boat years, heeled sharply to the challenge, clipping along at better than eight knots with a bellyful of catch. It was now important to make speed to Morehead City, sixty miles up the coast. It had been many years since *Kathrine*'s hold had been filled enough on the first week of dredging to make the trip back without another week in Bogue Sound before bringing in the catch. But for Josiah and the woman, Gabriel was tempted to come about and return to Wilmington. Never had he seen as many seven-inchers among the catch—and at a time when they were scarce, and cold weather appetites were coming. No, he would not go back. He'd found a gold mine in the runaway and it was worth anything to keep him.

With Willis Sickles on the tiller, Gabriel took advantage of Josiah in the cabin as Tenah cooked an oyster stew. Josiah had fixed the stove by fashioning a new grate and smokepipe.

"Aint had good, hot food aboard fer years," Gabriel exclaimed as Tenah set cornbread and stew before him. "I should get me a woman to cook like yer wife some day. . . ."

Tenah smiled at the word "wife". It was so reassuring—but would it really happen? She sat down and gingerly picked at her dish. Was this the beginning of freedom? To sit at the same table as a white man—to partake of the some food because of earning the chance? Because Josiah was as good and better than Mr. Sickles. She was glad that the other white man was not present. His eyes were frightening. Slits like those of a swamp snake. She didn't like the way the mate looked at her . . . with a sneering half-smile. She was sure that it wasn't by accident that Sickles came below while Josiah was off in the skiff that morning. She had come from the foc's'le where she was quartered with Josiah to the deckhouse cabin to use the tin tub for bathing. Old Tom was on watch in the cockpit and all hands had gone in the skiffs, leaving *Kathrine* anchored. As she was bathing—standing in the soapy tub, Sickles emerged from behind the bunk curtain, and passing very close, said he "had forgotten something". Tenah had not told Josiah, fearing that he would become violent. That he would do something that she knew was inside him and only needed a small excuse to come out.

"Josiah," Gabriel lowered his voice. "I can fix it so you an' yer wife can stay on this boat. With the right papers, nobody will bother you on the banks. You'll be freed slaves as far as anyone cares. I've been in need of a smart mate, and I don't care what color he is so long as I can make money—er, *we* can clear a good profit. I'm ready to offer you a good wage."

"Even a percentage of the catch?"

"Now that's just what I like about you, Josie. Yer smart an' ye got a sense of humor. If it's a percentage ye want, I'll agree. The more we catch, the more we make. The richer I get, the richer you get—and if we don't catch anything, we both lose. Is it a deal?"

"What about Mr. Sickles?"

"I'll take care of him," Gabriel cut his corn bread

with a bait knife and stuffed a piece in his mouth. "What do you say, Josie?"

"I'll think about it, Mister Pigot, and make up my mind when we reach Morehead City. . . ."

On deck, in the fading dusk, a figure leaning an ear against an open port, got up and went aft to take over the tiller from Cato.

Morning, and the wind had died. Fog hung so low that neither bank nor shore was visible. Old Tom rang the ship's bell every few minutes as a precaution to other vessels. The sails hung wet and limp as *Kathrine* wallowed in the swells. The last land seen at dawn before the fog descended was Cedar Point after *Kathrine* had slipped through Bogue Inlet into the sound under a full moon. Gabriel, not one to take chances, decided to anchor and wait for the fog to lift. Better to lose a few hours than be grounded on a full moon ebb tide. Morehead City was but twenty miles distant, at the other end of Bogue Sound.

Rising for his duty watch at eight bells, Josiah could not budge the foc's'le hatch. He pounded at it and shouted through the wood grating. Then he heard raucous laughter. Soon the jaundiced face of Willis Sickles appeared, leaning down to the hatch. "What's the matter, smart nigger . . . ain't strong enough to push up th' hatch?" Sickles spat a stream of tobacco juice through the grating. "Guess what happened? *Massa* Gabriel aint no massa no more. He's done taken sick an' I'm th' new captain of this boat. Cato, here, is th' new mate, aintcha Cato? We're still goin' on to Morehead City, but massa's goin' for a nice swim—an' Josie boy is goin' along. If ye don't want somethin' to happen to yer honeychile, ye better not make trouble. . . ."

"Where is Mister Pigot," Josiah called up. Noticing a pistol in Sickle's hand he ducked away.

"What did you say, smart nigger?"

Josiah pushed Tenah out of danger and rolled up the bunk bedding, then buttoned his red shirt around it. "I said where is Mister Pigot?" He held the red-covered bedding below the hatch. A revolver barrel came down through the grating and fired two half-inch balls into the red shape. There was a groan and Tenah screamed

"You've killed him," she cried out hysterically.

The hatch snapped open and Sickles slowly leaned in, weapon in hand. Seing a crumpled red and black form on the foc's'le floor, he took took careful aim and fired again. Before he could withdraw his arm, his wrist was locked in a powerful grip and slammed down against the hatch rim. Dropping the revolver, Sickles screamed in pain over his broken arm as Josiah catapulted to the deck and pinned the mate down. Looking about him, Josiah saw Pigot—lashed to the foremast, mouth gagged and a bloody stain on his shirt. Enraged, Josiah picked up the sniveling mate and flung him over the side. Sickles went under, then reappeared, thrashing out with one arm as the tide swept him astern and into the fog. There was another splash; Cato had jumped overboard. Old Tom appeared from hiding and untied Pigot, who uttered one "thank God" and collapsed.

At Morehead City, Josiah was introduced to the fish market merchants by Gabriel Pigot as *Kathrine*'s first mate. While Josiah supervised the unloading and took bids on the catch, Pigot had his stab wound treated and properly dressed, ascribing it to a fishing accident. *Katherine*'s catch brought a record price, merchants and fishermen alike making extravagant offers to learn the location of such wealth from the sea. Pigot, true to his word, gave Josiah a "percentage".

That evening, enjoying a supper of roast turkey and yams at a waterfront grogshop, Gabriel again offered Josiah the position of mate aboard the *Kathrine*.

"Tenah and I have discussed this, and we have decided there will be no peace for us and our children as fugitives. Even if you can do as you say," Josiah lamented, "we will know, we will be afraid. Somebody will find out. Rewards, as you know, will change friends into enemies. Find yourself a good, strong man who can dredge deeper for the diamondback and you will soon forget me. He will not seek percentages. I will now ask for one favor. . . ."

"Name it."

"I want to purchase your dinghy. We must go to New Berne tomorrow," Josiah broke off a turkey leg and wrapped it in a napkin. "For my wife. . . ."

"But you can't sail all the way around—"

"I will go north to the swamps; there is a creek. When you saw the doctor today, I asked a free Negro. There is a way to the big river through the swamp. I made a map from what he said."

"Take the dinghy. It's a gift."

"No, I have earned money. It will make me feel good to purchase it—like free men do."

"All right, Josie. For you—five dollars. It's an old boat. Been thinkin' of buying a new one anyway."

The next day, at dusk, the dinghy was lowered from *Kathrine*'s transom davits with Tenah aboard. Josiah climbed down and rigged the lateen sail on a short demountable mast. Provisions and belongings stowed in the bow, he was cast off with a last admonition from Gabriel Pigot:

"Keep yer weight low if the wind pipes up. . . ."

Acknowledging the advice, Josiah sculled clear of the schooner, then let out the lateen for a following breeze. Heading north, he unfolded his sketched map and looked for landmarks. Crab Point loomed up to port, while dead ahead lay a long, low belt of marshes. Josiah strained his eyes into the hazy contours and picked out an irregular notch which he was told led into Harbor Creek. Closing in on the shore, the breeze died and Josiah set his oars, pulling hard to reach the creek before dark. Thankful for a bright, though waning moon rising in the east, he maneuvered through the grassy marshes until he spotted a tangled cypress that marked the entrance to Harbor Creek. Making for it, the dinghy suddenly ran up on a sand bar. Josiah and Tenah got out and were hauling the boat over the bar when a menacing sight confronted them.

It was the largest rattlesnake Josiah had ever seen, its body as thick as a strong man's arm. In the stillness of the darkening swamp, the reptile's shrill rattle carried a long way. Spade-shaped head poised over the sand and tongue flicking under flashing yellowish eyes, the nine-foot-long scourge of the swamp drew back to strike. Concerned with Tenah's safety, Josiah picked up a driftwood branch and drew the snake's wrath to him by poking at it. The giant rattler struck viciously at the branch, leaving dark venom glinting on the smooth wood. Temporarily spent, the reptile retreated allowing the dinghy to be dragged across the bar, Josiah waded into the swamp, hauling the boat on a line lashed about his strong shoulders until out of the snake's dominion. Reaching a clearing in the marsh, he climbed aboard and resumed rowing.

"Josie, where we goin'?" Tenah had wrapped herself in part of the sail. The clear night had brought a chill.

"First to the big river, and then up to New Berne."

"That's north, isn't it?"

"Yep."

"We ain't goin' north—"

"Hell we ain't."

"The drinkin' gourd is over *that* way. It's real low in the sky. My father showed me many nights."

Josiah trailed his oars and looked up in wonder at the sparkling constellations. "That does look more like the gourd than what I was lookin' at," he confessed, and turned to port. After rowing through more marsh, the dinghy moved easier, as if it had a mind of its own. "We caught th' tide," exclaimed Josiah jubilantly. On either side he noticed trees and brush passing by against the starlit sky. "Damn, this mus' be the creek . . . we'll be in the big river in no time." He put an oar over the transom and steered clear of the overhanging branches and brush.

Suddenly the stars spread out wide above him and a rush of cold air swept the mosquitoes away. They were on the big river. Josiah leaned hard into his oars, but the river was too strong. What was a north ebb on the creek was now southeast on the river, sucking the water from the swamps to rush down into the sea.

The dinghy, caught in the river's swift grip, spun out of control, heavens swirling. Tying the bowline to his waist, Josiah slipped over the stern and swam frantically toward shore where he clung to a cypress root and pulled a bight of loose line around it barely in time to snub the dinghy. Securing the line, he followed it back to the dinghy, which had swung into the marsh below the cypress. After lashing the dinghy's stern to an overhanging branch, he climbed aboard, slacked up on the stern line and hauled the dinghy forward, thus mooring it safely against tide and predators. Next, he lashed the sail to the bow and gun'ls and folded the excess into a snug refuge wherein, after stripping off his wet trousers, he fell asleep in his beloved's embrace.

Refreshed, they awakened to the sounds of morning in the Carolina marshes . . . the *wock, wock* of the black-crowned heron and the *skeow, skeow* of the green heron . . . the *kideer, kideer* of the darting plover. Downstream, the clumsy splash of a brown pelican diving at a school of mullet, and, from the treetops the screech of a turkey vulture. It was a feeling of freedom and the runaways joyfully mimicked the sounds as they breakfasted on dried beef and cornbread.

Sail set, they glided upriver with the flood tide, wishing that the moment could last forever. It was their dinghy and the day was bright; no cotton to pick nor whips to fear. No sculleries to scour nor indignities to endure. They were alive and free on God's water—but in the company of man, in the town of New Berne, shimmering in the morning sun upriver, with its ship's masts and church spires—they would be fugitives.

SEVEN

A sidewheeler steamboat lay at the town wharf. In need of paint, the white hull had an enclosed foredeck with cavernous cargo ports. One-hundred-fifty feet overall, she was a small coaster, rigged with two raked masts upon which were furled smoke-darkened sails. Between the gaffed masts was a high black stack and a diamond-shaped 'walking beam'. Midships, on the paddlewheel housing, in peeling gold ornamental letters was *CATAWBA*. Forward of the foremast, which was stepped through a wood-paneled deckhouse, stood an octagonal pilot-house topped with a once-gilded cupola. To the pinnacle of this was affixed a wood-sculptured Indian head. A somewhat disheveled American flag hung limp over the stern.

"Where'd ye steal that dinghy, nigger," a gruff voice accosted the runaways as they tied up to the wharf.

"Bought it proper," called out Josiah as he helped Tenah up a short ladder. He unfolded his bill of sale and showed it to the roustabout. "I bought it from Mister Pigot, down at Morehead City."

The tar-smeared wharf-rat feigned reading the bill. "I heard o' the Pigots all right. Don't see any price here . . . How much did ye pay for it?"

"I might sell it for twelve dollars."

"I'll take a look at it then," the roustabout started to climb down the ladder.

"Can you tell me, sir—where can I find Mister Settles?"

"If ye mean th' young 'un, he's up in th' shippin' office. That house 'cross from the *Catawba*. You got business with 'im?"

"Not exactly, we're delivering something." Josiah tied an extra hitch in the dinghy's mooring line, picked up his satchel and took Tenah by the arm.

"Used to be called the *Medora*," David Settles drew back the drapes of his second-floor office window and looked across the wharf at the steamer being loaded. Hundreds of barrels of turpentine were lined up, waiting to be hoisted aboard by a donkey-engine powered boom and stowed by a gang of slaves.

"She was built in 1846 at New York for freight and passenger service between Charleston and Baltimore. There were berths for ninety gentlemen and twenty ladies. She even had a whiskey saloon forward. On the day of her first trip out of Baltimore, she took on some eighty special guests by small boats to a stream mooring because of the crowds wanting to board her at the dock. The paddles had only turned twice when both of her boilers exploded. Twenty-seven dead and forty hurt.

"She was rebuilt and most of her cabins converted to cargo areas as she seemed to be a jinxed vessel. Renamed the *Catawba*, she worked out of Norfolk for a time until my father hired her several years ago. There's not another boat in the Carolinas like her. Seagoing, but shallow draft enough to make it up this river to load. Saves us having to haul our products by keelboat or wagon down to Morehead City."

"We don't care how jinxed the boat is. It sure looks good to us, doesn't it?" Josiah smiled at Tenah who nodded.

Settles quickly closed the drapes and peeked out. "Is there any chance that you were followed?" He took a gold watch from his vest pocket and wound it. "Take a look; those men!"

"We came by water over the swamp; there was no one behind us. . . ." Josiah edged over to the window. "One of them's the man who was interested in buying our dinghy. We asked him how to find you."

"Then he knows you've come up to my office?"

"We told him that we were delivering goods."

The spectacled young man opened a ledger on his desk. "The other two men, the ones wearing boots and rawhide coats, are strangers to me. They could be slave-catchers. We'll have to hide you both until I work something out. You said you have a dinghy to sell; well, I'm buying it. What size?"

"Nine feet, with a sail. . . . Twelve dollars."

"A bargain," exclaimed Settles.

"We want to pay for our passage with the money—and I have more," Josiah reached into his pocket.

"You'll need your money," Settles led them from his office into the hall and then to a storage room where he removed a wall panel, behind which was an attic crawl-space. "Don't worry," he whispered as he ushered them in, "the Underground Railroad's steamboat service will not forget you."

* * *

"The nigger and his woman were seen going into this house—" Burly Jud Hines fingered the butt of his belted Colt navy revolver. He pushed back his weathered rawhide coat as if about to draw out his brass-framed weapon.

"Yea," added his accomplice. "They were 'delivering' somethin' to ye." Clem McCoy giggled as he laid the runaway slave newspaper notice on Settle's desk. "Kind o' funny seein' as he was a six-footer like it says here, and that the nigger girl was light brown. . . ."

"They were delivering something, that is true," David put on his best business attitude. "They brought me a dinghy which I had wanted to buy. Here's the bill of sale, signed over to yours truly."

Hines snapped the note from Settle's smooth fingers. "It says the seller is 'Dick Smith'. That's a phony name if I ever heard one. How do we know you're tellin' the truth?"

"That's the name he gave me. Said he was going up to the station to buy tickets. Why don't you run up and ask the stationmaster."

"Clem, you heard the man—get on up there. And Mister Settles, if you are lyin', we'll be back." Hines started for the door, then stopped and looked out the window. "Right purty boat. Does it take passengers, or just turpentine?"

"There are a few staterooms. Are you planning a trip to New York City? The boat will leave tomorrow at high tide," Settles offered Hines a cabin layout diagram.

"No thanks," roared the gun-toter. "Too damn many damn yankees up there." He snapped up the runaway notice and stomped out of the office.

Catawba's two copper boilers, on the truss braces port and starboard, aft of the paddlewheels, were fired up and building up steam pressure. The engineer, John Smart, opened a valve slightly, letting steam into the 120 horsepower side lever engine. Its 41-inch diameter cylinder slowly rose, moving a steel rod up, which in turn depressed the aft end of the diamond-shaped walking beam, pushing another rod down and turning the twenty-foot diameter paddle wheels halfway round. Satisfied that all was in order, Smart signaled Captain Henry Dobbs who was standing near the pilot house waiting for the gangplank to be removed. The captain signaled his engineer to stand by as David Settles walked hurriedly up the gangplank followed by another man.

"Now, Mister Settles," chided Jud Hines, spitting tobacco through his stubble beard into the river, "we're obliged to find out that the nigger bought a couple of tickets for today's train to Baltimore. But since Clem can watch the station by himself, I thought I'd mosey down here and look at the accomodations. Never know but I might want to send some freight m'self, eh. Now just act natural and I won't have to scare ye with my six-shooter again. We wouldn't want an 'accident' now, would we?"

They went forward and below, Hines examining the cargo holds and crew members in passing. "These barrels are too small for a big nigger to hide in," joked Hines as he tapped several with his pistol butt. He looked in the engine room and the firewood lockers, then went up to the cabin deck and searched the passages and life boats. After looking in the galley and pantry, Hines watched an elderly couple by the deck railing.

"I want to look in all the staterooms. Just tell your passengers that I'm a fire inspector. . . ."

"There are only five staterooms occupied," Settles studied his loading manifest and read off the passengers' names prior to each inspection. He hesitated before knocking at the door of the fifth and last stateroom. "Madame Dupré is traveling with her infant child. . . ."

"I said *all* the staterooms," sneered Hines.

"Very well." Settles knocked. "Madame Dupré, it's Mister Settles. Just a formality. May I show the fire inspector your cabin?"

"Just a moment, Monsieur Settles." There was a silence befitting a lady's privacy. "I am ready; please come in now."

Hines pushed open the door and stepped inside. There sat a slim woman, her back to the door. She wore a pale-blue silk shawl over her head and shoulders. A child's white legs were visible under her sleeved arms. "My little baby, she is so hungry. Please Monsieur inspector, do not mind us. . . ."

"That's all right ma'am," Hines backed out clumsily and tripped on the cabin door threshold. Without another word, he clomped down the companionway and off the boat.

Settles waited till Hines had left the wharf, then went below to the firewood locker. After taking a dozen split logs from the top of a stack, exposing a wooden crate, Settles opened the lid. "You can come out now. Remember," he cautioned, "that Mister Smart, the engineer, is one of us. If there is trouble, go to him, not the captain. As far as the crew is concerned, you've been hired on as a fireman's helper. Work hard, it's only a three-day trip at most. Mister Smart will have further instructions upon reaching New York City. Good luck to both of you."

Settles shook Josiah's hand and left.

Black smoke trailing from her stack, *Catawba* steamed smoothly down the zig-zag Neuse River, turning northeast past a windmill to Turnagain Bay and entered Pamlico Sound, a three-hour run from New Berne. Rather than go "outside" through Ocracoke Inlet and chance the weather around Cape Hatteras, Captain Dobbs set a course up the sound to Oregon Inlet, a channel that had been cut in the outer banks by a violent hurricane only sixteen years earlier. *Catawba*'s relatively shallow draft of six feet was again an advantage.

Aft of the pilot house, the "Texas cabin" served as a combination saloon, restaurant and belvedere for the officers and stateroom passengers of *Catawba*. The term was borrowed from Mississippi and Red River stern-wheelers. Enjoying the sundown view over ardent spirits, Cyrus Whitlock held up his glass to another cabin passenger, Philip Blackwing, a prosperous Indian merchant. "Philip, let's have a drink to our home states. Hurrah for Carolina. Come on now, join me in one more." The Indian, wearing a red velvet jacket, raised his glass of whiskey, hiccupped once, and shouted in unison with Whitlock. *"Hurrah for Carolina* . . . and *Hurrah for Connecticut."*

EIGHT

Unseen from New Haven's High Street, the firemen waited, water hose poised in the open doorway of the engine house near Alumni Hall. From the corner of Elm, raucous festivities had rung out for interminable hours; the 'Crocodile' eating club was over-run by fancy-dressed Yale undergraduates. The firemen clenched their fists and gritted their teeth in anticipation of revenge. Ever since the riot of 1854 there had been ill feeling between the disparate factions, fanned by smaller incidents in the interim.

In that year, a comic Irish singer at Homan's Theatre received too many curtain calls during an interlude act from a crowd of firemen in the gallery to suit the taste of a body of students in the orchestra seats. The orchestra hissed the gallery and vice-versa. After the performance—the main feature being a tragedy, *The Italian Wife*, featuring a celebrated English actor—the firemen, joined by a band of longshoremen, had a set-to with the students on the sidewalk. The police intervened and took a number of brawlers to the station-house. One Patrick O'Neill, a longshoreman, was put under bond.

The following night, 150 students attended the theatre again and the gauntlet was picked up by a larger force of firemen. Missiles were hurled from plebeian and privileged quarters alike, and shortly the firehouse alarm bell was clanging—a signal for the mustering of a great mob of roughneck townies on Chapel Street who were itching for a go at the 'gownies.'

The Chief of Police advised the students to leave in a solid body and walk back to the campus as quickly as possible. At one point, the striking up of a popular student song, 'Gaudeamus' was interpreted as an act of defiance and a fusillade of stones were thrown by the mob. In return, pistol shots rang out from the students. Enraged by the shots, Patrick O'Neill seized a student from Mississippi and roughed him up. The southerner, John Sims, drew a bowie knife and stabbed the longshoreman through the heart. The rioter fell dead

The next day, fire bells tolled again as the mob, with renewed fury, massed before South College, pelting the dormitories with bricks and stones. They broke into the armory, pulled out two cannon, loaded them with chain and stone, then leveled them at Old South. The mayor of New Haven read the riot act from the college fence, but the mob cried "Bring out the murderer," refusing to disperse. Meanwhile, the students had turned their building into a fortress, a professor of metallurgy instructing in the moulding of bullets. Fortunately, the mob could not get the cannon to fire and the weapons were captured by the police and citizenry. One of the cannon was so heavily loaded that it burst upon discharge some time later.

John Sims, who was incriminated by a lost hat with his name in it, hired legal counsel and the jury found that

O'Neill "came to his death at the hands of a person or persons to us unknown—the said Patrick O'Neill being at the time engaged in leading, aiding and abetting a riot." Sims, partly because of the tragedy, left Yale before graduation that spring.

With that score to settle, the water hose was turned on a group of students as they passed the engine house. The Crocodile Club emptied into the street and the fight was on. Reinforcements were called from the volunteer firemen's ranks. A townie, William Miles, armed with a hose wrench, called for an attack. Several shots were fired, mortally wounding Miles. Again, the students hired counsel, all former Yale students, and again the privileged won.

"Who killed Miles?" screamed the newspaper headlines and the townies, but there was no answer.

Fireplace flames danced on the brandy glasses. "It was you, wasn't it?" Nat Mather swirled the golden liquid and avoided his classmate's eyes.

"Let's say I *might* have done the deed—but I wasn't the only one to fire at the swine." Howell Clyburn spun the cylinder of his pistol after cleaning it, then admired its construction and finish from several angles, glinting in the firelight. "Are you going to reopen the case?"

"You know I would never do that—especially—"

"Especially because of Bess?"

Nat didn't answer Howell's probe. "It wouldn't have happened, Swanny, if. . . ."

"I know. If I didn't have a gun."

"Something like that. Well it's true. Six years ago it was a knife. Now it's a gun. Next thing we know, Chapel Street will blow up and there'll be more than one dead. What are we becoming, sages or slaughterers?"

"You sound like your father," Howell set his pistol into its fitted burgundy velvet-lined box and snapped the lid shut. "Where I come from, my city friend, a man doesn't get along on books and newspapers alone. He's got to tend to the livestock, fix fences, and travel a ways for food and supplies—makes no difference in what kind of weather. He's got to protect and fight for what he owns, be it against gators, snakes, wildcats . . . or men. There's always something that's tryin' to take it away or do a man in. Sometimes, taking the initiative is the way to survive. Miles came at us with a hose wrench. When a rattler rears back you don't wait to see what he's going to do.

"Up here in the Northeast, a man is not the same as he'd be out in the back country. You've got so many cities in this state, there *aint* any back country anymore. Instead of doing for himself, up here a man becomes dependent on bought services and little by little he's owned by other people and then it's too late. The government gets stronger and the man loses his self-respect. Man is an animal, king of animals and he doesn't want to lose that any more than a lion does in Africa."

"I agree with you—to a point," Nat spooned coffee into a pot that was ingeniously suspended over the fire. "Man has managed to alter his environment, an accomplishment that animals are incapable of. Today it's the savage who is most like an animal. . . ."

"Are you calling me a savage?" Howell laughed.

"No more than you intimate that I am losing my manhood. Swanny, you are a true enigma. As a medical student, you should be concerned with healing and the nobility of life, yet you cling to the baser instincts. . . ."

"What is wrong with survival? I thought you were an apostle of Professor Darwin."

"*Touché,* Master Clyburn," Nat poured coffee through

a sieve into Howell's cup. "Except that man may have a greater problem than animals. He seems to be the only species that kills its own kind without survival as the issue."

"Nathaniel—you know I only call you that when I'm riled up—I wonder what demons would possess you had you been brought up in my place. You would love the land and the river as I do. Damn, why can't we be left alone—to do what we've been doing for two hundred years? What right has the Federal government to change what the states have perfected? The almighty Constitution did not question state's rights. It did not question slavery. If it had, there would have been two separate countries here. For all we know, the south would have thrown in with Spain. But they lied, those conniving 'founding fathers'. All they really wanted was their own success and power. How different are our despots from those our people escaped from in England and France?"

"Perhaps there are fewer here—and they are not all in the North. There are, at least, free elections. Our despots do not last as long as Europe's. Our nobility is not rooted in blood but in enterprise." Nat ran his hand along the marble mantelpiece. "Toy penny banks," he exclaimed. "I wonder what Eli Whitney put on this mantel when he occupied this room. There was a man who didn't live in your 'back-country', yet changed the course of the South. A Massachusetts man who didn't shoot gators or wildcats. His quarry was knowledge. Why wasn't the cotton gin invented by a Southerner? They were too busy ordering slaves around and going on turkey shoots and fox hunts. You once said that the cotton gin was responsible for slavery. Surely you were joking . . ."

"Only partially," Howell blew on his hot coffee, "You must admit that prior to it, slavery was not a big issue, in fact it wasn't known by such a term. That's northern talk."

"Pardon us Northerners; shall we say 'indentured servants', or perhaps 'involuntary laborers?' Whatever the term, it was abolished in England and her colonies twenty years ago; in the French colonies, about ten years ago. In the Americas, only Brazil, Cuba and your southern states adhere to the practice. Legislation is under way in Portugal and Spain for abolition. That leaves *only* the American South. Would you say that the rest of the world is wrong?"

"All I know, Nathaniel, is that my father said 'If Lincoln is elected, South Carolina will secede.' He reckons that Georgia and Alabama will do the same."

"The Constitution holds that 'No state shall enter into any treaty, alliance or confederation . . .' Secession is a southern term for what is in reality, *rebellion*."

"Well, then, Nat. At least 'rebel' is easier to spell than 'secessionist'."

NINE

Steaming eight miles northwest of Ocracoke Inlet and approaching Bluff Shoal, the *Catawba*'s ruddy captain took a compass bearing on Royal Shoal Rock and set a new course to northeast as the sun settled into a bed of glowing clouds. Leaving his first mate at the helm, Captain Dobbs beat a quick retreat to the Texas cabin where Cyrus Whitlock was buying the drinks.

Recalling the alcoholic excesses of his Blue Ridge Mountains tribe, Philip Blackwing excused himself from the raucous table and staggered out on deck. Whiskey was bad enough without cigar smoke, especially in a confined space. His father's long-stemmed pipe had bothered him as a child—even outdoors, but the white man had made tobacco fit only for the devil to breathe. The Cherokee loosened his green silk turban and opened his cabin door. Stepping inside, his heady condition was abruptly cleared by the sight of a grimy seaman standing amidst the rifled contents of opened trunks and strewn boxes. Philip, never a hero, turned and ran as the intruder drew a derringer from his pocket. Losing his footing on the night-damp deck, he was pounced upon and immobilized by the feel of hard steel behind his ear.

"Back to yer cabin without a sound or I'll put a ball through yer brains. . . ."

Philip was about to comply when suddenly his attacker groaned and fell limp. He looked on with amazement as a Negro flung a piece of wood over the side then dragged the assailant along the deck and into the cabin. "Hurry in please; I will explain." Josiah closed the cabin door and bolted it.

"Whoever you are, I am indeed grateful, but shouldn't we call Captain Dobbs?" The graying Indian clutched at his turquoise and silver bead necklace.

"Please," Josiah noted a kinship of race, "I am not supposed to be on this deck. There will be trouble for me if I'm found here." Josiah looked about the cabin. "He robbed you?"

"No, he was searching for something."

"Wait a minute." Josiah handed Philip the gun. "Watch him." Josiah slipped out and returned quickly with a length of rope. "First we tie him good—and do you have something for his eyes?"

Philip rummaged and found a large polka-dot kerchief, which he handed to Josiah. He reached into a trunk and pried up a false bottom. "Here is what he wanted." The Cherokee unwrapped muslin from a gleaming object, the sight of which caused Josiah to recoil. It was a human skull, lined inside with wrought silver and bordered with the lustrous metal around the eye sockets, nose and jaws. The teeth were similarly capped and on the back appeared a calligraphic 'S', with the date, 1821. Philip rubbed it with the muslin. "Tarnishes so fast. . . ." Setting the grisly object down on his bunk, Philip regarded the bound figure. "Yes, I suppose they did find out."

"About what?"

"The secret of the skull. My father was the great chief of the Cherokee Nation called *Sequoyah*. In our tongue it means *sparrow*. He was the son of an American Colonel of the Army during the Revolution and a chief's daughter. At an early age he became lame and turned to other things than hunting and trading. George Gist, as he was also known, is famous as the inventor of the Cherokee written language, but he was also an accomplished silversmith. I wear his necklace. Now, this skull he bought from a tavernkeeper in the town of Bath when I was a child of seven. He resilvered it and it 'graced' our cabin for some years. Upon my father's disappearance in Mexico almost twenty years ago, I took possession of it. His papers tell that it is the skull of the pirate, Edward Teach, also known as Blackbeard. After the pirate had held the City of Charleston for ransom, he sailed to these banks and was grounded near the inlet we shall soon pass. The colonies were British at the time and the governor of Virginia sent two sloops of the Royal Navy to harass his efforts to build a fortress on Ocrocoke Island. Finding Blackbeard's ship, the *Adventure* fast on a bar, the sloops attacked and were devastated by Blackbeard's cannon. The *Adventure* worked loose and Blackbeard boarded the British commander's sloop intent on slaughtering the remaining crew. Shot in a duel with Lt. Maynard, the pirate did not fall, but instead bested the Englishman with the sword and was about to deliver a death-blow when he was stabbed in the back by a crewman of H.M.S. *Pearl*. Lt. Maynard ordered Blackbeard's head to be severed and tied to the end of the bowsprit for the sloop's victorious return to port. There, in Bath, it was seen and bought by an influential gentleman who had it silver-coated.

"For a time it remained in the gentleman's family and

toasts were drunk from the skull. It was then acquired by a secret society of a college where it was used for initiation pranks. After that it turned up in the tavern. In my father's papers, he described an inscription which he found under a silver plate on the back of the skull while repairing it. He said it had to do with the location of one of Blackbeard's treasure troves. After copying the inscription—which is not in his papers—he removed it from the skull with a file, much as one might remove the scrimshaw on a whale's ivory. Apparently he took the copy of the inscription with him to Mexico."

"*Sequoyah* disappeared with the secret of your skull?" Josiah, seeing the intruder stir, tightened the ropes and lowered his voice. "Then why does this man want the skull without the secret? Maybe he just wants the silver."

"No," replied Philip. "I believe that my father was murdered in Mexico, and the inscription has been found and translated from the Cherokee. It will take both the inscription *and* the skull to find Mister Blackbeard's treasure."

"Why do you take the skull to New York City?"

"There are people of great learning there. Philosophers who, with potions and elixirs, can make visible the inscription that remains latent in the bone—that is, what remains of it. If that can be done, I will become rich enough to build a school for the education of the Indian. A memorial to *Sequoyah*."

The bound seaman groaned and struggled on the floor. "I must go now," Josiah peeked out on deck. "Tell the captain that it was you who overpowered the crewman. He will be put in irons." Josiah closed the door behind him and went to Madame DuPré's cabin. He knocked lightly on the door twice, and twice again before he was quickly let in.

TEN

Gale winds buffeted the frail wooden house, howling through chinks in the driftwood siding and driving fine white sand under the door; impaling strands of beach grass on the small isinglass window panes. A bony hand cupped the streaming candleflame against the mounting storm's fury, then flicked at and twirled its unkempt owner's pointed beard ends. On the bleached plank table, fluttering in the wavering light, lay a half-rolled sheet of stained parchment, inscribed as follows after an initial letter "S" in the shape of a sea serpent:

Set ye Skull on the Highest Rock of
Duck Island at Midsummer's Dawn
With its nose and centre-line
Facing the rising sun.
Then spy through the centre of the
Bullet Hole in the back and
Sight over the lower right cuspid.
There on the bank shall ye dig
When the Tyde is Lowest.

Edward Drummond poured ochred rum into a chipped white china mug, then raised it to the rain-pelted window as his slip of a wife sat by the scrapwood-fired cast-iron stove, thin mouth moving to the turn of bent tarot cards.

"As I have the blood of Edward Teach, known by few as Drummond, I swear by this libation that his treasure shall be gotten by none other than myself. No one shall partake of it, not even the devil, in that which is rightly mine. . . ."

"Ye'll be wantin' to go out at first light providin' the storm has passed?"

"Aye, we'll catch the paddlewheeler as she slows down to make the inlet," Drummond dribbled rum from his beard.

"Too bad ye don't have a proper ship and crew like Mister Teach had," Leah Drummond turned a card and wheezed, "It's old number twelve again."

"The *Hanged Man*, eh. Do ye see self-sacrifice or treachery? Do ye want me tortured or dismembered?"

"You're already dismembered," she squealed.

"Mind what ye say *this* time, woman. The Cherokee is aboard and so is the confounded skull. We'll soon have property and niggers as good as the Governor. Edward Drummond does not need a proper ship nor crew. He shall triumph by his cunning—and why share with a motley crew anyway? Except, of course with you, my beach blossom."

"Edward," Leah hesitated as she turned up *La Mort*, with its scythe-wielding skeleton, "you'll never be like Mister Teach. Eleven wives 'e had, and he buried some of 'em in 'is pirate chests instead o' doubloons. I can't picture you doin' a thing like that to little me. Mmmm?"

* * *

Drummond's skiff wallowed at anchor in the Oregon inlet as he sat, fishing line grabbed tight in hand under his oilskin poncho. He hardly took notice as the steamship appeared rounding Duck Island, sails furled tight, belching black smoke. *Catawba*'s twenty-foot diameter paddlewheels churned up a white froth toward the bright red channel marking bouy. Captain Dobbs brought his boat in close to the marker and was leaving it in his wake when there occurred a rasping shudder along the keel. Clouds of silt and sand discolored the water as the paddlewheels dug into the bottom. The steam whistle screeched as John Smart cut the throttle. *Catawba* had run aground.

"Mister Smart," called Dobbs through the speaking tube, "put 'er in low reverse; careful now for the paddles. . . ." The walking-beam rod groaned and creaked, turning the camshaft slightly. Smart opened the cut-off valve, releasing the strain and shouted back. "We're stuck fast, Cap'n. Best wait a bit; tide's not quite high. . . ."

"Damnation," screamed Dobbs as he left the wheel-house, "what good are buoys that run ye aground?" Spotting a skiff anchored nearby, he fetched his speaking trumpet and hailed it. "What shoal am I on and what's th' best way off?" Drummond hauled in his anchor and rowed toward the steamboat. His plan had worked. It had been a simple matter to unshackle the buoy and move it to shallow water.

Drummond climbed up a rope ladder and onto *Catawba*'s lower deck. Followed closely by Dobbs, he pretended to survey the situation, looking over the side at various parts of the boat. He looked in vain for the crew-man he had bribed to appear with the package. Remembering his wife's tarot cards, he thought of *The Hanged Man*. So it was treachery—the stoker had accepted the money and fled, or was hiding below. Drummond led Dobbs up to the wheelhouse as the passengers and crew watched. "Captain," he grinned through his disheveled beard in the privacy of the octagonal wheelhouse, "I'll make a trade with you. I'll get you off the bank and through the inlet if you give me something I want. One of your passengers, a Cherokee called Philip Blackwing, has with him an object which is mine . . ."

"What right have you to make such a demand, and how do I know you will do as you say?"

"Only I know how far the buoy is from its proper position."

"This is ridiculous, and what's more it's piracy. Tampering with marking buoys is a federal offense. Now leave my boat immediately; I'll have nothing of this business. Better to send out a skiff and sound the channel, thank you . . ."

Drummond threw off his poncho, revealing a broad belt about his shoulder in which was holstered three battered naval revolvers and a wicked knife. In his hand, threateningly extended toward Dobbs's belly, was a four-barreled duckfoot flintlock pistol. "Take me to the Cherokee's cabin, or I'll cut you in half with this and then kill everyone aboard. I have nothing to lose since I've come this far . . . and it's your duty to protect the passengers."

Taking Blackwing along as a hostage, Drummond climbed down to his skiff, clutching the silvered skull to his body. Mind you aboard—no funny tricks or the Indian is dead."

"The Indian will be dead regardless," observed John Smart as the skiff moved away and passengers ventured from their cabins. Unseen, a dark, lithe figure slipped over *Catawba*'s side and disappeared. Moments later, the skiff, pushed by a force from below, rose high on one side and took a torrent of water. Drummond was thrown sprawling and grappling for his precious object as it went overboard, floating and taking water through an eye socket. In a frenzy, Drummond dove after it, oblivious of a school of hammerhead sharks that had come in with the tide and were foraging the shallows for food. Attracted by the flash of silver, an eleven-foot female swooped by and snapped up the sinking skull. Drummond, seeing this, went mad and swam thrashing toward the despoiler of his dreams only to be swallowed into a vortex of reddening water.

After bailing out the skiff, Josiah took aboard *Catawba*'s utility anchor and rowed it fifty yards to starboard where he set it. As the paddlewheels strained in reverse, a take-off steam winch took in the anchor line till taut and the boat shifted on its keel, allowing the paddles to turn. John Smart gave the winch another puff of steam and *Catawba* jolted from its sandy trammel, then slid backwards like a frightened turtle.

Cyrus Whitlock, leaning on the upper deck rail and puffing a cigar, stroked his sideburns and wondered where he'd seen that nigger before.

Contrary to expectations, *Catawba* encountered fair weather and an offshore breeze upon entering the Atlantic Ocean. Full canvas was set and the paddles retracted for the coastal run. Logging better than twelve knots, *Catawba* flew past the Delaware peninsula and the Jersey shore. At Sandy Hook, it hove to and picked up the harbor pilot. The run from Oregon Inlet, a distance of almost 300 miles, had been done in less than twenty-seven hours, equaling *Catawba*'s best time under steam.

In Madame Dupré's cabin, Josiah, lying in the bunk

nude, watched Tenah get dressed. ''My, my, don't you look like a rich lady from the Delta country way down Louisiana. Madame, are you going to take your white chile off the boat with you?'' Josiah dangled a lifelike toy doll by its ankle.

''It worked once,'' Tenah arranged her veil to maximum effect in a wall mirror. ''Now you best get dressed an' out of here. Suppose the Captain came in an' found you like that.''

''Aint any trees aboard to get lynched from,'' Josiah bounced out of the bunk and dressed hurriedly. ''But you better take a look before I go out anyway.''

They embraced, tingling with the excitement of being in a new world, yet fearful of the unknown. ''Now, just once more,'' Tenah cautioned, ''Where are we going to meet, and when?''

''As Mister Smart said, one hour after the boat docks, we are to be at a ship's supply store on South Street across from Pier Seven . . .''

''What's the name of the store?''

''Somethin' like a color. . . .''

''Brown's.''

''I would have remembered. And I walk in and ask to buy a tin mirror, while you—''

''As a high-born lady, I shall ask to see the best quality French spyglass as a present for my husband.'' There was a tear welling in the corner of her eye. ''Josie, be careful. I don't know what I'd do without you.''

''Been thinking about your offer, Mr. Whitlock,'' Captain Dobbs screwed up his craggy face while observing Fort Hamilton to Starboard in the Narrows. ''Double what I'm getting and more for the owners is an interesting proposition. The company is always looking for better situations, and cotton would be a damn sight better'n stinkin' turpentine."

"Good, then I'll see your New York agent and we'll work something out. Our little arrangement will be on the side—if the deal goes through."

"I'll use a bit of persuasion, Mr. Whitlock."

"I expect you to. By the way, Captain, you've got quite an unusual crew. I hope your engineer will stay on. My mills run on a stringent schedule."

"A little raise in salary will do wonders."

"And the Negro stoker—quite a resourceful fellow. The man who rowed out the anchor in Oregon Inlet. What's his name?"

"He signed on as Dick Smith, just for the trip to New York. Wouldn't mind having him on permanent. Mr. Smart brought him on board. Seems he's good in mechanics and knows how to read. Curious thing though—I couldn't help seein' what was written in one book he was readin' the other day. It said in ink handwriting 'Josiah Holladay's Book'. Well, I don't care what they call themselves so long as they earn their pay."

Upon entering Brown's Ship Chandlery, one was greeted by a painted wooden sculpture of a stocky sailor lad, knee propped on a barrel, holding a bulbuous brass binnacle containing a mariner's compass, flanked by protruding oil lamp chimneys. The boy's white-rimmed hat bore the motto, *Watch Your Helm*. His glistening lifelike eyes seemed to follow Tenah as she walked past.

"Came off the clipper ship *N.B. Palmer* last year, ma'am. You aint the only one it startles." A slight bespectacled sales-clerk stepped from behind the counter with a chuckle. "The *Palmer*'s crew thought it was haunted and they refused to sail on 'er unless the thing was taken off."

The clerk adjusted his glasses as he absentmindedly realized he was staring at Tenah's fashionably seductive attire. "May I be of some assistance?"

"Yes." she affected the airs of a plantation owner's wife. "I want to bring back a present for my husband in Louisiana." She paced down an aisle of wares, tools and knick-knacks.

"Ah, is the gentleman interested in something nautical to wear . . . something decorative, or perhaps utilitarian? The clerk held up a mercury barometer. "This is a very popular item. Well made, aesthetic and extremely useful. . . ."

Tenah did not understand several of the clerk's words, nor what the item was used for, but she waved it away nonchalantly. "Could you show me a spyglass—a French spyglass?"

The salesclerk's glasses slipped to the end of his nose and he looked Tenah up and down. "For *French* spyglasses, *Madame*, you'll have to see Mr. Brown. Follow me to his office please."

Tenah hesitated. "May I look about first?"

"As you wish, *Madame*."

She tugged at her gloves nervously and looked out the front window. Below the endless row of bowsprits, carriages and wagons plied busily, dodged by seamen, longshoremen and merchants. Tenah looked at a wall clock. Past four. Where was Josiah?

"Next," the doctor beckoned to the line-up of seamen. Josiah felt his heart in his mouth, afraid that he would be compelled to give more than his name. What if he was asked where he'd come from and where he was bound for? Had he known of the quarantine inspection he would have evaded it, or at least planned what to say. The *Catawba*'s engineer, John Smart, noticing the impending predicament, walked over to the doctor and whispered something to him. The doctor nodded, then waved Josiah out of the line. Smart strolled along the wharf, and as Josiah passed by, wished him luck, adding that it was past four o'clock.

Josiah ran north along the waterfront, weaving in and out of the crowds of businessmen, travelers and laborers. The complexity and clangor of the city confused him and with each block fear mounted within. He imagined that he was being followed by slave catchers and ducked into an alley, exhausted and trembling. He felt alone and lost. Then he thought of the whips and chains of the South, of Negroes put in barrels lined with sharp nails and rolled down hills, of children dying in the broiling cotton fields—and of Tenah, carrying *his* child.

Once more he was on South Street. Mr. Smart said Brown's Store was twelve blocks away from the *Catawba*'s wharf. Or was it more? Had he passed it already? A man in uniform approached him. The man had a wooden club in his white-gloved hand. Josiah was about to run, but instead, he stood his ground. He was tired of running, and it would only give him away. The white man eyed him suspiciously and Josiah knew that he would have to take the initiative. He steeled himself and smiled. "Sir, I'm looking for Brown's store . . . ship's supplies. . . ."

"Begorrah, the chandlery is almost in front of yer nose," the policeman gestured at a building on the corner with his club and walked on, shaking his head.

A face appeared at the window. Josiah's eyes spoke. "I am here. Everything will be all right. . . ." Tenah clasped her hands in relief and joy, then wheeled about and strode resolutely toward the back office.

* * *

The counter bell jangled furiously under Cyrus Whitlock's hand. "Just a moment," called the salesclerk from atop a ladder. In his haste to come down, the clerk slipped and stumbled into a barrel, scattering lignum vitae deadeyes across the wide-planked floor. Picking them up and rubbing his knee, he addressed the impatient customer. "I'm sorry, but we're short of help today. May I show you something?"

"I saw my Negro enter this establishment only minutes ago." The mill owner drew a handkerchief from his breast pocket and dabbed at his receding forehead. Regaining his composure, Whitlock walked through the store, searching all the corners.

"You must be mistaken, sir. Perhaps he went into the emporium next door. As you can see, we have no customers now."

"Where does this door lead?"

"To Mr. Brown's private office," the clerk put himself between Whitlock and the door. "Nobody is allowed in there without previous notice, sir." At that moment a wagon rumbled past the front windows, bound up South Street. Whitlock noticed that on its side was a panel emblazoned with *Brown & Co.* It was loaded with rope and rigging hardware.

"Henry, what the hell is all the commotion about?" the door sprang open and Jacob Brown stormed out.

"This gentleman is looking for—"

"Mr. Brown, I take it. . . . I am Cyrus Whitlock. My Negro hired man went into this store not ten minutes ago and he's not here."

"I'm sorry, Mr. Whitlock, but I know nothing of any Negro. What business might he have had here?"

"It makes no difference," grumbled Whitlock, noticing a double door in the corridor between Brown's office and the store. "Would you kindly open these doors please, or do I have to call the police?"

Brown snapped the latch open. "See for yourself . . . our storage and shipping room, and beyond, the stable."

Whitlock rushed in, and out to the stable. He found nothing, then remembered the wagon that had passed the window earlier. "Mr. Brown," he apologized, "I was mistaken."

The proprietor smiled graciously. "No harm done. If you'll excuse me now. . . ." He closed the door behind him.

Whitlock went over and examined the sculptured binnacle boy near the entrance. If only he could talk, he thought, then reached into his trouser pocket. He took out a twenty-dollar gold piece and expertly spun it on end on the counter, dazzling the clerk. "There *is* something I might buy." He picked up a pencil from the counter and wrote on a scrap of paper: 'I'll pay $20 to find out the destination of your last departed shipping wagon.'

Without a word, the clerk added below the query: 'Stamford, Benjamin Daskam.' Whitlock's expression changed from irritability to one of geniality. He picked up the scrap, leaving the gold piece on the counter and left the chandlery. Then he went into a Western Union office and sent a telegraphic message to Camden, South Carolina, after which he packed and boarded a horse-drawn railroad car at 26th Street. At 42nd Street, several cars were coupled to a locomotive—the noisy, fire-spurting engines being banned below that street—and the New York and New Haven Line train set out for points north, including Stamford, Connecticut.

ELEVEN

It was dusk when Brown & Company's wagon creaked to a stop at the Echo Bay Inn on the Boston Post Road north of Pelham Manor. The driver got off and had the horses back the rig into a stand of pine. Then he unlashed a barrel of trunnels and pushed it aside on the tailgate. "C'mon out now and do what ye have to. This is the only stop we'll be makin' fer a couple of hours." He handed Josiah a chunk of bread and a piece of dried beef. "Ain't much, but it'll do till we reach Stamford. Now stay out of sight." He tapped a keg on the wagon's side, filling two tin cups with water and setting them on the tailgate. "I'll water the nags after they've simmered down." The driver dusted his leather hat and walked around to the back door of the inn where he was greeted with a shout of recognition.

Tenah's eyes rolled. "I can smell somethin' real tasty comin' from the kitchen. MMMmmm," she rubbed her stomach and set her piece of bread down.

"Stale, aint it?" Josiah shrugged. He peeked around

the wagon. "You jest wai there, chile. Ain't no Holladays gonna go hungry if I can help it." He sniffed at the savory aroma of meat roasting, then cautiously made his way into the shadows about the inn and around back to the kitchen. A few minutes later, he returned carrying a sack. Tenah climbed back into the wagon hiding-place and Josiah followed, laughing under his breath. "Careful," he handed her the sack and she squealed with delight and reached in.

"Roast pork, MMMMmmm," she licked her fingers and held out a slice for Josiah. "I won't ask how you got this. . . ."

Josiah struck a match and lit a stubby candle. "Good," he answered, "I like a wife who lets her husband do what is necessary. Actually, it's sort of a magic trick. Now the cook sees it, now he doesn't. I jes' would like to see the cook's face when he gets back to his kitchen. He was drinkin' a whiskey with the driver in the storeroom when I *acquired* our dinner." He reached into his pocket and drew out a small bottle. "Cookin' wine—I took a swig and it's real good. Anyhow, we can celebrate comin' to Connecticut." Josiah took a small pewter plate from his other pocket. "This is for the meat. We're gonna eat in style." He poured the water out of Tenah's cup and replaced it with wine. "A toast," he held up the bottle, candlelight flickering in the redness. "A toast to th' North, and to th' Underground Railroad, without which we wouldn't be here."

She raised her cup, then drank deeply. "Josie, I'll be a good wife to you because you're so good to me. My, I aint had wine since. . . ."

"You people already back in there?"

"Yes sir," Josiah blew out the candle. "We sure like it in here—don't we chile?"

"It's so cozy," purred Tenah, snuggling up to Josiah.

"Well, I'll be hornswoggled," the driver lashed the barrel back in place. "C'mon," he patted a horse on the on its rump, "let's get ye some water."

As the driver held an oil lamp, Jonah Daskam signed the wagon manifest, acknowledging the receipt of two forty-yard bolts of long flax sailcloth. Josiah and Tenah were huddled under a blanket in Daskam's carriage, buffeted by a brisk easterly wind from Long Island Sound as nightlights sparkled and swayed from the moored ships in Stamford harbor.

Transaction completed, Daskam drove north on gaslit Atlantic Street, through the center of the village, then turned west on Broad Street. The operator of the Stamford Underground station, a severe, gray-bearded patriarch with a black high-hat, reined up near a Romanesque stone church. The runaways were quickly ushered through a side door by Daskam and up several flights of stairs into a secluded room a third of the way up the belfry tower.

"Just a precaution," announced Daskam while a plump old woman tidied up the room. "You'll stay here tonight and rest. In the morning we'll see about a place for you both. According to a communication from our agent in your home state, you are engaged to be married. Our New England practice of bundling allows for engaged couples to be in the same room overnight providing they remain fully clothed. Mrs. Fowler will see to all your needs. . . ."

"Mr. Daskam, implored Josiah, "my mother lives on River Street in this village, in a house that her grandmother, Mrs. Hagar owned some years ago."

"*Aunt* Hagar, of course," Daskam brightened: "She was the coloured woman who cooked dinner for General Washington when he was here. She passed away but ten years ago at an age of—people say, well over a hundred.

The house had been sold prior to her death and she rented a room over the bakery. Well then, this simplifies the situation. I'm sure you had good reason not to tell our agent."

"Yes, after my father died, I was sold to the new marse. Times were bad and Marse Maxwell and his son died of the fever. Missis Maxwell let my mother go free, but I had to go to Oak Hill. I wanted to—to help Missis Maxwell by going. I told Mr. Ross, but not Mr. Coffin. I was afraid the slave-catchers would hurt my mother when I ran away. They would know her name, and in hunting me would go to her house in this village."

"Quite understandable, Josiah. I'll take you to River Road in the morning. And after the joyous reunion we shall see about employment for you and Tenah. The groom must have at least a temporary position. There is a possibility at Oeffinger's Barbershop for a man who is willing to learn. We have placed several former slaves in such establishments and they have done well in New Haven. Why not in Stamford? I'm told that you are good with your hands and desire to become a mechanic. There is time. Well," Jonah Daskam tapped his hat down snug, "we're off to a fine start."

"Mrs. Holladay, she is no longer with us," the Negro woman's hands were clasped upwards. "She went to her divine reward in the heat of summer—jest like that. . . ."

Daskam gripped Josiah by his arm and Tenah's eyes welled up with tears. Daskam removed his hat solemnly. "I am truly sorry. Perhaps we should leave. . . ."

"No, Mr. Daskam, I want to see where my mother lived. I want to touch the things she touched," Josiah pushed past the woman and into the cluttered room.

"Oh, my dear God, I didn't know—" The woman

gasped and supported herself on the door frame as Josiah touched the arm of a sofa, then a tabletop. "She's still here. I can feel her presence." He collapsed onto the sofa and sobbed. "It's my fault. Why didn't I come home sooner . . . my fault that she's dead."

"But Josie," Tenah sat down beside him. "You couldn't have—not before Mr. Ross came to Oak Hill. . . ."

"Where is she buried? I must go to her . . . I must—"

"Mrs. Huggins, would you know where—"

"Yassir, she's laid to t' rest in the Baptist cemetery on Cottage Street—in the corner near the stone wall."

"My thanks, Mrs. Huggins." Daskam turned to the runaways. "Come, my children, let us go and pay our respects."

The four-storied red brick building on the corner of Main and Bank Streets was called the *Cornucopia* because of a white stone horizontal frieze between the second and third floors that featured a horn of plenty from which bounty flowed right and left. On the street floor were three shops. Henry Weber's shoestore, a dry goods shop and Frank Oeffinger's Tonsorial Salon. The latter, boasting four patent chairs of the latest mechanical versatility, also offered manicures and palmistry by one Madame Monique.

Josiah was beginning his second week as an apprentice barber and assistant. The proprietor had been amazed at his dexterity, and with one of the regular barbers taken ill, had given him the last chair. Receiving patrons' accolades about the new employee, Oeffinger half-hoped that the often-sick regular man would not return. Daydreaming of giving up his first chair to Mario, his senior employee at chair number two, allowing him to manage rather than clip and manage also, Oeffinger was startled as the doorbell jangled. "Good morning, Otto—er, I'm sorry, but I didn't expect you on a *Monday*. . . ."

"That's all right, Frank. I just want a quick trim. I see you have a new man," Muller gestured toward the rear. "He'll do. I don't feel much like waiting today."

"He's very good, considering—."

"So I hear, Frank," Muller unpinned his town marshall's badge from the inside of his coat and slid it into his trouser pocket. An immense man, with a lumbering gait, Muller ambled past the busy chairs and hung his coat on a wall hook near the vacant chair. Josiah, dusting bottles on the ledge, sprang to attention with a friendly smile as Muller struggled into the chair.

"Boy, I need a trim; don't take too much off, now."

"Yes, *sir,*" Josiah deftly arranged a cotton towel around Muller's neck and over his body.

"What's your name, boy," asked Muller matter-of-factly.

"Josiah, sir . . . Josiah Smith." He started clipping as Muller watched him in the wall mirror.

"Whereabouts you from, Josiah?"

"Near Philadelphia, sir." Josiah said what he had been told to by Jonah Daskam.

"Easy, there. Not too short in back, boy."

Josiah nodded and picked up another comb from the ledge. "Sorry, sir," He dipped his hand into the talcum powder jar.

Muller's voice suddenly grew angered. "Now how come you went lookin' for Mrs. Holladay, claimin' to be her son when yer name is Smith?"

Josiah gripped his scissors tightly and took a step toward Muller, his mind whirling with visions of whips and chains.

"Hold it right there, boy," Muller's hand emerged from under the towel. In it was a nickel-plated double-barreled Derringer pistol, pointed at Josiah's belly. "Drop the scissors, boy," snarled Muller as he rose from the chair and tore the towel from his neck. "Now just raise your hands over your head. We're gonna take a little walk down to the jailhouse. I think I got me a fugitive slave. . . ."

The scissors clattered to the floor and the sound of snipping stopped as heads turned toward the fourth chair. As Muller prodded Josiah with his Derringer, the fugitive suddenly flung a handful of talcum powder in his captor's face. Muller, temporarily blind, fired both barrels into a wall mirror as Josiah scrambled through the salon's back door.

Within minutes, Muller had attracted a crowd in front of the Cornucopia Building. "Anyone who finds out where that runaway is hiding gets fifty dollars in gold—and another twenty for the woman," he bellowed. The crowd dispersed and Cyrus Whitlock approached the marshal. "Otto, if you want to be marshal again next year, you'd better bring in Holladay. There's more than just money in this for me."

"You said seventy dollars for both of them," Abner Peaslee, the arthritic caretaker of the First Presbyterian Church wheezed as he hobbled along Main Street with the marshal.

"You'll get yer money after they're in jail," Muller turned up Atlantic Street and ran toward the church. The hulking marshal stormed through the front door, and drawing his pistol, clomped up the belfry stairs. At the third landing he found the room described by Peaslee and tried the doorknob. Locked.

"Holladay, I know yer in there," shouted Muller. "Under the Fugitive Slave law of 1850, I am empowered to seize you and the woman, and to bring you before the commissioner. Open up or I'll have the door broken in. . . ."

"Over here, quick. We are friends of Jonah Daskam," came a voice through the belfry window. "Don't ask questions now," whispered Nathaniel Mather. "We've rigged up an escape rope from the bell tower. Hurry, before it's too late."

Josiah looked out and saw a wagon waiting below. The rope was stout and had two loops tied into it. The 'friend of Daskam' pointed at a loop. "Put your shoulders through the loop and we'll lower you down . . . first the girl." Mather slid down, hand-over-hand till he was out of view.

"Holladay," the voice beyond the door boomed again.

"Jes' a minute, sir, we are getting our things together—"

"Your kind doesn't have anything."

Nat Mather hauled on the rope and the end ran through the block attached to the belfry opening, falling ninety feet to the church grounds. He coiled the rope and barely managed to climb into the wagon as it rumbled into Atlantic Street. Hidden under a load of hay, the runaways were headed toward the Boston Post Road, and the next underground station in the village of Norwalk. Jonah Daskam had written a ticket to Canada.

After a dinner in David Lambert's salt-box hideaway, which connected to the main house by a tunnel and a secret stairway, the group, refreshed and victualed, set out for the back-country and the village of Wilton, where Elias Wakeman was both station-keeper and conductor.

* * *

The Wakeman farm overlooked Street's Pond, a half mile from the Danbury Road in North Wilton. The main house, once a simple saltbox, had several wings, added in the past century as families grew and prospered. There was the usual red sagging barn, chicken coops and stable. Outwardly the typical Connecticut farm, it was also a hub of the Underground Railroad to points north.

Elias Wakeman communicated with other Undergrounders by ingeniously coded mail announcing the arrival of 'passengers'—as many as half a dozen at a time. His children having left and built their own houses, there were four empty bedrooms that were put to use for the passengers. When a passing neighbor saw Wakeman carrying wood to an outbuilding, or Mrs. Wakeman hanging out the linens, he knew that the "train" had arrived. As a conductor, Wakeman was diligent and bold, taking his "packages of hardware and dry goods" to distant towns. In rare cases he was threatened by contrary groups for his actions, but generally he was left alone, for he was feared for his temper and his shotgun.

Some years prior, he found that one of his horse's ears had been cut off in his barn as a protest of his activities. Elias cornered the culprit and, knee on his chest, ran a sharp knifeblade over his ear, drawing blood but not severing.

That evening, the fugitives and their rescuer were feasted by the Wakemans. Elias cooked venison on the clockwork spit in the huge stone fireplace while Mary baked herb bread and pumpkin pie in the beehive oven. It was as if there really was such a thing as a horn of plenty to Josiah and Tenah. This was freedom. To eat and drink of the bounty of the land . . . to live as equals . . . to share a table . . . to talk of hope instead of despair.

". . . Mr. Wakeman . . . Mrs. Wakeman," Josiah

was feeling the effects of too much claret. ''I wish that I had been able to go to school enough to use the right words to tell all you fine people of the Underground Railroad how grateful my future wife and I are for what you are doing. You place yourselves in great danger so we can be free. And my friend, Mr. Mather . . . you should have seen how he risked his life. Why he climbed down a rope from a high bell-tower window in the church we were hiding in and showed us how to escape through our window on the rope while a marshal was trying to break down the door. He saved us from goin' back to that land of whips and chains. He saved Tenah from bad Marse Clyburn. I can't say how much is in my heart, but to our dyin' days we'll never forget. . . .''

''A-men,'' seconded Tenah.

''It is not I, but my father, who deserves your thanks,'' replied Nat. ''Reverend Gideon Mather. He is a dedicated abolitionist, and I am but a student who happened to be visiting his family when the need arose. Any man might have done the same for my father. Jonah Daskam came to him knowing that he was a man of action and would get the job done.''

Elias got up from the table and tapped his clay pipe over the fireplace stone. ''Nat, I suspect that very few men grow up with church steeples to play in. I'll bet that wasn't the first time you climbed down from a belfry.''

''My brother David is the wild one; he did it first,'' confessed Nat sheepishly.

''Have you heard from him lately,'' asked Mary Wakeman.

''He's in Kansas. Dodge City.''

''That must please your father,'' quipped Mary.

''He's furious enough that I chose the science school

at Yale instead of divinity. David is trying to get into the cattle business—and Father a vegetarian."

"Mr. Mather," interrupted Tenah, "since you are going back to school tomorrow could you please write down your father's address so Josiah can send him a letter from Canada?"

"I can do that right now," Mary went toward the living room. "Tomorrow morning we might forget it."

"Jest think," Tenah's brown eyes flashed happily. "When we get to Canada, Josiah can write my folk in Charleston, and they won't have to worry no more—and maybe we can sign the letter . . . *With Affection, from Josiah and Tenah Holladay.*"

Huddled under a tarpaulin with a plow and a load of wire and fence-posts, the fugitives were driven in a steady rain to New Milford, a distance of twenty-six miles, and delivered to Augustine Thayer by Elias Wakeman. The next day, Thayer, a dairy farmer, drove the two amidst a shipment of cheeses to Torrington, where connections were made for Bennington, Vermont. From Bennington, they were whisked to Burlington, where they were put aboard a lumber barge which was towed by a screw tug up Lake Champlain to the Richelieu River. They were met by a Canadian Underground agent at the port of St. Jean, an hour's carriage ride to Montreal.

TWELVE

Six cotton-producing states received letters from South Carolina's Governor, William Gist. He asked the governors of these states for mutual support should Lincoln be elected and South Carolina secede from the Union. The replies were as he had hoped.

On November 6, 1860, the avowed foe of slavery was elected. Lincoln, while not receiving anything like a landslide popular vote, did garner an overwhelming majority of electoral votes. Two days later, South Carolina called for a secession convention.

Reconvened a few days before Christmas, the delegation cast 169 *yeas* against not a single *nay* and *The Charleston Mercury* rushed a special edition with gigantic front-page type proclaiming:

THE UNION IS DISSOLVED

Church bells pealed and cannon saluted as the populace celebrated in the streets. Blue cockades, symbols of secession, sprouted from hats and uniforms were taken from their closets to sprightly music of the Citadel Military College band.

Across the harbor, Major Robert Anderson stood on the parapet of historic Fort Moultrie, greatly concerned with the defense of his isolated outpost amidst the rebel fervor. Garrisoned by a peacetime force of sixty-one enlisted men, seven officers and thirteen musicians, the fort was vulnerable from the rear and short of ammunition and provisions. Anderson, a Southerner whose wife owned a plantation in Georgia, had been given Moultrie's command a month earlier to placate anti-Federal feelings. His pleas to Washington for reinforcements had not been answered. His next-in-command, Captain Abner Doubleday, who was also the recreation officer, wrote in his diary:

> Anderson has been urged by us to remove his command to Fort Sumter but he replied that he was assigned to Fort Moultrie and had no right to vacate without orders. Nevertheless, he had determined to make the change, and was merely awaiting a favorable opportunity.

The day after Christmas, acting swiftly and decisively, Anderson gave his officers twenty minutes' notice to form an evacuation company and take to the boats for the incompleted, though more defensible position of the island fort. Evading a steamer at twilight, they arrived at Fort Sumter only to be confronted by workmen wearing blue cockades. Captain Doubleday ordered a show of bayonets and soon the rebels were rowing back to the mainland to the strains of The Star-Spangled Banner.

Major Anderson's surprise move so infuriated the Charlestonians that they protested to Washington, insisting that the Federal troops return to Fort Moultrie from whence they would be paroled to return north as in any arrangement between independent countries. A prominent citizen expressed the mood of the day in a letter: "Anderson has united the cotton states."

A rabble-rousing Virginian, Roger Pryor, called publicly for South Carolina to strike a convincing blow that would induce the neighboring states to secede. All eyes were on Sumter.

Outgoing President Buchanan, finally budging under pressure from aging General Winfield Scott, sent an unarmed merchant steamer, *Star of The West*, with 250 recruits and military stores to reinforce the fort, which had only a few of its guns in position. On January 9, 1861, the shallow-draft side-wheeler arrived off the Charleston bar and anchored, to await daylight before attempting the harbor channel.

That evening, a party was in progress at the Charleston mansion of the newly elected Governor, Francis Pickens. Present were Confederate delegates, local businessmen and officers of the Citadel Military College, including the commandant, Major James Stephens. The mansion, once owned by a Colonel of Artillery during the Revolution, featured a basement that was used as a pistol range and frequented by the Citadel officers at the behest of the Governor.

After wine, dinner and conversation, as the women dealt with matters of recipes and the latest English fashions, Major Stephens, a ferret for finding adversaries, challenged a visitor from Baltimore to a target duel. The gentlemen, awaiting such a cue, descended in a body, glasses in hand, to view the contest.

The visitor, Ben Barker, who was in Charleston pursuing a possible arms order from the militia, lost the match. Stephens was in turn challenged by the Marylander's young companion, Jack Renfrew. Dark, slender and with sharply chiseled features, Renfrew doffed his gray velvet coat and picked up one of the .30–caliber *Volcanic Arms* magazine pistols furnished by Stephens. He handed it to a Citadel cadet sergeant for loading.

The Major fired first. Six discharges and six times the target bell jangled. Young Renfrew cocked his brass-cased pistol and fired, sounding the bell. After two more successful shots, he held the steel muzzle up and inquired of Stephens: "May I fire from a different position?"

"This is an informal match," answered Stephens.

Renfrew performed an about-face, still holding the pistol muzzle up toward the lamp-lighted ceiling. Poker-faced, he drew a small mirror from his vest pocket, turned his hand and rested the barrel on his left shoulder. The spectators were hushed as Renfrew took aim through the mirror, at the target, twelve paces behind him. He cocked and fired three times, each ball hitting the bell. The silence grew into applause and he bowed graciously to the awestruck onlookers. After handing the pistol back, butt first, to the cadet, Renfrew accepted a glass of wine from the Virginian, Roger Pryor.

"Bravo," shouted Pryor, shaking Renfrew's free hand.

"Where'd you learn to shoot like that?" Major Stephens rubbed his chin in amazement. "Are you some trick shot artist that Ben Barker brought here just to make me look bad?"

Wine corks popped and others, including the Governor, tried their skill with the target pistols. Laughter became raucous and talk rowdy, while a seventeen-year-old girl with honey-blond long hair, wearing a petticoated white dress watched from the top of the basement stairs. "Lenora," snapped the Governor, noticing his niece enthralled by the goings-on, whereupon she whirled and disappeared like a frightened fawn.

''Excuse me, Miss Pickens,'' a uniformed cadet bumped into her and almost tripped going down the stairs. ''Major,'' shouted the cadet, ''there's a Yankee boat headed down this way. We just got a telegraph message from Wilmington. The *Star of The West,* out of New York City, was seen roundin' Cape Fear—with a lot of blue coats on deck . . .''

''That's the boat that was rumored fittin' out to reinforce Fort Sumter,'' shouted Roger Pryor.

''But President Buchanan gave me his word . . .''

''What has *he* got to lose by lying?'' roared Pryor, ''He's as good as out of the White House already.''

''Let's get a big pistol and blast the Yankee boat out of the water.'' Jack Renfrew imitated a weapon with his hand and thumb.

''Excuse me,'' Governor Pickens looked askance at the youth.

''Well, sir; we might just scare 'em with a few close shots.''

''That's just what it'll take to bring Alabama and Georgia into our tent, your honor,'' Roger Pryor's long black hair swung wildly as he took the floor. ''We've got to stand up to the Federals or nobody will. The longer nothin' happens, the stronger the lazy Yankees will get. We've got to take 'em by surprise. This here state wants to be the leader? Well then, it should lead.''

''Major Stephens,'' Renfrew enunciated clearly, ''The *Star of The West* will have to pass close in to Morris Island to get to Fort Sumter. Is that correct?''

''It will have to take the channel, yes.''

''And you have a battery on Cummings Point?'' asked Renfrew.

''Old cannon from the War of 1812. We use them for practice.''

"Well, there it is, Major," the Governor patted him on the back. "Take your cadets out to Morris Island and have them practice on the Yankee steamer if it tries to come up the channel. Put a ball across her bows. Then if she doesn't turn round, you're on your own. If they want a war, we'll give 'em one."

"Governor," snapped Renfrew, "I'd like to go along."

"Major," joked Pickens, "sign him up."

Laurie Pickens surprised Renfrew as he was about to leave the mansion. "Don't go just yet, Mister Renfrew," she tugged at his coatsleeve and led him into the anteroom, choosing a secluded corner for her purposes.

"Is my uncle sending you away because of me?"

"No, I volunteered," replied Renfrew, noticing a fragrance about the girl that attracted him. "Besides, the Governor need not fear about my intentions."

"I'm afraid he may be worried about mine," Laurie confessed coyly. "But I did so enjoy our conversation before you all went downstairs. That poem about animals—could you recite it once more before you leave?"

"It's not a poem," Jack recoiled in mock horror. It's from Shakespeare's Julius Caesar . . ."

"Oh, please," Laurie crowded him into a window drape.

Jack slipped nimbly away. "Very well, if you insist. . . . The Conspirators are concerned that Caesar, forewarned by augurers, will not come to the Capitol. Decius Brutus has this to say:

> Never fear that. If he be so resolved,
> I can o'ersway him; for he loves to hear
> That unicorns may be betrayed by trees,
> And bears with glasses, elephants with holes,
> Lions with toils, and men with flatterers. . . .

"Oh, that's absolutely marvelous," Laurie moved closer to him and straightened his necktie. He felt her body against his, her warm, moist breath on his cheek. Then he thought of his promise to the former Secretary of War, John Buchanan Floyd, an acquaintance in Washington. Floyd, a staunch pro-slavery Virginian, had been asked to resign over charges of profiteering. The politician, a man of deviate pursuits, had confided to him of a plan to send large stores of government arms to Southern arsenals in anticipation of war. His promise, in exchange for a lucrative position as a secret agent of the secessionists, was to avoid social entanglements that would impair his efficiency and endanger the cause. Floyd had instructed him to go to Charleston, observe the proceedings and await further orders.

Miss Picken's loquacity seemed potentially dangerous to his assignment, considering her *milieu*, and his own weakness for unsullied young women.

"Miss Pickens, I've had a delightful time, but now I must leave. Perhaps another day—"

Laurie extended her hand, expecting him to be *galante* and kiss it, but he'd already turned toward the door. Piqued, she kicked her shoe across the room after him.

A bright red flag, with a yellow palmetto tree emblazoned on it, flew gaudily over the sand dunes at Cummings Point on the northern tip of Morris Island. Captain McGowan, master of the *Star of The West*, ignored it as the sidewheeler ran up the channel, approaching the point. Two miles ahead, in the morning haze, loomed Fort Sumter. On the shores to either side of the beleaguered bastion stood the secessionist batteries of Forts Moultrie and Johnson. Below decks on the *Star of The West*, 250 'bluebellies' waited anxiously with loaded muskets.

Suddenly, a puff of black smoke appeared near the

palmetto flag on Cummings Point off the port bow, and a geyser erupted, a hundred yards short of the steamer. McGowan ordered the stars and stripes up the foremast and called for more speed.

Another shot screamed from the hidden emplacement, struck the water in line with the *Star,* then bounded over the steamer. Increasing in rapidity as Major Stephen's cadets zeroed in, the balls came closer to their target, one narrowly missing the *Star*'s wheelhouse and another striking the forechains. Realizing that being fired upon was not part of the leasing agreement with the Federal government, McGowan swung his helm around and made for the open sea.

The *Star of The West* incident set ablaze the fuse that had been laid out by Major Anderson. Mississippi seceded on the same day, with Florida and Alabama following. By February 1, Texas and Louisiana had left the Union as well.

Slowly, the sleeping Federal giant stirred, its powerful warships moving from idle moorings to head south. One by one, the Union forts in the "secesh" harbors were taken by the state militias, hungry for cannon and shot.

Officially, the South did not want war and their reactions were dependent on whether the Federals would try to reinforce their threatened forts. The USS *Brooklyn,* an intimidating warship, was sent to Pensacola to strengthen Fort Pickens, while several other ships stood by for Sumter, despite President Buchanan's pledge to the Charlestonians. It was not until Lincoln's inauguration on March 4, 1861, that the Federal gauntlet was thrown. Lincoln took a firm stand on the forts and ordered relief boats to Sumter. Despite the initial secrecy of the mission, the armada's departure became known and Charleston was warned. A

Confederate peace commission, in Washington at the time, hastily made for home.

Colonel Pierre Beauregard, having resigned as commandant of West Point upon the secession of his native Louisiana, was appointed by Jefferson Davis as Brigadier-general of the new Confederate Army and put in charge of the Sumter situation. The relief ships were due in Charleston on April 10, but were delayed by an Atlantic gale. Well prepared, the harbor was lit with flares and calcium lamps, in anticipation of a night foray by the Union navy.

Beauregard advised Major Anderson to evacuate or be fired upon, but the latter declined, stating that he had provisions to last a few more days. Finally, at 3:30 on the morning of the 11th, a Federal fleet had grouped at the Charleston bar, with orders to wait for the powerful warship *Powhatan* before entering the harbor.

Not knowing of this order, General Beauregard had the harbor batteries commence firing. After two days of incessant bombardment, Fort Sumter, depleted of supplies, hauled down its flag.

Advised of this by telegraph, President Lincoln called for 75,000 volunteers. On the 16th, General Robert E. Lee was offered command of the Union Army, but instead, he resigned. Lincoln then ordered a blockade of all Confederate ports.

A civil war had started!

THIRTEEN

It was ten o'clock in the morning, a time when the good citizens of 'the state of steady habits' were industriously occupied, and unconcerned with the splendid young man who sprang off the train from New Haven. Bess Mather had written Howell Clyburn and asked that he spend a few days in Stamford before going on to Charleston. He'd agreed and sent his luggage ahead. They were going to carve some time out of the war for themselves, and Bess had worked it all out. A *necessary surprise*, she'd called it in her letter.

Howell Clyburn was among the first in the class of '61 to leave for the South. He notified the dean shortly after the news of Fort Sumter had been received, and then he organized a group of Southerners who "appropriated" a palm tree from its pot in the lobby of North Church and fastened it to Alumni Hall's proud tower as a symbol of secession—South Carolina's palmetto. He felt like the enemy at Yale—in New Haven, the center of industrial New England and bastion of Union arms production. And there was the William Miles case . . . fanned again by the events in Charleston . . . and by the attack upon the 6th Massachusetts by a mob in Baltimore. High time that he went back to his home and his own people. Lincoln had called for 75,000 volunteers. Three-month volunteers! Hell, he mused, it'll take a lot longer than three months for a recruit blue belly to come anywheres near to bein' the equal of a Santee-bred soldier. No, there was too much had been done to be undone in three months. Too long simmering on the fire to be put out so quick—if at all.

Carrying a striped blue gripsack, Howell walked round the side of the station house and sat on a baggage wagon. Bess had written that she'd come by in a buggy and pick him up as fast as possible so as not to chance "people knowing." As far as her parents knew, she was on her way to spend some of the Easter recess with the family of a classmate in Rye town. He took a small package from his grip, untied it, then sprinkled tobacco on a piece of thin linen paper. The newest fad at school; little cigars to be made upon demand. *Cigarettes,* as the French called them. Hardly had he licked the paper when a one-horse calash-topped buggy careened to a dusty stop just short of the baggage wagon. Bess motioned to him from under the hood and he climbed aboard, sliding his gripsack under the seat. The French linen paper was stuck to his lip.

After a quick embrace, Bess snapped the reins and shortly they were racing along the Boston Post Road, joyously alone under the buggy's black hood.

"Where are you spiriting me off to?" Howell tugged at the cigarette paper to little avail, then let it be.

"It's my surprise—a place of legend and dreams," Bess shook her flowing auburn hair from her eyes. "As a very young girl I used to go there and wish for someone just like you. My wish came true and now I want to show you off to the Indian spirits in the valley that made it possible. About 200 years ago a seventeen-year-old girl from Holland was traveling on this road, on her way to marry a friend of her father's whom she had never met. The father had 'arranged' the marriage upon his death-bed and sent his daughter to America to be the bride of a man three times her age. While brooding of this unhappy prospect, a young Indian disrupted the party by shooting arrows past the wagon. Never had she looked upon such a man. His long, black hair hung about his shoulders and his sharp, dark features shone in the afternoon sun. For a moment, his eyes caught hers. The brave walked calmly up to the wagon's guide and spoke in a strange language, whereupon his statement was translated to English, which Hilda understood well enough:

'Tell Sunny Hair that Lone Heart never will shoot a woman. His arrows are for the rabbit.'

"Afterwards, the guide warned Hilda to beware of Lone Heart. The brave was husband to old Chief Cos Cob's only offspring. She was a bad woman, much feared by the tribe. Lone Heart had not wanted to marry her but she bewitched his arrows so he was unable to hunt well and had to marry her for his own survival. The squaw was a jealous woman and threatened to kill him if he even spoke to another woman. . . ."

"This sounds like a story in *Leslie's Weekly.*" Howell hung tightly to the buggy seat as they rounded a sharp curve.

"Except, there *is* a real place where the legend comes from. Hilda married her father's friend, Cornelius Labden. He was called 'Laddin' by the townsfolk and neighbors."

After a while, Bess turned the buggy into a narrow road that zig-zagged down through the woods. Arriving at a clearing, Long Island Sound was spread before them, and beyond, a ribbon of sand cliffs and blue hills extended as far as they could see in both directions. Leaving the horse and rig under a shady oak, they strolled along a forest footpath and came to a precipitous rocky bluff, jutting out over a hundred-foot deep ravine.

"This is called Laddin's Rock," Bess held Howell by the arm as she dared look over the edge. The ravine had an awesome, silent beauty. Giant hemlocks flared up from the distant ground, their tapered tops hardly higher than the couple's heads. A silver-flecked stream threaded its way through the mossy, fern-covered valley and a solitary bird-call added an unworldly loneliness to the vista. It was as if time did not matter, and it could have been a thousand years earlier.

They carefully descended by a side path until they reached the fragrant fern carpet and breathlessly looked up in wonder at the shafts of light playing through the lofty hemlock tops they had earlier stood level with.

"This," announced Bess, pointing at a massive rock imbedded in the earth, "was where Hilda and Lone Heart lay when they were spied upon by Chief Cos Cob's daughter. It had been their meeting place for the entire summer. Laddin's house, since burned, was a short walk from the rock that bears his name, and Hilda, after the wedding, came down here to wash clothes and linens. One day she was surprised—pleasantly—to encounter Lone Heart at this stream. Noticing that one of his feet was cut and bruised, she tore her linen and bandaged him. That was the beginning. The legend says that this rock, by the stream, was not here when they met and came here by a curious way."

"It looks natural enough to me," Howell walked around it, examining its strata and fissures. "But I think we should consult your brother, the scientific genius."

"Swanny," Bess exclaimed facetiously, "don't irritate the Quinnhitituckss. That's the tribe's name. This is a very sacred place. . . . Though married to genial Cornelius, Hilda felt little remorse at having her first true love affair.

"One evening, when Cornelius was in New Amsterdam—that's New York City—to buy her a spinning wheel, she met Lone Heart, as usual, who took her down to the beach to a secluded cabin he had built for her on the long point where the water sparkles on the many pebbles. They spent the night in that cabin, sleeping by a romantic fireplace, unaware of the Indian woman who had followed them.

"Cos Cob's daughter spoke to the braves at a conclave, inciting them to vengeance against the white squaw in the name of her father. She pointed out that the white settlers had built their cabins on Indian lands and now the Dutchman's wife was defiling the tribe's remaining grounds by washing clothes in the ravine. The white squaw was evil. Lone Heart had been bewitched by the Sun spirit in her yellow hair. The braves, said she, must free Lone Heart to be the next chief and protect the valley from being taken over by the white squaw's people.

"The braves, bound to do her bidding, attacked the settler's houses, killing and scalping several families. Meanwhile, Cornelius, returning to his own cabin, found Hilda gone. Assuming the Indians had carried her off, he loaded his fowling piece and shot one of the braves. Jumping on his horse, he led the maddened braves to that rock," Bess pointed upwards. "When Cornelius looked down here, he saw his wife lying with Lone Heart. His horse reared and jumped, followed by a horde of Indians, whose weight broke loose a part of the rock ledge which fell into the ravine—upon the lovers, upon Cornelius, and upon Cos Cob's daughter, who was spying on them. This rock marks their graves."

"You may call me 'sunny hair'," joked Howell as he took her in his arms, backing her against the rock.

"Just a minute," Bess cautioned him, then wet her finger and dampened the cigarette paper, of which a small part still clung to his lip. She peeled it off carefully and his mouth found hers. The magic of the rock tingled through her body and she responded, struggling but giving. Deep forest fragrances overwhelmed her as the Southerner took those liberties that she had always secretly desired. Not since the boathouse rendezvous in New Haven almost a year earlier had she been alone with Howell—and then they had been rudely interrupted by Cyrus Whitlock. She closed her eyes as she felt his hand under her petticoats and his hot breath on her neck. "Darling," she protested, "there's a cabin down near the beach. It was where I thought we could go. . . ."

"Fine," he murmured. "Later . . ."

Suddenly Bess felt deliciously weak, his gentle manipulations having achieved their intended result. He drew her down and she felt cool air in her most secret place. Leaves clinging to her hair, she opened her eyes and, with his weight heavy upon her, his head buried in her shoulder, she gave herself to him. At first there was a hint of pain, changing into sublime pleasure as, high above, the hemlock tops wavered in the sunlight and myriad meteors seemed to explode inside her. Then, all was still once more, and a blue and purple butterfly, iridescently shining, alighted on his shoulder.

The cabin, secluded by a grassy knoll near the beach was well-stocked for the tryst. Bess had borrowed it through a classmate whose father used it as a hunting and fishing lodge. She had made sure there was good, dry wood for the fireplace and food enough to satisfy an outdoorsman such as Howell. After starting the fire, they crawled under fresh linen and heavy bearskin covers and fell asleep for several hours. Awakening, they made love again, then dashed down to the gently rippling moonlit water to bathe before returning to the cabin, refreshed and hungry. With a leg of succulent lamb sizzling on the fireplace spit, they poured wine with the door bolted against Indian squaws and chiefs. Potatoes and green beans, carrots and corn bread, stewed plums and vanilla pudding graced the rustic cabin table in steaming succession. "I spent most of yesterday preparing for this," Bess proudly opened a bottle of brandy and poured excitedly.

"And now, for entertainment. . . ." With a flourish, she set a deck of cards and a cribbage board before Howell.

"One of the reasons this game is such a favorite of mine," observed Howell as, to Bess's chagrin, he scored a pair royal, "is that it's reputed to have been invented by one Sir John Suckling." He advanced his peg six holes on the board. "According to Aubrey's *Short Lives*, Sir John, a poet, was also handsome, rich and popular. He was, in addition, the best card player and bowler in King Charles' court. Anyone who can succeed in life with a name like Suckling has my deepest respect."

"Did Sir Suckling ever get married? Bess moved her peg.

"I believe he did elope—after being exiled for opposing the king. However, Sir John committed suicide by poison in Spain after learning he had lost his riches by Royal decree. . . ."

"Then he didn't succeed in life."

"He did very well in England. Many people never succeed at all. Isn't it possible to succeed *at first,* contrary to the nursery school proverb?"

"If at first you don't succeed, try, try again," recited

Bess. "Does that mean one might change it to 'If at first you *do* succeed?' Then what?"

"One might still *try, try again.*"

"You've succeeded with me," she smiled.

"And vice-versa," Howell counted off three more peg holes.

"But you're going off to war . . . so very far away. We won't even be able to play games anymore. Swanny," she pouted, "I want to go with you—or I'll come to Charleston when school is out."

"Bess, it'll be too dangerous for you—"

"You should talk about danger—with all those southern belles. They're worse than a war for me. I'll just have to come down and protect you. You're so handsome and brilliant, *Doctor* Clyburn. And you're so *good.*"

"I'm not sure your brother would agree to that."

"Oh, you know what I mean—and don't worry about Nat. He's just a little stand-offish, like father. I'm more like my mother. Pies, jams and warm puddings . . . One for his nob. Seven." Bess laid her cards on the table.

"Sorry, Bess." Howell moved his peg five spaces. "Fifteen two and a run of three. That's the game. I think, as my prize, I shall demand that. . . ." He didn't finish the sentence. She was on him like a cat, so he lay back and watched the firelight flickering on the cabin ceiling.

FOURTEEN

Gustavus Vasa Fox, a former naval officer, had directed the unsuccessful attempt to relieve Fort Sumter. A visionary, with 18 years' service, he'd resigned his commission in 1856 because of stagnation and outdated promotion procedure in the United States Navy. But for confusion between Lincoln and Gideon Welles, Secretary of the Navy, the USS *Powhatan* would have gone to Sumter instead of Pensacola, in time to assist the beleaguered Federal outpost and probably prevent its surrender. Fox, a fair and respected businessman, complained through channels and received a letter of apology from the President. Lincoln offered Fox a commission and a ship. Well advised, Fox instead took a position in the Navy Department and soon a new post was created for him; Assistant Secretary of the Navy.

His appointment rejuvenated the service. An advocate of steam, he had commanded mail steamers and even gotten experience while out of the navy as an executive with a Hartford textile mill. The first thing he did was to scour the country for new talent, especially in science and mechanics. Among the sources contacted was the Sheffield School of Science at Yale College.

In June of 1861, Nathaniel Mather was commissioned as a Lieutenant in the Naval Ordnance Bureau under Captain John Dahlgren, Commandant of the Washington Navy Yard. Several weeks later, Secretary Fox briefed Dahlgren's staff. . . .

"The South will have to compensate for its lack of industrial power by developing expedient and novel weapons. The Navy Department has received intelligence that the Confederate Navy, such as it is, is concentrating on two things—the building or purchasing of ironclad warships, and the development of torpedo weapons. England and France have built ironclads . . ." Fox gestured at an easel, upon which was exhibited a print of the French warship, *Glorie*. ". . . but unfortunately, our navy has been top-heavy with old-line sailing admirals. The President has just authorized Secretary Welles to proceed with a program for building an ironclad. The department is advertising for offers to build armored vessels of not less than ten nor over sixteen feet draft. . . . The vessel to be rigged with two masts and wire rope standing rigging. The date for bids is September 9th, and the date for commissioning will be late in January of 1862.

"We have little experience in this field. Some work has been done on a floating battery covered with iron plates, but we need a maneuverable vessel, fitted with the latest of Captain Dahlgren's guns. Our esteemed inventor is responsible for our present dilemma. He has developed guns that no wooden ship can withstand. And what happens? The Norfolk Navy yard is abandoned to the rebels along with fifty-two Dahlgren 9-inchers. We have reason to believe that nine of these guns will be installed in a

Confederate ironclad. That boat is our own USS *Merrimac*, a large steam frigate which had been scuttled and burned to the waterline at Norfolk. The rebels have raised and hauled her to a drydock. Tredegar Iron Works in Richmond has just put on extra shifts to roll 2-inch iron sheets. Captain Dahlgren, can your new 11-inch gun pierce 2 inches of rolled iron plate backed with two feet of oak and inclined at a sixty degree angle?''

''Most assuredly, Mr. Secretary. We have test-fired to that effect with a 15-pound powder charge.''

The secretary walked over to the easel again and slipped a second drawing over the *Glorie*. ''This, gentlemen, is the CSS *Merrimac*, as we think it will look. Note the ram at the bow. Two tons of iron to terrify any wooden boat. The Union Navy has no match for this proposed vessel. With it, the rebels intend to smash our blockade. Unless we can stop it, even our northern seaports will be in grave danger. Now, Commander Davis, you will report to Captain Dahlgren regarding any promising designs submitted—as soon as you get them. We don't want to have to wait till the deadline date.

''The second thorn in our side is the submarine torpedo. The Confederate Navy engineers—officers we have sailed with—are devising infernal machines to blow up our ships in the rivers and harbors of the South. We have to find out what they are doing, where they are doing it, and how to stop them. This brings us to Lieutenant Mather. Lieutenant, your assignment is to penetrate the secrecy of such projects and prepare ordnance reports for Captain Dahlgren. As an engineer from the acclaimed Sheffield School, your expertise in metallurgy, chemistry and ballistic sciences will be welcomed by the Navy Department.

''Gentlemen,'' Gustavus Fox extended his hand to each of the officers in turn, wishing them the best of luck.

As he shook Nat's hand he cocked his head. "Lieutenant, you be extra careful. Tall men make good targets."

"Good afternoon, Bob." Old Clem Hodges stopped in front of a trim red brick house on fashionable Clay Street in Richmond, Virginia, the newly designated capital of the Confederacy. "We sure beat hell out of th' Yankees at Manassas, eh."

"Looks like the young'uns will do well enough without us old codgers," Robert Maury sat down on the top step of the stoop.

"Hell, Bob, you weren't even born when I was with Jackson at New Orleans. How about Matthew? I hear he's stayin' with you. Is Jeff Davis gonna give him a ship?" A sharp explosion from inside the house startled Hodges. "What on earth. . . ."

"Cousin Matt is in the Governor's defense council," Robert gestured nonchalantly behind his back. "He's doin' some research."

Matthew Fontaine Maury, stocky and balding, hopped lamely around the cast-iron bathtub as his sixteen-year-old daughter, Betty looked on. "That was too deep, Pa. The charge has to be closer to the boat." Betty pulled a pair of wires out of the tub and dried the exposed ends. She then spliced them to a fine platinum wire that ran through a goosequill of fulminate. After waterproofing the explosive cap with molten wax she handed it to her father who positioned it carefully atop a tower of bricks under the surface of the tub water. Next, Betty placed a toy wooden rowboat on the surface over the joined wires.

"Mind you now, stand back," Maury warned his daughter as he turned a magneto hand crack vigorously, hand poised over a telegraph key contact switch. "One

. . . two . . . three—'', he pressed the key down, closing the circuit. A sharp, muffled report echoed through the house as water erupted out of the tub. Father and daughter rushed to the tub. Of the toy rowboat, only pieces remained, bobbing in the water. Dripping wet, they joyously hugged each other.

The coopers, Talbot and Son on Cary Street, built a large oak cask to Maury's specifications, while Governor Letcher ordered two barrels of gunpowder for him from the Richmond arsenal.

On a sweltering day in late June, the prominent civil and military dignitaries in Virginia gathered at Rockett's Wharf on the south bank of the James River for a full-scale test of Maury's apparatus. With his son Richard aboard, Maury rowed out to midstream in a skiff where he floated his torpedo cask and set the percussion cap trigger. He was disappointed that not enough insulated wire was available so that instead of electrical detonation, he was demonstrating a mechanical device. At a prudent distance, his son yanked a long lanyard and a column of water rose twenty feet. Scores of dead and stunned fish popped to the surface as the onlooking officials appluaded.

On a ridge overlooking the river, a tall figure in clerical collar and a black suit, sitting on a horse, closed up his telescope and tucked it into a saddle bag. He patted the horse on its neck and then cantered on his way.

As a result of the demonstration, Maury was appointed Chief of Confederate River and Harbor Defenses. Given the rank of captain, he was provided with a troop of assistants and ample funds for development of his weapons.

The first targets Maury chose for his torpedoes were the Federal blockading flagships USS *Minnesota* and

Roanoke, lying at their moorings in Hampton Roads off the mouth of the James River.

On a hot Sunday night in early July, with a comet blazing in the sky, Maury set out with five skiffs carrying four keg torpedoes and two lengths of floating bridle rope. At a point upriver from the fleet, with the tide running out, Maury's crew bent the ropes to the kegs and put them overboard. They were close enough to the *Minnesota* to hear voices from the fo'c'sle. The kegs, with 400 pounds of cannon powder in copper boilers suspended beneath them, drifted into the darkness on a five-knot current.

Meg, Betty Maury's elder sister, wrote in her diary:

> They rowed for some distance and waited for the explosions, which never came. Thank God, for had the Union ships been blown up, Pa would certainly have been caught and hung . . .

"You did a fine Christian deed." Nat Mather patted Meg on the shoulder, then withdrew his hand, realizing that his touching her did more to him than proper for a man of the cloth.

"Oh Reverend Cotton, the good Lord, through you, heard my plea and rendered the torpedoes ineffective. Mother is also very happy. She's always told Pa that it is barbarous to blow up your fellow men without giving them a chance to defend themselves."

"You haven't told your mother about me. . . ."

"No, Reverend Cotton—we do have an understanding. You came all the way from Louisiana to study the morals of the South first-hand . . . and you can't do that if everybody knows just who you are and what you're about doing. . . ."

"Call me Nathaniel."

"Oh, this is so exciting. It's like having my own personal preacher and confessor—You're not Catholic, are you? Bein' from Louisiana and all. Pa wouldn't like me to—"

"Quite the opposite, I assure you." Nat unfolded his copy of the *Richmond Dispatch* and sat down on the park bench, a discreet distance from the dark-haired belle. Immersed in the newspaper's pages, Nat spoke softly. "Now, we don't want people to get the wrong ideas. . . ."

"Nobody I know comes to this part of Byrd Park," Meg moved closer to Nat. "I used to come here when we visited Uncle Robert—that's when Pa was in the Navy in Washington."

"In the Union Navy?"

"He had thirty years in until they retired him, but because he was so good they reinstated him three years ago." Meg leaned forward and read the headline of the *Dispatch*. "Nathaniel, do you think it's fair that part of Virginia has refused to secede?"

"No slaves . . . no reason to secede. Miners and mountain people are different from planters. But, in effect, the western counties are seceding from Virginia. If the Union can be broken, why not a state?"

"You men are so much better at politics."

"Meg, what was your father's duty in Washington?"

"He was commander of the Naval Observatory until he resigned—the day after Virginia seceded. My father is not pro-slavery, nor did he agree with secession, but he is a Virginian. What the Navy Department did to him was no help either—retiring the one officer of the Navy who had distinguished himself in his field. It very nearly broke him. He bears a heavy grudge."

Nat reflected for a moment. "It seems that I remember the name . . . a scientific book. . . ."

"He wrote a book that was translated into several languages. It's called *The Physical Geography of the Sea*. Much too complicated for a small-town girl like me. Nathaniel, it's too bad you have to wear that collar all the time. . . ."

"How's that?"

"Well, if it weren't for the collar, we might go over to a charming little inn on the river and have some tea." Meg smacked her lips. "It's only a short walk from here."

"Done." Nat tore his collar off, stood up and bowed gallantly. "To the inn, madame?"

"Nathaniel." Meg's glistening black hair had become partially undone and she occasionally slurred a word. "Is li'l old Meg Maury gonna be an example of lascivious Southern morals in your study?" She squeezed his hand on her lap, sitting in a snug wooden booth in a secluded corner of the Old Bridge Inn. "Don't be bashful, Reverend Nathaniel, this is the most notorious establishment in Richmond." Meg, her glass empty, reached for Nat's brandy. He took it from her reach.

"You said you were worried about your father's next experiment. Tell me about it," Nat held up his glass.

"That is a Confederate secret," whispered Meg.

"Is there a more southern name than Nat Cotton?"

"That's true." she absentmindedly moved her hand under the table to Nat's lap, then blushed and withdrew quickly. "Where are you staying?"

"What have you in mind, young lady?"

"I'm not used to brandy . . . and . . . if you were staying upstairs, I could borrow your room and rest for a while. My father wouldn't take well to my comin' home in this condition. He's very religious. Just for a short time. . . ."

"Very well, wait here. I'll arrange for a room in my name and give you the key. Then I'll hire a carriage to my hotel and bring my things here. It shouldn't take more than an hour—or, if you find you need more rest. . . ."

"An hour will be enough."

Nat waited until the lobby was clear, then slipped up the stairs to the second floor. Setting down his bag, he tapped lightly on the door of his room. "It's me, Nathaniel."

"I'm ready, Nathaniel. The door is open."

Nat turned the knob and entered. The bed was made and not a sign of Meg. Suddenly the door swung shut behind him, and before he could turn, soft arms encircled his neck. The window curtains were drawn. He looked sidewise at a wall mirror, then closed his eyes in disbelief. It seemed as if he saw a woman embracing him from behind—a woman without shame, and utterly without clothes.

"I'm not sorry I took advantage of you." Meg Maury gazed out over Hampton Roads where the Federal blockading fleet of five warships lay placidly at their moorings.

"I was equally at fault." Nat focused his glass on a fishing skiff that was being rowed out from the shore below his vantage point on a wooden elevation. There were three men in the boat and a quantity of fishing net.

"Nat," Meg entreated, "I've never done such a thing before. You have to believe me . . . it was the brandy."

"I believe you—and what's more, I'm not sorry either."

"Oh, Nathaniel." Meg threw her arms around him. "I just *knew* you were the right man. We *do* have an understanding. I so wish that you could meet my father some day. You'd like him."

"I'm not so sure he'd feel the same way."

"Let 'er go." Matthew Maury gave the signal and his son cut loose the 200-pound mushroom anchor that had been lashed to the skiff, invisible below the water line. Next, the other crewman made a show of heaving the fishing net overboard as the buoyed torpedo was also cut loose, the skiff lying athwart the ebb tidal flow. A sailor aboard the USS *Roanoke,* a steam frigate of forty powerful guns, watched the proceedings from the bowsprit, unaware of the fishing skiff's real mission.

Descending with the mushroom anchor was a doubled insulated wire reeved through a pulley on the shank. One end was fixed to the copper-clad torpedo magazine while the other ran from the pulley all the way to shore, about a quarter-mile distant. Captain Maury had calculated the delivery of his torpedo through precise measurements of the magazine buoyancy, depth of water, and velocity of tidal flow. It remained only to row back to shore and feed out pre-marked lengths of cable to insure that the 1000 pounds of explosive would be carried by tide and buoyancy from the anchor to within yards of the *Roanoke's* vulnerable hull.

Leading his horse, Nat made his way down through the woods, where he spotted a wagon, concealed from the sea by a covering of pine branches. Tethering the horse, he crept closer until he could see, on the wagon, a series of glass cells connected by copper wire. It was a Cruikshank galvanic battery, similar to one used by the Sheffield Scientific School at Yale. Careful not to be seen by a solitary guard, he mounted his horse and trotted down to the narrow beach, where he again assumed the posture of a traveling man of God. By this time, Maury's skiff was approaching the shore so Nat took his cue and trotted in the water along the shore, passing between the battery-wagon and the boat, where he noticed, half-buried in the sand, a telegraphic cable. Then he realized it was not one, but two cables, a certain indication that the purpose was not communication, which used "earth-return" for the circuit completion, but rather activation of some insulated object. An electric current to be sent into the water in the general direction of the enemy's fleet with a return cable meant just one thing: electrical detonation of a torpedo or mine.

Nat dismounted, slapped his horse and sent him galloping into the brush, then crawled behind a large rock close to the cables. Drawing his large-bore boot pistol, he put the muzzle against one of the cables and fired, parting the copper wire within. Then he buried the cable in the sand and crawled away before the lookout ventured out from his hiding place. Seeing the cable apparently intact, the guard waded into the river to take the bowline of Maury's incoming skiff.

Once again on the bluff overlooking the fleet, Nat took note of the sun's position, then sighted a signaling mirror on the *Roanoke*. Over and over several times he flashed SOS . . . TORPEDO . . . BOW . . . SOS . . . TORPEDO . . . BOW. . . . From the approach of the skiff and the direction of the cables, Nat had deduced that the torpedo had been placed forward of the warship.

Within minutes, *Roanoke's* anchor chain rattled out scope as the two-masted steamer backed off with the tide and fired up its boilers. A gig was lowered from its davits, manned by a detail of sailors brandishing long boat hooks and muskets. Plying the water forward of the warship, the detail picked up one of the telegraph cables and severed it with wire cutters. After attaching a float to the shore-directed end, they hauled carefully on the other until the torpedo was visible just under the water surface. Wary of a possible percussion detonator, the officer-in-charge ordered his men to tow the magazine to a reef where it was lashed to leeward, presenting no danger to the blockading fleet.

"Your father will not be hung for this attempt either." Nat kissed Meg quickly. "But he'd better hide. Those Yanks don't take too well to inhumane warfare. They'll probably send a shore party in to look around."

"This time it wasn't God, was it?"

"Well," Nat imitated Howell Clyburn's manner, "you might say I did what he tol' me to."

They rode together for a while, then said goodbye; but not before Nat promised to write from the next city he was to stop in as part of his "morals of the South" tour. Nat galloped on to the town of Smithfield and the home of a clandestine Union sympathizer, where arrangements were made to be picked up by a small boat from the USS *Minnesota,* flagship of the blockaders. In uniform once again, he was transferred to the *Marblehead,* a fast gunboat, which sped him, along with the fleet's mail, to the Navy yard in Washington, D.C.

Commander Davis tidied up his desk, then held up a letter. "You've done a hell of a job, Lieutenant. If I may read:

> Through information provided by your department, we have apprehended, and have in custody an agent

suspected of being the purchaser and procurer of insulated telegraph wire for the Confederate States. The President is mightily pleased.

signed, Gideon Welles,
Secretary of the Navy.

"If I may ask, Lieutenant—off the record, of course—how did you come across this information?"

"Off the record, Commander—there's a certain young lady, now in Richmond, with whom a certain man of the cloth was not entirely celibate. . . ."

FIFTEEN

The populace of the town of Brandywine had turned out to welcome Orton and Older's Traveling Fair. Shouts of "Johnny Rebel" were mingled with the cheers for the performers and officials since the company was fresh from a tour of the South. One of the partners, P.A. Older, freely admitted that his friends included General Lee and Jefferson Davis as well as General Scott and Abe Lincoln—depending on where he happened to be at the time.

Nathaniel Mather, like many others from the Navy Yard in nearby Washington, had chosen to spend a sunny July day taking in the sights and ballyhoo of the midway. "Lieutenant," a man drawled from within a rope enclosure, "Try your hand at my artillery?" He held out a handful of wooden hoops and pointed to three waddling white ducks. "Six throws fer a dime . . . ring 'em and win 'em."

Children on various rides were shrieking—a merry-go-round driven by a cantankerous steam engine with a calliope . . . and ups and downs wheel powered by dray horses. Garish barkers pitched their wares to sailors, enticing them into a tent emblazoned with a thinly-clad Princess of the Nile, while young ladies in hoop-skirts excitedly peeped into a 'lantern magica' apparatus to the drone of a hurdy-gurdy.

A group of Union soldiers, dressed in *zouave* regalia, blue jackets, scarlet trousers and white turbans, sang popular ditties in front of a tent operated by the Sanitary Commission, a group devoted to the welfare of prisoners of war. Nat dropped a new dollar greenback into the collection box and the zouave chorus cheerfully saluted without missing a note. Dodging a trained bear on a chain led by a rawhide-attired trapper, Nat was drawn to a commotion beyond the fair grounds where a multi-colored tent seemed to undulate above the crowd in a non-existent breeze.

The "tent" proved to be a balloon being inflated by workmen operating hydrogen gas generators. A sign announced:

Jean LaMont
AERONAUT
Ascents Hourly
starting at 1 PM
$1 per person

The aeronaut, dressed in a French military uniform of the previous century, held the crowd's attention. ". . . and my grandmothair, she marry a montgolfier—that means in English, 'master of the mountain'—and then my mothair, she marry a LaMont, which means 'ordinary mountain.' My family, we come to Montreal and I come to this country to work for the famous aeronaut, Professor John Wise. I go with him on the longest balloon trip in history—

from St. Louis to Syracuse in New York. Then I make my own balloon, and my little sister, she come from Canada to help me . . ." LaMont held up her hand. "Ladies and gentlemen, thees is Micheline. Soon she become the best lady aeronaut in ze world. Now who will be first to go up wiz me? I take two passengers at one time . . . and my sister, she take your money . . ." LaMont bowed courteously, then went over to the balloon to direct the preparation.

With an invisible force urging him, Nat got on the line, ultimately realizing that the attraction was as much the aeronaut's lovely sister as the balloon itself. Standing tall in line, Nat studied the shapely young beauty, her somewhat careless sable hair glistening in the morning sun. She possessed a perpetual smile that tempted him to smile in return. There was something about her that was very refined, yet at the same time naughtily elfin—quite unlike the young ladies he'd known in Connecticut.

When she gave him his ticket, the accidental, casual touch of her hand affected him as nothing ever had before. Was this the effect of a month behind rebel lines? He looked long and deep into her lavender eyes, and she became so flustered that she forgot to give him change from his five-dollar gold piece. Realizing her mistake was the reason he didn't leave, she blushed and counted out the change. "I don't usually—Please be here five minutes before three o'clock . . . Mister. . . ." her pencil was poised over a manifest.

"Nathaniel Mather; Lieutenant, U.S.N."

At first, it was like viewing the fair from the topgallant yard of a frigate, but then the realization set in that there was nothing between him and the hard earth except a few ropes. Nat swallowed uneasily as he looked from his wicker basket perch at the silvery Potomac, meandering north to the nation's capital city. A sudden gust of wind caught the gas bag above him, swinging the car like a pendulum and throwing the occupants off balance.

"You'll get used to it, Lieutenant. Just theenk of air as a three-dimensional ocean." shouted Jean LaMont.

"I'll remember that—if I ever go up again. Do you mind?" Nat reached for a sheathed telescope and the aeronaut handed it to him with a nod of approval. "Don't look west," he joked, "or the rebels will start shooting at us."

Nat took off his service cap and drew the glass out to its full length. The idea of looking at the rebels intrigued him, especially looking for the rebel's boats. Certainly a boat as large as a first-line frigate would be easily spotted from a balloon. He focused on a ferry that was leaving Port Washington, then turned the glass toward the lush, green Virginia shore . . . toward Mt. Vernon. It was all so tranquil . . . farming country . . . grazing fields for spirited horses, broken only by the occasional puff of smoke from a railroad locomotive heading west.

Yet there were slaves in those green fields far away and below—and somewhere out on the horizon, perhaps a stop for the puffing train, lay the quiet town of Manassas Junction, near where General McDowell's Union forces had been routed in the first major battle of the war. Where a thousand men had fallen.

"I send letter to your generals in Washington about looking at the rebels from my balloon. My friend, Professor Wise—he got a job with your army, but his balloon, she get caught in the telegraph wires and she fly away with Union soldier's rifles to the rebel lines. Army pay good money for good look . . ."

"Maybe the Navy could use you too," Nat thought

of the Confederate ironclads. A balloon might be able to direct Union guns against the ironclads. Simply run a telegraph wire down to the gun emplacements, regardless that the target is hidden from ground observation—or run it down to a floating battery, to a gunboat lying in the river. A marine compass in the gondola . . . transmit the azimuth reading, the balloon's altitude—or the altitude could be marked on the guide rope in calm air—then transmit the declination angle of the target. "Mr. LaMont, I hope you are not one to get seasick. The Navy needs you."

SIXTEEN

The tall, gaunt Commander-in-Chief walked slowly around the table eyeing the painted gray cardboard model like a stalking pelican. Lincoln stroked his beard pensively, sighed, and continued his pacing. The war room at the Navy Department in Washington, under a Marine guard, was host to a gathering of high Naval officers, their aides, and several officials and business dignitaries. Secretary of the Navy, Gideon Welles and Assistant Secretary Vasa Fox looked approvingly at two-foot long flat hull upon which was set a squat cylinder—appearing like a hatbox, with twin adjacent slots showing gun muzzles. Two smoke-stacks aft and a tiny cubicular pilot house forward of the turret were the only other visible structures of the bizarre vessel.

Commander Charles Davis, junior memeber, at 55, of the newly created Ironclad Board, regarded the exhibit with deep scorn. Wedded to the old Navy, where only wood floated, he complained that Mr. Ericsson's invention did not comply with the requirement that the vessel was "to be rigged with two masts and wire rope standing rigging, to navigate at sea." The senior board members, Commodores Hyram Paulding and Joseph Smith, both veterans of the War of 1812, were more receptive to the novel design, while Cornelius Bushnell, a New Haven shipbuilder whose influence had brought Ericsson's *Monitor* to the attention of the Ironclad Board, waited breathlessly for the President's opinion.

Turning to the seated and standing group, Lincoln's deep-set eyes twinkled before he spoke. "All I have to say is what the girl said when she stuck her foot into the stocking: 'It strikes me that there's something in it!' "

Nat Mather, present in his capacity as aide to Commander Davis, was awestruck by Lincoln.

The President took his seat and squinted over his glasses at the naval officers. "Gentlemen, whether the claims put forth by Mr. Bushnell are valid, I cannot say—my experience on the water being restricted to a flatboat trip down the Mississippi. You are the experts and I'm sure you will make the right decision. But do it quickly. We have little time left to deal with the ironclad that's already being built by the enemy." The President rose briskly. "Mr. Bushnell, shall we?"

There was a hush as the double doors swung open and the two men walked arm in arm across the gray marble floor.

"Here," Commander Davis flung a report on the table near the scale model of the *Monitor*, "is a description of a similar ironclad battery, designed by Mr. Ericsson and presented to Emperor Napoleon III at the time of the war in Crimea. The Emperor rejected the proposal because of the small number of guns that could be brought to bear, considering the expense of the vessel."

Commodore Smith, favoring an arthritic elbow, looked over the *Monitor's* plans on the table. "Eight-inch thick armor on the turret! Maybe the Emperor didn't care as much as we do about the crew's safety. We should consider the design's attributes as well as its deficiencies. Why there isn't a gun made that can penetrate eight inches of iron—especially curved and reinforced iron. And her very size is an advantage . . . difficult to hit, and certainly more maneuverable than an ironclad frigate."

"That all *may* be so," scowled Davis, "but let's not forget Ericsson's other folly, aboard the USS *Princeton*. A 12-inch gun of his design exploded during a demonstration, killing both the Secretary of State and the Secretary of the Navy . . ."

"But, Commander Davis," Nat blurted out, "Captain Stockton of Naval Ordnance built the gun, without proper. . . ."

The junior, but vociferous member of the Board shot a withering glance at his 22-year-old aide. Thereafter, Nat contented himself with staying clear of the controversy.

The following day, Cornelius Bushnell was called in by the board for another session. The senior Commodores voted for the *Monitor's* acceptance, provided that Davis agreed. With a stone face the Commander handed the cardboard model back to the shipbuilder. "Take it home and worship it," he concluded caustically. "It is in the image of nothing in heaven above, or the earth beneath—or in the waters under the earth."

The genial old sea-dog shrugged nervously in a huge leather chair in his room on Vermont Avenue in the Northwest quarter of Washington. "Lieutenant Mather, if the Board of Ironclad Ships had wind of my calling you here I would probably be courtmartialed. By Commander Davis, of course," added Hyram Paulding with a canny grin. "But I've been in this navy too long not to sense when something is wrong. When Commander Davis stopped you from giving your opinion this afternoon, I almost objected. But, then I thought I'd first find out on my own. Better tactics in some cases. Now, Lieutenant, what do you, as a man schooled in today's sciences, think of the Ericsson Battery? Don't worry, what we say here will go no further, and I assure you that I am within certain areas of naval protocol."

Nat leaned back against the tufted Chesterfield sofa and deliberated for a moment. "Sir, as an engineer in the physical sciences, I am extremely taken by the *Monitor*. The ironclads *Galena* and *New Ironsides,* which we are building now, are of the same basic style as the *Merrimac*. A wood boat clad in iron. Aside from the amount of armor, the idea is not new. A thousand yards ago the Norsemen attached strips of iron and steel to the sides of their longboats, and the sixteenth-century Koreans built an ironplated turtlebacked sampan. What is new—aside from propulsion and the complete iron hull—is the use of steam power to turn a heavy turret. This makes the pivot gun safe to man, unlike those guns on all of our present warships. The crews are at the mercy of sharpshooters in the tops.

"According to the scientific journals, the English foundries, using the new Bessemer process, are starting to produce low-carbon steel, which upon sudden cooling, becomes much harder than any steel the world has known before. Large hydraulic presses are being built which will form compound-curved armor plate of this steel. Armored vessels will become lighter and stronger. It is time that our Navy takes the initiative . . . especially with the rebel agents contracting for arms in Europe. The new English rifled guns could be devastating to our fleet."

"That's all very impressive, Lieutenant." The Veteran of the War of 1812 took a decanter of sherry from a sideboard and filled two cut crystal goblets. "Consider yourself off duty." He placed one on an end table near his guest. "However," Paulding continued, "Commander Davis is not convinced of the vessel's stability. There is so little underwater profile. I must say that I don't disagree with him."

"Well, sir, the *Merrimac*—or the *Virginia*, as they call it now—is underpowered for its weight and mass as an ironclad, and not likely to venture into rough weather or water, even with its frigate's hull. Ericsson's battery is not a vessel designed for a seaway either. Its shallow draft is essential for harbors and rivers where ocean stability is not the question. Larger, ocean-going monitors can be built, but now there is no other solution for engaging the *Merrimac*. *New Ironsides* will not be ready until the summer and we can be certain that the *Merrimac* will not wait that long." Nat toyed with his goblet, but did not drink.

The baldish gray-haired officer, mutton-chop whiskers almost touching his cravated collar, looked up at a framed print of the USS *Ticonderoga*. "I was a lad of seventeen when I served under MacDonough at Lake Champlain. That was my ship, a schooner of twenty guns. During the engagement, our lieutenant was wounded and I was put in command of the port battery. When my guns were brought to bear on the approaching British boats, I found that the slow-matches were useless, so I fired the guns personally with the flash powder of pistols prepared by the boys. When the enemy came within pistol range, I had balls put in and fired at them as well.

"Sometimes, now, I think that I'm losing my nerve. One gets that way at my age. But then I think of the battle again, and what I was capable of when I was a young man. No responsibilities, no wife, no children . . . and I say to myself: Paulding, it's time to pick up that ol' pistol again—and do what you know in your black heart that you have to do. You're a line officer in the Navy, and you know that all those braided chair-sitters in Washington—like yours truly, I do confess—are not going to lift a finger to change anything at all while they're waiting for a promotion. Just listening to you has brought back some of my old fire. It looks like I ought to pick up my old pistol again . . ."

"Then you'll countermand Commander Davis' decision on the Ericsson Battery?" Nat had not touched his wine for the importance of the situation. This was a moment of grave decision.

"Son, if you join me in a little drink—mind you, I don't say that a man has to be a drinker to make a choice in life, but I must say I never trusted a man who couldn't imbibe when necessary—I'll propose a toast to the USS *Monitor*. The battle of the Ironclad Ship Committee is by no means over."

Commodore Hiram Paulding, who was, besides advisor to the President, in charge of the Naval facilities in Brooklyn, was the advocate of the innovative *Monitor*, and spared no efforts in his lobbying for that vessel. He telegraphed Mr. Bushnell regarding the importance of bringing, in person, the inventor to confront the Philistines of Washington. It was up to Ericsson to explain his theories of stability directly to the old-line Admirals.

The Swedish inventor, who had become an American citizen, out of conviction that the democratic system was the way of the future, traveled to Washington and spoke to the Committee, with the result that Secretary of The Navy, Gideon Welles, authorized that the *Monitor* be built immediately.

The vessel's iron keel was laid on October twenty-fifth, at the yard of the Continental iron works in Greenpoint, Brooklyn, overlooking New York City's wide bay. Aside from John Ericsson, the proudest man was Commodore Paulding, who naturally relished the effects of the increased business potential for his home port of New York City. The contract called for one hundred days in building the vessel—which projected to the first week in February of 1862. One of the things that the venerable old Naval salt was able to obtain was the services of Lieutenant Nat Mather as an advisor to the project.

Not only was the Union Navy Yard booming with contracts for the depressed Brooklyn economy, aside from the *Monitor* contract, but so were the local services in the area such as the Ferry Hotel, The Metropolitan House, Knock's Cafe, and Poppy Smith's Tavern. On November seventeenth, the *New York Herald*, one of the city's newspapers, lay on a table at Knock's Cafe. Commodore Paulding gestured at an article on the front page.

"Nat, look what I found in the press. It seems that free enterprise is much more informed than the military."

Nat set his coffee aside and read the article:

> "The *Merrimac* is still in the dock, and it is the opinion of intelligent men that she will never float. She is encased in three layers of one-inch boiler iron . . ."

"Yet," scowled the Commodore, "other sources have said she will be ready this month. Perhaps it's a scheme to keep us Yankees off balance. There's only one way to cope with this menace—and that is to destroy the monster before she comes out of her lair. But the rebel batteries on the Elizabeth River would make short work of our gunboats if they ventured in. Our *Monitor* will not be ready until the hundred-day deadline. That means the end of January, and another week or two of working up . . ."

"Sir," Nat's dark eyes brightened, "I have an idea. We might possibly observe the Confederate ironclad's progress by sending up a balloon. Perhaps we could have one launched from Fort Monroe—or even from a boat moored in Hampton Roads, out of range of the Rebel batteries. . . ."

"There may be some merit in your idea, Mather." Pauling stirred his coffee. "I'll bring it up at my next meeting with the Navy Department. Too bad we don't have a balloon big enough to carry a torpedo, and drop it on that damned ironclad."

"That, sir, is the best idea of all. I volunteer."

"Agreed, Nat," Paulding envisioned the *Merrimac's* demise in his mind's eye with relish, "but not until you've looked at Novelty Works' turret drawings. They're being altered for taking eleven-inch Dahlgrens. You've got to go over to the *Dacotah*, by the way, and pick out their two best guns. It's the only way we can get some ordnance on the *Monitor*. Damn, I'm still worried about the concussion that turret will take if she gets hit by a couple of nine-inch solid shot. I say the gun crews will hurt.

"Sir, we *could* line the interior with gutta-percha—"

"Good, lad. Do inquire about that and report to me."

SEVENTEEN

The old woman sat on an empty keg near the receiving tent of Chimborozo Hospital, eyes glazed and oblivious to the activity, as wounded and maimed Confederate soldiers were borne past her in wagons and on stretchers to the hastily-built complex on a promontory in Richmond, Virginia, overlooking the wharves of the serpentine James River. Calcium lamps turned night into day, casting geometric shadows among the tents and barracks.

The wounded were being brought in from battlefields in the north of the state: a hundred and forty from Drainesville, thirty-four from New Market Bridge, and more from the skirmishes at Alpine Station, Cacopan Bridge and Hancock. The hospital camp, orginially called The Tompkins Facility, after Sally Tompkins, a Richmond woman who organized it, had a capacity of about five hundred patients. It was already overcrowded because of the carnage at the Battle of Ball's Bluff several weeks earlier. A victory for the rebels, but a defeat for the fallen.

Lieutenant Howell Clyburn dismounted, and an orderly led his horse away. About to enter the receiving tent, he stopped momentarily at the sight of the old woman and drew a small silver coin from his pocket which he dropped on her lap. "Thank you, and God bless you." The hag's wrinkled hand closed about the coin and she sang in melancholic tones:

"Take thy beak from out my heart,
And take thyself from off my door.
Quoth the raven, 'Nevermore,' "

Swaddled in ragged, once grandiloquent, theatrical costume, she opened a torn, beaded purse and extracted a small, brass locket which she snapped open. A tiny, elliptical daguerreotype stared blankly at her as she held it up to the tent's light. It was a sepia portrait of a sad-eyed man with abundant dark hair and a drooping mustache. Facing the picture on the inside of the locket lid was an engraving of a raven. "Edgar," she implored the likeness of her departed younger brother, "I too, am an actress. You must admit that mother's talent was not lost on me. See—the soldier gave me money. Now don't you fret; the bird will eat well tonight, and the bells, bells, bells will ring, ring, ring." Old Rose Poe gathered up her voluminous skirts and raised herself feebly from the keg. It was time to go home. Tomorrow she would go down to Libby Prison on Carey Street and see what she could cajole from the garrison there.

* * *

LIBBY & SON
SHIP'S CHANDLERS & GROCERS

The framed sign hung on the northwest corner of a large three-storied brick building on the waterfront in

Richmond. But there was no such business being transacted within. The sprawling structure had been taken over by the Confederate government and converted into a prison for the captured Union officers and camp followers. To one side were the garrison tents, and to the rear flowed the James River. Behind one of the tents, two Negro servants were tending to their masters' equipment.

"Gus, why didn't you tell me your daughter was goin' to follow the drinkin' gourd?" James Weeks set a pair of boots upright and picked up a cavalry belt to work in some saddle soap.

"Didn't know myself, till I got a letter from Charleston. Tenah and her husband are in Montreal. My little Tenah—she's got a real name now. Tenah Holladay. Not like her Pa who goes by the name of his owner. They went up by way of the Underground Railroad jes' before I came with the Major to this abode. It wouldn't have made much difference, Jim, since your diggins are up through Kentucky and Ohio. They were dead set on goin' to Connecticut to stay with Mr. Holladay's mother.

"When they got there, they got into a scrape with some slavehunters but they were saved from bein' sent back to South Carolina by the son of a Yankee preacher by the name of Mather." Gus set Major Turner's saddle on a saw-horse. "My, my, I don't know how this leather gets so dry."

James Weeks sighed and scratched his white hair, cavalry belt dangling from his knee. "You know, Gus; if we weren't so damn-fired old, I'd get my brother-in-law to write us out a couple o' tickets on th' railroad an' we could go on up an' have us a good time in Columbus, or even Chicago. Damn, if the Major knew about my relatives in the railroad he'd have me up fer a necktie party fer sure." Weeks got up and walked over to his friend. "Now here I be, shootin' off my mouth when I should be asking about your wife. What else did the letter say?"

"The Deacon says she's not long for this world. Althea never got over the fever, he says. So I'll be goin' home as soon as I can—" Augustus buried his head in his hands.

"Hell, Gus. You go on an' ask the Major. Tell 'im about Althea, and tell 'im that I'll do all your chores fer a few days. Show 'im the letter from Charleston. . . ."

"Then he'll get somebody else, fer sure, Jim, and there won't be any more money, little as it is. Nobody gonna hire me out anymore. No, this ol' darkey gonna wait some more. The good Lord will watch over her, an' th' doctor will get his money."

EIGHTEEN

'Young Napoleon,' Major General George Brinton McClellan, looked out of his window overlooking the parade grounds at Fort Monroe on the Federal-held shore of Virginia's Hampton Roads, entrance to the James River and the Confederate heartland. A balloon was being inflated with hydrogen gas, from an apparatus whereby dilute sulphuric acid was applied over iron filings in closed containers and the gas purified by bubbling through a tank of water. The general, only thirty-five and a brilliant railroad engineer before his recall to service, was enjoying fame brought on by his earlier victory in the West, after which part of the state of Virginia elected to remain in the Union. A close relationship with outgoing veteran General Winfield Scott had further helped his star in rising and his request to start a Balloon Corps had been quickly approved by his superiors.

If McClellan had one phobia, it was his concern that the enemy's numbers were greater than reported. Now he would find out for himself—by observing from a balloon. 'Professor' Jean LaMont was the first aeronaut to offer his services.

"She is a beauty, no? She better be. I spend all my money for her in New York." LaMont beamed as the colorful silk envelope slowly took form like some breathing antediluvian monster fettered within its diamond network of knotted rope. The glistening oiled balloon rose higher, restrained by ground ropes, until a large portrait of President Lincoln was visible over a star-spangled name: U N I O N in letters ten feet high.

"I call her the *Union,*" laughed LaMont, "because when I get back to our own lines I don't want to be shot down by our own guns. It's enough to take a chance with the rebels, no?"

"Yes," agreed Nat, "but I have another idea that will help attain our objective. Now suppose we had a banner prepared with the Confederate colors, and attach it over our own when going over rebel territory. When we return, it can be hauled down."

"My friend, I see what you mean. Maybe we have painted a picture of General Lee. The rebels will not shoot at him, eh?"

"That's a better idea than just putting up a flag or the name 'rebel' since most of the southerners can't read anyway. . . ."

"Excuse me," a young man hiding behind a handlebar mustache walked up to them. "I am Timothy O'Sullivan." He handed Nat a calling card. Below his name, it said '*Photographer*.'

"Mr. Sullivan," Nat handed the card back, "I don't think we have any need for portraits at this moment—"

"But, wait, Lieutenant. There's no charge. I have a

pass from General McClellan. You see, sir, I was formerly in the employ of Mr. Mathew Brady, in Washington—and now I have my own rig." He pointed to a horse-drawn wagon standing among some government supply carts. "Just give me a chance to explain what I can do for your campaign. I won't be in the way."

"Brady," pondered Nat. "Doesn't he also have a fancy gallery on Broadway, in New York City?"

"Yes, of course. But he opened another facility in Washington to cater to the important government officials. Welles, Stanton, Vanderbilt . . . I've photographed them all. Dozens of generals and naval officers. Commodore Paulding suggested that I get in touch with General McClellan if I wanted to see some action, and here I am. In a way, the fact that Mr. Brady does almost nothing with the camera—his eyesight is failing—is a good thing for his assistants. Since the pay was minimum, at least we got to know some interesting people—and improved our skills. Several of the operators, like myself, gave notice to Brady rather than continue without getting credit for our work."

"Mr. Sullivan, a recommendation from Commodore Paulding is good enough for me—but I don't think Mr. LaMont or I are in need of having our portraits taken."

"But I propose to take an image from the balloon," O'Sullivan bowed graciously toward the billowing mass of fabric.

"Why not take a picture *of* my balloon, young man?" LaMont, erstwhile performer in circuses, was intrigued, though outwardly nonchalant.

"By all means; if you will please pose before it . . ."

"Micheline," shouted LaMont, "come, quick. We need a pretty girl in ze picture." He ran to the supply tent, looking high and low for his sister.

O'Sullivan climbed into his darkroom wagon and

emerged with a large, wooden wet-plate camera as his Negro driver set up a tripod. Nat excused himself from the picture on the pretext that the balloon was a civilian project, as yet unassigned and unproven to the military. His real reason was to remain anonymous, considering the nature of his assignments.

* * *

"But why can't I come along?" Micheline expertly pulled a valve rope, letting out some hydrogen gas from the top of the balloon. The *Union,* responding to the imbalance, descended toward Virginia's historic southern peninsula. A thousand feet below, the Federal blockading fleet lay at their moorings under the protection of shore batteries.

"A naval vessel is no place for a . . . girl." Trying to avoid a squabble, Nat set to recoiling a guide rope.

"But I am an aeronaut," Micheline pouted. "What difference does it make that I am a girl?" She moved closer to Nat, backing him into a corner of the wicker gondola.

"All the difference in the world," the lieutenant assumed an air of propriety. "Careful, we're not on the ground yet."

"But I can dress up like a man—"

"Sorry, Micheline, it will be too dangerous, and besides, you know the gondola can't carry more than three people."

"Then I'll stay on the boat and help with the lines. Sailors don't know anything about balloons. . . ."

Nat ignored her pleas as the craft's shadow passed from Hampton Roads to the narrow beach of Newport News. "We ought to go lower before we overshoot the fort." Nat pulled the valve rope.

"Very well, Lieutenant when do you plan to return?"

Suddenly Micheline's face paled. "You may *not* come back . . . you and Jean—Oh, Nat, I couldn't bear the thought that. . . ." she threw herself into his arms, dangerously jolting the gondola.

It was, for the middle of January, a mild day, and the sun's warmth was welcome. This, the last test ascension before the mission, had gone well. Micheline had implored her brother to let her go up with Mather and prove her ability to pilot the new craft. The *Union* had traveled westward at five hundred feet to the lighthouse in Burwell's bay on the rebel side of the James River, then ascended to ride a high-altitude prevailing breeze back to Fort Monroe.

Now the euphoria of flight stirred their passions. Free as soaring eagles—and alone. Away from war, from misery and mud. Micheline pressed her vibrant young body into his and he responded. First, an impulsive kiss, then another, fired with unrequited desire and abandon. Together, they slipped down to the floor of the gondola, azure sky and bright clouds reeling through the myriad support ropes attached above them to the complex netting bridle of the huge multicolored balloon. Micheline giggled and said something about 'love in the sky', whereupon Nat jokingly unbuttoned her coat.

"Yes, yes," she purred, and reciprocated by unloosening his uniform collar.

"Then it's war you want . . ." Nat undid her blouse and she drew him down upon her.

To a seaman, far below, on the frigate USS *St. Lawrence*, the balloon's wicker gondola seemed to be buffeted by unusual updrafts for a short period before regaining its stability and descending toward Fort Monroe.

* * *

Three mooring ropes were let out through dead-eyes by sailors on the stripped foredeck of the gunboat, USS *Miami*, as the *Union* rose slowly into the morning sky. Lieutenant Commander Charles Flusser, on the starboard sidewheel bridge, swore through his mustache and side-whiskers: "What in damnation am I in command of? A nursemaid to a gas-bag?" Flusser could hardly wait till the umbilical ropes had been untied and the strange craft had taken its leave. He secretly hoped that it would not return.

At five hundred feet the last line was let loose from the *Miami* and hauled up by Jean LaMont into the *Union's* square wicker gondola. With Gallic abandon, he threw a kiss at the gray gunboat and saluted Lieutenant Nat. Timothy O'Sullivan also saluted, and with a broad grin added: "Ready for duty, sir."

As Lynn Haven Bay came into view beyond Cape Henry, Nat and Jean LaMont hauled up sheets of canvas, port and starboard, bearing the portrait of Jefferson Davis, thereby covering up the likenesses of Lincoln and the name, *Union*. "The rebels, they won't shoot at their president; no?" LaMont let go a bag of sand ballast from the gondola rim and the balloon leapt up, correcting for a sudden downdraft. "Too bad—I was going to save it to drop on the rebels, but we 'ave more," he counted the bags.

A chill, but clear morning, the adventurers were bundled in heavy clothing. Even O'Sullivan's cumbersome camera, lashed to the gondola's gun'l, ws covered with a blanket. The young photographer rubbed his hands, keeping them warm and nimble in excited ancitipation of accomplishing something, that as far as he knew, had never before been accomplished. A reconnaissance image taken from a balloon. It had been determined that from the approach height of five hundred feet, not only could a vessel be photographed, but also the defenses of Norfolk and Portsmouth—yielding information that General McClellan needed for his proposed landing on the rebel-held peninsulas. Already, one hundred thousand Federal troops were being mustered in the north for the assault.

Far below, in the narrow streets of Kempville, and on the roads leading to Norfolk, knots of people were gathering to observe the balloon. "You know, Nat," commented LaMont, "next time we do this, we bring a keg of gunpowder with a fuse. Then we finish the whole job. *Poof*, no more *Merrimac*, eh?"

"You may be right, Jean, but it would be very difficult to hit such a target while we're moving. We'd first have to practice, and devise a whole new system of ballistics based on height, speed and wind. I'm afraid there's not enough time."

"Maybe your admirals would let me try. I can go very low, and I hang a torpedo-keg on the long rope with percussion caps. Then the rope, she swing like a pendulum till she hit the *Merrimac*. No?"

"If you don't get shot to pieces first, yes!"

After a flight of barely one hour, the *Union*, sporting the initials, C.S.A., floated over the bustling port of Norfolk and approached the opposite shore of the Elizabeth River. There were several small tugs and gunboats moored before the Navy Yard inlet, above the city of Portsmouth, Norfolk's twin on the west bank. Nat scanned the scene through LaMont's new French-invented 'binoculars'. Nestled along a mile of shore, composing the complex, were machine shops, storehouses, shiphouses, sail and rigger's lofts, barracks and administration buildings. Only when the *Union's* noon shadow was near the shore did he finally spot the objective—the dark granite drydock. He focused on an angular shape that lay within. Pierced with gunports, four on each side, and two, fore and aft, he recognized it as the much-vaunted Confederate ironclad. Straining for a glimpse of the *Merrimac's* ram and underbody, Nat pointed down and O'Sullivan stripped the blanket clear, then tilted his camera down. Taking off the lens cap, he pulled the black viewing cloth over his head and reached out to turn the focusing screw on the brass lens mount. An upside-down image of the navy yard danced on the camera's 4¼×5½-inch ground glass. With the focus set at infinity, O'Sullivan pulled out the ground glass and inserted a lightproof collodian negative plate, a new item that allowed development to take place at a later time than the standard non-fixed wet plates. He removed the slide panel, then took off the lens cap again, counting audibly to four seconds.

Sighting over two brass nailheads on the camera's wooden frame, he exposed his quota of nine fixed plates, saving three for 'unexpected events'. After each exposure he quickly and privately asked the blessing of St. Patrick and crossed himself. If his immigrant parents only knew that behind this mechanical and chemical breast beat the same heart they brought from the old sod. . . . One of the exposures should work, he convinced himself. There *were* some moments when the gondola was relatively still. He packed the plates into a padded case and slumped back, exhausted.

Turning toward his companions, Nat put the binoculars back in their case, a look of deep concern etched on his tanned face. "I'm afraid that the *Merrimac* looks ready to launch. All the armor seems to be in place. It's only a matter of putting her afloat. Let's get back to friendly territory."

The Frenchman jettisoned several sandbags and the *Union* bolted up toward the sun until, finally, her westward progress was stayed and she was borne seaward by the high-altitude winds.

NINETEEN

January 21, 1862

HON. JEFFERSON DAVIS
President
Confederate States of America
Richmond, Virginia
SIR: Through certain contacts in New York City, I have found that the Ericcson floating steam battery, now called the USS *Monitor*, under Lt. John Worden, is scheduled to be launched by the end of this month, after which it will be completed and given sea-trials. The vessel shall depart for Charleston on March 1, fully manned and ready to do battle.

The ironclad's turret armor, being applied at the Novelty Works is 8 inches thick and reportedly impervious to our heaviest shot. Fortunately, the proposed 15-inch Dahlgren gun will not be ready and she will be equipped with two 11-inch smoothbores.

My adversary in the Federal Secret Service is becoming a nuisance, so I propose that communication be done by cipher; either the Vicksburg Code, the Route system, the Dictionary code, or those methods we have worked out privately, depending on the complexity. My name shall be 'PET' and yours, 'HOSANNA'. The courier will remain as usual, one of the players.

I have the honor to be
your most obedient servant,
Renfrew

The planter from Mississippi stood by a window of the executive mansion and looked over the greensward, beyond which a regiment of militia was marching toward the railroad station to the sprightly strains of "Dixie". How many of these boys, thought Davis, knew that the song was composed by a Yankee. How many of these exuberant sons of the South, bolstered by early Confederate victories, were aware of the great disparity in strength—of the sleeping, ponderous giant of the North? Distinguished for gallantry during the Mexican War, he had seen, at Vera Cruz, the Federal behemoth in action: hundreds of ships disgorging swarms of well-equipped, fresh troops . . . mortars and field-pieces, so thick as to turn the white beaches black . . . shell and shot more numerous than shoals of pebbles.

The Alamo massacre had been remembered, and the overwhelming American superiority in arms and provisions defeated General Santa Anna's legions in short order. While he and other Southerners were the most decorated of the American combatants, it was northern logistics and ordnance that had determined the outcome.

How long can the confiscated Federal pistols and

rifles last? Can the southern gunsmiths produce reliable weapons? Can warships be purchased abroad and run through the blockade? Will the few southern factories clothe the troops well enough? Can the boys be fed and cared for?

President Davis crumpled the letter in his hand. We didn't want this war, he scowled to himself. We went out of our way that no blood should be shed at Fort Sumter. We sent peace missions to Washington. We *knew* in our hearts that we were the Davids, and the Federals were Goliaths. Our only sling is a quick victory, such as may be accomplished by our ironclad being built at Norfolk. Even this boat has a hull built for the United States Navy. The engines and most of the guns were manufactured in the North. Only the armor can be claimed as a confederate product—plates rolled by the Tredegar Works in this city, from ore mined in the western mountains of this state . . . Davis flung the crumpled letter into a fireplace and watched it burn. Those traitors, those turncoats—part of our great state, going over to the Union . . .

"Hold on there, Jeff," a voice within him reverberated. "It's not that the people of west Virginia are *going over*. It's more like they've never left the Union. Fair's fair. You've read philosophy, law and the English classics. You were a successful military leader, planter and senator. And what was your reaction in the garden with Varina when you received notice of your election?"

Davis smiled. "Yes, my inner Devil; you know me well. I still feel the same as when I said to my wife, 'Oh God, spare me this responsibility. But I would love to head the army.' "

"Then why didn't you refuse the nomination? Others did."

"You know I like to be liked—and Varina . . ."

"She is the archetypical Southern woman, only more

so as she is almost twenty years younger than us—or you. She is young enough to yearn for a monarchy—a court with fancy dinners and entertainment. Quite the opposite of Buchanan's and Lincoln's solemn simplicity. You weren't *elected* as far as Varina cares."

"That's correct, my devil. I was *crowned*."

"Varina likes Richmond better than Montgomery."

"So do I; I'm something of a martinet, but militarily it is a disadvantage, requiring so much protection that we need a separate army. The Mississippi valley is the real strategic center of this conflict."

"May I remind you that the lovely courier awaits a response from her leader. You did see her walk across the grounds. . . ."

"Yes, but my interest in women has waned of late."

"But not in her friend, young Jack Renfrew!"

"Begone, my inner devil. Mr. Renfrew is a valuable agent to our cause and nothing more . . ." Davis sat down at his desk and unfolded a letter that had arrived earlier from the Secretary of the Confederate Navy. He read from it:

> . . . I submit for your consideration the attack on New York City by the *Merrimac*. Can the vessel steam to that city and burn it? She can, I doubt not, pass Old Point safely, and with good weather and a smooth sea, could go to New York, and once in the bay, could wreak havoc.
>
> Such an event would eclipse all the glories of naval combats, would place every man in it preeminently high, and would strike a blow from which the enemy would never recover. Peace would inevitably follow as bankers would withdraw their capital from the city's vaults. The Brooklyn Navy Yard, its magazines,

and the harbor commerce would be destroyed. The machine works where Union naval engines are manufactured would be destroyed, and so with the shipyards that are building ironclads, along with Ericsson's revolving battery . . .

Davis put the letter aside, opened a desk drawer and drew out a packet of penny post cards. Each one had been pre-addressed to The Winter Garden Theater in New York City. On the message side was the simple printed form:

PLEASE RESERVE______SEATS FOR THE PERFORMANCE OF__________186____

Davis penned in the numerals, 5, 3/1 and 2, then rang for a servant. He inserted the card in an envelope and sealed it. The card was to be carried beyond the Union lines and posted. If Jack Renfrew's *dramatis personae* could not get through the Federal pickets, no one could. The message, a simple one, confirmed receipt of the *Monitor's* departure date by repeating it in a different context, and arranged for future cipher communication with the insertion of the numeral '5', which signified the dictionary code, utilizing identical out-of-print volumes.

An aged Negro servant bowed and proffered a silver tray, upon which the Confederate President placed his envelope. "Gilbert, give this to Miss Partington."

"Thank you, Gilbert." Sally Partington rose from the anteroom settee and accepted the letter with a quick curtsey, which ruffled the old darkey, besides amusing him. He looked around nervously, then content that they were alone, broke into a grin. 'Missis' Varina was known to appear at odd times.

"Take this." The actress, wearing a somber dark wig and a spinsterish costume, pressed two theater tickets into the servant's hand. "Wednesday—a comedy you will enjoy. Bring Mrs. Hunt . . ." Sally sidestepped Gilbert's attempt to return the tickets. "Now, don't make a fuss," she whispered. "It's about time you got over that fright of yours. Two fires in fifty years aren't all that bad—and besides, nobody was hurt at the Marshall Theater. Mrs. McGill is already starting to have it rebuilt."

"Who's to say that th' ol' Exchange Hall aint goin' to burn down too?" stuttered Gilbert. "And sittin' upstairs aint th' best place to be in a fire . . ."

"Gilbert, I'll bet you my five dollars to your two bits that there won't be any fire."

"Well . . . ," Gilbert scratched at his ear, "if yer that sure, maybe we'll come on over. In that case, I'd better pay up now 'cause if there *is* a fire—" He reached into his trouser pocket. "Oh, oh; plum forgot t' bring some money," Gilbert grinned again. "Tell ye what—let's bet like ladies 'n gennlemen. No money. It's luckier that way." Gilbert escorted Sally to the door. "See you all on Wednesday night."

President Davis watched from behind a window curtain as Sally descended the front steps and walked toward Clay Street. He felt a jealousy rise within him. Since moving the seat of government from Alabama to Richmond, it had become a practice to go to the theater with his cabinet—often without the womenfolk. He'd gotten to know Sally, first through Jack Renfrew, who before the war had been a manager and actor in George Kunkel's stock-company. Sally was a great favorite with the soldiers, playing opposite the most celebrated male actors of the day, including Edwin Booth.

But what was he jealous of? Did he envy Sally's attentions to Renfrew—or Renfrew's to Sally? Or was it his own age—over fifty—that bothered him? Perhaps he envied youth, missing his own hell-raising days prior to his first marriage. His first wife, General Zachary Taylor's daughter, had succumbed to a fever less than three months after the wedding day. She was eighteen, and he, a dashing lieutenant, fresh from the Indian Wars. Resigning his commission, he brought his bride to the family plantation in Warren County, Mississippi after building a house for his own section. He brought his bride to *Brierfield* in the hot summer—against his mother's advice, and she caught the fever.

For ten years, he isolated himself at Brierfield, shunning both social and political involvement. He planted cotton and read law, and, by careful management of his estate, acquired considerable wealth. In 1843 he entered politics as a Democrat, and demonstrated great eloquence as a public speaker. Soon after, he became a representative in Congress and married Miss Varina Howell of Mississippi, a granddaughter of Governor Howell of New Jersey. She came to be known socially as "Queen" Varina.

Now, after seventeen years of marriage and seven children, Davis again felt isolated, even from his own cabinet. He was in a no-man's land between his family and his governmental appointees. Already, the Secretary of State, Robert Toombs, had opposed his policies, calling him "a fool and utterly incompetent." But then, Toombs had earlier been passed over for the Presidency despite his popularity, because of a propensity to alcohol. Would that he'd never accepted the nomination. The cares of his office had drained him in less than one year.

And all this because of one man . . . Abraham Lincoln. He brought upon us death and privation in his quest of immortality and fame. He was the one who said that he was against hasty emancipation. In his debates with Stephen Douglas, Lincoln declared he was willing to wait a hundred years for the abolition of slavery, and that the practice, while legal, should enjoy the same protection as any other private property. Now that he has tasted victory in politics, he has changed. Lincoln, the opportunist . . . Lincoln, the Illinois volunteer whom Davis himself had sworn into the Union Army during the Black Hawk War. Lincoln, the Captain who was twice in disgrace; once for firing a pistol near camp, and again because his entire company was intoxicated. His company was mustered out in several weeks, having engaged in no battles. Davis wondered whether Lincoln remembered him as a young lieutenant. No matter. He agreed with the secret agent he had sworn in. If Lincoln could be eliminated. . . .

Gilbert Hunt didn't sleep well that night. Ever since the fire fifty years earlier he'd had recurring dreams that woke him up in a perspiring frenzy. Agnes, his wife, had gotten used to the nocturnal seizures and was always ready to muffle his screams with a pillow, lest the Marse think he has raving demons living in the attic.

The servant's dream would start with a coffle of strong, young slaves walking up Shockoe Hill, chains rattling as they followed behind their mounted overseer. It was the night after Christmas in the year 1811, and the slaves were returning to their quarters after being hired out to clean the capital's stables. The Governor, George Smith, had complained of the condition of the stables before departing for a dinner party and evening of theater.

Suddenly the sky was ablaze as tongues of flame leapt from the upper-floor windows of a wooden building on the hill. Frantic screams attested to the plight of the theatergoers and brought out the citizens. The Shockoe Hill Playhouse was buring out of control with a capacity house which had come to see 'The Bleeding Nun.'

Silhouetted against the interior flames, parents were seen holding their children out of the windows of the third floor. The overseer, a resourceful minion of the State, shouted, "The Governor is in there," and dismounted. He unlocked the leg irons of several slaves and commandeered them to batter down the front door of the theater. Try as they did, the doors would not budge, for behind them were piled up trampled, asphyxiated, and burned bodies. The audience had panicked and rushed to the front of the house to escape the fire that had started in the stage scenery only to confront double doors that opened inward. Evading the rushing inferno, many of the audience climbed the stairs in the hope of being rescued through the upperfloor windows. Several were injured by jumping and others by climbing out and falling. Gilbert, a strong, muscular young man of twenty, braced himself, held out his arms and shouted, "I'll catch the children . . ." One by one, the parents dropped their crying young from a window that was still spared the fire. Gilbert caught eighteen children and was set to catch the women when the playhouse roof gave way with a volcanic eruption, belching flame and smoke from all the upper windows.

The screaming had stopped. Seventy-two souls had perished, including the Governor and most of the actors. Among the latter were David and Elizabeth Poe, whose three children were among those caught by Gilbert Hunt. The eldest, William, died shortly after of the fever. Rosalie became mad, and the two-year-old, Edgar, was adopted by a wealthy tobacco merchant to satisfy his wife's desire for a child. Gilbert, given his freedom as a result of his heroism, had little trouble finding employment with the relatives of the disaster survivors including Edgar's foster-father, John Allan. The former slave, an apprentice blacksmith, enchanted the local children, especially Edgar, with his tales of adventure, one of which concerned a Caribbean treasure and a gold scarab.

Young Edgar, displaying character more akin to actors than businessmen, was frequently in scrapes. He was expelled from the University of Virginia for gambling and drink. Mr. Allan refused to honor his debts, so Edgar enlisted in the Army and did well, rising in a short time to the rank of Sergeant-Major. On this account, Mr. Allan secured his discharge and a nomination to West Point—from where he was again expelled. With the premature death of the merchant's wife, Edgar lost his position with regard to the Allan family fortune. He was left nothing, which advanced his intemperance, ultimately leading to his death at the age of forty.

Gilbert relived those years in his agonizing nightmares. "Lawd," he often exclaimed to Agnes, "That po' little boy, gettin' dropped out of that burnin' window—and his mother and father dyin' in the window. . . . For sure that did no good for his soul."

And Agnes would reply, "Ain't nothin' you could of done. Edgar had the play-actor in him. Ain't like real folk, those 'uns."

The Shockoe Theater fire raged on in Gilbert's dreams. Screaming people, play-actor's faces in the flames. Famous actors . . . William Mcready, Edwin Forrest, James Walleck . . . burning playbills and charred scenery . . . Junius Brutus Booth in Richard III . . . Edwin Booth, his son, in Romeo and Juliet.

And the youngest, who worked as a stage manager at the Marshall Theater just before the firing on Fort Sumter. The moody son, John Wilkes.

And now the Marshall Theater had also burned to the ground, almost fifty years to the day later. During the holiday season. Fires . . . actors! Yes that was it. The young man called Renfrew who called on Marse Davis late one evening. His voice; it was familiar—Ah, yes. Why not a blond wig?"

It was Wilkes Booth!

"Wouldn't put it past Wilkes Booth to set fire to the Marshall playhouse," Agnes confided. "The boy was mad that he never got a part there like his father and brother. And what's he doin' in Virginia anyway? He's supposed to be up North. I tell you, Gilbert, there's no good in having him come to this house."

TWENTY

"But how will your vessel ride in the sea with all that weight?"

"The sea shall ride *over* her," thundered John Ericsson, "and she will live in it like a duck!"

James Lenthal, the ablest ship's model constructor in the Union Navy, scoffed, "This man is crazy." He tore at his thinning hair and stared at the wooden model of the double-ender he had built from the inventor's plans. Why, even President Lincoln had voiced his skepticism with a quip: "I have often heard of a vessel with two bows but have never before seen one with two sterns."

Lenthal possessed great talent, but too many years of modeling sloops-of-war and frigates had made him over-cautious and conservative. He had no patience for examining plans or calculations relating to Ericsson's *Iron Pot*, as he called it. Had this government employee been more enthusiastic about the *Monitor*, the warship would already have been on its way to confront the *Merrimac*.

* * *

Commander David Dixon Porter, of the distinguished American naval family, was ordered to report to the Secretary of The Navy concerning the progress and potential of the new ironclads that were under construction. In New York City, Lieutenant Mather was assigned to him and together they went to the Swedish inventor's office.

Ericsson's office was on the second floor of 36 Beach Street, near City Hall. He had arrived with his wife from England almost twenty years earlier, then became so absorbed in his projects that Mrs. Ericsson, out of boredom, returned to England, expecting that he would soon follow. He didn't, and never saw her again even though they remained married. His workroom had five bright windows and several drawing tables. There were chairs for guests, but the balding mutton-chopped inventor preferred sitting on a rollable upholstered piano stool.

Commander Porter showed his orders to the Swede, who read them and exclaimed: "You are no doubt a great mathematician and are familiar with the advanced calculations that enter into construction of my vessel, so help yourself and take what you will of the drawings and specifications."

"I'm no great mathematician," replied Porter, "but I am a practical man, and think I can ascertain whether or not your vessel will do what is promised for her. As far as calculations are concerned, Lieutenant Mather will deal with them. He is a graduate mathematician among other things."

"Well," stormed Ericsson, "at least the government has done the minimum. One would expect—" he looked Mather up and down while coasting on his stool, "an older man for such a calling." He watched quietly as Nat spread out a sheet of plans on one of the tables. "Commander Porter, I want men who can work out the displacements, horsepower, impregnability, endurance at sea during a gale, capacity of stowing man and gunpowder, stability as a gun platform, and so on. Now, if the Navy cannot fathom these things, you had better go back to where you came from.''

''Mr. Ericsson, I do know a few equations. I know the rule of three and that twice two are four. . . .''

Ericsson bristled at the naval officer and his sideburns twitched uneasily. ''Very bad that the United States Navy sends such a man to examine John Ericsson.''

''Perhaps, sir, you might instruct me about the features of your celebrated steam battery. Certainly, if *The Scientific American* could get sketches and information on your vessel, which they published in November, the Navy could be granted as much.''

''It was not from me that the information was gotten. I am now a citizen of this country, and I abhor the policy of slavery. If the Navy wants secrecy, they should appropriate money for a security guard.''

''I'll make a recommendation. Meanwhile, show me some important detail and I'll see what I can make of it.'' Porter caught Nat's eye and winked.

''Yes, of course,'' grumbled Ericsson. ''With your limited knowledge of simple equations you will run aground in a short time.'' Ericsson took a detail sheet from a stack of plans and handed it to Porter. ''Tell me what this represents.''

Porter looked at the drawing, turning it around several times and then looked up with a serious and concerned eye. ''I take this to be some sort of coffee-mill—a large one at that.''

The inventor slapped himself on his high forehead and spun around on his piano stool. ''Commander, you are vexing, and I am a fool to waste my time on you. I have spent so many sleepless nights over this drawing and now you call it a coffee-mill. Now what do you make of this scale model?"

Porter picked up the cardboard model and held it upsidedown. He passed his hand over the flat bottom. "This must be the topside armor, and this," he pointed at the round turret, "is undoubtedly the engine compartment. . . ."

Ericsson was flabbergasted at Porter's reaction. He fumed briefly and then broke into a hesitant grin. "You Americans—always joking. Even with a war going on!"

Porter, noticing Nat tidying up a set of plans, called to the junior officer, "What are your findings, Lieutenant?"

Nat marshalled his thoughts carefully before responding. "Sir," he cautiously addressed the inventor, "while I concur with most of your claims and calculations, I'd like to make a few personal observations. . . ."

Ericsson's eyes narrowed to slits from which guns might have been run out loaded with grapeshot.

After a nod from Commander Porter, Nat counted on his fingers: "*One*—the vessel will not be capable of eight knots, taking into consideration loaded weight, hull shape and shaft horsepower."

The Swede drummed his stout fingers on his flannel-trousered knees and stared out of a window.

"*Two*—The joining of the forward hull to the deck armor may not be strong enough to withstand the pounding in a gale."

Ericsson, fumbling with his gold watch-chain, pulled the timepiece from his vest pocket by mistake.

"*Three*—The pilot-house location will prevent an efficient depressed elevation use of the battery at close quarters.

"*Four*—Eighty tons of coal in one bin aft of the

center of gravity could affect the vessel's stability and trim."

"There was no other place to put the coal," Ericsson rose from his piano stool. "A larger vessel will be needed. . . ."

"*If* another vessel is ordered," interrupted Porter as he playfully pushed the cardboard model about on the table upside-down.

"*Five,*" continued Nat, touching his pinky. "The protected anchor well may be hazardous by creating a vacuum and drawing in seawater through the hawse-pipes. . . ."

"Is that ALL, young man?" thundered the inventor.

"No sir," replied Nat, "Just my first findings."

"I must say, Commander Porter, that the Navy is outdoing itself today. Lieutenant, for a mere child you seem to have acquired some knowledge beyond your years."

"I was fortunate to have been a student of Professor Brush at the Sheffield School of Science."

"Brush," pondered Ericsson. "Metallurgy?"

"The foremost authority in this country," added Nat.

"He's capable, but the real advances are being made in England today, my boy. When this war's over I'd advise you to look up a Professor William Fairbairn at Cambridge—" Ericsson shook his head. "What am I doing? Let's get to the business at hand. Commander Porter, if you have something to say, do it now. For each day we lose is a day gained for the enemy."

"I say let's go out to the Continental Iron Works and inspect your craft before it is launched and before—as Lenthal says—it sinks!"

The entourage of three crossed the East River by ferry and landed at Greenpoint. A chill January day made them thankful that the *Monitor* was being built in a closed shed, and they availed themselves of a cherry-red iron stove before crawling into the cold, dank recesses of Ericsson's vessel.

An hour later, Porter emerged through a forward deck opening. "Now, sir, I know all about your machine, especially the coffee-mill. There are a few—" He stopped in mid-sentence as an attractive woman appeared out of the yard office and climbed a ladder up to the *Monitor's* iron deck.

"Excuse me gentlemen," called out Ericsson. "May I introduce Miss Sally Parsloe. She is helping me out with the enormous volume of paperwork necessary on this project."

Nat Mather, climbing down from the turret roof, almost lost his balance due to distraction. There was something about this woman that was different. She had a presence of no mean sort.

"I'm so pleased to meet you, Commander," Miss Parsloe extended her gloved hand to Porter, who though normally a social *roué,* was taken aback by her libertinism. Dressed in a pert and suggestive fashion she walked the deck as if it were a stage. Nat, watching her as if he were in a trance, managed a gullible smile upon being introduced to the shapely, blond-tressed woman.

"Sally was good enough to take over when my office assistant suddenly quit last week," Ericsson proudly announced.

"Have you worked in a boatyard before, Miss Parsloe?"

"Not really, Commander. But I just *love* boats."

"Gentlemen," the Swede helped Sally down the ladder. "Miss Parsloe will be happy to take down any comments that you want to make about the *Monitor* before you leave. Now, you have inspected my vessel. Are you satisfied?"

"Mr. Ericsson," answered Porter, "I have borne a great deal from you today. You have mocked my authority and have not treated me with the respect due my station. I am about to have satisfaction, for on my report depends whether or not your 'iron pot' is accepted by the Navy Department, so I will say my piece in plain terms before presenting a written report. . . ."

"Say what you please," boomed Ericsson in the hollowness of the ship shed, "the Secretary of The Navy will decide."

"Well, sir—I have looked into this whole affair from A to Izzard, and conferred with Lieutenant Mather. I have come to an inescapable conclusion from which there is no return."

"Go on, sir, go on," said the inventor, "you will run upon a reef soon enough."

"Very well," continued Porter as he watched Miss Parsloe and Nat chatting in front of the yard office. "I will say that Mr. Ericsson has constructed a very small iron vessel, which in the opinion of our best naval architect, is in violation of well-known principles and will sink the moment she touches the water."

"Oh," lamented Ericsson, "you are a fool!"

"But," smiled Porter, "I shall also state that Mr. Ericsson has constructed the most remarkable vessel the world has ever seen—one that, if properly handled, can destroy any ship now afloat, and whip a dozen wooden ships together, providing they could not maneuver so as to run her down."

The Swede looked at Porter with astonishment, then seized his hand and almost shook it off. "My God," he exclaimed, "and all this time I took you for a damned fool, and you're not a damned fool after all.'' They both laughed heartily and climbed down from the cold deck to partake of hot cocoa and cake in the office.

''John,'' confessed Porter to the inventor, ''I must admit that Mr. Lenthal's recommendations and calculations could not be lightly dismissed, so I was bound to make an issue of it—before accepting 'too easily.' The Navy is still the old Navy.''

* * *

Acting Paymaster Henry Watkins admired the reflection in the fitter's mirror. The deep blue Union Navy uniform added extra verve to his flagging demeanor, replacing what the years had shorn. Even though he'd asked Captain Worden if he could serve in his civilian attire, as did some other specialist volunteers, he was secretly pleased when advised to see the tailor. And sixteen dollars more for the ceremonial sword! Well, it *would* look fine in a photograph.

The tailor was on his knees attending to the trouser's length: a servant to the pasha. Watkins felt a momentary wave of superiority bordering on arrogance. Yes, this is what rank does for the ego. Visible, incontrovertible rank! Gold epaulettes and braid on the sleeves. He was inwardly ashamed of his feelings, but then he'd always envied such trappings on others. Perhaps it was a natural inclination as a jeweler—one of his many pursuits—to want to decorate his own body.

''All the way from Illinois,'' the Commodore's clerk had gasped. ''We don't get many sailors from the prairies.'' What the clerk didn't know was that Henry Watkins had gone round the horn with the 49ers. then across to China, and back by way of the Indian and Atlantic Oceans. His wife, Regina called it 'wanderlust' when he went off for two years after their first son was born. Others said he 'had a roving disposition' when he left the wealthy family nest in Utica, New York.

Failing to find his fortune in California and the Orient, Watkins applied himself to some family holdings in LaSalle, Illinois, and by 1853 was a prosperous watchmaker and merchant, dealing in clocks, looking-glasses, guns, toys, fishing tackle and stationary. He then invested the proceeds of his success in The LaSalle Iron Works as senior partner, to the delight of Regina and her father, who was head of the Law School at Yale and shortly to become Governor of the state of Connecticut. His company manufactured steam engines, mill gearing, horse powers, corn shellers and machinery of all kinds.

The mustachioed paymaster tweaked his upper lip and wondered if waxing would enhance his image. The cavalier assignment he had wrangled aboard the *Monitor* through an Illinois Congressman demanded a dashing appearance.

There were those back home whose eyebrows arched when Henry, a mature forty years of age, volunteered. What, with a growing family and a business? Unheard of. The Army and Navy were asking for men under thirty-five, and men without such responsibilities. Was it wanderlust again, or a roving disposition?

No; it was a business failure brought on by the financial panic of 1858. Watkins had sold out to his partners to cover his debts. The transaction had been confidential, thus sparing the family's honor and reputation. In addition, there had been an increasing tedium between Henry and his wife. Fifteen years of marriage, a business reversal—and a touch of wanderlust. It was time for a sabbatical, and the war was a convenient reason. Another consideration was that Regina's father should be proud of his son-in-law, and not have reason for scorn. Governors and ex-Governors should be kept happy, especially if they are wealthy.

That evening, Henry, in uniform, boarded the East River Ferry, intent on sampling the Saturday delights of the big city.

Brooklyn
Sunday, Feb'y 2, 1862

Dear Regina,

Instead of going to Church this morning, I am sitting in my room writing you. There is little to do until my vessel is delivered to the Navy Yard. I am in charge of provisions for the crew, such as soap, candles, buttons and whatever a sailor will need at sea.

The *Monitor* was launched this past Friday morning at Greenpoint, Long Island, and I was present at the ceremonies. There were bookmakers taking bets that the vessel would sink, and boats in the water waiting to rescue survivors. Mr. Ericsson stood gallantly on the bow as the blocks were knocked out and the ironclad slid down the ways. She hit the water, wavered a bit, then floated like a log.

The New York *Daily World* reported afterwards that The *Monitor* had not the slightest intention of sinking, as her skeptics foretold. Naturally this gives great assurance to yours truly and the rest of the crew.

I found a good-looking darkey for a servant but he wasn't of age so tomorrow I shall hunt for one aboard the receiving frigate, *North Carolina*.

Making the acquaintance of our surgeon yesterday, I found that he was one of my fellow sufferers aboard the *Anna Reynolds* on which I sailed around the Horn to California. Small world!

Your father came down from Bridgeport yesterday and we went aboard the vessel during one of the severest snow storms I have ever seen. He was impressed by her armor but not convinced of her stability. All in all it was a worthwhile trip for him as I introduced him to Commodore Paulding, who is quite well-connected.

As soon as the vessel is in the Yard there will be more visitors, including President Lincoln. I wish I could add your name and other good LaSalle friends to the list, but there is no time.

In the midst of all this excitement, my home and loved ones are not forgotten, and the farther I am from you, the more precious you all seem. Please imagine the rest of this letter filled with hugs and kisses for you and the children. I will write again before we sail. Till then, goodbye.

Henry

Watkins addressed and sealed the envelope. He felt some remorse at lying about being in his room in Brooklyn, but war was war and he was not about to incur suspicion. He got up from the writing-desk and parted the window curtains a trifle. Among the carriages on Fourth Avenue were occasional sleds drawn by spirited horses and driven by fur-swathed families from the rural up-island communities. Barking dogs and rowdy snowball-throwing boys completed the winter scene. "Would you have a stamp, my dear?"

"Henry, I don't *live* here you know," a woman answered from a tangle of down comforters in a huge four-poster bed. "The Cary sisters were so decent as to allow us to stay over. As poets they understand life more than . . . oh, my God. It's Sunday, isn't it?"

"Past ten," Watkins wound his watch and put it back into an inside coat pocket.

"Ten," shrieked Sally Parsloe. "The sisters have a reception and a buffet lunch at noon every Sunday. We've got to hurry, and tidy up the room." Sally jumped vigorously out from under the lavish comforters, unconcerned with her nudity. "What are you staring at?" she giggled, facing him with hands on her hips.

Astonished, Henry took off his reading glasses. "Frankly, I thought—never mind; it's nothing."

"I told you I was an actress before taking the job at the shipbuilder's. Actors are never what they seem to be. Hair color is just another hat, depending on the part."

Watkins steadied himself. "Perhaps I'm still a bit hazy from last night. Alcohol and I do not mix very well." He buttoned up his uniform jacket. "I hope your Cary sisters are discreet. My position with the Navy is very sensitive."

"Don't worry about them. They just love people who are themselves. Woe be to those who are pretentious, pompous or devious. The sisters will make short work of them." Sally gathered her clothing from the back of a chair and tip-toed into the serpentine verde-antique bathroom. "Ooh, it's so cold. When this is all over, I'll go back south. People were not meant to live in the cold. . . ."

"Have I been sleeping with the enemy?" joked Watkins.

"Of course not, silly. Cain't you tell a Maryland girl?"

"I'm sorry, dear." Henry was on his hands and knees, looking for an errant boot under the bed. "It's just that this war is getting on my nerves. The waiting, the preparation, the confusion. I'm used to getting things done on time and in an orderly fashion.'' He slipped into his boot. ''Sally, about last night—was I . . . really *myself?* Not that you should know what I am, but. . . .''

''I understand, dear. Sally has been through the mill more than once.'' Her voice echoed hollowly from the cavernous bathroom as the tap water was running. ''Henry, you were just marvelous—especially when you tried to dance with the coat-rack. Everyone was in hysterics. . . . And those stories you told me last night, after we—You couldn't be forty years old. You were magnificent.'' She came out of the bathroom dressed and freshened up. ''It must be so exciting; meeting all those important people at the Navy Yard.'' Henry held up her Siberian sable coat and she slipped it on. ''When did you say President Lincoln was going to visit the *Monitor?*''

''He's to come a week from this Wednesday. By then the vessel will be at the yard and ready for sea trials.''

''I suppose there will be the usual reporters. . . .''

''By invitation. The public will not be allowed.''

''Do you suppose a very brilliant photographer friend of mine could get an invitation?''

''By all means,'' Watkins succumbed to a kiss on the cheek as they descended the brownstone stairs into the snowy street. ''Give me his name and I'll have a pass waiting for him at the yard office. He can pick it up anytime.''

''Renfrew,'' she spelled it out letter by letter. ''Mr. Jack Renfrew.'' Sally tucked her gloved hand under Henry's elbow as they walked down Fourth Avenue. She knew what men liked.

''I just can't believe it.'' Abraham Lincoln ducked his stovepiped head as he followed Commodore Paulding down the *Monitor's* companionway to the berth deck. ''Why it seems only a few weeks ago that I held Mr. Ericsson's cardboard model in my hand."

"It's been just four months, Mr. President," replied John Ericsson proudly as the group gathered round below decks. Included were Commander Porter, Lieutenant Mather and the Mayor of New York City, Fernando Wood.

"My congratulations, Mr. Ericsson," exclaimed the President, "but I still don't understand how iron can float."

"No different than a prospector's tin pan—except that it's must bigger," replied the Swede.

"I wish I'd said that." Lincoln examined the seaman's bunks, five high from deck to ceiling. He slid into a lower bunk and shook his head. "The sailor's life is for shorter men than I," he quipped and stood up again. "You," he addressed Nat Mather, "were at the Navy Department last summer, eh? I never forget a tall man. How do you find sleeping at sea?"

"He spends most of his nights on land," laughed Porter.

"Understandably so," Lincoln turned toward the Mayor. "Mr. Wood, did you ever think you'd be invited aboard an 'enemy' warship?" The President was referring to the proposed plan that New York City was to secede from the Union a year earlier, before the war started. "What was the proposed name of your new country, Mr. Wood? It always escapes me."

"Tri-insula, Mr. President," replied the natty politician sheepishly. "But it was not to be a country; merely a free city such as are common in Europe."

Lincoln grinned sagaciously. Wood had proposed secession to the City Council after the initial rapid Southern State secessions in December and January, following Lincoln's election in November of 1860. Fearing war, the many feuding Democratic factions of the city were prepared to unite in a common cause and "receive the whole and united support of the Southern States." A secret association was formed to carry out the project but the firing on Fort Sumter roused the population's patriotic fervor so that the politicians changed their minds. Even so, New York was still a smoldering hotbed of opposition to the Republican President and his policies.

Lincoln doffed his hat and went forward to inspect the wardroom and officer's accomodations. He marvelled at the liberal use of black walnut, damask and tapestry.

Sensing what the President was thinking, Commodore Paulding set him at ease. "Mr. Ericsson fitted the cabins out at his own expense, Mr. President."

"In that case," joked Lincoln, "we have many more vessels for him to fit out so handsomely."

After looking at the boilers and engines, the party went up into the turret to look over the twin eleven-inch smoothbores. A gun crew snapped to attention, then opened an iron port and ran one of the Dahlgren cannon through as a demonstration.

The President sighted over one of the guns through the open port. "If we fired now, we'd sink the *North Carolina.*" He ran his hand over the bulbuous polished breech. "Commodore, have these guns been tested?"

"Not aboard this vessel yet, Mr. President."

"When will the fifteen-inch model be ready?"

"In April, sir."

Lincoln shrugged and followed Paulding back down to the berth deck and up the companionway exit. The group emerged on deck and strolled once around the turret, inspecting the various pipes and stacks. Ericsson explained how they telescoped into the deck when clearing for battle and pointed out the unique anchoring system and the protected propeller access.

On the dock, an artist was hastily sketching the scene as marine guards held back a group of anxious reporters. A young photographer wearing a cape was setting up his view camera on a tripod directly in line with the boarding gangway. Content with the camera's angle of view, he slipped his hand under the focusing cloth and cocked the hammer of a large caliber percussion pistol that had been fastened to the inside, with its muzzle just behind the lens cap. Sweating finger curled around the trigger within the camera, Jack Renfrew smiled pleasantly and waited.

The President, preceded by Commodore Paulding, walked erectly across the wooden gangway. Paulding, noticing the camera, stepped aside upon reaching the dock to allow an unimpeded view of Lincoln for the exposure. At this moment several of the reporters surged through the cordon of marines, one of them accidentally tripping over a tripod leg and knocking the camera to the cobblestoned pier. Lincoln shook his head sadly at the photographer and continued toward a waiting carriage as the guards cleared the way. Nat picked up a lens cap and handed it to the photographer who was examining the downed instrument. Their eyes met for an instant.

"Thank you," said Renfrew acidly as he covered the camera's empty lens barrel with his cape. "I can handle this—alone." Nat would never forget the incandescently greenish eyes of this chalky face—nor the ethereally fragrant and heady perfume that attended it.

* * *

"It's so nice of you to show me the vessel, Henry," Sally called down from the cubicular pilot-house. "I just love all these contraptions. . . ."

"Hurry up, Sally. We've got to leave before the next

watch is on. Some people are averse to having women aboard.''

''Just one minute, dear,'' she took a small wrench out of her purse and dropped it into a tube through which the steering wire ran aft from the wheel. ''I'll be right there—'' She climbed down the ladder to the engine room just as Watkins approached. The paymaster's concern was pacified by a deliberate display of petticoats and legs in lamplight.

Watkins handed a greenback dollar to the Sergeant at the gatehouse. A paymaster, like a captain, had his privileges. There were no questions—a quick wink sufficed. They took a carriage to the ferry landing and went across the East River. This was to be the last night of liberty before the test run and departure. Sally was especially frolicsome, for she had been given a difficult assignment by *Hosanna* through *Pet*, one that only a woman could do.

TWENTY-ONE

A heavy snowfall had transformed the city into a winter stage set, almost obliterating the carved and gilded letters over the icy latticed window of a restaurant on the corner of Bleeker Street and Broadway. Desoto's, a rendezvous for actors and theatergoers, hardly needed a sign, for the succulent aroma of the house special, broiled kidneys and rarebits, had led the blind to its door.

At a table in the rear, comic actor Charles Parsloe balanced a spinning dinnerplate on his index finger as John Wilkes Booth and Sally Partington egged him on. "Would that I had room enough for another helping."

"Or money enough to pay for one?"

"Must you rub it in, Wilkes?" emoted the deadpan actor. "We genuine thespians aren't as concerned with Mammon as are the Booths . . ." Parsloe's expression suddenly changed. "But pray, what is the secret of your recent affluence? You're not doing anything in Gotham. I don't see how your road appearances could—Now, your brother Edwin—there's a man who's really raking it in.

First a successful New York season, and now the Haymarket in London. That will put him at the top. . . ."

"Charles," interrupted Booth irritably, "I'm very grateful that you cared so well for Sally while I was away."

"Always glad to lend a hand, or a leg—or my name. All of it was so cloak-and-dagger. Ah, Miss Partington-Parsloe, how I wish you were indeed my sister. We might have had such good sport together."

Wilkes peeled a greenback from his billfold and handed it to Parsloe. "Here, this should clear your arrears with this establishment. Consider your services paid for."

"A more propitious bequest has never been made. I shall surprise the old man in his counting-house—and order more of everything." Parsloe skipped joyously past the tables toward the proprietor's office.

Wilkes leaned eagerly toward Sally. "Now, before he returns, what have you found out about the adversary?"

"The *Monitor,*" she whispered, "went out into the bay yesterday, intent on leaving for Hampton Roads. After leaving the dock in the snowstorm, with families and friends waving, they found that the vessel would not answer to its helm. They went back and forth, pushing off buoys like a drunken man, even running into the gas works across the river before signalling for a tow back to the yard—Something I 'arranged'—"

"Marvelous," Wilkes loosened his lavender cravat, poured a shotglass of anisette and downed it with a grimace. "How long will the vessel be laid up?"

"Watkins told me Ericsson will have it fixed in four days."

"That means they won't leave til the third or fourth of March. I've got to get word to Hosanna. Captain Buchanan needs all the time he can get, especially for his engines. Leaving on the fourth, the *Monitor* will arrive at the Roads on the seventh."

Sally's hand clasped his under the table. "Which cipher are you planning to use?"

"The Reid Dictionary—I'm afraid that Secretary of War Benjamin is shrewd enough to have intercepted and solved Hosanna's personal cipher messages, especially the 'checkerboard' types. Hosanna is suspicious of Benjamin's ambitions and would like to maintain control over his cabinet. . . ."

"How clever of you to find a rare book to base code messages on. It's no wonder that he personally engaged you." Sally knew that John Wilkes Booth thrived on flattery.

"There will be an important position in the Confederacy when this war is done, should I want it. Hosanna promised. And there will be money, the likes of which an actor has never seen—arrangements with a Canadian bank are already in progress." Booth raised his glass to an invisible benefactor. Just then, Parsloe gamboled over to their table, bottle in hand and a girl in tow.

"Let's celebrate," he shouted, "a toast to Wilkes Booth, without whose largesse, we struggling actors would pale and shrivel away for lack of nourishment." Several more players suddenly appeared, brandishing empty glasses. Booth had no choice but to accept the honor and order yet more champagne.

"A toast," repeated Parsloe, and it was completed by an anonymous shout from another table:

". . . to the Romeo of the provinces!"

"Stand up, whoever said that, stand up like a *man*." Wilkes sprang up atop his table with a steak knife poised like a sword, parrying at the startled diners. "I challenge my detractor to the field of honor—if he dares. If I do not get satisfaction, then heed this. Cowards die many times before their deaths. . . .''

''Wilkes,'' pleaded Sally. ''Think of Jack Renfrew. What good will it do for the *cause* if you get hurt?''

Booth shook off his tipsiness and thought of his pledge to Jefferson Davis. As Jack Renfrew, he would be the most dedicated of Confederate secret agents, letting nothing stand in the way of victory for the South and the destruction of the despotic Union. Now, was he going to stumble over the bantering of jealous actors? It *did* bother him, though, that he did not receive the acclaim of his peers, and of the big cities. His blood curdled with rage at the New York critics, especially William Winter of the *Herald*, who called his debut in *Richard III*, 'raw, crude and much given to boisterous declamation'. How close Mr. Winter had come to being the recipient of a Derringer bullet!

It rattled him that his stage success—what there was of it—had been generated by swarms of dewy-eyed adolescent females who knew nothing and cared even less about Shakespeare. One of his co-actors, Clara Morris, had said of Booth: 'He had an ivory pallor that contrasted with his raven hair, and his eyes had heavy lids which gave him an oriental touch of mystery. Girls in restaurants always gave him extra food and women naturally loved him.'

This was all very well—*then*, but not *now*. He succumbed to Sally Partington's entreaties. ''True, my dear, let us ignore the rabble; they're only envious.'' Wilkes climbed waveringly down from his table and settled into a chair.

At the opposite end of the room, a table broke out in song. There were several Union soldiers among the carousing group . . .

The Union forever! Hurrah, boys, hurrah!
Down with the traitors, up with the stars;
While we rally round the flag, boys,
Rally once again,
Shouting the battle-cry of freedom . . .

A lively cheer followed the chorus, intermingled with toasts for the Union field commanders: "Hurrah for General Burnside . . . Hurrah for Grant . . . Hurrah for President Lincoln."

Booth's eyes ignited and color flushed his face. "Lincoln," he snarled, "what a glorious opportunity there is for some man to immortalize himself by killing Lincoln. Just as the ambitious youth who set fire to the Ephesian dome outlived the pious fool who built it. . . ."

"Who was this ambitious youth?" asked Parsloe.

"What difference does it make?" Wilkes, not knowing who, passed it off as trifling.

Sally observed Wilkes with apprehensive admiration. There were times when he exhibited the madness of his late, famous father, and other times, the shrewd eloquence of grandfather Wilkes, the maverick English politician. Some had pointed out that the Booths had a strong strain of their wealthy ancestor, Israel Wilkes, a distiller—except that they drank whisky instead of making it.

Dark, thick-set and stout, Judah Philip Benjamin reached for a gilt-bordered book in his legal library at his office in Richmond. The spine read "Principles of Estate Transactions." But the inside title page announced a different volume: "Reid's English Dictionary." Benjamin, a prominent New Orleans lawyer before becoming Secretary of War under Jefferson Davis, took no chances in peace or war. Finding out about the dictionary code, he scoured the

South for a copy of *Reid's* and had it bound into a legal cover. The informant was well-paid. It was not that he differed from Jeff Davis' policies, but rather that he kept a lawyer's eye on all sensitive communications lest the president act rashly or without tact as his opposition had charged. Furthermore, the secretary was especially interested in the loans that were being transacted with European banks using Confederate cotton as collateral. This was an area where the president had given power to others, including Benjamin's former law partner, John Slidell. Petty jealousies were rampant among the Confederate agents in Europe, and Benjamin meant to keep an eye on the proceedings, as well as on certain of his own investments in France and England. His appetite had been whetted with knowledge that a brilliant Confederate naval officer, Lt. John Maffitt, had been given a copy of *Reid's English Dictionary* by Jefferson Davis before leaving for the Bahamas to take command of the first of several powerful commerce-raiders being delivered from British shipyards.

After locking his library door, Benjamin unfolded a copy of a telegram received that morning from Fredericksburg, near the Union line. He set it down next to the dictionary and gleefully deciphered it while stuffing preserved figs into his wily mouth. It was quite easy compared to the Vigenère variations of the checkerboard cipher. The first word was indicated by the numbers 13, 4—which meant page 13, fourth word down in the first column: *adversary*. The next word was on page 468: *to;* then *leave*, and finally, the date: *March four*. It was 'signed' *Pet*.

The Secretary of War burned the message in his fireplace, savoring the idea of the next sunrise, when he was officially to take over the position of the highest cabinet member, second only to Jefferson Davis—that of Secretary of State. He felt a surge of power within his "beer keg" body. He had been called names by the Southern aristocracy, as well as the common run, and he had kept smiling, perhaps only to anger them more. But he was a gambler and he knew when a card was worth playing. Judah Benjamin, son of a dry goods merchant who had come to Charleston, South Carolina from the Virgin Islands, had been a child prodigy, entering Yale College at the age of fourteen through the generosity of a wealthy family friend. Despite his standing at the head of his class academically, he fell in with the wrong people and became addicted to gambling. He was expelled in his junior year for "ungentlemanly conduct." There were rumours of thievery at the time. Despite his cloudy beginnings Judah completed his education while employed in New Orleans—a less stratified city than Charleston—and was admitted to the Lousiana bar at twenty-one. A consuming ambition led him to pursue several fields, including language tutoring. He married one of his students, the sixteen year-old daughter of a prosperous Creole family, gaining as well a dowry of two mulatto girls and a generous amount of gold.

During a childless decade that saw him become one of the most successful lawyers in the South, his marriage faltered, and Natalie, his wife, tired of being mistress of a plantation, left for Paris. That a daughter was born after ten years of marriage was the subject of some tongue-wagging, especially with Natalie spiriting the child off with her to the continent.

Compensating for the misfortune, Judah built a new, very elaborate mansion on his plantation and entertained lavishly, with a widowed sister, Rachel Levy, as surrogate mistress.

For a while his eyesight almost failed him and he devoted himself to planting sugar, using the most ingenious and advanced technology that could be bought. Recovering his sight, he resumed practice in New Orleans, becoming famous by his handling of an insurance claim case involving a slave mutiny aboard the brig *Creole*.

Appearing for the underwriters and disputing the claims of slaveowners for the loss of 26 slaves on a trip from Norfolk to New Orleans, Benjamin argued that the Negroes who escaped after forcing the ship to land in the British Bahamas were technically no longer slaves. In addition, the course change, away from the agreed destination of New Orleans, invalidated the owners' claims of compensation. The Louisiana Supreme Court decided in favor of Benjamin's clients and the *Creole* cases became important precedents in international insurance law.

Known to some as "the smiling Jew," Benjamin had his share of detractors. He was being held responsible for the loss of Roanoke Island to the Union amphibious forces a month earier—for not heeding the call of Confederate General Wise to fortify the seaward approaches to this strategic island within the North Carolina Banks that was the "back door" to Norfolk and Richmond.

The Federal Navy then sent an armada through Hatteras Inlet and the vastly outnumbered garrison of Roanoke Island fell under a relentless bombardment. The 2000 raw-recruit defenders had been bolstered by two companies of Virginia's best, the Richmond Blues, under command of Captain Jennings Wise, son of the commandant who had implored Benjamin for aid. Though the rebel losses before surrender were small, they included Captain Jennings, a prime target in his crimson-lined cape.

Because of this and other allegations, Benjamin was being 'removed' from his position as Secretary of War. The newspapers were carrying spurious accounts of his high-living in the face of shortages and his frequenting of gambling establishments. Even his penchant for devil fishing in Port Royal Sound came under fire. In addition, his expulsion from Yale College was disinterred, branding him through anonymous disclosures as a habitual thief.

But for his 'relationship' with Jefferson Davis, he would shortly be back in New Orleans, pleading cases. Instead, he was to be the new Secretary of State, where 'his great mind would find ample employment' and not collide with the military establishment.

"So be it," the chubby politician said to himself. "I am a fish out of water, but I shall not be netted. President Davis called me, in private, a 'scapegoat' for the recent military reverses. Such is the lot of my people!"

Judah Benjamin had acquired a taste for power, and what better odds to succeed than to be Secretary of State? Next in line for the Presidency itself, should anything happen to Davis! Ha, then he would show these self-righteous 'aristocrats' of the South. Benjamin felt a tinge of fear. What would be the reaction of the Southerners should they have access to his innermost feelings about them, and about slavery? He most probably would be lynched. The injustices of the practice bothered him . . . the imperious attitude of the slaveholders over these Africans who were, after all, human.

Yes, he would stop by at the telegraph station and send a cipher message to Captain Buchanan in Norfolk. After all, he was *still* Secretary of War. There was no way to prove that he did not have his own informants on the progress of the *Monitor*. Besides, a stroll downtown would be relaxing after the strenuous pressures of his war office. Perhaps a short furlough at Worsham's Faro Bank after sending the wire.

* * *

The guns of Fortress Monroe looked down over the broad, calm expanse of Hampton Roads, entrance to the James River, above which, only sixty miles away, lay the capital of the Confederacy, Richmond. Captain John Marston, standing on the quarterdeck of the USS *Roanoke*, looked apprehensively toward Craney Island, to the south, which marked the mouth of the Elizabeth River, beyond which was Gosport, lair of the dreaded rebel ironclad. It was shortly after seven on the morning of March 9th, a Saturday, and the promise of an early Spring was in the air. A southerly breeze wafted the sounds of Confederate emplacements along the muddy shores below the Federal blockading squadron's anchorage to the breakfast mess tables of the bluejackets aboard their splendidly equipped vessels.

Marston knew, from reports of escaped Negroes and avaricious Southern traders, that *Merrimac* was 'out' and counting the minutes before being let loose on its much-heralded foray against the proud wooden fleet that was choking the lifeblood out of Richmond's industrial capacity and denying the shipment of war materiel from Europe. And the crew of some four hundred knew that without its drive-shaft, which was being repaired in New York, the *Roanoke* would be a sitting duck for the underwater ram-equipped *Merrimac*. Still, the boilers were kept stoked—not only for heat and hot water, but to blow off steam occasionally and appear to the Confederate look-outs that she was in fighting trim.

The captain had taken heart that his fleet was held to be more than a match for anything the rebels could come up with. Commodore Goldsborough had devised the "trap" personally before leaving for the North Carolina sounds. The combined firepower of the *Cumberland* and *Congress*, moored off Newport News, and that of the larger *Minnesota*,

Roanoke and *St. Lawrence,* waiting in reserve, totalled about 250 guns, against 14 on the *Merrimac.*

250 guns behind wooden hulls and parapets against 14 guns behind heavy iron plating. Two thousand well-trained and well-fed sailors against two hundred ragtag landlubbers! Yet Marston was secretly glad that his flagship was lying under the protective guns of Fortress Monroe, shaft or no shaft. It would be up to the *Cumberland,* 24 guns . . . then the frigate *Congress,* of 50 guns to first challenge the *Merrimac.*

Lieutenant Joseph Smith, newly assigned, was in command of the *Congress.* Perhaps it helped to be the son of Commodore Smith of the Ironclad Board. Coincidentally, the previous commander, due to go ashore that afternoon was also named Smith, though no relation. Another coincidence was that McKean Buchanan was paymaster of the *Congress,* while unbeknownst to him, his brother, Franklin had been appointed Captain of the *Merrimac.* Both from Maryland, Franklin had hastily resigned his commission in the Union Navy in anticipation of his state's secession. When Maryland elected to remain in the Union, he asked to be reinstated but Secretary Welles, furious, said the Navy did "not need irresolute officers." Franklin, like his brother a veteran of almost fifty years' service, rebuked by the North, split the family and joined the South.

Old "Buck" Buchanan stood erect inside the conical ironsheathed wheelhouse of the *Merrimac,* a fringe of white hair protruding from under his gray cap and his Roman nose quivering.

"Mr. Ramsay," he addressed the chief engineer, "Clear the engine room; all workers ashore. . . . And Jones, we can't wait for any more powder. Clear the decks and be ready to cast off at half flood tide." The executive officer saluted and followed Ramsay out of the pilot house.

Buchanan winced as one of the 600-horsepower engines sputtered erratically, sending vibrations through the double layer of two-inch iron plate that covered the slanting sides of the 3200-ton 'iron diadem of the South'. Ramsay had done his best with the engines and had it not been for the fortuitous extra week gained by dint of the *Monitor*'s delay in leaving New York, *Merrimac*, or CSS *Virginia*, as it was to be called in the Confederate Navy, would not have been ready. As it was, the starboard engine had been juryrigged with wire and makeshift components, such as would drive an engineer from its Northern manufactory to drink.

The supply of powder and shells were barely enough for a limited engagement, and the prospects of receiving more within the week were negligible. Secretary of The Confederate Navy, Mallory, had instructed Buchanan to depend on the vessel's ram as much as he could in order to save ammunition.

The ship's surgeon, Dinwiddie Phillips, noted, "Many of those who watched us predicted failure, and others suggested that the *Merrimac* was an enormous burial case, and that we were conducting our own funeral, thereby saving undertaker's fees."

Nevertheless, Old Buck's wizened blue eyes narrowed like the viewing slit in the pilot-house armor. A distinguished veteran of the Mexican war, he had been the first Superintendent of Annapolis and had commanded Admiral Perry's flagship on the expedition to Japan in 1853. Now he had a score to settle. This was one of the reasons he had been picked over several others for this important post. "Vile vagabonds," he called the Union Navy. "That bewigged bureaucrat Welles. I'll show him. First, the

Cumberland, because of its dangerous new rifled guns, and then the *Congress*."

The flag officer's red ensign was hoisted at 11 A.M. and a signal gun was fired. Hardly had the vessel left its mooring when scores, then hundreds, then thousands of townspeople from Norfolk and Portsmouth appeared on the shore vantage points, traveling by land to Sewell's Point and Craney Island. Spectators crammed into oyster skiffs and dinghies, and made for the Union anchorage.

"Lieutenant," Buchanan observed the steam tugs *Raleigh* and *Beaufort* swinging into a leading position, "I am going to ram the *Cumberland*. The moment we're in the Roads I'm going to make right for her and ram her."

TWENTY-TWO

Under cloudless blue skies the 'cheesebox on a raft' rolled heavily as rough seas slammed over her flat hull, sending spray high over her single turret. Far to starboard lay the misty hills of Cape Charles, and dead ahead chugged the tow-tug *Seth Low,* eight-inch hawser snapping rainbows in the spindrift. Following off the quarters were the watch-dog gunboats, *Currituck* and *Sachem*. Now and then, the *Monitor's* bow would pitch deep and its stern would rise clear of the waves, exposing its whirling, 9-foot diameter propellor, racing and whining free.

On the grated turret roof, protected from seaspray by a makeshift canvas barrier, the crew, by turns, welcomed the drying sun and fresh air. Three days of battling a sea it had not been designed for had left the novel ironclad in miserable straits.

Down below, Paymaster Henry Watkins sloshed in seaboots through his tiny cabin, wrung out a sodden rug and hung it dripping on his open door. The small glass portlight in the cabin ceiling flashed white and green as waves rolled over the deck. A stench of burnt rubber and acrid carbon pervaded the vessel, having belched out from the engine room during the night. This was a result of sea water entering the blower pipes and wetting down the drive belts. The shortage of combustion air in the furnaces disrupted the draft and soon the engine room was filled with carbonic acid gas combined with seawater steam. In escaping the deadly fumes, the stokers and engineers threw open the bulkhead doors, spreading the noxious gases throughout the vessel's lower deck. In addition, there was a constant seepage of seawater onto the berth deck from the rotating turret junction.

After making sure that the ship's safe was secure and dry, Watkins took his soggy rug and went up into the tower, climbed to the top, and elbowed his way into the warming sun, where he draped the rug over a railing and lit a pipeful of tobacco. The Paymaster sucked on his pipe and daydreamed of his comfortable dry home in LaSalle, Illinois.

"Hey, Henry," a tall Lieutenant slapped the older man on his back. "I heard you're a hero. Isn't that so?" He winked at Chief Bosun's Mate John Stocking.

"Right you are, sir; if it hadn't been for Mr. Watkins, Sunstrom might not have made it. He was almost gone from the fumes when Mr. Watkins found him in the engine room."

"It was nothing, Nat. Anybody would have done the same. I was in the right place at the right time. . . ." Watkins looked quizzically at the ship's flag. It was upside-down.

"Distress signal, Henry." Nat Mather was amused at the apparent insult to Watkins' sense of order. "Doctor Logue wants to sample the other medicine cabinets of our fleet for remedies to sea-sickness . . . but right now it's too rough. . . ."

"Did I hear my name?" The surgeon appeared, stifling a yawn. "Ah, *el sol* is the best medicine of all."

"How is Captain Worden?" inquired Watkins.

"Still under the weather. Lieutenant Greene is spelling him in the pilothouse—"

There was an ominous rumbling in the distance and all eyes turned landward.

"Doesn't look like a storm to me," Bosun Stocking sniffed at the offshore breeze and uncased a spy-glass, which he drew open and handed to Nat.

"Smoke," called out Nat as he focused on the shore ahead.

"That would seem to be Hampton Roads," exclaimed Stocking.

"Damn," shouted the surgeon. "Are we too late?"

"Shells exploding in the air," said Nat as he passed the glass to the Paymaster. "Notify the Captain."

"Aye, sir." Stocking climbed down through the tower hatch.

"If it hadn't been for the damn steering, we'd have been here a week ago," Surgeon Logue shook his head.

"Sure looks like they beat us to it—by one day." Nat bit his lip. "We can only hope and pray. . . ."

"If the *Merrimac* is out, it's more than a coincidence, I'd say." Logue pensively rubbed his beard.

At 4 P.M. Cape Henry light was picked up, and exploding white puffs of smoke could be seen without the glass. Captain John Worden, shaking off his sea-sickness, concluded that the *Merrimac* was indeed "out" and ordered that the *Monitor* clear for action. As darkness descended, the horizon flashed with gunfire and the little ironclad slipped her tow hawser. Taking on a pilot, *Monitor* stood in for the harbor under her own power. It was learned from the pilot that the *Merrimac* was out and "making a terrible havoc" among the Union blockading squadron.

As they entered the Roads, vessels were leaving like "frightened quails, their lights dancing in all directions." The firing had slackened as *Monitor* approached the flagship, *Roanoke*, moored under the protective guns of Fortress Monroe. At midnight Captain Worden was ordered by Flag Officer Marston to steam to Newport News and protect the frigate *Minnesota*, which was aground and a vulnerable target for *Merrimac's* next attack.

Such was the fear, upon hearing of the destruction and sinking of two powerful Union warships by the rebel ironclad, with a calamitous loss of life, that no one slept aboard the *Monitor* that night. Among the mourners was Commodore Joseph Smith. When told that the *Congress* had surrendered to the *Merrimac* during the carnage of splintering wood, the old officer simply said, "Then Joe is dead." The Commodore was right. His son had died on the first day of his command, along with almost 400 others.

The next morning, *Merrimac* realized that what they took for a floating water tank during the night was a formidable opponent. Fought to a standstill from eight in the morning to one in the afternoon, the weary "diadem of the South" withdrew upriver. Aboard the *Monitor*, Captain Worden had suffered temporary blindness and powder burns when a point–blank shot from the *Merrimac* had struck the pilothouse. The next in command, Lieutenant Greene decided not to pursue the adversary.

It was a tactical victory for the Union. The *Minnesota* had been saved and a new era of naval war had dawned.

Steadying his flamboyant gray wig with one hand, Secretary Gideon Welles paced excitedly before a gathering of military and war department officers. One of those present was Allan Pinkerton, former head of the Secret Service. Welles had called for a closed session in his office at the Navy Department in Washington after a suspicious telegram had been intercepted and decoded by a brilliant team of young cipher-operators known as the 'Sacred Three'. It had been intended for delivery to Taltavul's Tavern, a known haunt of Confederate sympathizers in the city.

Wells held up the decoded message triumphantly, then read aloud: "To Pet . . . Bravo for wrenching victory from the jaws. Signed, Hosanna." The Secretary turned on his heels slowly. "Hosanna, we believe, is none other than Jeff Davis. We don't know who 'Pet' is, but we can be sure he's no angel. The devastation wreaked on our noble fleet this past Saturday in Hampton Roads is most likely linked to this message. Washington is swarming with rebel spies, and we must—we will do something about it lest more of our plans go astray. Thank God we have stopped that monstrous rebel ironclad, but had it not been for wanton sabotage—of which we now have evidence—so many of our gallant boys would not have died."

The Secretary hesitated a moment, as if in silent prayer, then picked up an object from a table and brandished it. "This, gentlemen, is the reason for the ignoble butchery in the Roads last Saturday. A wrench! A wrench treacherously slipped into the steering mechanism of our illustrious *Monitor*. This piece of metal delayed the steam battery from leaving New York for one week, giving the

Merrimac the time it needed to repair its engines and take on shot and powder, the bulk of which was loaded on the vessel on Thursday, the 7th of March—two days before she came down the river. Somebody knew the *Monitor's* exact schedule. Somebody communicated that information to the Confederate schemers, and somebody slipped this wrench into the steering cable channel. We are now planning to build a fleet of larger *Monitors*. Ocean-going vessels. Thirty of them will have their keels laid within a month. In addition, we are proceeding with several large armored vessels, more potent than *New Ironsides*, which is now under construction. And there is an immense program under way for building shallow-draft river gunboats.

"How many more 'wrenches' are poised in our shipyards—to delay and destroy our vessels? We must strengthen our vigilance against this wave of treachery. We must find this 'Pet', and others like him . . . or *her*, before they can strike!

"Commodore Paulding will be in charge of a commission to enforce security on these programs, and I expect that everyone present will submit his recommendations. . . ."

Commander David Dixon Porter and Lieutenant Nathaniel Gideon Mather exchanged knowing glances. The Secretary had said "or *her*." There was one woman that came to mind—and a saucy one at that. And she *did* have a Southern accent.

John Ericsson wired Porter that Sally Parsloe had left his employ the day after his *Monitor* had sailed, and he insisted that the steering had been bench-tested before the zig-zag trial in the East River. That he didn't report finding the wrench initially was because he'd thought it was due to a worker's negligence and would cause a delay in sorely needed payments from the Navy to satisfy his suppliers.

Allan Pinkerton's man in New York advised the commission that a little pressure exerted on actor Charles Parsloe completely vaporized his 'sister' Sally. The comedian denied meeting any such person and claimed that it was most likely a joke.

"Lieutenant Mather," the venerable Commodore tried to maintain the dignity of his station. "Commander Porter has recommended that you be assigned to this 'Wrench' affair. . . ."

"*Wench* affair, sir," corrected Porter.

Paulding squinted over his reading glasses, first at Porter, then at Mather. He pursed his lips and continued. "I agree with the Commander, Lieutenant. You *did* meet the lady—and I suspect you will recognize her face should you encounter her again."

"He might recognize more than that."

"Now, Commander," chided the Commodore.

"Sir," piped up the youngest by far. "Commander Porter knows as much about her as I do. Perhaps he would do better."

"Now, I might at that—were I twenty years younger, and without this long, black beard—and the responsibility of a fleet. I have to join Admiral Farragut at Ship Island. I'm afraid this is my last day in Washington. Besides—it's simply a matter of tactics, Nat. When one wants to catch a fish, it's much easier when using fresh bait."

Before going to New York to see John Ericsson, Nat reported to Captain Dahlgren regarding the *Monitor's* ordnance performance at Hampton Roads. First he gave an account of the flaws in the turret design: "The chalk marks on the turret deck were soon obliterated and the gunnery officer could not tell which way his guns were pointing relative to the fore and aft line of the vessel itself. Captain Worden's instructions from the pilothouse were totally useless during the last hour of the engagement."

"I see," lamented the impeccably uniformed Dahlgren, sitting behind an enormous oak desk cluttered with reports, blueprints and numbered shell fragments. Dominating the exhibit was a small scale model of his newest creation, a fifteen-inch gun. He swung it around toward Nat. "If Worden said '*Merrimac* bearing off the port quarter', Greene would have no idea just where the port quarter was."

"Exactly," continued Nat. "So it became necessary to fire as the turret revolved and the target came into view through the open gun port. And what's more, the voice tube only functioned when the turret was lined up fore and aft. When Captain Worden was blinded by the shot that hit the pilothouse, the vessel was blind as well. Perhaps the pilothouse should be on top of the turret, and revolve with it. . . ."

"Yes, yes, Lieutenant, but that's another matter, one that I am not concerned with. What about my guns? I hear they performed well. No misfires, no recoil problems—"

"True, except that the guns cannot be depressed far enough to roll a shot out in case of a defective primer or canister."

"That is the fault of the turret port. I was afraid of that. The same thing will happen with elevation." Dahlgren leaned forward, his sharp features suggesting a predatory eagle, ready to pounce on any criticism of his deadly iron progeny.

"Of the 41 rounds fired, sir, I believe that at least half struck the Merrimac. At one point, Captain Worden brought the *Monitor's* bow against the enemy's quarter and both guns were fired point blank. They did not penetrate the casement, which appeared to be constructed at a 45 degree angle and was covered with grease.''

''No penetration at all?'' Dahlgren winced.

''Only once—''

''Yes, tell me!''

''We loaded one charge with twenty-five pounds of powder—''

Dahlgren jumped to his feet. ''Why that's out and out insubordination. Fifteen pounds is the absolute maximum. Who gave that order, Lieutenant?''

''I was just testing, sir. You see, the guns have never been tested. I recommend that—''

''You'll recommend nothing. It is I who will make the decisions regarding this ordnance. You might have blown up the gun. . . . Destroyed ten years of hard work.''

''To say nothing of the gun crew—''

''Mather, I'll not have your insolence to boot.''

''Then will you approve my application for a transfer? I would like to get sea duty.''

Dahlgren settled down and thumbed through Nat's report. ''Are your 'recommendations' in here too?''

''Sir, the *Merrimac* would be on the bottom now if the *Monitor* had used a stronger charge.''

''That's enough, Lieutenant,'' the senior officer cautioned Nat abruptly. ''I understand you are investigating the *Monitor's* steering mishap for Commodore Paulding. When you get back from that, I'll have a new challenge for you—perhaps a berth on one of our new vessels.''

* * *

''Sally was—what you might call variable,'' John Ericsson turned on a swivel stool toward Nat who was sitting adjacent to the engineer's drawing-table. ''She could be a rum doxy one day, and a ladybird the next. . . .''

"A rum *what?*" Nat was bewildered by the British term.

"Rum doxy means a fine lass. Ladybird is quite the opposite," he plucked at his steel-gray side whiskers and emitted a long, low whistle. "Very trim lines, that woman."

"It follows; we think she was an actress."

"I can't believe that a woman would be capable—but then, times have changed since I was a young man, what with all these feminist movements and Bloomer girls. But it was suspicious that she left when she did. Took her pay the day after my vessel left and never returned. The bookkeeping is still in chaos." The Swede threw up his hands in despair.

"We don't *know* whether she was involved or not, Mr. Ericsson, but nobody is above suspicion in wartime. Did she have any friends? Gentlemen callers, references aside from Mr. Parsloe?"

"I hoped for a while that I might have—now fancy me. Old enough to be her grandfather. We had coffee, now and then at Poppy Smith's. I was angling to take her to Delmonico's. . . ."

"And what happened—sorry, it's none of my business."

"Nothing, that's just it. I saw her walking with a Naval officer one afternoon, and that was the end of it."

"Could you describe him? His rank, his age. . . ."

"Sorry, I only saw him at a distance. My eyes are not that good anymore. They were headed toward the Navy Yard."

"You're certain, sir, that the steering was functioning well on the day before the first trial?"

"Trial, Lieutenant? That was the day before the battery was to leave. The trip down the East River was the only trial planned. She was provisioned and carried a full load of powder and shot. The 'good-byes' were all said. As far as I knew, she was ready to go. When bringing her from the Continental Works to the yard, we had no trouble steering under tow. A defect would have shown up at that time."

"What you say makes sense." Nat buttoned up his coat collar against the blustery March weather. "My next stop will be the yard."

"If you catch her, give 'er a squeeze for me—around her pretty neck. And please convey my respects to Commander Porter."

"You think it was done *here*, under my very nose?" Commodore Paulding was aghast. "And with *me* the man in charge of the inquiry!"

"Would you rather I didn't, sir?" Nat replied.

"Of course not, son. It just bothers me that one of my own men might be involved. We've had such a good record here." The aging officer looked out of his window at the bustling facility. "Where would you like to begin?"

There was no listing of Sally Parsloe in the main gate visitor's book, so Nat interviewed the Marine guards individually. Among them was Corporal Bruce Hall. Nat was struck with the stocky Marine's resemblance to another "little corporal," Napoleon. But this corporal had weak, evasive eyes despite his glitter and polish.

"No, *sir*, I certainly would not have missed a wench such as you've described, sir. If I may ask, what did she do, sir?"

"Thank you, corporal. That will be all."

The blue and gold-trimmed Marine stepped back inside his guardhouse and watched Mather through the window. There was no turning back now. The Paymaster's lady had not been listed in the book that night. Therefore there was no lady.

TWENTY-THREE

Sporting the eight gold stripes of a Rear Admiral's rank, earned by taking Port Royal Sound and establishing a Federal foothold in South Carolina, Samuel Francis DuPont, scion of the Delaware industrial family, proudly pointed out the features of his next flagship to his new engineering officer. "Nathaniel, I'm glad to have you aboard, even if it is only a paper boat at this stage." The tall, sixty-year-old officer turned one of the plan drawings several ways before he had it right-side up. "It's about time someone was assigned to me who could decipher these blasted drawings."

Nat held a drawing up to the window in the Admiral's office overlooking the Philadelphia Navy Yard. "Sir, according to this plan the engines are amidships and the wheelhouse slightly aft."

"So they are, Lieutenant. Something to do with trimming the vessel—there's so much iron plating to protect her boilers that they had to be placed more forward than usual."

"Can the wheelhouse be moved forward?"

"Not without changing the interior layout, and that would take weeks by the time we got approval from the department. The contracts have all been let and much of the equipment is already being manufactured—" DuPont paled. "Why do you ask?"

"It's just that this elevation does not show the funnel, and from what I can see, it looks like the funnel will sprout up forward of the wheelhouse," Nat traced his finger up from the engine room and through the gun decks.

"I see," DuPont steadied himself against his desk. "I mean I *won't* be able to see out of the wheelhouse very well—at least not dead ahead. Damn it, Mather, can't something be done about this without going through the Navy Department again?"

"We could have a telescoping funnel built."

"Good, I'll put you in charge of it," DuPont, relieved, sat down behind his desk with a sigh. "Anything else?"

"The drawings show keel steppings for two masts—"

"All boats should have masts," boomed the admiral. "The Bureau of Naval Construction will not allow a boat to be built without masts, and that's that."

"Rigging will be shot away in an engagement," cautioned Nat. "Masts, spars and sails will only get in the way—hanging over the sides and covering the gunports . . . and fouling the propeller and rudder. Impossible to cut away on an ironclad during battle."

"We know that, Mather."

"We can 'remove' the spars after commissioning."

"You're in charge of that too, Lieutenant."

"Curious that the *Monitor* was commissioned without masts, even though the specifications demanded them."

"Not so curious, Mather. That vessel was built so fast that the Bureau didn't have time to get out of their chairs. Had it not been for Hampton Roads, the Bureau would have tracked down the boat and forced it to have masts installed."

"Then let's not say anything, sir . . ."

"Definitely not. Lieutenant. We'll do the alterations ourselves. *New Ironsides* will bring the South to her knees. Our ultimate impregnable vessel will lead an armada to the Rebels' harbors and annihilate their fortresses. Nothing can withstand her firepower. Almost five thousand tons, and armed with 16 eleven-inch Dahlgrens—and escorted by a fleet of monitors. I can see it now . . . The Trafalgar of our time . . . sea-going vessels against the despots of the enslaved land . . ." DuPont closed his eyes and smiled.

Nat set the plans back in place and couldn't help wondering if professional military people thrived on war and its toys. DuPont was a midshipman at the early age of twelve, back in the War of 1812. War and destruction had been drilled into him instead of peace and building. How fitting that the nation's largest munitions manufacturer would have an Admiral in the family—someone to be counted upon not to spare powder and shot, since each gun fired added to the profits of his rich uncle. Table talk in the DuPont mansion at Wilmington must certainly center not on the outcome of an engagement, but rather on the number of rounds fired.

"Mather," DuPont opened his eyes. "It will be Christmas before the vessel is launched, so the Navy can be generous with furloughs. You must be anxious to see your family in Connecticut—or," the Admiral smirked, "the girl you left behind."

"There is no *one* girl . . . yet," confessed Nat. "what I mean to say, sir, is there have been several, but none permanent."

"Good, you had me worried for a moment. Mather,

we're planning a little get-together at my home this weekend. Perhaps you could come up with me on Saturday. Lovely country along the Delaware, and some interesting people."

"Thank you sir, but I've already plans for the day. My father's birthday. I'm going to scout the city's shops."

* * *

PROCLAIM LIBERTY THROUGHOUT ALL THE LAND UNTO ALL THE INHABITANTS THEREOF . . .

Nat read the inscription cast in the cracked bronze bell on exhibit at the base of a stairway in Independence Hall.

". . . ALL THE INHABITANTS THEREOF . . ."

He thought of Josiah Holladay and his betrothed; certainly *inhabitants* of our fair land. Was the great crack on the Liberty Bell an omen? A symbol of the hypocrisy and disgrace of slavery?

According to a handbill, the bell had been originally cast in London, England. It cracked when first struck in America to try the sound, in the newly completed belfry of the Pennsylvania State House in Philadelphia. It was melted down and re-cast by a local foundry with more copper added. Lasting for some years, it again cracked in 1835, while being tolled in memory of Chief Justice John Marshall. The tone was somewhat impaired, but still serviceable. On the 22nd of February, 1843, the crack widened upon tolling in observance of George Washington's birthday. The sound was permanently destroyed.

Washington and Marshall! Nat recalled that John Marshall had written a popular biography of the President. So were they both related to the Liberty Bell by cracking it. Curious that the bell should single out these two in its injury and decline . . . that the name 'Liberty Bell' was applied to it by abolitionists during the decade of its cracking.

The strange coincidences preyed on Nat as he searched the shops on Chestnut Street for a gift worthy of his father. In front of a silver shop he noticed several elaborately appointed saddle horses tethered to a ring in the hand of a cast-iron Negro servant boy. Philadelphia, the cradle of liberty and hub of the Underground Railroad! Then it came to him:

The two statesmen had something else in common. They were Southern aristocrats and slave owners. Washington, childless, set his slaves free in his will. Marshall maintained a mansion on Shockoe Hill, the citadel of Richmond, and was there interred. Each man had pursued his self-righteous calling, borne by slaves!

"It's a very rare item." The salesclerk proudly held the ivory pipe tamper up to a ray of sunlight that beamed through the display window. "Made in the Hebrides . . . a true conversation piece." Two young Rittenhouse Square belles, shopping with a haughty *grandedame,* tittered as they watched Nat examine the curiosity, an exquisitely carved woman's index finger. The clerk gave the silver cap on its base a twist. "Voilá, Lieutenant!" He triumphantly extracted a pipe reamer and demonstrated with circular gestures.

"I'll take it," Nat's cheeks flushed when he suddenly realized the object of the girls' amusement was his purchase. "Please put this in the box and wrap it for mailing." He handed the clerk an envelope with his father's name on it. Leaving the shop under the matriarch's penetratrating stare, Nat walked along Arch Street, stopping at a billboard in front of a theater.

Now in its Fourth Year &
Direct from New York City
Laura Keene presents
OUR AMERICAN COUSIN
A Farce by T. Taylor
with
L. Keene & J. Jefferson III

"Thet's a purty good play. Sure is funny."

Nat turned toward the voice and was appalled at what he saw: an elderly Negro, dishevelled and tipsy. His first impulse was to leave, but there was something in the old man's presence that deterred him.

"You've seen the play, then?"

"Yessir, Mister Admiral," the Negro's drawl changed into educated English. "I'm the custodian of the broom for this establishment. I've seen all the productions. So many that I have committed much to memory." He assumed a dramatic stance.

"Get me some poison, Iago; this night. I'll not expostulate with her, lest her body and beauty unprovide my mind again. This night, Iago."

Springing to another position and changing the timbre of his voice, he continued: "Do it not with poison, strangle her in her bed, even the bed she hath contaminated . . ."

Nat was amazed at the Negro's transformation. "You should be *on* the stage, not in the street. That was Shakespeare—"

"The Moor, sir. Othello. As if you didn't know."

"I wasn't sure—Mister . . ."

"Lingard. Justin Lingard."

"And I am Nathaniel Mather."

"Ah, sir, you said that I should be on the stage. Well I was . . . once. Ten years ago in this very city, I was the leading man, one might say." Lingard laughed, then coughed and held his black hand to his tattered breast. "My name was on the playbill . . . in the newspapers, and on the lips of the nation. That is, I was in the name of the play. Uncle Tom. Uncle Tom's Cabin. They said that my performance was flawless, and in almost every instance I was as pathetic as the author had meant to make the poor African." The elderly actor contorted his face to signify pathos.

"But I wanted to play Othello, not a pathetic—" Lingard coughed and caught hold of the playbill post for support.

"You must have many stories about your profession."

"I'll say I do, Mister Mather. I've seen them all. Forrest, Garrick, the Booth brothers, Fanny Kemble. Those Booth brothers, they are something. Edwin is the best, and th' youngest, John Wilkes; I've never seen so much jumping around in my life. Even more than his father, Junius. And Laura Keene, she's no slouch either. Does everything, even makes the scenery and costumes. I first knew her when she came back from Australia. She went there with Edwin Booth, and came home without him. Guess they might of had an argument," Lingard snickered. "She's sure had a ring in all the Booth noses, besides two young'uns—and a husband in Australia."

"Husband?"

"She was married to a Captain in the British Army. He resigned and opened a tavern. She'd been a barmaid anyway, and called 'Red Laura' by the clientele. Then her husband got in trouble with the law and he was sent to a prison in Australia for life. It was peculiar when she came back from an unsuccessful tour and opened the most expensive theater in America. All white, gold and damask, while poor Edwin came back with no money at all. That was when we all were with the Baltimore Street Stock Company. I came there with old Jimmy Wells. We had been minstrels with Ordway's Aeolian Vocalists up in Boston. Laura was the life of that company but somehow she never made it big on the stage except in comedies, and that ain't real theater like the Booths are in." Justin Lingard looked Nat up and down. "Now a feller like yourself might make a good actor."

"I'm afraid I don't have a good memory, and I'd probably trip on the stage. Engineering is my business."

"That's too bad for the ladies, sir."

"My name is Nathaniel. Call me Nat."

"Where are you from, Nat? Don't sound like around here."

"Connecticut."

"The land of steady habits."

"That's what they say, Justin. This playhouse, is it the best in the city?" Nat studied its brick facade.

"Right now it's the only one going. Managed by a lady, Miss Drew. She's from a long line of English actors. She played with Junius Booth and Joe Jefferson's father. Before Miss Drew's Arch Street Theater there was the Walnut Street Playhouse. It closed when I was about your age. Got my first job actin' there back in 1825. But the most famous was the old Southwark, accordin' to my father. It burned down when I was a little child, and it was fixed up to be a distillery. The Southwark was the first playhouse in America. That's how Philadelphia got to be the center of our profession in this country—before New York.

"Come to think of it, Nathaniel, one of the best actors to play the old Southwark was a soldier with a fancy uniform, But it was bright scarlet, not blue like yours. Handsome fellow and a dandy with the ladies, even if he was the enemy. When the British held this city—and it wasn't too difficult with all the loyalists livin' here—this soldier-actor, who you may have heard of, appeared at the Southwark. Major John André."

"The spy who was hanged," replied Nat. "He was captured out of uniform while passing through the American lines with plans for the betrayal of West Point hidden in his boot."

"The very same, Nathaniel. To Major André, a change of clothes was merely a change of costume."

"But for a soldier, it means death by hanging if caught out of uniform behind the enemy's lines." Nat was glad that his 'Reverend Cotton' was behind him.

"Do you know what the Major's undoing came from? I'll tell you, Nat. It was a woman."

"Isn't it always?" Nat was amused.

"But this woman was one of the belles of the city. André had every possible grace. He wrote poetry, both serious and comic. He sketched well, did water colors and brushed scenery for the dramatic clubs. He played the flute and was an expert dancer. Fluent in four languages, he was a companion to the two most beautiful young women in Philadelphia. Both named Peggy. When the British quit the city late in the Revolution, André organized and produced a gala celebration, called a 'mischianza' or medley. It featured a water pageant and a joust of fourteen knights—young British officers in medieval costume with fancy names like 'Knight of the Blended Rose'. Each knight had a lady, and Major André chose Peggy Chew, leaving Peggy Shippen to a fellow officer. And each knight had a black slave. My grandfather was Major André's Moor, and he was dressed splendidly in oriental robes and jewels. After the joust, everyone danced, gambled and drank wine, 'til at dawn the mischianza was ended with a great display of fireworks.

"Peggy Shippen, to spite André, married the new American commandant of Philadelphia, Brigadier Benedict Arnold. She was only nineteen, Arnold being twice that and divorced. A year later, she initiated the espionage between her husband and André, which led to his capture and demise."

"A touching story, Justin, but if Major André was such a talented man, why was he in the army, in America?"

"My grandfather, being a servant of André, was privy to his secrets. The Major was from mercantile origins, and his father blessed his early marriage to a girl who lived a literary life—one Miss Honora Sneyd. But . . . her family forbade the union. He then obtained a commission in the army. When she married another, André volunteered for service in the colonies. When captured with the plans in his boot, he had yet another secret hidden in his mouth: a miniature portrait of Honora Sneyd, which he took with him to the gallows."

"And the moral of your tale, Mister Lingard?"

"Be careful of beautiful women, I suppose."

"Are there any lovely ladies in this comedy, aside from Laura Keene of course? She seems too experienced for me."

"And old enough to be your mother," added Lingard, struggling to overcome the effects of drink. "Yes, there is Augusta, played by Sarah Partington."

"Then I'll buy a ticket for tonight's performance." Nat reached into his pocket, then flipped a silver coin, which Justin caught and handed back. "Keep it. Buy a steak dinner."

"No thank you, Nathaniel. Don't feel you must pay

me for my song and dance. It is I who am grateful to be talked to as an equal. I hope you enjoy the play."

Hunched over somewhat, concerned with those behind him whose view might be obstructed by his unusual height, Nat wondered where he'd heard that voice before. The voice of Augusta . . .

No heir to the fortune, Mr. Trenchard?
Oh, no!
What? No fortune?
Nary a red . . . barking up the wrong tree. . . .
Augusta, go to your room!
YES, MA! THE NASTY BEAST!
I am aware, Mr. Trenchard, that you are not used. . . .

Nat looked at his program. Sarah Partington. Sarah. Sarah could also be Sally. Sally Parsloe? Sarah's hair is dark and long; Sally's was ash blond—but the anatomy is the same. Could this be a coincidence? The voice aboard the *Monitor*. Here in Philadelphia? With *New Ironsides* being built at Merrick's yard on the Delaware, just a few blocks away! But it all seemed to fit. The girls' initials were the same and Sally Parsloe's reference in New York City was an actor, a comic actor. And the *Monitor* incident was anything but a laughing matter. Old Justin Lingard had warned him that afternoon to be wary of a beautiful woman.

After the next performance of *Our American Cousin* on the following Monday evening, the usual stage-door Johnnies and a few Jills were queued up, awaiting their idols' exit. One of them sported a dapper new suit of clothes in place of his usual blue naval uniform and carried a bouquet of spring flowers.

Laura Keene and Joe Jefferson were assailed by the older, more dedicated theatergoers while Sarah's following were of more basic instincts. One of the swains, a stout, middle-aged admirer, with the air of a snake-oil pedlar and garb to match, reached for her in an ungentlemanly manner, almost pinning her to the brick theater wall.

"Excuse me," Nat stepped between them with one hand clenched around the back of the philanderer's neck and a bouquet in the other. "Sorry I'm late, Sarah dear, but there was a little trouble at the jailhouse. . . ."

The pedlar, gasping for air, tipped his hat several times before Nat let go, then backed fawningly away, to turn on his heels and run into the night.

"You're quite persuasive, Mister. . . ."

"Nathaniel," he handed Sarah the bouquet and they strolled down Arch Street, very much a proper couple.

"Mister Nathaniel, I do appreciate what you've done, but I have an engagement. . . ."

"You can break it for me—Sally Parsloe!"

The actress turned pale and almost dropped the flowers. "Just who are you!" she scoffed nervously.

"A friend of John Ericsson, the inventor. Didn't we meet on an ironclad boat in a Brooklyn shipyard? It was in January. I was in uniform accompanying the illustrious Captain Porter, the naval officer who has just taken the rebel forts below New Orleans."

Sarah started to run across the street as Nat called after her, "Four hundred men died because of Sally Parsloe. . . ."

She stopped, sobbing and oblivious of the careening coach and charging team of horses that was racing along Arch Street. Nat jumped into the street and pulled her aside just as the coach rumbled by. Instinctively she fell into his arms.

"They made me do it. I didn't want to, but he said he'd kill me if I didn't. I had no idea what would happen. You've got to believe me." Sarah fell limp and almost fainted. Nat, supporting her, led her into a coffee-house where he eased her into a cozy booth.

"Just who are *they*?" Nat stirred Sarah's coffee.

"I can't say, Mister Nathaniel," she warmed her slim hands around her coffee cup. "They are desperate men."

"I'm Lieutenant Nathaniel Mather, by the way." He looked up at a wall clock. It was past eleven and the proprietor had begun setting chairs atop the tables. "Suppose I said that I'd have to report you . . . bring you in?"

Dabbing at her tear-streaked cheeks with a napkin, she implored his mercy with her eyes, and, finding him resolute, tried other tactics. "But there is no proof—I was just upset. I didn't know what I was saying."

"Mister Ericsson's identification of you will be adequate grounds for your detention. There is a wartime law under which suspected spies can be held without proof of conviction."

"Held?"

"Confined to jail until proven innocent."

"My God." She trembled. "If they found out, they'd kill me. Even in jail. Please . . . you can't."

"Sorry, Miss Partington, you'll have to come with me." Nat slipped a ten-cent piece on the table.

"Very well, but I'll have to pack a few things." Sarah stoically accepted her fate.

"I'll have to accompany you."

"Of course, Mister Mather. You have your orders."

Sarah set a full bottle of brandy and two glasses on a baroquely carved oak table in the living room of her apartment on South 8th Street and went about packing in the adjoining bedroom. Nat leaned back on a tufted maroon velvet sofa and thumbed through the April issue of Harper's Monthly Magazine.

He noted an article about 'Caricature', which, according to Webster, "is a figure of description, in which beauties are concealed and blemishes exaggerated, but still bearing a resemblance to the object . . . Thus the flat nose and the thick lips of the negro may be exaggerated; or the long legs of the crane and the mane of the lion . . . The word itself is derived from the Italian *caricare*, to load or charge . . . in attaining the end of caricature: ridicule."

Thumbing through a piece on 'Building of Ships', he read the praises of the 'axemen' who recklessly swung their tools in 'close proximity' to the fingers and toes of watching children.

A title caught his eye.

THE CONTEST IN AMERICA
by John Stuart Mill
As it appeared in Fraser's Magazine

He was absorbed by the famous philosopher's stand on slavery and his repudiation of England's support of the Confederacy. Nat was heartened by Mill's closing sentiments:

> . . . but war, in a good cause, is not the greatest evil that a nation can suffer . . . A war to protect other human beings against tyrannical injustice . . . In effecting this, the Free states will have raised themselves to that elevated position in the scale of morality and dignity which is derived from great sacrifices consciously made in a virtuous cause. . . .

Nat put the magazine down and was surprised upon finding a glass of brandy on the end table next to him. Picking up the glass, he sniffed it quickly and set it down again. Determined to resist the temptation of a drink, he rose and walked about the lavishly appointed chamber. Stage properties and memorabilia abounded. Crossed spears and sheilds with lotus motifs, exotic oriental robes and ostrich-plumed hats on ebony coattrees. Noh masks, elephant tusks, Javanese shadow-puppets, silver-trimmed tiger heads and elaborate gilt-framed paintings. . . . One wall was covered with posters and playbills. An announcement of *Uncle Tom's Cabin* or, 'The Death of Eva' for the Pine Street Theater in Troy, New York caught his eye. It featured 'The World-renowned Child Actress', Little Cordelia and her talented parents, Mr. & Mrs. C.G. Howard.

While examining a Scottish nickel-plated broadsword, Nat became aware of a vaguely familiar redolence, a combination of sweet lilac and pungent camphor. Try as he did, there was no recollection of his previous encounter. Accepting it as a déjà vu phenonemon, Nat dared inhale and let his imagination and senses loose momentarily. He imagined himself on the stage, amidst the profusion of curious and arcane artifacts, an existence that Reverend Mather would equate with the nether regions. Now and then the rustle of fabric and the light, quick footsteps in the next room excited him.

Absent-mindedly, Nat reached for the glass of brandy. "This is quite an apartment for one woman. . . ."

Sarah parted the bedroom drapes. "It belongs to friends; John Clarke and his wife. They're away at present. He's a theater manager as well as an actor." She was folding a sheer negligee in a provocative manner. Nat turned away and poured more brandy. "Is that him?" Nat pointed to a framed, hand-tinted photograph hanging over the white marble fireplace mantel. "No. That's Junius Booth, the late, famous British actor." Sarah disappeared into the bedroom, wary of being questioned and trapped into compromising her associates. She unsnapped the catch of a leather satchel and reached inside for the little derringer that she had seen John Wilkes flaunt on occasion. Wilkes, the brother of Clarke's wife, Asia, had been staying there, but had left for Boston a few days earlier to attend the funeral of Edwin Booth's wife, Mary Devlin, who had died suddenly at the age of twenty-three. Sarah drew out the deadly little weapon gingerly by the end of its walnut handle, barrel facing down. Was it loaded? She couldn't tell . . . nor could she point it at the drapes. The idea of death, real death, frightened her so that she put the gun back where she found it and stashed the bag under the bed. There was another way, a better way.

Choosing her most daring 'costume', one with overtones of a Turkish harem, Sarah made her entrance once more.

The brandy bottle was now half-empty and Sarah was lying on the divan, her radiant dark hair tumbling from Nat's lap as she looked up into his eyes reciting Shakespeare. "Can we steal love's sweet bait from fearful hooks?"

"If I weren't in the Federal Navy I might say 'yes'," Nat tried to extricate himself but Sarah wiggled tighter, pressing the back of her head against his rising passion.

"Pray, do not fall in love with me," emoted Sarah, "for I am falser than vows made in wine. . . ."

"Exactly what I am afraid of." Nat blinked and saw the brandy bottle wavering. The spears and swords seemed to swoop from the walls, challenging him to be a man, not a captor. Voices mocked him and boisterous actors sprung from the confines of their baroque frames. "En garde," a swordsman in codpiece tights lashed out with a flashing rapier. An invisible chorus sang a paean of approval, accompanied by thunder and lightning over a field of lilac; over a pink and lavender landscape bordered by delicate white lace.

Sarah lay with her head in his lap, blouse undone and singing a lilting air of elves and fairies in the Elizabethan woods. She'd kicked her shoes to the carpet and stretched out on the sofa. Fearful of what was happening, Nat turned away from her nakedness to look at the pictures on the wall behind him. There hung a photograph of three young men in Roman togas, to which signatures had been added, each in a different color ink. Edwin, in blue, Junius Jr, in green, and John W., in crimson.

But try as he did, his gaze returned to Sarah and he put his hungry hand on her bare shoulder. She flung her head back, looked into his eyes and took his hand in hers. He tried to draw it back but it was too late. She pressed it to her pulsing breast and leaned her head against his rising excitement until he could stand it no longer. Slipping out from under her Nat knelt on the carpet and kissed her tenderly on the shoulder as his hand moved across her smooth waist and under the hem of her petticoat. Sarah deftly wiggled out of her skirts and Nat suddenly realized that he was fully clothed. He fumbled with his coat and started to apologize but she put her hand over his lips and then undid his necktie. Eyes closed and with a relaxed smile, Sarah lay patiently awaiting him, allowing him to visually devour her in the soft, multicolored radiance of a stained-glass lampshade.

Sarah awakened Nat at dawn. She was dressed and sprightly. The aroma of fresh-brewed coffee had replaced the incense of the night before. "If you're in the navy, don't you have to report for roll call?"

"How did I get here?" Nat was befuddled to find himself in a huge four-poster bed amidst a profusion of decorative quilts.

"First you carried me," laughed Sarah.

"I apologize."

"Why? You were wonderful."

"Sarah," Nat got out of bed half-wrapped in a quilt, "I feel the same way about you. I know I had too much to drink, but I would have wanted this to happen anyway." He embraced her and the quilt dropped to the floor.

"I'm all packed, Nat. We can go after you've had some breakfast. It's on the kitchen table." She kissed him lightly on the cheek and slipped out of his arms.

"Go where?"

"Aren't you going to 'take me in?' " Sarah left the bedroom as Nat bathed at a washbowl.

"But it wasn't your fault. These people forced you."

"Your government will never believe that," she replied.

"But I do," Nat walked out of the bedroom with a towel around his waist, looking for his clothes. Sarah handed them to him, neatly folded. "Thanks . . ." Nat got dressed as Sarah turned her back on him. "I can't take you in, Sarah. Not after. . . ."

"Last night," confessed Sarah, "I had a pistol in my hand while you were in the living room. I just couldn't. . . . It's in a satchel under the bed. It's not mine. I'm not a murderer. How I wish that I hadn't— All those poor sailors, and their families."

"It can—it will—be different from now on, Sarah. You don't have to be afraid anymore." Nat took her in his arms.

"Last night, you said you might go west after the war, to build bridges and railroads . . . and you asked me if I'd like to go with you. I don't expect that you were serious."

"I meant it, Sarah."

"But you're from such a different background. Your family wouldn't approve. Your father especially."

"Things like that only matter when the son needs to inherit his family's money. I intend to find my own way. My older brother David is out in Kansas herding cattle. Reverend Mather did not take very kindly to *that* either."

"What will you tell your commanding officer about this?"

"Nothing," Nat let Sarah adjust his necktie. "Just promise me that you won't drop any wrenches in the steering mechanism of *New Ironsides*, the boat I'm assigned to."

Sarah nodded seriously. "You have my word." She sealed it with a kiss. "But I have to go on tour. The production is going up to Boston this week. I'll write you, if I may."

"Headquarters, Philadelphia Navy Yard."

Noting the address, Nat walked to Arch Street where he hailed a carriage to the Navy Yard. For the rest of the week he was not himself; such was the impact of the short affair. Would she write? Did she lie? Did she use him? Was he a fool for believing her? On Saturday Nat went back to South 8th Street as a gentleman and called on the apartment. He was relieved when a woman opened the door, and apologized for having the 'wrong address.'

TWENTY-FOUR

In the ice-glazed windows of the Negro quarter in Montreal, multitudes of candles burned in vigil on New Year's Eve. 1863 was to ring in a new era for the enslaved and oppressed below the border. Candles burned in windswept Kansas and industrious Connecticut as well, while in the Confederacy there were none to burn.

The new world awaited the day of emancipation, and the great cheer that would arise when the hour came.

In a second-floor window of a frame house on the Rue Moreau near the waterfront of Canada's historic city, a candle burned low, casting a halo over the sign below:

HOLLADAY'S CARRIAGE REPAIRS

A letter lay open on the windowsill, flame flickering across the uncertain handwriting. . . .

Charleston, S.C.
Dec. 24, 1862

My Dearest Children:

Praying that you are both well, I write on this holy night. Please, Josiah—tell my daughter gently that the

Good Lord has taken her mother. She departed in her sleep and we should all thank God that she was spared unnecessary suffering.

For me there is no more joy in this city and I'll have no regrets in going back to Libby Prison as Major Turner seems to value my services, especially in grooming his pet poodle. I shall content myself with remaining in the South since I am not well enough to travel on the train that you and Tenah went North with.

If the Lord does not allow us to meet again, I shall join my beloved wife, thankful that my daughter is well cared for and that I have a grandson with a proud and proper name—not one ill-gotten from his master. Let God's will be done. Amen.

Your loving parent, Augustus

At noon the next day, the great bell of Notre Dame of Montreal, largest in all the Americas, rang out joyfully.

"We are free," shouted Josiah as he embraced his wife. "That bell ringin' means that Mister Lincoln's words have come over the telegraph wire. Benjie," he picked up his year-old son and held him up to the window. "You see out there—over that river. That's where the United States is. Now we'll be able to go 'cross that river and not be afraid of slave catchers."

Tenah looked dolefully at the bright winter sky over the ice-strewn St. Lawrence River. "Yes, *we* are free, Josiah—but not my father. I'm so worried about him, now that mum is gone. If he admits that he's not well, then he must be sicker than he lets on."

"It would be worse if Major Turner was in the cavalry. At least we know where your father is going, and it's a lot closer than Charleston. And easier to get to. . . ."

"What do you mean, Josiah?" Tenah clutched Benjie.

"I could *go* to Richmond and bring your father back. Hell, that lady Underground Railroad conductor brought most of her kin back, even from Alabama."

"But that was before the war. Now there's too much shooting, and besides, Mister Lincoln's soldiers ain't in Richmond yet," declared Tenah. "In fact the Union Army has been pushed back out of Virginia."

"They'll go back in come spring, and I might just be joining them." Josiah mimicked a marching soldier. "In Springfield, Massachusetts, there's a new regiment callin' for recruits."

"To do the white man's chores," replied Tenah.

"No, ma'am, this here's all Negroes, except for the commissioned officers. Another regiment, the First Carolina Volunteers, all Negroes, are already down in Port Royal. Can you imagine old Marse Clyburn seein' a regiment of colored soldiers comin' across his cotton fields?"

"Josiah, I do think you are serious."

"If I don't try now, Benjie will never meet his grandpa. It'll just be for six months, maybe a year. Sam and Otis are good workers. You just have to keep an eye on them, and if we get too many carriages, just tell Otis to bring his brother around."

Tenah smiled at her husband. "You've made up your mind, Mister Holladay, haven't you?"

"Yes ma'am, Missis Holliday, and I also have made up my mind about tonight—" Josiah pinched Tenah's behind.

With the occupation of New Orleans by Federal forces, the war took on a new tone. The South had lost its life-line river to the interior. The Mississippi was now crawling with shallow-draft Union gunboats and ironclads, carrying destruction and privation relentlessly northward, closing a gigantic ring about the Confederacy.

The bloodiest single day of the war had seen ten thousand killed and twice that number maimed at Antietam Creek in Maryland with neither side able to claim a decisive victory. General Lee's army, dug in near Fredericksburg, then repulsed the Union army's foray into Virginia with heavy losses. With this defeat, the Army of The Potomac retreated and regrouped with a change of command.

Answering the first call for the blood of Charleston, the famous USS *Monitor* sank during a storm off Cape Hatteras, taking half her crew down.

Meanwhile, the South continued to build armored vessels with rams, to the extent that the Union Navy became afflicted with 'ram fever;' fear of the 'barbarian' ironclads.

As a prelude to a rebel offensive, the Federal steamer, *Isaac P. Smith* of Admiral Samuel Du Pont's blockading squadron at Charleston, South Carolina, was allowed to go up to the Stono River for reconnaissance. As she lay off a plantation upriver, a battery of hidden guns opened fire from an island. It was a trap and the former ferryboat was caught in a crossfire. Badly raked, she suffered many casualties and was forced to surrender.

The loss of this vessel to "deceitful" Southern tactics enraged the North. It became a rallying call, in the towns, in the cities, and in the White House. . . .

Mary Todd Lincoln, chubbier than she'd been at the inauguration two years earlier, read aloud in the library from *The Washington Star:*

" 'The Federal gunboat, *Isaac P. Smith,* allowed its normal passage up the Stono River, was mercilessly shelled by masked Secesh cannon, killing eight and wounding seventeen Union boys. The engine was hit by solid shot, and Captain Conover surrendered for the safety of his wounded—'

"Abe, are you listening?"

The President put down his volume of Shakespeare's plays. "Mother," he addressed his wife. "I received the very same unfortunate news last evening by direct telegraph from Admiral DuPont."

"Then you know about the *Chicora* too!" Mrs. Lincoln went on reading in a more irritated tone:

> '. . . Taking advantage of a thick fog at dawn, two Confederate ironclad warships attacked the USS *Mercedita*. Rammed and fired into by the CSS *Palmetto State*'s bow guns, the Union vessel was forced to surrender.
>
> Using a new incendiary shell, the CSS *Chicora* set the USS *Keystone State* afire. The Union Captain tried to run the ram down, but rifled shells crashed into his wooden hull, killing scores of men while the Union shot merely bounced off the ram's armored sides. His decks covered with blood, the Union Captain struck his colors but still . . .'
>
> Mrs. Lincoln screamed,
>
> 'the *Chicora* kept on firing!
>
> The Confederate Captain, a plantation aristocrat, called Handsome Dan by his crew, claimed that he kept on firing only because he thought the *Keystone State* was attempting to escape after surrendering.'

She slammed the newspaper down on her settee. "Abe, are you just going to sit there, allowing our Navy to be humiliated? The people in Charleston are barbarians. The city should be destroyed; burnt to the water's edge. Are you listening to me?"

"I heard you, mother." The President put his shoeless, stockinged feet on an ottoman and wiggled his toes at the fireplace. "Mary, the newspapers are more sensational than truthful. These were fair fights. We had no business going up the river unless we were sure of our scouting. Those Rebel guns took some time to be dug in. Masked batteries are a part of all river wars. I don't mean to be unsympathetic, but as to the *Keystone State*, it will take an enquiry before blame is cast on either adversary."

"But that nest of traitors—"

"Mother, for a lady with some ties to the South, you're pretty hard on them," Lincoln chuckled. "Eleven half-brothers in the Carolina Light Dragoons alone. You ought to be careful what you say, lest they take offense. That's no small army."

"Father, you know very well that I have hardly ever spoken to any one of them."

"You only call me 'father' when you're riled up, *mother*. I was only joking. But the newspapers are sure concerned about your rebel relatives."

"They lie; the filthy reporters are only interested in selling their filthy rags. . . ."

"Ah, mother," chimed the President. "We do agree that the newspapers twist the facts. The masses of people feed on such fiction, but it is the government's task to keep hysteria in check, to be cautious and rational."

"Well, the quicker we send a fleet to Charleston, the better. What are we building all those expensive ironclads for?" Mary Todd Lincoln rose and stormed out of the library.

* * *

"Lisbeth," Mrs. Lincoln addressed her dressmaker and confidante, a handsome mulatto who had been in the services of Mrs. Jefferson Davis three years earlier, "arrange for an immediate sitting with Mrs. Laurie."

"And what is the topic, ma'am?" Elizabeth Keckley rummaged in her skirt pocket for her notebook.

"I want to consult her about certain of our Admirals. Let's see; there is Farragut . . . and Sam DuPont . . . and John Dahlgren . . . and the one with that long, black beard."

"That might be Mister David Porter, ma'am. But he's only a Commodore." Mrs. Keckley quickly noted down the names.

"He'll do, Lizbeth."

"And ma'am, Mrs. Laurie will want to know all their birthdays. Whether they're Aquarius or Scorpio. . . ."

"I'll have that information by tomorrow morning. I'll wear my black moiré afternoon dress and my white point lace shawl. And Lizbeth—I don't like the horses we had on our last trip to Georgetown."

"Yes, ma'am."

In February, General Grant and Commodore Porter joined forces and blasted a canal from the Mississippi to the Yazoo River in an attempt to take the Confederate stronghold of Vicksburg from the rear. With the help of a pilot who had traveled the route years earlier, before the levee had cut off the passage, Porter sent six thousand men in advance vessels to cut away timber and obstructions. In two weeks, nine vessels had clawed up the pass with great difficulty. Adverse currents raced through the channel, pushing the Federal gunboats into the quagmired banks, tangling their rudders in cypress roots. The unwieldy iron-clads thumped into ancient, overhanging trees and shook a downpour of poisonous snakes and vermin from the flowering branches upon the invader's decks. Sitting ducks, the bluebelly sailors were soon raked by sniping guerrillas and Porter called for an additional army regiment before proceeding.

The next month, Congress passed a conscription act applicable to all men between twenty and forty-five, providing exemptions for those who could pay $300 or hire a substitute. After two years of war the patriotic volunteering had abated in the North and Lincoln was forced to show his hand as commander-in-chief of the army. The unassuming president turned his talents to repeating rifles and incendiary projectiles. An erstwhile inventor himself, the Illinois lawyer's favorite legal pursuit had been the business of patents and now his technological bent would find its satisfaction in a vigorous search for the deadly tools of war . . . a peculiar incongruity to his avowed love of humanity and his gentle nature.

"My, our cat has a long tail tonight," the president joked as he watched his wife promenade her newest trailing gown prior to a formal dinner on the first Saturday in April.

Mary Lincoln smiled contentedly, for she had gotten her wish. "Father," as she called her husband, had sent a telegram to Admiral Sam DuPont of the South Atlantic Blockading Squadron. The fleet of turreted monitors had been alerted.

Charleston Harbor was protected by at least seventy-six large-caliber guns, most of which had been pre-sighted to fire projectiles to land in marked areas. There were three "circles of fire," outer, middle and inner. If a vessel survived the first circle, it was then subjected to the second and third, besides the danger of electrically detonated mines.

The 'Font and Head' of the rebellion was not a strategic city in terms of manufacturing or military stores. It was a symbol and target for a vengeful North and the attack on Fort Sumter was not the only reason. In South Carolina's arrogant and conceited public officials and wealthy landowners were seen the ultimate aberration of slavery. The slaveholders of this state demonstrated, more than those of Virginia, the effect of the system upon judgement and character. Lust and pride of power so controlled these men that as absolute monarchs of their holdings and regions, they taught defiance of national law and asserted that their doctrine was a chivalrous practice of the rights of free men.

Assuming a superiority over Northerners, they underrated, even more than the "savage" Indians, the vast military power and resources of the Union. South Carolina was the intellectual center of the slavocracy. Far enough from the commercial and social influence of the North to nurture their own businesses and mores, and far enough from the lethargic gulf states to be vital.

Public sentiment in the Union compelled the government to make an early move against Charleston and it was immediately blockaded by the Federal Navy. Simultaneously, a fleet of stone-laden vessels were towed into her harbor and sunk in the shipping channels to discourage trade and the delivery of arms from Europe. Initially, Great Britain protested, until it was found that the sunken hulks also served as channel guides. By the second year of conflict, British blockade runners of great speed had some success in evading the Federal Navy under cover of night or fog.

The Federal government, anxious to gain moral support after its serious setbacks on land and sea during the first year of war pushed forward the completion of a fleet of Monitors armed with the new 15-inch Dahlgren gun as well as the smaller 11-incher that had not been able to pierce the *Merrimac's* armor plate. With this 15-inch gun, the largest seagoing weapon on earth, it was expected that the forts of Charleston harbor would be demolished and surrender terms would be dictated to the city from these novel ironclads lying at the wharves.

"In order to be effective, we will have to ascertain the ability of our new monitors to stand up against the enemy's guns and silence them before attempting a 'major' mission. The only way to accomplish this is under actual battle conditions." Admiral Samuel DuPont gripped his ceremonial sword handle solemnly before his flotilla commanders in the sumptuous wardroom of the USS *New Ironsides*, safely anchored beyond the Charleston bar and out of range of the harbor batteries. "Gentlemen, I am going to send several vessels up the Ogeechee River to attack Fort McAllister. The capture of this installation is of no great importance but I want you to subject your boats and crews to a real test. The various new mechanical appliances of your monitors have not been adequately tested, and it will be better to have them break down on our terms rather than the enemy's. And, naturally, we are all anxious to find out what the new guns will do. . . ."

"He wants to go into Charleston harbor next," whispered Lieutenant William Cushing to his senior counterpart, Nathaniel Mather. "Fort Sumter's the plum that would make him the highest-ranking man in the navy. . . ."

Nat put a discreet finger to his lips to soothe the impetuous young man from Wisconsin. Cushing, a head shorter than Nat, was an Annapolis man who resigned after graduation and rejoined after Sumter, distinguishing himself in action aboard the gunboat *Ellis* in the Carolina sounds. "You just wish you were not attached to the flagship so you could go up and capture Fort McAllister by yourself," joshed Nat as they filed out of the wardroom to take up their posts.

One evening later that week, Dick Osborn, a reporter with the *New York Herald,* approached Nat, who as officer of the deck was scanning the harbor with his 'newfangled' glass.

"Is that one of those French binary glasses, Lieutenant?"

"Have a look," Nat handed the instrument to Osborn.

"You'd never think there was a war on," the white linen-garbed reporter's walrus mustache drooped around the double oculars as he focused on the glittering chain of horizon lights beyond Fort Sumter. "Reminds me of Manhattan Island as seen from the narrows, except there's no Brooklyn." Osborn shrugged uncomfortably as he returned the glasses to Nat. "Who would think that there are a hundred guns on those sleepy shores that are itching to blow us all out of the water. Guns that only yesterday, it seems, protected us all from foreign men o' war."

"What can I do for you, Mister Osborn?" Nat turned away from the deck railing and took a step toward the pilothouse entrance.

"Nothing much, Lieutenant. Just a word or two."

"Such as?"

Osborn feigned indifference, pushing his coat back and tucking manicured thumbs under his red-striped suspender straps. "I don't suppose the admiral is going to chance getting his fleet caught in that crossfire out there . . . and those hideous torpedoes. . . ."

"Why don't you ask him yourself," replied Nat indifferently.

"He'd just as soon put me ashore. You know how he

is about reporters.'' Osborn's pearled coat buttons flashed reflections of the pilothouse oil lamps. ''Look, Nat—I mean Lieutenant. I heard Cushing say something about attacking Charleston. What do you think are the chances of taking the city with a dozen ironclads?''

''That might depend on the Fort McAllister outcome.''

''But, Lieutenant . . . the fort has only ten guns. One-tenth the firepower of the harbor forts!''

''There's your answer,'' smiled Nat. ''But don't quote me. You came up with the figure yourself.''

''True; that's true. I did.'' The sunburned reporter reached for his notepad. ''I'll take the mail steamer to Port Royal in the morning.'' Osborn excitedly scribbled by the pilothouse entrance.

''Sorry, Mister Osborn,'' rebuked Nat, ''there will be no communicating of rumors concerning the flotilla's plans. Admiral DuPont's orders. All telegraph messages and letters will need the Admiral's consent until further notice.''

''That certainly will not apply to personal letters,'' Osborn scoffed haughtily.

''Of course not,'' bantered Nat, ''only to the personal letters of reporters who work for big newspapers.''

Captain John Worden's bearded jaw set taut, with ashen gray splotches extending from his left temple to the corner of his mouth. The explosion of a shell from the *Merrimac* on the *Monitor's* pilothouse over a year earlier had left the officer with a permanent memento of the renowned engagement. At first blinded by the flash that penetrated a viewing slit in the armorplate, Worden had no ill effects save appearance and the need for amber-tinted eyeglasses, which gave him the aura of a mechanical commander, much in keeping with his new ironclad. He berated himself, however, because his injury at Hampton

Roads was the reason that his second-in-command had not chased the *Merrimac* to its lair and destroyed it.

Now with DuPont's squadron, in command of the *Montauk*, a monitor armed with the new 15-inch Dahlgren, he was disappointed that his first mission was to bombard a useless rebel fort. Nevertheless, he lead his five-boat flotilla up the Ogeechee River, thankful that an escaped slave, or 'contraband' in military terms, had come to the flagship and given the locations of Rebel torpedoes to the Admiral's staff. An advance party in a skiff had gone up the river the night before and cleared the approaches to Fort McAllister of these 'infernal machines.'

With reporter Osborn taking notes and Nat Mather observing in the relocated cylindrical pilothouse atop the revolving turret, *Montauk* opened fire, followed by the other vessels.

The action continued for almost four hours, the Rebel's shot striking the *Montauk* forty-eight times. The pilothouse was hit several times, snapping some armor plate bolts and sending them ricochetting inside. One bolt narrowly missed Nat and struck Osborn, breaking two of his ribs.

Dented and bearing one bandaged casualty, the *Montauk* led its brood back to the blockading fleet off Charleston Bar where Admiral DuPont eagerly awaited the battle report.

"Well, Mather, your report indicates that our monitors should be able to absorb anything that Charleston can throw at them." Admiral DuPont thumbed through a sheaf of papers and slapped them down on his exotically carved and inlaid desktop. "What do you make of our chances to take Charleston, Lieutenant?"

"Off the record, sir—with converging fire from six Rebel batteries, the monitors' gunports would have to be closed much more than in an engagement with a single opponent, thereby reducing the flotilla's firepower by a corresponding factor. The advantage gained by our rotating turret would be greatly diminished."

"Mather, I trust your judgment, but I'm afraid I have my orders. I don't know how long we can put this operation off."

Several days later, the CSS *Nashville*, scourge of Union shipping lanes, which had burned the clipper *Harvey Birch*, ran aground above Fort McAllister where it had been lying and preparing to run the blockade with a load of cotton through a swamp by-passage. Advised of the British-built raider's dilemma, Admiral DuPont ordered the *Montauk* into action.

At four in the morning Captain Worden took his monitor up the fog-shrouded Ogeechee and waited just outside the range of battered Fort McAllister's guns. When the *Montauk's* first 15-inch shot landed near the *Nashville*, the raider's crew scrambled into the woods. The fifth shot, finding perfect range, smashed into the grounded vessel just forward of her paddlewheel, setting her aflame. Shortly the fire reached her magazine and she blew up.

The press releases from DuPont's flagship created a jubilant furor at this victory, calling for a raid on Charleston, thus supporting the President's prime aspiration.

After making the harbor by an advance party, DuPont's squadron crossed the Charleston bar on April 7th, led by the *Weehawken*, a monitor equipped with a raft-like bow dredge, designed to set off Rebel torpedoes. Following the *Weehawken* were three monitors, then the eccentric *New Ironsides* with eight guns on either side, then three more monitors with the rear brought up by an experimental small ironclad, the *Keokuk*.

It was noon on an ebb tide as the procession steamed into the harbor, the most suitable water condition for heavy ironclads to maneuver in a narrow channel. Nat Mather had again been assigned to the lead boat to observe the torpedo guard as well as the ordnance and damage control. Looking through the one-by-six inch horizontal slit in the six-inch thick armor plate of the pilothouse atop the turret, he was amazed to see thousands of pale yellow butterflies clouding the balmy sky and almost obliterating the *Weehawken's* dun-gray bows. Was this an omen, or nature's attempt to stem the carnage of war? Or was it a foreboding of flowery petals on an iron crypt?

A sudden breeze sprung up from the south, pocking the smooth swells, unfurling the ensign and dispersing the yellow cloud of butterflies. Dead ahead, levitating on the shimmering horizon lay the dark patch that was Fort Sumter. Anchored by wisps of tenuous illusory tentacles, it was a somber diamond in the blinding bay.

To port lay the palmetto-fringed dunes of Morris Island, behind which waited the anxious guns of Fort Wagner and Battery Gregg. To starboard loomed the rolling heights of Sullivan Island, bristling with the bastions of Forts Beauregard and Moultrie. Beyond Sumter lay yet another island fort: Ripley, flanked on the shores by Fort Johnson and several batteries. In the far distance, the spires of Charleston's churches pierced the low-lying fog and glinted gold in the hazy sunlight.

"Hard to port," shouted Captain John Rodgers—but it was too late. A clump of floating debris disappeared under the wooden torpedo raft. The helmsman gritted his teeth and the others in the tiny pilothouse held their breath and braced themselves.

Nothing happened! It was not a torpedo.

At 2 o'clock obstructions were sighted, extending

across the channel between Forts Sumter and Moultrie. Suddenly the monitor's bow lunged out of the water in a profusion of smoke and spray, almost tearing the raft away. The line of ironclads slowed down and ran out their guns; two in each of the eight small vessels and eight on the port side of *New Ironsides* as she turned and brought one broadside to bear. The bulky slant-sided warship, responding erratically to her helm, swung around, bumping into the *Nantucket* and the *Catskill* as Forts Sumter and Moultrie opened fire.

"Commodore," Admiral DuPont addressed his flagship commander in the oppressive darkness of the pilothouse, "Send this signal: 'Disregard motions of the flagship.' " The venerable, elderly officer squinted through an observation slit and despondently sighed. "Turner, we're a worse hazard than the Rebels. Get off one broadside, then fall back out of range."

"Aye, sir."

Eight eleven-inchers boomed, signalling the monitors to commence firing, and *New Ironsides* turned its sandbag-protected tail to Sumter as crowds of onlookers cheered along the shores.

The battle raged for only forty minutes, after which the Union fleet drew back. Over two thousand shots had been fired at the fleet by the Confederate guns while the ironclads had managed to return only a hundred and thirty-nine. *Patapsco* fired ten minutes and was hit forty-seven times! Fortunately, only one seaman was killed; and that by a dislodged armorplate bolt.

That evening, the monitor commanders reported to DuPont aboard *New Ironsides*. To a man they agreed that another twenty minutes of such pounding would have destroyed the turrets, several of which had been pierced and sprung. The attack had failed!

Captain Percival Drayton of the *Passaic* pointed out that his battered vessel did not get off many shots because "the enemy's fire was all around and required the ports be kept closed while loading his guns."

Licking its armored wounds, DuPont's fleet resumed its inglorious blockading duties while in Washington the Navy Department came under furious fire for the failure to capture Charleston. Heads would soon roll.

Word came up from Savannah that the CSS *Atlanta* was ready. Originally a powerful English blockade runner, she brought a cargo of arms and ammunition across the Atlantic in November of 1861 and safely ran past the Union blockade and into the harbor.

Now she had been cut down and converted into an ironclad with inclined armor four inches thick, backed by eighteen inches of oak and pine. Armed with new Brooke heavy rifles and propelled by Glasgow-built engines, the *Atlanta* was the Rebel's greatest hope. Her bow, a deadly underwater iron ram, was also armed with a percussion torpedo at the end of a long spar. In anticipation of the vessel's appearance to challenge the blockade, two monitors were sent down to welcome her in Wassaw Sound, south of Savannah. One of the monitors, the *Weehawken*, had a newly assigned gunnery officer, Lieutenant Nathaniel Mather. At his own request he had been given a post that would promise more action than could be expected on the cumbersome flagship, *New Ironsides*.

At dawn, on June 17th, the *Atlanta* came down the harbor quickly, intent on attacking the two monitors as they lay at anchor. They slipped their cables and turned seaward as if running away, but it was only a feint. After ten minutes, ready for action, the *Weehawken* and *Nahant* turned again—toward the enemy.

A shot screamed across the *Weehawken's* stern, as the *Atlanta,* over a mile distant, opened fire.

"What are we waiting for?," Captain John Rogers called down from the pilothouse.

"Can we go in to a five-hundred yard range?" asked Nat.

"I don't see why we can't return fire while closing in."

"I'm using a higher charge than specified, sir."

"Lieutenant, I hope you know what you're doing."

"It's a precaution, sir. The fewer shots, the better for the gun," Nat shouted above the engines' roar.

Rogers did not argue. Someone had to do it and it might as well be the *Weehawken*. Battles were also won by twisting the orders and it was known that Admiral Dahlgren was overcautious when it came to his precious guns.

The *Atlanta* lay across the channel, her broadside bearing at the approaching monitors. "Five hundred yards," called out the pilot as spumes of water spouted port and starboard.

"Four hundred. . . ."

Rogers squinted through the observing slit at the smoke-belching ironclad ahead. He ducked instinctively as one of the three heavy rifles spewed flame. Two steamers from Savannah, crowded with boisterous spectators were anchoring a safe distance away. The townsfolk had turned out to see the *Atlanta* destroy the bluebelly navy.

"Three hundred yards."

"Fire," Nat called out and the gun-captain jerked the percussion lanyard of the 15-inch Dahlgren. The turret shuddered as 50 pounds of gunpowder detonated, sending a 330-pound explosive shell hurtling toward the rebel vessel. *Weehawken's* gun crew covered their faces with their caps as thick black fumes oozed through the smoke box into the turret. The Union monitor swerved to starboard.

Commander Webb, his invincible new ironclad shaken to its keel by a tremendous impact, scurried below to the gun deck. There, between two Brooke cannon, was a maelstrom of shattered men and equipment. The protective armor side-plating had been pierced, and its thick wood backing splintered. Solid shot had been driven from the *Atlanta's* racks by the *Weehawken's* first missile, further wounding and demoralizing the *Atlanta's* inexperienced crew.

The deep-hulled ironclad swung around and grounded on a bank as *Weehawken* closed in for the kill. Two more shots stuck the wounded vessel—piercing her below the water line. Another shot blasted off the top of *Atlanta's* pilothouse. The rebel commander, his dream of challenging the Union blockade shattered, sadly struck the stars and bars. In a fifteen-minute engagement the future of naval warfare had been changed for all time. England and France awoke the next morning to find out that that their latest warships could be sunk by an American gun.

Admiral DuPont, disheartened by his failure at Charleston, was relieved of his command. The next in line, Admiral Foote, was assigned to the blockading squadron. Death intervened and the important post went to Admiral John Dahlgren, to the delight of Mary Todd Lincoln, one of whose best friends was Dahlgren's wife.

The *Weehawken*, a renowned hero, rested on her laurels. While moored in Maffit's Channel off Fort Moultrie in September, a gale blew up and the monitor was dragged and grounded on a bar. While awaiting high tide, the crew fell in for target practice.

Well-stocked with powder and shell, the gun crew took turns at aiming. The first shot arched over Fort Moultrie and dug up the parade ground behind it. The second tumbled some masonry ramparts.

Smiling broadly, Nero Brown dusted his black hands off ritually as he put his eye to the top of the Dahlgren's 'soda bottle' breech and sighted along its barrel through the open turret port.

"One turn up, elevation." Worm screws creaked.

"And a finger to the right," Nero pointed and the turret chugged on its circular brass track. "Too far," he added. A lever was thrown in the engine room and the turret jolted slightly.

"That's perfect," Nero squinted once more as a shot from Fort Moultrie splashed down some yards away. "Okay . . . fire!" Nero winced and put his hands to his ears. Flame spurted into the twilight sky and a shell whizzed over the tidal flats. A flash of light sprang from one corner of the fort and erupted into a series of orange explosions, culminating in the complete disintegration of a tower.

"Nero," shouted Nat Mather. "What do you think this is; the Fourth of July? Looks like you hit the powder stores."

"Just a lucky shot, sir," the Negro shrugged. "But maybe, de lord, he tell me where to aim—for all those bad things that done happened to my people."

* * *

"Mister Welles," The President addressed his Secretary of The Navy. "If all of our vessels were as gallant and successful as the *Weehawken*, I should expect that Charleston would be taken by now. I authorize that the commander and crew be given a special citation—and let's take a good look at her promotion list. We can't afford to ignore our heroes."

"Excellent idea, sir; it will set a valuable example."

"One thing more, Gideon. I want to take a look at Charleston harbor *personally*. The sooner, the better."

The rotund secretary's gray wig slipped sideways and he discreetly repositioned it. "Mister President, it's much too dangerous. Any other city but Charleston, that den of assassins."

"Gideon," the President rose from his desk like a threatening squall. "Arrange a visit with Admiral Dahlgren aboard his flagship. I'll go incognito, but don't have me dressed up as a woman again. Once is enough."

"That, sir, will be a herculean task in itself."

TWENTY-SIX

No more driver's leash for me,
No more, no more.
No more pint o' salt for me
No more, no more.
No more hundred lash for me,
No more, no more.
No more mistress call for me,
No more, no more.

The men of The Fifty-fourth Massachusetts Colored Infantry were gathered round their campfires near Culpeper, Virginia. They clapped their hands and tapped their boots to the rhythm of the voices. A flute trilled from within a lamp-lighted tent. A drum beat its somber message, as here and there, a dark, shining figure, caught up in the ancient African moods, strutted and whirled, a reincarnation of his ancestors.

Some cleaned their rifles and spoke of General Meade's retreat across the Rapidan, and others, of the battles that would come in the spring.

". . . and I say that if we'd gotten here in time to go to Mine Run, the General would have beaten the pants off of ol' Robert E. Lee."

"You mean the Army of Virginia would turn tail at seein' two thousand screaming Negroes with loaded guns runnin' at them," joked Corporal Josiah Holladay.

"Well, it *could* have happened," replied Private Rivers. "Surprise is one of the elements of warfare."

"Be thankful that we weren't among the hundred Union men that won't come back. A hundred men just to prove that Lee's defenses are too strong to take." Josiah rubbed his hands in front of the fire. "It's going to be a cold winter."

"Tomorrow we start building the cabins. Let's build a real nice fireplace in ours, eh corporal?"

"I won't be here."

"You going to desert?"

"Not exactly. I'm goin' south. To Richmond. The Lieutenant and I had a talk." Josiah puffed contentedly on a cheroot.

"You cain't go in that uniform."

"That's true, Private Rivers."

"And if you don't wear a uniform, you'll get shot as a spy."

"*If* I get caught, and *if* they find out. Two if's are good bettin' odds in any game," smiled Josiah.

"What you gonna do in Richmond—if you get there?"

"That's between me and the Lieutenant."

"You're on your own, Holladay," Lieutenant Trowbridge extended his hand. "Good luck." A white hand shook a black one.

"Thank you, sir," Josiah waved at a group of colored picket soldiers and ducked into the woods. Wearing a tattered brown coat, denim trousers and a gray wool scarf, he looked like a farmhand or a runaway slave, his few possessions and scraps of food bundled in red calico and slung over his shoulder. He had memorized the key features of a campaign map. Some seventy-five miles of rebel territory lay between the Union lines at Culpeper and his destination, sprawling Richmond. Ahead to the west loomed the summit of Lost Mountain, herald of the Blue Ridge range. The plan was to follow Robertson's River down to its juncture with the Rapidan and cross at Dugan's Ford, thereby avoiding the Confederate Army post at Rapidan Station. After that he was to follow the Orange and Alexandria Railroad track till it spurred off to the Virginia Central at Gordonsville. The object was to contact a Union sympathizer in the station baggage office who would arrange transportation to Richmond upon being given the codeword "tuckahoe."

It was the first week in December and the dun-gray sky promised a chill rain. Stately pines and hemlocks were shedding the last of their enormous brown cones, while the white oaks, hickorys and walnuts tenaciously held on to their crimson-sprinkled mauve mantles. Along the river's bank, among the patches of withering wax myrtle and wisteria, rose the stalked remains of the trumpet and passion flowers, dead of an early killing frost.

Arms bruised from thickets of thorns, Josiah stumbled upon a clearing by the river's bend, sending a cloud of screeching turkey-buzzards flapping from the banks accompanied by a gush of putrid air. Choosing a dry, flat rock to spread open his calico on, he unwrapped his vittles and took out a strip of dried beef and a hard biscuit. Laying them out like offerings Josiah shook his tin cup upside-down and walked down to the river to fill it.

There were many curious white rocks imbedded in the

muddy sand of the bank. He shrunk back upon realizing that the "rocks' were human skulls. One of them still had a lock of blond hair. Attendant to the skulls and buried deeper in the mud were bones and remains, some still covered with cloth.

All about the scene, trees were shattered and rocks were chipped white. The further he walked, the more evidence he found of a recent battle. Dead horses and broken sabers, bloated bodies, both in gray and blue. Lifeless, staring eyes and glinting belt buckles. The initials 'U.S.' on a buckle seemed to call out to him:

I am a soldier of the Grand Army of The Republic.

I have died that you may be free . . .

Josiah held his arm against his face to offset the stench as he made his way back to the flat rock. Rebels and bluebellies alike had fallen and been picked clean by the buzzards. These were the victors—hunched in the high branches, waiting for him to be on his way. Waiting to finish the feast. Dozens of bodies; fathers, sons, brothers and husbands that may never be found, come the winter storms, come the swollen, rushing river to carry the remains to the Rapidan and then to the Chesapeake and the sea. Brothers and husbands floating past Fredericksburg, and unheeded as spirits in the bay passing the Union blockading fleet.

One incredible sight caught Josiah's tired eye. Propped up against an oak were two dead men, one dressed in the Confederate hodgepodge of tattered gray and homespun. He had been shot through the head and his hand was still in the coat pocket of a Union private.

* * *

"Ain't gonna ask a nigger fer papers if he wants to go back south," laughed a sentry as he watched a solitary darkie shuffle across Dugan's Bridge. The sentry, a grizzled mountain man, peeked from the window of the bridge shack, then reached for a jug. His companion was already nodding and dozing from the effects of potent corn 'likker.'

Playing the role of a dim-witted slave, Josiah swirled and wheeled sycophantically as he crossed over the timber bridge toward the beckoning road beyond.

Clowning done with, he walked briskly along a path that followed the Rapidan River toward its source in the Blue Ridge range. This was the river that the Union Army had crossed up near Fredericksburg in retreat after failing to penetrate Lee's lines, the outer perimeter defenses of Richmond. Josiah held his head high, for he was a free man and he was proud to be in the service of his benefactor nation and the great emancipator, President "Linkum." It gave him strength to have a cause other than himself and his family. For now, he belonged. Only one more bridge and he'd be on the road to Orange Court House; deep behind the Rebel lines and within several hours of Gordonsville. He hitched up his trousers, re-tied his calico sack and set out with new vigor.

Suddenly, the ground went out from under him. Sky and trees whirled as his ears thrummed, pounding into his brain. "Tenah", he shouted as though the world were ending. "Tenah", he repeated weakly before all went black.

A cold, pelting rain revived him. Lightning flashed as Josiah struggled to his feet. He reached down for the pain in his left shin and realized the wetness was blood mingling with rain. Snatching up his bundle he noticed a charred hole in the footpath. He had set off a Rebel torpedo. Those infernal machines. Lieutenant Trowbridge had warned him. It was a miracle he was still alive.

Hobbling to the safety of a rock ledge he crawled under as far as possible where he washed his wound with trickling water and bound it with a strip of his red calico bandana. Drawing his coat over his head he fell asleep, thankful that his wife and child were safe and far from the cruelty and ravages of war.

"Hey, you, boy," a voice boomed down from atop a side-stepping dapple-gray stallion. Startled by the splashing apparition, Josiah stumbled, falling to his knees among the submerged stones and musselshells of Barnett's Ford on the Rapidan River.

"What's your name?" The rider, wearing the tattered trappings and braid of a Colonel of Confederate cavalry shouted again with a bombastically accented tone. "Never mind, boy. I'll call you *Elijah,* just like my last boy. He was killed back at Lost Mountain. Same damn Yankee shell that did *this* to me." The officer raised his right arm. Its sleeve was folded and pinned at the elbow. "You're going to take Elijah's place from now on, boy. Go on back and get on my pack mule, unless you want to walk all the way to Yanceyville." The colonel gestured behind him with a toss of his head. "We're going home and we're going to plant tobacco. . . ."

"But suh, Ise gwine to Gordonsville where I got a job comin' to me." Josiah started to wade toward the river bank.

"Hold on there, boy. When a Tazewell goes back home, he goes with a manservant." The colonel flicked back the hammer of his service revolver and pointed it menacingly. "Who has hired you out and where are you going to work?"

"I'm a free nigger, suh."

"Show me your papers, boy."

"Aint got no papers, suh."

"That settles it. Get on the mule or float in the river with yer brains blown out. Take your pick, boy."

"Ah jes changed my name to Elijah, suh."

Colonel Wyatt Tazewell rode proudly erect into the town of Orange Court House. Deep-set eyes and grim mouth were framed by long prematurely gray hair, shaded from the noon sun by a wide-brimmed cavalry hat. Tethered behind, Josiah clung to the mule's bare back between a bedroll and several gunny sacks.

Mysteriously empty of people for a normal weekday, the main road showed signs of having been quickly and quietly left. There was a carriage in front of the general store and a chair leaning by the door. A child's toy wooden horse lay on the courthouse steps. A hand pulled down the door shade of the barber shop.

"They don't understand, Elija." Tazewell gestured with the reins in his hand. "It was an evasive action at Lost Mountain. We were outnumbered by the bluebellies. Ammunition was running out so I *had* to go. The column was intact when Elijah and I left. It was the only thing to do—go and get help. And then the shells! We didn't expect artillery. You agree with me, don't you, Elijah? . . ."

They crossed the North Anna River at Mallory's Ford on a ferry raft hitched to overhead wires by wheels and pulled by ropes. Negro Run, Roger's Run and Hickory Creek were shallow and could be waded across. At dusk they rode into Louise Court House and took the road to Yanceyville, nine miles south.

"Sorry to have to do this, Elijah," Tazewell, gun tucked under his right shoulder, tightened the ropes around his captive's wrists and ankles. "Too dark to make the plantation tonight so we'll take a rest and go on in the morning. Can't take any chances with you running away or doing something bad while I'm sleeping. Now you sleep well and I'll wake you at sunrise. Maybe even give you some real bacon. That is if you can cook and look after your new master as well as the real Elijah did." Tazewell blew out the lantern flame and slipped cautiously under his blanket. "Mind you, my new Elijah, I usually sleep with one eye open and I'll put a ball through the first thing that moves."

Josiah could hear the Colonel's stallion snorting and rustling at its tether. In the distance a wolf howled and high above, the winter-clear belt of Orion glittered bounteously. If only he could break free. It would serve the rebel Colonel right to have his horse taken for a Union mission, and that by his manservant! Did he talk of planting tobacco? Now wouldn't that be the clincher? From chains to freedom to chains again. Josiah Holladay, you are a fool. But then, planting tobacco is a lot better than pushin' up daisies after being hemped as a spy. That's it. Settled. He would cook for the Colonel. Get on his good side and bide his time till the opportunity for escape came along. Yes, he'd catch a catfish in the morning, with the Colonel's permission, and cook the best gol-darned breakfast ever ever eaten by a one-armed rebel. There were some makin's in the gunny sacks.

Now a nigger like himself didn't even need a hook and line to catch a fat ol' bullhead catfish. Been doin' it ever since he was a kid back on the Maxwell Plantation in Santee country. All catfish are the same, whether in Carolina or Virginia. Jes' wade on in behind the critter and slowly put yer hands into the water and gently rub him on the belly. Then when he starts waggin' his tail, grab it. Josiah forgot about his bound hands and feet, recalling the mouth-watering aroma of a Carolina fish-fry.

Take one large catfish and gut it. Then rub his insides with salt and pepper. Mush up some tuckahoe root and mix in wild chives and ground nuts . . . and chopped bacon. Stuff it in the fish and sew him up with grass or sweet vine. Next, make three slits on both his sides and stick a slice of salt pork in each slit. Then into the bacon-rubbed fryin' pan, and sprinkle a little wine on now and then as it sizzles. . . .

"That, Elijah, was the best damned fish I ever tasted." Tazewell smacked his narrow lips as he reined up to a clearing on a ridge overlooking the South Anna River just above Beaver Creek. "Just a little ways more and you'll be seeing the pride of Virginia's tobacco country. Woodbine; built by my father before he went up into the mountains looking for gold. He found iron instead and in this war it's better than gold." Tazewell spurred his steed to a gallop, then stopped abruptly. He sat, mute in the saddle, hand shading his squinting eyes.

"It can't be," he moaned loudly. "Not Woodbine. Those dirty, damn bluebellies. . . ." The Colonel slumped forward, leaning on his horse's neck and whimpering softly. All that remained of the main house were two chimneys and charred rubble. Another chimney stood where the curing-house had been. The barn and drying sheds were hardly more than ashes on rectangular stone foundations.

The Colonel pushed back his hat and stared into the sky. "God, you just look what they've done. After all my praying and church-going. Elijah," he shouted. "Take heed what devils those Yankees are; burning a man's house when he's gone." He backed his horse from the precipice. "We're going down there, Elija—and you're going first."

* * *

Searching through the ruins they found little of value, only a few iron tools, handles burnt away. Tazewell picked up an ax head and held it out to his 'boy.' "Now you go on out there," he gestured at a stand of pine, "and find a proper branch for a handle, Then you're going to cut down enough trees to build a cabin. It'll take a while, Elijah, but you'll get it done. As for me, with this arm I'll be the supervisor. And when the cabin's done we'll get on to the barn."

"But, suh, I'm only one man—"

"Take heart, boy. I'll buy a few more niggers just as soon as I get my bearings."

"Where are the boys that used to work here, and where. . . ."

Tazewell hunkered down in the shade of a chimney. "Were you going to ask about my family, Elijah? About my wife?" He toyed with his revolver, pressing a cartridge out of the cylinder, examining it, and replacing it. "That's no business for my niggers. I live my life the way I see fit and it's going to stay that way until something better comes along. Now get out there before the day is gone and cut me some twelve-foot logs. When you've cut enough and trimmed them I'll tell you to stop."

Blisters! Josiah, alone in his tiny tent, held his stinging hands out before a candle. Were these the hands of a free man, or was this his fate? Perhaps he deserved this lot . . . and there was something to be said about working for a massa. No concern for tomorrow. Work and git your vittles an' bed. Yes, it was easy, not having to think for yourself. Two-legged black dog; jes wag yer tail at massa, lick his feet and roll over when he tells ye to.

For three days, from sunup to sundown, he'd been cuttin' and trimmin' pine. Almost enough, he reckoned, to start building. His only rest had been from about midnight to dawn. About six hours. The rest of the time he'd had to wait on the Colonel. Prepare breakfast, wash and lay out his clothes, come back from cuttin' timber and cook supper. Mostly a late supper because massa liked his bottle of coffin varnish. Half the mule's pack was corn whisky. How he hated to tend to the Colonel like a nursemaid, especially washing his liquor-sotted clothes. But there was always the gray persuader. The Colonel's ever-present revolver.

"Elijah, dammit, come on over here, boy."

Now what? Past midnight and he calls. Josiah crept out of his tent and stifled a yawn as he approached the Tazewell's tent. "You called, massa?" Josiah used his best fieldhand drawl.

"Come on in. I wanna talk to ye."

Josiah eyed the glowing tent, edged with frost glinting in the moonlight, a shadow cast on the canvas. The shadow, looming larger than life, threw its scraggly head back and drained its glass, then slumped forward.

"Where th' hell are ye, boy?" the shadow boomed.

Cautiously, Josiah slipped through the tent fly. There, sprawled on his back and leaning on his saddle, the Colonel waited, liquor dribbling from his mouth and features sharply lit by a candle next to him. A spurred riding boot lay on its side near an empty bottle between Tazewell's splayed legs. His hand lay rigid on his crotch. "C'm'ere, boy, an' get this other boot off."

Josiah knelt down, then froze as Tazewell burst into bawdy laughter. A glistening alabaster pillar of muscle had sprung up from nowhere. To the right of it was the muzzle of a wicked-looking weapon. It shook nervously. "Elijah, boy," Tazewell sputtered between his yellowed teeth and drooping mustache, "You wanted to know where my *wife* was? Well, I'll tell ye she didn't cotton up to some things I like to do. Now, you can sort of see what ol' Wyatt Tazewell might like, eh? Wha'samatter, boy? Don't fool me any. You damn well know your massa's gotta be happy—and all niggers are in this world to make their massas happy. You're grown up, boy. . . . Now git on with it an' suck me off or I'll blow yer nigger head off." Tazewell rubbed the barrel of his revolver against his penis, stroking it up and down with his loosened thumb till it was once more erect. "This here gun's got nine balls in the cylinder, boy, and a load o' buckshot in the lower barrel. As sure as Jeff Davis likes little boys, I'm gonna cut ye to pieces with this here gun, and the last shot, the load o' buckshot will go right up yer black ass. . . ." Tazewell faltered, letting the muzzle dip, then corrected his aim right at Josiah's face.

"Okay, massa. I'se gwine to do anything you say, suh so ah kin be jest like your Elijah." Josiah smiled pearly white and gripped the Colonel's knees. "But for th' Lord's sake don't point that thing at me. I caint do m' best under th' circumstances." Josiah reached for the white appendage.

"I knew you'd come round, Elijah. The moment I saw you at Mulford's Ford, I knew you were my kind o' nigger. I got yer vibrations, boy. Hell, if we can't have a good time in this war we might as well shoot ourselfs, eh?" Tazewell slumped back against his saddle as Josiah stroked his penis. Eyes closing, the Colonel set his revolver down limply. One eye on the gun, Josiah took the enemy gently into his mouth.

"Elijah," moaned the Colonel, "I always knew. . . ."

Summoning up all the strength his strong jaw could muster, Josiah bit down as hard as he could.

The Colonel screamed bloody murder and fired his gun blindly, holes peppering the tent canvas behind Josiah.

Now an animal of prey, the former slave leaped on the weapon and wrested it to the ground. Jumping to his feet, Josiah picked up the gun and clicked a lever, then pointed the barrel between the Colonel's pained eyes. "Colonel Tazewell, you are now the prisoner of Corporal Josiah Holladay of the United States Army, Fifty-fourth Massachusetts Colored Regiment." He cocked the revolver hammer. "I am well acquainted with this weapon, *suh*. Made in France for the rebels." Josiah moved his finger on the trigger, savoring his moment of victory against all that was bad about the South.

Josiah reached for the tent fly. "Sorry, Colonel, but now it's my turn to tie you up." He motioned with the gun barrel for his prisoner to accompany him outside the tent where rope was to be found. The Colonel didn't respond. His eyes were open and glazed.

Wyatt Tazewell was already dead.

"Sorry, Colonel, but this is war." Josiah searched through Tazewell's saddle bags. Finding a leather pouch with money in it, he extracted a portion of each denomination; Confederate notes, English shillings and U.S. half-dollars. He was surprised that the backs of the half-dollar silver coins bore the stamp of the Confederate States of America, a cap propped over a shield, in place of the familiar eagle. Riffling through a packet of papers, he noticed a letter with a familiar name on it:

> . . . this is to certify that the bearer, Elijah, is the personal negro servant of W. Tazewell, Col. CSA. He should not be detained as he is on an errand to . . . . for the undersigned.

Josiah found a pencil and in a studied hand similar to that of the note, he entered on the dotted line:

Richmond.

Josiah carefully repacked the Colonel's saddle bag and tidied up the tent. There was nothing that could be done about the bullet holes in the tent but the empty bottle might suggest that the Colonel had emptied his revolver at some booze-born demon and expired from heart failure.

Traveling as a servant might, on a mule and carrying a sack of assorted edibles, he arrived at the town of Louisa Court House before eight and tied his sullen mount in the shade. Then he nonchalantly walked over to the Virginia Central ticket office and waited for it to open.

TWENTY-SIX

"What are you doing in Richmond?" Major Howell Clyburn unlatched the chain and let the door swing open.

"Now, now, Swanny boy." The dapper blond visitor danced into the room with a swirl of his silk-lined cape.

"I thought you'd given up the cause, with all that money you've been making up north," Clyburn took Wilkes' cape and gloves.

"In my capacity I have to appear neutral. One never knows from where the zephyrs blow." Wilkes brandished a letter with General Grant's signature on it. "I came right through the Union pickets with this pass."

"What do you want, Wilkes?"

"Don't use that name here."

"I suppose you have a pass for Jack Renfrew too."

"Certainly," the actor accepted a glass of brandy. "Ah, the perquisites of a surgeon's profession. I could never be a doctor, with all this medicinal liquid around."

"Well, Renfrew. . . ."

"Suppose I told you that in reality I'm a Colonel in

the Confederate Secret Service, receiving a commission directly from President Davis?"

"Actors can be anything they desire. All it takes is another costume in the trunk and a script."

"Then you don't believe me?"

"If you mean that you can order me to do something by outranking me, the answer is 'yes,' I don't believe you. Besides, I've been given no notice of a 'secret service.' "

"Swanny, I'm on a very important assignment for the . . . let's say, War Office, and I'm here because I need something that is in Richmond. Something that you can provide me with."

"I give up," Clyburn refilled Wilkes' glass.

"I need chloroform—a gallon of it."

"There is none to spare. Haven't you seen the hospital at Chimborazo? Over 400 wounded just came in from Mine Run. We haven't even enough beds. . . ."

"Major Clyburn, this is such an exquisite apartment. I'll bet the ladies just adore it. Fashionable neighborhood . . . away from the stench of death. . . ."

"What do you know about death, Renfrew? You only *act* it."

"I know that spies go to the gallows."

"What does that mean?"

"A Mrs. Van Lew has a house on Grace Street. That's just a block from here. She's called 'crazy Liz' because of her inane actions and mutterings. A woman of means nevertheless, she distributes food and clothing to the Union prisoners in this city."

"Commendable, since General Winder can't."

"But we have reason to believe that her daffyness is a cloak for espionage. When McClellan was marching on Richmond almost two years ago, Mrs. Van Lew prepared a room for him. Amusing at the time. It seems that she carries on a spirited correspondance with an uncle who is behind the Union lines in Norfolk. The 'service' is about to get to the bottom of this."

"What has it to do with me?"

"Not with you. With Miss Mather. She has been observed entering and leaving the Van Lew house on several occasions. For a northern woman with an abolitionist father, and a brother on Admiral Dahlgren's staff to tète-a-tète with Mrs. Van Lew—well really, Swanny."

"Miss Mather is a very accomplished nurse, and I resent your accusations," Clyburn brooded through a window, hands wrung behind his back.

"She's also quite a morsel, Major."

"Leave her out of this, *Wilkes*."

"You have my word, providing I get the chloroform."

President Lincoln took off his stovepipe hat and cautiously peeked out of the armorclad porthole in Admiral Dahlgren's cabin aboard the USS *New Ironsides*. A fresh north wind etched rippling patterns across Charleston's broad harbor. Closer in, anchored just out of range of the rebel shore batteries, lay the fleet of blockading Union monitors.

"Gol darn it, John," the President exclaimed to his long-time favorite naval officer and confidant, "I'm getting itchy just sitting around on this floating fort. What's holding up my inspection plans? I told Secretary Welles that I wanted to see all the vessels. By now I should have been aboard the *Weehawken*. We've got to resolve this fiasco. God knows we've got the firepower to take the city."

"But you *are* going aboard the Weehawken, sir." Dahlgren handed a telescope to the President. "Look over there. The launch."

The gaunt statesman put the glass to his weary eye. "But that's absurd." His thin lips trembled and the mole on his right cheek vibrated as he watched a ship's cutter being rowed toward the monitor *Weehawken*. Sitting aft in the boat was a tall man wearing a stovepipe hat. "That's me, but I'm here!"

"Exactly as we wanted it to appear, Mr. President. Perhaps you remember Lt. Mather, another tall fellow. We just dressed him like you and added a beard. Colonel Baker of the Secret Service has intelligence that an attempt on your life will be made here."

"What else is new," quipped Lincoln sardonically. "I don't see how an assassin could get onto these boats—unless he is already a crew member."

"We can't take a chance, sir, especially here. These Charlestonians are the most fanatical of all the rebels."

"That is so, John. It's too bad their efforts are so misdirected. Wasn't it a regiment from South Carolina that broke through the Mexican lines at Buena Vista?" The President watched intently as his double disappeared below deck on the monitor.

"Cast off," Bosun Selby called out to his cutter crew. "On the double, Hanrahan." The bosun didn't see Hanrahan take a jug from under his peacoat and upend it into one of *Weehawken's* deck ventilators before jumping aboard the cutter.

Choking, and eyes seared from chloroform fumes, Nat Mather struggled aft from his cabin, only his physical strength and knowledge of the monitor's interior saving him. Tearing off his false beard, he stumbled over unconscious seamen and reached the turret, where panicked men were fighting to get through the ceiling hatch.

Up in the pilothouse, the wheel, unattended, turned as

the anchored vessel swung with the current, jamming the rudder hard to one side. The jolt shifted solid shot and coal in the lockers, tilting the deck as the ponderous vessel broached into the waves. Torrents of water came through the hawse-holes and the turret gun ports, quickly settling the vessel by its stern.

It became 'every man for himself' and primal instincts prevailed over rank and heroism as the once-proud *Weehawken*, belching bubbling black smoke and resounding with trapped shouts, slipped quickly beneath the whitecapped waves.

Coughing up seawater, Nat crawled up on the beach at Sullivan's Island. It was almost dark. For hours he had battled a strong ebb tide, finally clawing himself onto a reef, resting and swimming the last leg at slack. Bleeding from razor-sharp barnacles, he stumbled toward the beach brush, away from the lights of Moultrieville and the rebel batteries overlooking the main channel. Slipping and falling on stones and seaweed, he was struggling to his feet when a sharp command stopped him.

"Hold on there, bluebelly. One move and I'll blow ye into fish bait. Now jes' keep yer haid down."

Nat felt cold steel prodding the nape of his neck; then hands going through his trouser pockets.

"Gawd-damn shee-it," a gruff voice complained. "Blow his brains out, Bee-jay. Fucker ain't got nothin', not even boots to contribute." He unbelted a revolver and cocked the hammer.

"Jes' a minute," drawled the rifleman. "I ain't gonna stretch hemp for murder. How do we know he's a bluebelly for sure—and he aint armed. Put yer piece down an' we'll bring 'im in." Putting his rifle up, he leaned over to examine the captive. "This 'uns got a tailored shirt." He touched the material on Nat's back. "Only 'shoulder-strappers' wear shirts like this. Hell, we're gonna get a week-end pass fer this 'un."

* * *

"I just loved Mrs. Malaprop." Bess Mather balanced her teacup as a Negro servant poured.

"If you've heard her once, you've heard enough—that is, I speak for myself Miss Mather. Frankly, I prefer Elizabethan drama. It's more universal, though I must admit *The Rivals* has its moments. The author, Sheridan, was quite above his contemporaries."

"Mrs. Renfrew, you speak so knowledgably. Are you in the business of theater?" Bess was admiring his impeccable attire and feeling guilty for it. She hoped that Howell hadn't noticed.

"All the world is a theater, my dear," the mustached young blade swirled his brandy and sniffed the bouquet. "I am presently an observer of the war on a certain level."

"You certainly picked up the best party to observe."

"Very good, Miss Mather, or may I call you Bess?"

She didn't answer, being wary of Renfrew's motives.

"Ah, yes," he allowed. "Mrs. Chesnut does attract the more influential people to her theater parties. Over there," he gestured, "talking with Howell, the gentleman with all the gold stars and braid. Jeb Stuart. . . . And in the midst of those tall Kentuckians . . . General Morgan, just escaped from the Federal prison in Ohio. I wouldn't be surprised to see Jeff Davis walk in."

"It's all so exciting, Mr. Renfrew."

"I should think so, especially for a northern girl whose father is an abolitionist and whose brother is on Admiral Dahlgren's staff. Is it true that your father gave rifles to John Brown?"

"Mr. Renfrew," replied Bess indignantly. "I am a

nurse and I was with the neutral Sanitary Commission in Brandywine Station, Virginia, before coming to Richmond. My services were most needed in the hospital at Chimborozo."

"I agree with Major Clyburn's choice. A fine person and an even better surgeon. He's an old friend of mine, or didn't he tell you that we used to frequent the same establishments in the fair city of Charleston."

"What do you mean, establishments?"

"Nothing vulgar. A pistol range, a gentleman's saloon."

Bess was furious and frightened. "Excuse me, Mr. Renfrew, I've just seen someone I have to speak to."

"Not Mrs. Van Lew, I hope," teased Renfrew. "I don't think she was invited." He feigned searching about.

As Bess turned to leave, he caught her by the elbow. "Of course you're excused, *Bess,* but one of these days I hope we get to know each other better. Much better." The actor-operative smacked his lips as Bess fled through the garrulous guests.

"Renfrew." A smiling, portly type sidled up, nodding to various acquaintances in passing. "It didn't work."

"But I saw him go aboard."

"He's back in the White House. Take my word for it."

Renfrew stared at Secretary of State Judah Benjamin. The Jew must be wrong. Too much black market anchovy paste and loaf sugar. Hallucinations born of pederasty and faro tables. Maddened, he squeezed the bell of his brandy snifter and it shattered, dripping a mixture of cognac and blood on the white marble floor.

* * *

Both the Blue and the Gray dug in to winter quarters, north and south of the Rapidan River, an unofficial truce during which time the mutual observance of the holidays held sway. It was a time for boxes of sweets from home and extra-long letters to loved ones. It was a time to give thanks that one had survived the minie balls, the Parrott gun shells and the dread sicknesses of the era. The fortunate went home and the less fortunate were captured and went to prison camps. It was better to be less fortunate than mutilated or dead, but, for many, the camps with their primitive conditions were a slow death and a worse one.

Thirty-one seamen and officers perished when the monitor *Weehawken* went down for 'unknown causes'. A small number survived, including the commanding officer, who by some quirk of fate or plan was not aboard. A subsequent Naval inquiry ruled that the vessel had foundered because the ammunition was improperly stowed, causing a bad trim that allowed the ingress of water.

Admiral Dahlgren was not satisfied with the findings of the inquiry but the incident was soon lost amidst the sheer enormity of the conflict. Outside of Secretary Judah Benjamin and Jack Renfrew, there was only one person who knew of the Chloroform Plot, and that was Seaman Hanrahan. But the compromised sailor would be telling no tales. Shortly after the sinking of the *Weehawken*, Hanrahan, on leave, went to a tavern in Port Tobacco, Maryland to collect the balance of his fee but instead received a half-inch lead ball in the brain behind his ear from Jack Renfrew's favorite derringer. During this period, Nat Mather had been held in a Charleston jail before being sent with other captives to Richmond in a cattle car.

After arriving at the Richmond railroad depot, the group of Union prisoners were hurried off the train and marched through the main streets toward the James River. Taunted by the populace with epithets such as 'hirelings, mudsills, greasy mechanics' and 'Northern vandals', they marched for a mile until halting before a large four-storied brick building on the river at 19th Street. A faded sign on the northwest corner proclaimed the building's earlier function as a ship's chandlery and grocery. The contingent of prisoners were lined up brusquely on the front grounds under threat of prodding bayonets.

"Show proper respect for your superiors, bluebellies . . ."

"Lincoln ain't gonna free your asses from here . . ."

The guards' taunts subsided as a tall officer with a white plume in his gray felt hat emerged from the building, accompanied by two subordinates. With the gait of peacocks, they walked through the files of the prisoners, examining each one in turn and stopping longer in front of those who were announced as being of high rank. Of the forty-seven prisoners, there were three majors and eight captains, the balance being lieutenants. Several had been treated and bandaged for minor wounds.

The head peacock gripped his uniform lapels like a clergyman about to give a revelation to his flock.

"I am Major Turner and this building is my command. I have been in charge of Libby and Belle Island since the first Union prisoners were taken at Manassas. In these two and a half years I have developed a system in my command, no less than that of an infantry or cavalry regiment. In fact it may be compared with a man-of-war because of the close confinement.

"There are, no doubt, some among you who might already be thinking of escaping. Take my advice and forget it. The consequences for yourself and your fellow prisoners will be drastic. We will shoot to kill, should there be anything left after our hounds have caught you.

"Bear in mind that no prisoner shall look out of any

window in Libby prison. The guards have orders to fire at any such person, and they have in the past, as you will find out from the messes you are to be assigned to. Libby Prison has a record of efficiency that in unsurpassed and I shall not tolerate any blots on that record. You will now be processed and given specific instructions for your stay here. I warn you that any disorderly conduct will be reported directly to me and you will be disciplined accordingly.''

Turner took one last searing look at the lined-up captives, then nodded to his subordinates and walked briskly back toward his headquarters in the northwest corner of the ominous building.

The two elderly Negro servants chuckled at Major Turner's speech as they tended to their masters' riding saddles behind one of the garrison tents. ''Gus,'' whispered the leaner of the two, ''the Major sure is buckin' fer promotion. Thas' all he cares about; bein' a colonel.''

''You know it, Jim. I've heard 'im say—in private of course—that he'd kill anybody that got in his way. He said that to 'is wife one day when he was mad at somethin'.'' Sam suddenly rolled his eyes and started singing: ''. . . I wish I wuz in de land ob cotton, old times dere are not forgotten. . . .''

''Ain't you niggahs finished with those saddles yet?'' Corporal Jackie Lee Stowers swaggered by, tripping on a tent peg. ''Gawd damn,'' he measured the distance with his musket, butt down, then swung the musket violently at the tent peg, splitting it and collapsing the tent. ''Now, you niggahs, hurry up an' fix 'at before I tell the Major whut ye done.'' Stowers grinned malignantly and continued on his way to the big red brick building.

* * *

"G'wan, you." A gruff Confederate sergeant prodded Nat Mather with the point of a Union cavalry saber as he sat balanced on the back legs of a chair in the processing tent. Nat drew up the collar of his cast-off rebel coat and left the tent, ushered out by a scrawny guard.

"Next," called out the sergeant, ticking off a list. "Well," he tapped his pencil on the list expectantly as a bearded Union major was led into the tent.

"Percival Nelson, Major. Sixty-sixth New York Infantry."

"You from New York City, Major?" Sergeant Lynch ogled the major's uniform.

"I'm originally from the town of Westchester in the State of New York, Sergeant."

Lynch chewed on the end of his pencil. "Now ain't you the uppity type, Major. Ah think you are much too uppity and fancy brought-up to chew tobaccy, eh? Spit it out, quick!"

The guard slapped Nelson resoundingly on the back. "you heard the sergeant. Spit, or I'll—"

Coughing, the major obliged. A wet, brown mass fell onto the dry and trampled grass near Lynch's boots. "Pick it up, open it and set the greenbacks on thet there table," sneered Lynch.

Nelson's eyes bulged as he complied, peeling five ten-dollar bills from the tightly pressed wad he'd separated from the tobacco and unfolded. "This is my property and I'll have to ask you for a proper receipt."

"Lem, you heard the Major. Give him a receipt." Lynch winked at the guard.

"Yes, siree," Lem tore a sheet of paper from Lynch's notepad and took the pencil from his mouth. "Le's see now." he printed laboriously. "One chewed-up plug o' tobaccy. Received from Major Nelson, February 6, 1864. . . ." He handed the note to Sergeant Lynch for his signature. Lynch then gave it to Nelson and motioned for the next prisoner to enter.

"Just a minute, Sergeant," Major Nelson shook the receipt, "there's no mention of the fifty dollars on this."

"What fifty dollars, *sir*?"

"On the table—"

"You must be mistaken, Major. Lem, did you see any greenbacks on that there table?"

"No sir, and I've been here all the time."

Nelson gritted his teeth, then rolled up the receipt into a ball. The table was bare. He made a motion to toss the ball on the table but reconsidered and instead looked up as if to a deity, shook his head and left the tent. Raucous laughter followed him out.

Jackie Lee Stowers drew a large key from the lock on the door of Room #4 on the third floor of the building. Brass-trimmed Colt revolver poised, he kicked open the door. "Git on in there, bluebelly." He shoved Nat Mather in, gave a rebel yell and shouted "fresh fish" before slamming the door and locking it.

"Welcome to Room 4," a stocky, gray-bearded prisoner stepped out of a crowd of bedraggled men, offering his hand to Nat. "I'm Colonel Streight, Arthur Streight. Fifty-first Indiana."

"Lieutenant Nathaniel Mather, United States Navy."

"Well, it's rare that we get a sailor here. I see they took your uniform very fast, those scavengers. What ship were you on, Lieutenant? Come on now, the men are anxious for news from the outside. Precious little recreation around here." A murmur of agreement rose among the prisoners.

"I was aboard the *Weehawken*—"

"Sunk in Charleston Harbor," replied Streight. We get all the news about Rebel victories. How did it happen?"

"I don't know. It didn't seem to be by enemy action. No engagement, no torpedo. I was lucky to swim ashore."

"Luckier that some ignorant Johnny Reb didn't pick you off in the water. Shooting men is like rabbit hunting to them. Were you a line officer, Mather?"

"Acting, but my specialty is engineering and ballistics."

Streight rubbed his beard. "Well, now that's something we can use around here. A practical calling, the engineering part, as we do not possess any cannon, much less chairs, beds nor the amenities of civilization."

The prisoners crowded around Nat. "What's the news from out West? . . . When's Kilpatrick coming?"

"I'm afraid the last I heard was about a month ago," apologized Nat. "Longstreet fell back to Virginia and Knoxville held." A scream of delight erupted from the captives.

"All right, men. Let's all introduce ourselves to the Navy," pleaded the Colonel, "and for God's sake, then let him be. By the way, Mather, how are you at cooking?"

"I can manage. Why do you ask?"

"Well, each man in every mess takes his turn at the stove and we are all anxious to see what you can do with boiled rice and corn cakes." Colonel Streight took Nat by the arm and walked him around the room, stepping over sleeping men and passing by groups playing chess and others carving chess pieces out of scrap wood. "There are over 300 men in this room at night, and there are seven rooms like this. That's twenty-one hundred men guarded by about one hundred rebels. And these are dumb rebels." Streight guided Nat to a relatively empty corner of the vast room. He looked around casually and, satisfied that nobody was listening, whispered to Nat, "You're just in time for an escape. Seeing as you're Navy, we'll squeeze one more man into the operation. And seeing that you're an engineer, I want you to check out the tunnel we've been digging for three months, that is if you can do some underground navigation and figure out about where we should come up. Colonel Rose is in charge of this and he's a little rusty in his mathematics and geometry. We don't want to come up next to a sentry and have our heads blown off. The tunnel's entrance is in a closed-off room in the basement below the cook-room. Our access is through a chimney. So far we've tunneled about sixty-five feet due East. There are two men working night and day with mason's trowels and a blanket to haul out the earth. We've got barrels hiding the opening in the chimney in the cook-room."

"Do you have a pocket compass?"

"Colonel Rose has one."

"Good," replied Nat, "I think I might be able to bring the tunnel up into an empty pickle barrel at under 100 feet."

Vivacious Belle Boyd, acclaimed the most famous distaff rebel spy, sauntered gaily into Libby Prison, accompanied by General John Morgan and Major Turner. The Major brought up the rear, with his prize corded poodle 'Beauregard' straining on a leash. The white dog, paraffined curls dangling to the floor from head to tail, had been specially groomed for the occasion.

General Morgan, recently escaped from an Ohio prison, was one of the most dashing and feared of Confederate raiders. Wearing an ostrich-plumed hat and sporting a Vandyke and waxed mustache, he personified the famous Dumas character, d'Artagnan. His escape was a marvel of determination, cutting through two feet of cement and masonry with tools fashioned from table utensils.

Miss Boyd, equally at ease in the latest fashions or in bushwhacker's garb, epitomized the beribboned Southern woman, gloved hand on Morgan's gold-braided arm. Belle, a honey blonde, all of nineteen, had just been released from a Federal prison in Washington, where she had been held for, among other things, the fatal shooting of a Yankee soldier.

The illustrious couple were saluted by guards as they went from one prison room to another, inspecting the Union captives. As the guard opened the door to Room number 4, Major Turner snapped off his poodle's leash. "Watch this," he snickered.

Beauregard sniffed once on the inside of the door, then lifted his leg, to the amusement of his master.

"Sure got him trained," Morgan laughed.

"These bluebellies are being disciplined for disorderly conduct," explained Turner. "This is their second week with no meat rations." The Major opened a small paper bag he'd been carrying and fed Beauregard a few pieces of red meat as the prisoners looked on indignantly.

"Serves 'em right," agreed the General from Kentucky.

Belle disapproved of these tactics but dared not contradict the rebel officers. She found herself wondering about the prisoners, men in their prime, and starved for love as well as for food. While in prison Belle had gotten to know some of her captors as decent, intelligent beings, and what interested her most about Northerners was their literacy. Her dormant flair for writing had been kindled by the availability of books and instruction at the prison to the degree that she'd written her memoirs to date in a lively style. On the whole, she'd found Southern men less stimulating and rather more conceited than Northerners.

Suddenly, there was the sound of a dog barking among the inmates. This so frightened Beauregard that he turned tail and ran from the compound. After a quick search of the floor and stairway for the poodle, Turner addressed the prisoners. "If the man who did that does not step forward, you'll get an additional week without meat rations." The Major waited, impatiently leering at the prisoners, then spun on his heels and left.

"Beauregard," Turner conjectured to his guests, "has most likely gone down to the cook room, which is on our itinerary."

"Here, Beauregard. Where are you, puppy?" Belle called out in a corner of the cook room. Hearing this, Nat Mather crawled out of the unfinished tunnel below a storeroom and scrambled up the ladder inside a chimney. Emerging through a hole in the chimney in the storeroom, he hastily pushed two large barrels to against the hole, picked up a broom and started sweeping the floor.

"Hello." Belle entered the storeroom. "Have you seen Major Turner's dog?" She lifted her dress to step over some tumbled firewood, revealing white lace petticoats and a shapely leg.

"No Ma'am," replied Nat, sweeping briskly.

"The Major thought Beauregard might have come down here to the kitchen." Noticing the barrels against the wall, Belle walked toward them. "What's in those barrels?"

"Kitchen slops."

Belle turned up her nose and retreated. "You sound like a Yankee. You're a prisoner?" She fumbled in her handbag and Nat held his hands over his head. This amused her so that she drew out a handkerchief instead of her nickel-plated derringer. "I've seen you someplace before."

She studied his chiseled, lean features. "Were you in the Yankee Cavalry?"

"Horses don't like me, so I went into the Navy."

"All Union officers in this prison?"

"That's right; the enlisted men are at Belle Island."

"And you have to work in the kitchen?" Belle was appalled.

"I'm new here," explained Nat, "and I've been told that originally Libby had Negro cooks, but the food was prepared so badly that the inmates volunteered to take over the kitchen themselves. I'm just taking my turn. Next week I start cooking."

"What can you do with bread, bacon and rice?"

"The most important factor in cooking here is to leave out hemp, pebbles and roaches as condiments." Nat picked up a bag of rice and slung it over his shoulder.

Admiring Nat's raw-boned strength, Belle tagged along to the cook room in which three broken-down stoves were besieged by a score of officer-cooks, each clamoring to get his pot or pan on a hot spot. On the other side of the kitchen Major Turner was questioning the prisoners about Beauregard while General Morgan looked on with amusement. "Damn," he chuckled to a group of cooks, "this is the *rankest* kitchen I've ever seen."

Nat heaved the bag of rice onto a table and started back toward the storeroom. "Nice talkin' to you, Miss. . . ."

"I'm Belle Boyd, from Shenandoah country," she replied.

"Nathaniel Mather. Connecticut." Nat stood up to his full six feet, four inches and bowed facetiously.

Belle pondered a moment. "Now I know who you remind me of. Don't take me wrong, but you could pass for a handsome young Abraham Lincoln. Before he grew that beard."

"I didn't know that rebels had any liking for the man."

"I never said I *liked* him, but he sure gives good speeches. Anyone who comes from a poor family and gets to be President has got to be admired somehow. At least he ain't one of your fancy, rich types—the ones who all went to Harvard and Yale." Belle followed Nat back to the storeroom.

"Won't your friends be looking for you?" Nat held the storeroom door from swinging closed. Belle didn't answer. Instead she looked up into his hazel eyes, curled up the corners of her mouth and casually pushed his hand away from the door. It swung closed and the storeroom became a separate, dark island; lighted faintly by a small window behind some stacked crates.

"You knew it too, didn't you?"

"Knew what?" Nat asked hesitantly.

"That our very opposite natures are intriguing to each other," purred Belle. "North and South . . . tall and small . . . dark and fair-haired . . . silent and talkative. . . ."

"Rebel and bluebelly," joked Nat as Belle pressed her agile body into him. He thought of the others—the encounters of war. Sarah . . . Micheline . . . Meg Maury. And the places! A bizarre actors' apartment, a balloon high over Hampton Roads, and a notorious inn on the James River.

And now in a *prison*?

But Nat was not a Puritan like his ecclesiastic ancestors. With a reckless shrug he slid the door bolt home, then took Belle in his brawny arms. "What do you want, *rebel*?"

Belle smiled impishly, then feigned innocence. She closed her eyes and whispered, "The same as you, Yankee."

Taking the cue and offer as well as the challenge of an enemy in gray, Nat's right hand was sent on a reconnaissance mission. It slipped beneath a mass of gingham and lace, intent on a nor' by nor' west course. The tactics included the placing of the enemy's main body on an empty shelf, which was accomplished without great casualties because of a strategic retreat by the aforesaid enemy. While the gray heroically resisted the blue's adamant thrusts, it had no choice but to ultimately yield to a superior force—which was part of the original strategy of the weaker force.

"You're wonderfully insane," brooded Nat as he disentangled himself and stretched his limbs out on the broad shelf.

"I like danger—" Belle didn't finish the sentence as she pounced upon Nat's body, heedless of the faraway shouts:

"Miss Boyd, Miss Boyd . . . where are you?"

Meanwhile, from a large pot on one of the kitchen stoves wafted a savory aroma that weakened rebel and Yankee alike. Major Turner complimented the cook, a Lieutenant-Colonel from Boston and requested that a sampling be immediately ladled out for his own epicurean appraisal. The Major, upon tasting the stew, smacked his lips. "Colonel Joslin," he addressed the cook, "this is the tenderest veal I've tasted in years. Where did you get such fresh meat?"

"We caught a lost calf while on firewood detail." Joslin had all he could do to keep from laughing as the other cooks looked on in disbelief at the Major finishing his plate ravenously.

Offering a spoonful to General Morgan, who declined, Turner cautioned, "Always sample prison food from the pot. One never knows what the bluebellies will put in it behind your back. By the way, Joslin; what do you call this recipe?''

''Veau de Libby,'' of course, replied the Colonel.

After Major Turner and his guests had left, a sign was hung on the pot of stew:

''VEAU De BEAUREGARD''

TWENTY-SEVEN

The cobbled streets of Richmond were walked by hundreds of one-armed Confederate soldiers, while in the fashionable West End, well-to-do young women in the latest riding attire cantered their elaborately groomed mounts to luncheon and afternoon tea.

Speckling the seven hills upon which the city had been built were fresh graves as bodies waiting in crude pine coffins burst unattended. The more avaricious of the city's doctors were busy with the booming trade of embalming and the whiskey purveyors had tripled in as many years. So unsure was life that even men of the cloth invested in gambling halls. Richmond was the Rome of the South.

Prominent citizens wrote of 'swarms of prostitutes' in Richmond, and others reported that 'even the most hardened observer could not imagine the intemperance.' The hundred whiskey shops on Main Street and its adjoining alleys featured a concoction called 'white mule' which, after several drinks, assured that the imbiber would be swacked for a full two days. From these establishments issued songs such as 'Mother, I've Come Home to Die,' 'The Vacant Chair,' and 'Listen to The Mockingbird.'

A regiment in faded gray and butternut homespun marched West on Broad Street, past the Capitol grounds and the First African Church toward the Virginia Central Railroad Depot. Gone were the ornate knapsacks of '61 in favor of blanket rolls—and the proud tassled kepis had given way to soft felt hats. Scraggly tooth brushes sprouted from buttonholes and frying pans were stuck by their handles into musket barrels alongside bayonets. Tin coffee pots dangled from aching hips, and feet sloshed in boots taken from the enemy dead. A soldier tamped his smoking pipe down, thankful for the South's only resource, tobacco, as his marching brothers sang to the tune of *Yankee Doodle*:

> But Doodle knows as well as I
> That when his zeal has freed 'em
> He'd see a million niggers die
> Before he'd help to feed 'em.

The column passed by the Exchange Hotel where a painted young woman huddled in the darkening shadows of an adjacent alley. Above loomed the spire of Trinity Methodist Church, catching the last rays of the lowering sun.

The rear ranks of the regiment cleared the Capitol Green, deceptively peaceful with its illuminated portico and fountions. A soldier in the last rank turned about in quick step and thumbed his nose at the Seat of Government.

A chorus of highly-polished brass ceiling lamps reflected on the black and white diamond marble floor of the Exchange Hotel Lobby. Standing near the cloak-room, a comparatively well-uniformed Confederate corporal was posted to discourage his superiors from consorting with the ladies who gave James Ballard's hotel its renowned reputation.

In the gentlemen's room beyond the sumptuous rosewood and mirrored bar, a golden-tressed dandy astride a carved wood 'throne' was having his hand-tooled leather boots oiled and shined. Hidden behind a newspaper, he did not notice a rotund though well-dressed businessman enter.

"Why hello, Mister Renfrew," greeted the ever-smiling Judah Benjamin. "What brings you to this part of town—as if I didn't know," the Secretary of State winked knowingly. "Of course it's to break our famous Faro Banks." Benjamin took a Confederate dollar from his billfold and handed it to the shoeshine boy, adding "keep the change," and motioning the Negro to leave them alone. The Negro bowed and scraped before disappearing into the bathroom.

"Wilkes," whispered the older man, "you've no idea how I've missed you. I couldn't talk at Mrs. Chesnut's party. . . . Why not come and stay at my house while you're in the city. *Hosanna* need not know. We can have a good time—just like we used to in New Orleans. I have everything you like, in spite of the damn blockade."

"Even African candied figs?"

"But, *naturellement,*" Benjamin put his hand on the actor's knee but was quick to remove it at a sharp look from the recipient.

"Those days are over, *Judy*."

"No; let's always leave some doors open," advised the legal genius. "You never know what's just around the bend. By the way, I think you're positively smashing as a blonde. Look; I have an idea. You're so lucky, why don't we take a look at Ballard's table—and, guess what? I'll back your bets."

"I can't turn down that offer," laughed 'Renfrew' as he sprang down from the ebony throne. "But please. No more Wilkes—not even in private."

Jack Ballard was proud of his illustrious clientele. Not only was the Secretary of State at his Faro table, but so was General John Morgan and the impetuous heroine, Belle Boyd. He took Benjamin's dandy friend to be one of his many indulgences. The upstairs room was exquisitely appointed with silk moiré panels and a ceiling tent of gold and white stripes. On one wall, a decorative painted panel had been hung depicting an elaborately robed and jeweled Egyptian King or 'Pharoah'.

The Faro dealer sat within a circular table to which had been added rectangular wings, one on each side. Before him was a green felt 'lay-out' upon which was enameled a complete suit of spades, from ace through the numbers to king. Thirteen cards in all. Next to the dealer, a 'case-keeper' sat, fingering an abacus-like counting frame that corresponded to a duplicate suit of spades.

"Place your bets, please." The dealer waited, shuffled and cut his deck of cards, then placed the deck into a black velvet-covered dealing box, face up.

A dozen red chips were placed at various positions on the lay-out by the players or 'punters', who were gathered round the table. Benjamin's group was sitting, along with a few town cronies, while the rest of the players stood behind and to the sides.

The dealer waved his hand to signal the end of betting, then turned the face card from the deck, exposing the first betting card. Placing that aside the box, he turned up the second. As the chips were raked in, a groan arose from the players, all except for Belle Boyd whose stakes were increasing.

"Miss Boyd," joked Jack Renfrew, "Jefferson Davis should send you to Monte Carlo to raise money for our cause."

"I'm afraid that I'm not very consistent, Mr. Renfrew."

"Belle, if I may call you that, have you ever thought of being an actress? You're a fascinating type."

"Oh, thank you, sir, for the compliment." Belle stacked her chips neatly. "If it pays, I might be interested." Belle puffed on a cigarette. "Are you offering me a position?"

"No, I'm just an *aficionado* of the theater. Always interested in types of people. Characters and so on. The supporting cast is the salt of the play. A comic, a fool, a despot. A shrewish old woman. They will always make the difference. In my travels, on river steamers and railroads, I have been tempted to recruit a company of extras. Like collecting costumes and exotic props. Here, in Missouri, a perfect Helen of Troy, there, in Boston, a Napoleon. . . . a Columbus, and so on."

"Or a Lincoln?"

"What did you say, Miss Boyd?

"I met a man who resembles Abraham Lincoln—as a young man."

"Interesting. Very interesting," Renfrew placed his bet. "And where did you find this . . . gentleman?"

"Here. In Richmond at Libby Prison. I was given a tour along with the General." Belle poked Morgan in the ribs.

"How extraordinary," Renfrew bit his lip. "But I don't think I know of any part for him as yet. . . ."

"I don't think you could get him anyway."

"Why is that?"

"He's a prisoner of war," replied Belle.

"From the Army of The Potomac? Chickamauga?"

"No. He's a Union Naval officer." Belle gathered in more chips. "What's wrong Mr. Renfrew? Have you seen a ghost?"

"Nothing, nothing at all." Renfrew clenched his fist and broke a playing chip.

"RAID . . . RAID!" shouted Ballard.

Instantly the Faro room was transformed. The gaming table was covered with a white cloth, and religious pamphlets and icons placed upon it. The dealer donned clerical trappings and opened a large bible as the players assumed pious bearings.

"Let us sing," the dealer rose and bade his followers to do likewise. "A Mighty For-tress is our God,

A Trusty Shield and Wea-pon;
He helps us free from ev-ery need
That hath us now o'er-taken. . . ."

As the song rang out, Judah Benjamin was helped through a window and he crawled perilously across a pitched slate roof to make his escape. For the Secretary of State, there could be no reason to attend a Christian service, much less an illegal gaming table. As it turned out, the 'raiding party' of provost troops was looking for an escaped Yankee prisoner.

TWENTY-EIGHT

A small piece of broken mirror was canted above the sill of a window on the third floor of Libby Prison's east side. The jagged glass had been meticulously positioned, without arousing the suspicion of the guards pacing below with orders to fire upon anything that moved in any of the windows.

Kneeling unseen below the sill, Nat lined up the sights of a pocket compass with a line inscribed through the mirror's silvered backing. This line, in turn, had been positioned to line up with a carriage shack diagonally across Carey Street in an empty lot. The compass reading of ENE was five degrees in a more northerly direction than the reading of the tunnel axis as far as it had gone. Nat quickly sketched a long triangle on a scrap of paper, the shortest arm of which was marked *27 feet,* which was the distance from the ground to the window vantage point as measured the night before with a string and attached weight. By sighting through the mirror along a makeshift protractor he determined the carriage shack to be at an angle of 65 degrees relative to the vertical 27-foot arm. By applying trigonometrical variants to the reciprocal 25-degree angle at the carriage shack Nat calculated that the tunnel would have to extend 58 feet to emerge within the shack providing that the last eight feet turned directly north.

Junius Henry Browne, prisoner and special war correspondent for the *New York Tribune*, read over his notes on the evening before the scheduled escape attempt:

> Since my incarceration in Secessia's morbid prisons, I have had a profound respect for civilization's successful tunnels.
>
> I have always been a stockholder in a planned tunnel. I've helped to plan them, crept in and out of them, but, alas, never *through* one. I fancy Adam must have crawled to Paradise through a tunnel.
>
> A woman's humor is no less uncertain than a tunnel.
>
> I never knew any man to make a correct calculation for a tunnel's completion regarding the time needed.
>
> Tunnels linger longer than rich relatives whom expectant heirs are waiting to bury.
>
> Though there be an engineer now who deigns to lead us to the promised land by his mathematics, I am convinced that tunnels, at best, lead all moles back to where they began.
>
> The only implements in our possession for digging are an old trowel and a broken canteen. Two of our number are continually and vigorously digging at all hours. The digger, advancing slowly, places his loose earth on an old blanket, which his helper conveys out of the tunnel and into a corner of the hidden room. Now that the tunnel is at an advanced stage, we have

> been retrieving the loose earth from a distance by pulling a brass spitoon back and forth, the length of the tunnel.
>
> One of the fears of tunneling is that in burrowing horizontally, the human animal tends to work upward toward the surface. We work in constant fear of emerging in front of a trigger-happy rebel sentry.

Informed of the 'upward digging tendency', Nat devised a trough consisting of two long, narrow sticks, planed smooth and joined in a vee shape longitudinally. Upon this was set a glass marble. The angle of digging the last ten feet was determined by cumulative rolling of the marble in the trough the length of the undertaking. This assured that the last leg dug was strong and parallel to the surface.

Just when it seemed that the tunnel was within a yard or so of its objective, the diggers were confronted with wooden pilings that had been driven deep into the ground at some earlier period in the lot bordering on Carey Street. A call was sent out for extra pen-knives and candles to overcome this final obstruction. Relays of men chipped at the pilings for two days before they could be removed and the digging resumed.

After nineteen days digging, a furtive eye peeked up through a small hole atop the vertical shaft at the 'calculated' end of the tunnel. The only light to be seen was from cracked cedar shingles on the roof of the carriage shack. Further enlarging of the escape exit was impeded by stacks of packages and boxes bearing the labels of the Christian and Sanitary Commissions. The carriage shack was chock-full of clothing, food and provisions sent by Northern organizations to be distributed among Libby's inmates.

Word was passed that the tunnel was ready and escape a reality. In all, 109 prisoners, chosen for various reasons, such as age, military importance and resourcefulness gathered up their meager possessions and formed groups of three and four, waiting for final instructions from Colonel Thomas Rose, the project's mentor.

The ranking officer, General Neal Dow, declined an invitation, citing that an escape was contrary to the agreements of prisoner exchange. Others, more forthright in their reasons, thought escape more dangerous than confinement and chose to remain.

Shortly before midnight on the 9th of February, the prisoners started out, Colonel Rose leading the van. Rose was followed by Colonel Streight, Captain Vanderhoef and Lieutenant Mather. Each man had stripped naked and rolled up his clothing to be pushed ahead while crawling through the tunnel in which candles were set in niches at ten-foot intervals. Each group was to take as different a route as possible and push for the Union Lines.

At midnight, the rear guard of prisoners, led by Colonel Kendrick of Tennessee made a loud racket in the kitchen with pots and pans, carrying the noise up and down the stairways to create a diversion for the prison guards who were expected on their hourly rounds. The clamor was also the signal for the advance group to emerge from the tunnel into the carriage shack.

Huddled among the boxes in the shack, Nat's group waited anxiously as the sentries outside exchanged calls:

"Midnight and all's well at post number seven. . . ."

After unlocking the door, Colonel Rose slipped out of the shack, then Streight . . . then Vanderhoef, all dressed in their citizen's clothes. From a third-floor window in Libby, Colonel Kendrick watched as the solitary figures emerged from the shack across Carey Street, caught in the glow of the gas street lamps and walked hurriedly toward the safety of nearby building shadows.

"They made it!" The word spread quickly.

* * *

After waiting for Vanderhoef to disappear in the shadows, Nat took his turn only to be surprised by a southern drawl.

"Hol' on there, you—" A bayonet glinted.

Nat reached back into the shack and held up a box to the lamplight. "Jes' thought I'd help m'self to some o' these bluebelly goodies." He ripped open the cardboard lid and offered the box to the sentry.

"Don't mind ef ah do," Corporal Stowers reached into the box and drew out a package of dried fruit which he tucked under his jacket. "Now, you git on back to wherever you came from," ordered Stowers, "or I'll turn you in." He took the box from Nat and waited for him to leave, then examined the carriage shack door. The lock showed no signs of being broken or forced. The quartermaster must have left it open by mistake, thought Stowers as he filled his pockets with the contents of the box and stashed it in the brush. Snapping the door locked again, it never occurred to him that it had been an inside job. The corporal shouldered his musket and marched back to the guardhouse. His four-hour watch was over and he was looking forward to enjoying the rewards of the evening. All this because he walked across Cary Street to take a leak!

The word was out and the prisoners stormed down to the cook-room, pushing and shoving regardless of the agreed order of escape and chosen participants. Hundreds of the two thousand inmates converged on the stairs in their mania to get to the tunnel's mouth. Muscle became the trump-card and the weak, regardless of rank, were pushed aside without ceremony.

At one point, someone shouted "GUARDS! GUARDS!"

and the kitchen was cleared in an instant. It was a ruse, the shouters taking advantage of their own alarm and scurrying into the tunnel. It was a wonder that the guards did not suspect what was going on, but rather attributed the noise to a mounting insanity.

One guard was heard to call out to a companion, "Halloo, Bill, there's somebody's coffee-pot upset fer sure in there."

"What's holdin' up everything up ahead?" cried out a mud-spattered escapee halfway through the tunnel.

"It's the big root," came a distraught reply. "Randolph can't get through; he's stuck fast."

"Push him, damn it!" Frantic voices echoed.

"Get some grease from the kitchen for the fat one!"

"Cut him up and push through the pieces!"

There was a cheer as Randolph finally slipped through. Then his group scampered the last few yards and stealthily climbed up into the carriage shack where they quickly dressed, offering a silent prayer before going off into the night.

By dawn, over one hundred prisoners had fled and at roll-call that morning certain men were designated to cross the room slyly and be counted twice by the guards. This ruse was discovered and a recount by the prison clerk came up one hundred and fifteen short.

Major Turner was called and his count verified the clerk's findings. Subsequent questioning of the inmates were of no help since all had sworn to be silent. The escape was made public, and the local newspapers advised, with offers of rewards for information leading to the capture of the Yankees.

Nat caught up with his group several blocks away at a rendezvous near Gillies Creek in the valley between Church and Chimborazo Hills. The fugitives caught their breath, then set out to the southeast, keeping the York River Railroad tracks to their left. They had previously decided that the best route to take was not toward the Union Lines in the North beyond the Rappahannock River, but toward Norfolk or Fortress Monroe since there were fewer rebel units and pickets in that direction. Setting out for the Chickahominy River, they reached the village of Seven Pines and turned Southeast toward the White Oak Swamp, where they waded in water up to their necks to throw off the bloodhounds they knew would be let loose in the morning. Following the Swamp River till dawn broke, they clambered up on a small, wooded island where they rested and shared their rations. It was a chill day, all the more so for their wet clothes, so they dug a pit in a grove of thick oaks and Colonel Rose demonstrated his expertise at Indian fire-starting.

* * *

Bloodhounds were baying ahead as Major Turner, leading a column of mounted guards, held up his hand. The column came to a halt as a lone rider caught up with them.

"Major," the rider called out, "do you mind if I tag along?"

"This is not a civilian matter; there are over one hundred escaped Yankees out there somewhere."

"Ah, but I am on a special mission. My name is Jack Renfrew." The rider unfolded a letter and handed it to Turner, whose expression changed upon seeing the signature of Jefferson Davis. "Major," continued the actor, "there is reason to suspect that one of the escaped Yankees is a dangerous Union agent, wanted in Charleston and other cities."

"Mr. Renfrew, I can't argue with your credentials, but could you tell me just whom you are after?"

"That's confidential, Major. We don't want him to know that we're onto him."

"I understand, Mr. Renfrew." Turner handed the letter back and motioned his troop to procede along the Old Williamsburg Road to Seven Pines. "What makes you think your man is going this way rather than to the Rappahannock, Mr. Renfrew?"

"Major," Renfrew grinned as he spurred his horse into a canter, "why are *you* heading east instead of north?"

"Very perceptive, Mr. Renfrew. You might have become a good field commander, had you the inclination."

"I may surprise you some day, Major."

The column raced along the Old Williamsburg Road through Seven Pines. On a rise above the White Swamp Ford, row on row of small gravestones shimmered through the morning mist, testament to a battle almost two years earlier when a vast Union army under General McClellan was repulsed and turned back only five miles from Richmond, thus ending Northern expectations of a short war.

At a fork in the road, the column split, with Renfrew following a detachment south toward White Oak Bridge. The wily actor was playing a hunch. If the elusive Lieutenant Mather was with the instigators, Colonels Rose and Streight, the group might try to make contact with one of the Union gunboats that were plying the James River down by City Point. This would mean that the fugitives would have to cross the White Oak River. That the hounds had lost the scent was an indication that his hunch had some merit.

* * *

Rested, fed, and somewhat dryer, Nat's little group made its way south along the bank of the White Oak River until the sun's position told them that the river was turning east. As the river was very deep and swift, the party was fortunate to come upon a massive pine tree that had fallen across and tangled with another on the opposite bank. The elder Colonels were first to struggle across and gained the bank without mishap. Captain Vanderhoef was next and as he approached the center of the natural bridge, holding on to branches to keep from slipping on tar resin, shots rang out from upriver. A branch was splintered in front of him and the next minié ball caught him in the back. He pitched forward, jamming a leg in the sharp crook of a branch and dangled head down over the rampaging river.

Focusing his field glasses on the tall figure that was crouching low on the fallen pine tree, Renfrew shouted to the riflemen, "I want him alive. Just scare him."

"But the Major said—" Corporal Jackie Lee Stowers accepted a three-dollar gold piece from the actor. "You heard the man," he shouted to the other guards. "Scare th' hell out of him."

A withering fire chipped and slotted the pine bark under his feet and Nat flung himself down on the trunk, clinging to the downriver side. A ball grazed his arm and another tore through the bark, inches from his head. Nat studied the river and its currents for a moment, then let go of the trunk. He hit the water and dived under, letting himself be carried as long as his breath held out. Lungs almost bursting he sputtered to the surface in the shadow of a large, mossy rock. Head barely above the water, Nat spotted a clapboard cabin, gray smoke swirling from a fieldstone chimney. It lay in a clearing on the south bank, wood stacked against the weather side. Beyond it was a small, leaning barn and a meadow. He dove under again and swam toward a grove of trees and brush overhanging the bank near the clearing. Relieved that there were no dogs about he dragged himself up on the muddy bank, teeth chattering from the freezing water, and stealthily made for the inviting cabin.

First going around to the barn, he was heartened to find it empty save for some roosting chickens and an old mare. In the waning daylight he selected a scythe blade from its wall hook and crept up to the cabin's front window. A candle sent soft halations against the small, cold windowpanes. Gripping the cold scythe in his hand, Nat apprehensively peeked in.

Inside, silhouetted against a meager fire in an enormous fireplace, a woman sat, spinning thread on a large wheel. On the wide plank floor before a beehive oven, a young girl of about three years' age was playing with a toy carriage. Over the fireplace were two pegs, the kind that were accustomed to holding a rifle. Nat felt a tinge of shame for his affront to a mother's privacy. But hearing bloodhounds in the distance, he forgot his qualms, placed the scythe against the cabin and knocked sharply on the door.

"Who's out there?" The woman jumped up and ushered her daughter into another room. She picked up a fowling-piece, cocked it and stood squarely behind the door.

"Can you be Christian enough to give a rebel some supper?"

"You can have the best this house affords, but first tell me who you are and where you're from."

"I'm Nathaniel Cotton, Fifty-first Alabama Mounted. I've escaped from th' Yankees, Ma'am, and I'm on my way to Richmond to rejoin my company."

"How come you got this far without runnin' into some of our own boys?" The woman's finger tightened on the trigger.

"Ah jumped off a bluebelly gunboat goin' down the river by Bermuda Hundred," Nat drawled as best he could. "I guess I got lost. Well, thank you anyway, Ma'am, I'll be goin' now."

"Hold on Mr. Cotton, I'll unlatch the door, but mind you, I've got a load of buckshot aimed right at you. Amelia—" she motioned to her Negro servant to go up to the sleeping loft and look out of the loft window. In a moment the servant was back downstairs. "Ain't no one else I kin see, he ain't got no gun."

The woman nodded to her servant. "Let him in."

Amelia opened the heavy door slowly, then stepped back as Nat walked in, his hands raised and open.

"You're drenched," the woman pointed to a chair near the fire. "Sit over there. I'm Mrs. John Fisher. My husband is off to war." She sat down by the spinning wheel, shotgun on her lap.

Nat watched the woman. Her face was young, but drawn. Her clothes were plain, yet well-tailored. There were dress patterns pinned to the wall next to the fireplace. On the mantel stood a small, framed photograph of a Confederate officer.

"Ain't seen my husband for nearly a year, nor heard from him since before Thanksgiving. His last letter came from Missionary Ridge in Tennessee." Mrs. Fisher spun her wheel slowly.

"I've seen a lot of misery, Mrs. Fisher. I was shocked at the dastardly conduct of those Yankees that came up from Norfolk back in '62. The citizens were driven from their homes and treated like bushwhackers. Their property was confiscated and their hounds were shot down because they tracked escaped prisoners."

"Mr. Cotton," replied the woman, "the Yankees were no worse than our own soldiers. In passing through the state they took from the rich the surplus necessary for sustenance, but when our illustrious cavalry followed in pursuit they took nearly all that was left, seeming to care little for our wants and often stripping defenseless women and children of their last morsels of food."

"I regret, Ma'am, that the conduct of our troops has given you such cause for complaint—but remember, our Commissary Department has been completely wrecked. We are dependent on the citizens for our very survival."

"What do you think about the war, Mr. Cotton? Does the South have a chance?" Mrs. Fisher set the shotgun against the wall next to her and signalled to Amelia.

Nat quickly responded. "Our future looks bleak, but the sacrifices of our gallant dead must be avenged. We will fight to the last man, and die in the ditches if need be."

"Amelia," Mrs. Fisher digressed, "you can prepare some supper for our guest. I'm sure he won't mind smoked turkey and yams. And we'll both have some cider."

"Yes'm," Amelia fluttered away.

"Mr. Cotton, you seem to think there is little hope for our cause. I should think if that were true it would be better to lay down our arms at once rather than die in the ditches."

Nat did not argue that point. "And who's that?" he asked as a child peeked from behind a door.

"She misses her father so. I told her he was on a trip and will come back soon," whispered the woman, "but *soon* never seems to happen. Jenny," she raised her voice, "you can come out now."

* * *

Given dry clothes and a bandage for his grazed arm, Nat slept in the barn that night. The next morning he repaid Mrs. Fisher's hospitality by splitting and stacking a half-cord of firewood.

Hidden in the woods beyond a meadow, field glasses held by nervous hands scanned the cabin and barn, then became rigid at the sight of Nat stacking wood. A grin formed under the glasses and one of the hands reached into a saddle bag for a flask of brandy.

TWENTY-NINE

The gray garrison tents in the shadow of Libby were for the most part empty. Here and there a dusky servant did his chores, slower than usual since the troops were off on a manhunt. Patriarchal Augustus, Major Turner's man, sat near the well, rinsing his master's linens in a wooden tub. It was good to be outside, to be free in the bright afternoon sunlight of an unseasonably mild winter day. Free of petty orders and constant degradation.

"Gus?"

The white-haired Negro squinted at a newcomer who was pumping water into a cooking caldron. "That's me. You be one of the new boys from town?"

"Gus; it's Josiah. It's me! Now don't let on. Just talk natural. I've come to get you out of this place."

"And my daughter, is she. . . ."

"She and the baby are fine."

"I can't believe it. You, here. How. . . ."

"I'll tell you later, but first we've got to figure out a way to get back north. Both of us."

"But I can't go. I'll never make it."

"Come on, Gus; don't be scared. We're as good as they are. Now you just get your things together and meet me here in 10 minutes. We've got to get a good start while everyone's gone. I'll work out the details as we go. There's an underground station up in Mechanicsville. We can get there by sundown. . . ."

"But you don't understand, Josiah. I should have written you, but I didn't want to worry Tenah about me."

"What's wrong, Gus?"

"It's my heart. Ain't been tickin' too good lately. Major Turner doesn't know either. If he did I'd be out of m' job."

"But Gus; we can make it. I'll get you to a doctor in Montreal. You'll be all right and we'll all be together."

"I'm sorry Josiah, but I can't—" Augustus clutched at his chest and gasped for air. "The pains are comin' faster every day. I just know it's time. I've known since my dear wife passed away." The old man wheezed and tried to steady himself.

"Here, Gus—I'll tend to the laundry. We'll wait a few days and see how you feel. Hell, I just signed up with the rebels to work in the officer's mess. Can't quit right away!"

* * *

"Lieutenant Mather!"

The shout startled Nat and instinctively he dove into some high marsh grass. A carbine ball sliced above his head as his pursuer called out, "Mather, give up. You're my prisoner."

Nat crawled through the grass and hid behind a cypress where he waited till Renfrew had passed, carbine at the ready. "Mather," shouted the actor, scattering a flock of red egrets, "You must surrender or be executed. I warn you now. . . ."

Seizing the opportunity, Nat made a break for it. He leapt into a stand of pine and zig-zagged for his life. The 50-caliber Sharps carbine cracked once more, its deadly projectile whistling through the tall pines. Renfrew, stopping to reload, doubled back to get his horse. Still running at full tilt, Nat spotted a church spire and headed for it.

The Willis Congregational Church was holding a Saturday afternoon benefit for the Chimborozo Hospital in Richmond. The church was surrounded by rigs and wagons of every description, with women, children and older men scurrying back and forth, laden with blankets, clothing, cakes and jars of 'put up' fruits and vegetables. A fiddler was tuning up and the minister was directing the proceedings from the church steps and noting the contributions as they were carried inside.

Nat slipped into a group surrounding a wagon and was handed a sack of sweet potatoes which he dutifully slung over his shoulder and followed the others into the church. After depositing his sack on the proper table, he went up the balcony stairs and climbed into the spire. Looking out from behind a bronze bell he saw a rider galloping down the road. The rider had flowing blond hair and a carbine in his saddle holster.

"I saw a big man go up there." A freckled schoolboy bit into the ten cent piece he'd just received. Renfrew, unarmed, went up the stairs as the townsfolk prattled about an escaped Yankee and hurried out of the church.

"So, we finally meet." Renfrew emerged from the opening in the belfry floor with a grandoise gesture. "Shall we go, or shall we have to make a scene?" Renfrew drew a silver-handled knife from his coat and stalked his prey slowly. A pungently fragrant aroma wafted through the bells and all at once Nat remembered. The photographer on the pier in Brooklyn . . . the Monitor . . . the President!

The actor lunged at Nat, who parried the knife thrust with his arm and sidestepped his assailant who slammed into a bell, ringing it erratically. Before Renfrew could recover, Nat grabbed his wrist and forced the weapon out of his grip. It fell through the bell rope aperture and clattered down the stairs.

Green eyes raging and pinned against a bell, Renfrew kicked his knee up into Nat's groin. He broke free and attempted to climb out of one of the belfry windows but was dragged back by Nat who wrestled him to the narrow catwalk. Holding Renfrew down, Nat grabbed a bell rope and looped it around the actor's legs. In a desperate effort, Renfrew lashed out with a free arm and Nat countered with a blow to his adversary's jaw.

Tightening the rope around Renfrew's legs, Nat turned the groggy actor over and started to hog-tie his arms.

Then he saw the tiny pistol in the actor's hand.

Saw a finger move.

Felt a searing pain in his stomach.

On the following Monday, The *Richmond Dispatch* printed a front-page article recounting the escape at Libby and the recapture of twelve prisoners. Listed as wounded was a Lt. N. Mather, USN, who was admitted to Libby's hospital ward. Shortly after the newspaper was delivered to Chimborozo Hospital, Confederate Army surgeon Howell Clyburn and a nurse were in a carriage on their way to Libby.

* * *

Lieutenant Colonel Clyburn shook his head disconsolately. "It's a bad wound, Bess, and I don't know that I can do any better than the resident surgeon. Wounds of that sort can be fatal because the attendant infection is usually uncontrollable." Clyburn thumbed through the pages of Chisholm's *Manual of Military Surgery*, then rose from his chair in the hospital office and looked out into the ward. "What's his condition now?"

"The quinine brought his fever down some, but he's very weak and still in delirium. He doesn't recognize me at all." Bess mixed ground-up jimson weed seeds and maypop root with alcohol, then poured the tincture into a small bottle. Next, she put chips of slippery elm bark and mauva leaves into a stone mortar and started grinding the mixture. "It's so odd." Bess wiped a tear from her eye. "If Nat hadn't been caught, much less shot, we might never have known that he's been right here in Richmond, hardly a mile away."

"The exchange list would have reached your parents in a few weeks," replied Howell, "but getting a letter from Connecticut to this god-forsaken city is another matter." He closed his book and laid out his surgical instruments, checking them one by one. "Did you manage to find some sponges and silk thread?"

"No, but I brought laundered cotton cloth and boiled horse hair. We could ask the medical orderly here. . . ."

"Wait," exclaimed Howell. "The last stomach puncture we treated at Chimborozo—I sutured with boiled horse hair and dressed the wound with fresh linen. Do you remember? There was no inflammation. Poultices were unnecessary. . . ."

"Yes, the young private from Michigan," recalled Bess. "What are you getting at?"

"It may only be a coincidence, but there was yet

another time I used cloth instead of sponges on an abdominal puncture. There was no suppuration in that case either. Quick recovery, too."

"Are you saying that the sponges used in cleaning a wound may have something to do with its infection?" Bess added alcohol to her mixture.

"I'm not sure, Bess, but there *could* be something in a sponge that causes infection. Perhaps a poison, that, while harmless to unbroken skin, could affect the blood or open wounds. Since sponges contain large amounts of silicon and carbon, they might also contain toxic salts. The tropical waters where sponges are found are host to many poisonous creatures as well."

"And clean cloth does not contain these poisons," contributed Bess excitedly.

"Bess, what did we do with the linen and the horsehair that we didn't do with the sponges and the silk thread?"

"We boiled them—"

"Exactly," replied Clyburn. "We boiled them; boiled off whatever poisonous salts they may have contained— He picked up a scalpel and examined it. The instrument glistened in the lamplight. It was clean, but he wondered whether it, too, had invisible, toxic salts clinging to the blade.

Howell decided to operate early the next morning. But first he had the orderly bring a pot of boiling water from the kitchen. He tied string to his instruments and immersed them, one by one in the bubbling water and laid them out on a strip of clean cotton cloth. "What's sauce for the goose," he crossed his fingers, "is sauce for the gander."

THIRTY

On Saturday, February 18th, the *Dispatch* headline was set in unusually large type:

> CSN TORPEDO BOAT SINKS BIG UNION WARSHIP IN CHARLESTON HARBOR. USS Housatonic, of The Atlantic Blockading. . . .

"It says here," Augustus squinted, holding the newspaper at arm's length, "that the torpedo boat also sank with all hands drowned, and there were no casualties aboard the Yankee boat."

Josiah hung a kettle of water in the brick fireplace that commanded one end of the Libby Garrison kitchen tent. "Major Turner's tea water will be ready soon, *massa*." He walked over to the table where his father-in-law was sitting and leaned over his shoulder to read the newspaper. "One less boat in the Union Navy won't make much difference,'' he whispered confidently. Then another article on the page caught his eye. Josiah read aloud:

> LIBBY PRISONER FOUND
> GUILTY OF ESPIONAGE.
> Court-martial decrees hanging. Lt. N. Mather convicted of charges brought forth by Confederate Agent. The Union Naval Officer, recovering from wounds sustained in recapture after the tunnel escape of last week has been identified as the Union operative who posed as a clergyman in this city last year, using the name, Rev. Cotton for the purpose of making a reconnaissance of the James River defences . . .

''Oh Lord,'' Augustus flinched. ''The good man who saved you and Tenah from whips and chains is in mortal peril. Not yet recovered and already sentenced to hang. That means Massa Mather will be locked up in the cellar jail where he'll not see th' light of day till the hangman comes. Lord have mercy on us all. . . .''

''There's nothing we can do, Gus. I'm here to bring you back with me and we must go as soon as you are strong enough. Tenah has waited so long and I've written her that I hope to return by next month. A year away is a long time.''

''How wonderful, my son. You've *written* her. You've taught her to read. Ol' Augustus is so proud of his daughter.''

''I write with small words,'' joked Josiah. ''By the way, Augustus, I've noticed you reading a book. What is it about?''

''A new volume I've borrowed from the prison clerk. It's by an Englishman. Very popular in this country too. It's called *A Tale of Two Cities*.''

* * *

Assignments accomplished, it was time for Jack Renfrew to nurture his other life. Shedding his blond wig, and brandishing a pass signed by General Ulysses Grant, raven-haired John Wilkes Booth was escorted through the Union picket lines near Fredericksburg, where he boarded a train for Washington. He met his brother, Edwin Booth, at the National Hotel to complete arrangements Edwin had managed, and go to New Orleans to play Richard III in the theater where their father had given his last performance before expiring of a fever on a Mississippi steamboat in 1852.

The elder, more famous brother proudly showed Wilkes an invitation to the White House from the President's wife.

"Is she still smitten with you for saving the life of that mollycoddled son of hers?" Wilkes helped himself to the brandy decanter, booted feet crossed over a red velvet ottoman.

"Don't be too hard on the woman; she's still in mourning for her youngest." Edwin moved the decanter. "It *was* a curious coincidence: Robert Lincoln and I, on the same train platform in Jersey City of all places. Anyone could have done what I did. . . ."

"It was clumsy of him to slip just as the train had started to move. Maybe he wanted you to save him; after all, it was dear Robert who recognized *you*," scoffed Wilkes.

"Perhaps it was fate." Edwin gestured grandly. "The upshot is that I'm to do a special appearance at Grover's for the President and his lady. Hamlet." Edwin bowed.

"Nooo! Really?" Wilke's eyes bulged.

"Yes, *really*! And Mrs. Lincoln wrote that I could

bring my younger brother, should he so desire. She likes actors, I fear. Especially actors with trousers."

"How nice of that parvenu bitch."

"Now, now, John. This could be advantageous to both of us. I'm going to bring up the Shakespeare Statue fund."

"Is the President going to be there?"

"No, this is an afternoon tea."

"Well, it might be amusing." John Wilkes Booth toyed with the end of his mustache.

* * *

Pert Belle Boyd peeked through the flag of Major Turner's tent. "Here I am. One o'clock, just like you said."

"I'm sorry I've been so busy, Belle, but there were many reports to make regarding the escape. The tunnel has become a circus side show. People are clamoring to see it."

"Maybe you should sell tickets and let the public crawl through it. The money could be used for better wash-rooms."

"Always the entrepeneur, my dear." Turner rose from his desk and took Belle by the arm, escorting her outside his tent and toward the James River behind the sprawling prison complex. "Enough of my problems. What brings you here—aside from my charm?"

As they strolled, workmen were erecting a gallows. The structure cast an ominous shadow on the parade grounds. Belle stopped and watched. "Is that for the Yankee I read about?"

"Justice will be done," lamented Major Turner.

"What exactly did he do?"

"My dear, it's enough when a soldier is out of uniform in the country he is at war with. If he is caught, he knows the consequences. It was true in Caesar's time, and it still is. Come, come, Belle; you know the rules of war. Why such sudden concern?''

''I thought I might write an account of the escape and capture for Harper's. A woman's point of view. . . .''

''And, of course, you know prisons from experience. Marvelous idea, Belle. You should have no trouble getting it accepted—by the Southern edition, I presume.'' Turner took off his broad-brimmed felt hat and fluffed up its white ostrich plume. ''How are your memoirs coming along?''

''I've just included you and General Morgan.''

''Wonderful. I could use a *promotion*; get it?''

Belle conceded him his pun. ''But getting back to my question, the *Dispatch* said the Union officer was found guilty of espionage—spying around the James River defences. How could it be proved that the officer who was captured was the man who posed as a clergyman, and why wasn't he tried before he escaped?''

''I give up, counselor.'' Turner raised his arms.

''Please, Major. . . .'' Belle walked closer to Turner, her dress rustling against his leg.

''My dear,'' he weakened, revelling in the envious glances of the garrison officers and sentries, ''you may have heard of the Secret Service. The North does not have a monopoly on the art. One of our cleverest operatives, appointed by Jeff Davis himself, has been on Lieutenant Mather's track for some time. Reverend Cotton, as the Yankee called himself, tarnished the honor of one of the daughters of an illustrious Virginian who also was the head of our coast and harbor defence department. After compelling the young lady to compromise her father's secret projects, the rascal absconded. Fortunately, her sister told her father of the despicable ruse and it was reported to our Secret Service along with a description of the bogus minister. . . ." Turner looked back at the gallows. "Belle, you understand I'm telling you much of this in confidence. There must be no mention of the affair. I've said too much already."

"You've been working too hard, Major. Why don't we have dinner this evening at Ballard's? You must be tired of prison food."

"Are you staying there?" Turner's pulse quickened.

Belle popped another grape into the Major's mouth. His head was on her lap and he was sprawled, uniform askew, on a dimpled red leather couch in a third-floor room of Ballard's Exchange Hotel.

"You promised to tell me more about Lieutenant Mather." Belle pushed Turner's hand from her knee.

"So I did, my dear. Whiskey has never helped my memory. Where was I?" Turner closed his eyes.

"Reverend Cotton was reported to the Secret Service."

"Ah, yes," Turner slurred his words. "Our operatives were apprised of the intelligence, including the gentleman who ultimately captured the culprit."

"And shot him?"

"The man was resisting. Renfrew had no choice."

"Renfrew?"

"Fictitious name. I made it up." Turner quipped uneasily. Belle encouraged his wandering hand. Taking his cue, the Major continued. "Prior to the escape, our operative was already suspicious that his quarry might be in Libby Prison, especially after finding the name 'Mather' among the recently arrived prisoners. There was an eccentric Congregational minister by the name of Cotton Mather in Boston during the late sixteen hundreds. . . . It seemed more than a coincidence: Reverend Cotton and Lieutenant Mather!"

"A clever operative, as you said." Belle crossed her legs, temporarily stemming the Major's advances. "But he still had no proof."

"He had enough to satisfy his suspicion," replied Turner. "But I must admit that he seemed to have a personal grudge against Mather. As if they had met in some other life. After the escape, Mather made the mistake of impersonating a Confederate soldier in gaining the hospitality of a woman whose husband was off to war. She fed him; she provided dry clothes and discoursed on the future of our cause with him. After he was seen leaving her house, our operative inquired about him. Private Cotton of the Fifty-first Alabama, indeed!"

"Thomas," cooed Belle as she ran her fingers across his chest, "be a darling and write me out a pass. As part of my story I would like to interview the condemned man."

Leaving the Libby orderly room, Belle was startled as an old Negro came toward her. "Missie Belle," pleaded Augustus, "I seen you go talk with Massa Mather down in the jail. Are you a friend o' his'n?"

"Why do you ask?"

"Fo'give me Ma'am, but we have to do somethin' before—" Augustus rolled his eyes at the gallows, silhouetted against a reddening sky.

Belle took a notepad from her purse. "You are Major Turner's manservant, Augustus?"

"That's right Missie Belle—"

"Just pretend that I'm interviewing you. What do you mean by 'do something?' "

"Massa Mather is a good Yankee, Ma'am. Somebody got to save him like he save my daughter and her husband from slave-catchers jes' before the war. They have a baby now—in Canada."

"Do you have any idea how he can be saved?"

"Yes'm. Old Gus knows what to do. My son-in-law, Josiah come down here from Canada to bring me home with him, but now we both try to save Massa Mather. Maybe you help. . . ."

The exchange boat lay at the dock behind Libby's main building. Little more than a shoal-draft scow to which had been fitted an ancient steam engine, the *Malvern Hill* flew a frayed white flag from an improvised mast abaft the wheelhouse. The vessel might have been impressed into the rebel navy but for its uncertain range, which, at best, included the exchange landing at City Point, some fifteen miles down the serpentine James River.

The exchange system was based upon a table of equivalents in which the private soldier was the prime unit. A lieutenant was equivalent to four privates, a captain to six, a colonel to fifteen, and a commanding general to sixty, with other ranks in proportion. Because of restrictions placed on exchange by General Winder, commanding the Richmond District, after the tunnel escape only a few sick prisoners were to be ferried to City Point.

"Do as I say, Lieutenant." Belle kept an eye on the guard in the dimly lighted hall leading from the cell to the stairway. "Rub this on." She set a small container between them. Nat spread the mixture of lamp-black and ash over his face and arms. "It's almost dark and the garrison is at supper. You have a good chance. Put this in your pocket." She handed Nat a small bundle. "You'll be hungry and thirsty."

"Why are you doing this, Belle?" Nat winced from pain as he slipped into a gray oilskin coat, of the style worn by guards and orderlies during rainy weather.

"Let's say it would be a shame for a man of your many talents to simply *hang* when we might—After the war is over, I'd like to go North; see the big cities, and perhaps get my book published—that is if I ever finish it."

"What is it about?"

"A little southern girl who ran messages for Beauregard and Jackson, and who told your General Butler to go to Hades. When I go North I'd like to look you up, if it's all right."

"Please do," Nat tried to kiss Belle on the cheek but held up his blackened hands in dismay. "You can find me through the Fourth Congregational Church in Stamford, Connecticut. My father is the minister. Reverend Gideon Mather."

"My folks are in Martinsburg, Virginia. Just write care of the post office. Everyone knows us there. . . ." Belle held up her white-gloved hand. "Shhh, I think he's coming."

"Hell, Gus," the guard bellowed. "Ain't gonna rain anymore tonight—" Private Ivy Duncan teased Augustus about his raincoat. "What ye got there, the Yankee's last meal?"

"Not quite, Massa Ivy, but the Major, he wants to treat the poor man good." Augustus balanced a tray with soup and biscuits. "Here's somethin' fer you." Augustus handed Private Duncan a tin of "Lone Jack" tobacco.

"Damn," exclaimed Duncan as he took out his briar and stepped outside for a smoke. "There's a lady in with the Yankee now. She's got a pass from the Major."

"Thank you, Massa Ivy, I'll be back in a minute." Augustus felt in his pocket for the duplicate key he had fashioned after pilfering the original from the orderly room.

Shortly after, even as Private Ivy was still lighting his pipe, musket leaning against the outside prison wall, a dark figure wearing a gray oilskin coat and carrying an empty white tray emerged into the night. Hunched over to appear smaller, Nat waved to Private Ivy and walked briskly through the back door, humming *Dixie* before slipping into the shadows on the loading dock.

THIRTY-ONE

The next morning at eight, a guard carried a breakfast tray down to the basement cell. "Come an' get it," he slid a bowl of grits and a tin of water under the cell door.

"Not hungry," came a muffled reply from under a blanket in a dark corner of the dank cell.

"I don't blame ye." The guard retrieved the food and sampled the grits with his fingers. "I'd sleep all day m'self if I could. Of course I probably couldn't sleep if I were you 'cause I'd have bad dreams about that contraption out in back. . . ."

A few minutes before noon, *Malvern Hill's* steam whistle emitted a quavering wail and her lines were cast off. Lazily the old flat-bottomed scow swung out into the James, catching the down-river current. Straw-hatted Jehu Hanks, a one-legged veteran of Chickamauga, sat comfortably at the wheel in the vessel's boxlike pilothouse, forward of a slender, rusting smokestack. He called out occasionally to a Negro fireman to put more wood into the patched-up copper boiler, and to another, standing on the bow, to watch for floating logs and shoal water.

Six convalescent prisoners to be exchanged lay on the deck, aft, on blankets under a makeshift canvas awning. In theory these former inmates of Libby, all officers, could be exchanged for one Confederate Major-General, also convalescent, or two other combinations besides head for head, as worked out by the exchange agent. Down below, hidden behind the wood bunker, crouched Nat and Josiah. The latter, with the late Colonel Tazewell's revolver cocked, kept an eye on the open hatchway.

At quarter past one, *Malvern Hill's* whistle blew again as it was abreast of Cox's Ferry. Ashore, a Confederate soldier dipped his musket barrel to roll out the ball, then fired his powder charge into the air. Powder, in Secessia, was plentiful but lead was scarce.

Rounding Farrar's Island, Jehu Hanks' heart jumped up into his throat. He swung the wheel to port; better to take a chance at running up on a shoal than being caught in a crossfire. Ahead, lying motionless with steam up, in the middle of the river off Aiken's Landing, was a double-turreted Union monitor. The crew's wash hung on lines strung from the central stack to the decks, fore and aft. Each turret was capped by a squat conical canopy, under which could be seen the ship's duty watch. Two menacing cannon muzzles protruded from the upriver, or forward turret.

Jehu Hanks nervously scanned the river banks, knowing that bands of soldiers were watching from cover, and at any moment might open fire on the Union gunboat. It would be just his luck.

Noticing the abrupt change as *Malvern Hill* fought to cross the river's current, Josiah crawled up from behind the firewood and cautiously peeked out. A look of elation came over him and he passed on the news to Nat over the rattling chug of the engine. "It's a monitor, flying the stars an' stripes, sir. Two turrets and one stack."

"That might be the *Onondaga,*" replied Nat.

"Would it be a better chance than City Point, sir?"

"You're right. Josiah. If the exchange agent is a stickler for procedure, we could find ourselves back at Libby."

"Why don't we hold up this stagecoach?" Josiah blew on the barrel of his revolver. "This beauty belonged to a rebel colonel who I met up near the Rapidan."

"You killed a colonel?"

"Not exactly, sir; I scared 'im to death."

Nat tried to get up but his wound was too painful.

"You stay put, sir. This is a job for the Fifty-fourth Massachusetts." Josiah climbed up behind the pilothouse unseen, as the crew's attention was focused on the Union Monitor.

There was no door on the back of the pilothouse. Jehu Hanks was silhouetted against the front window as Josiah crept up behind him. Putting the steel muzzle of his revolver against Hanks' broad, red neck, Josiah snarled. "Don't move, Mister Rebel, or I'll blow your head off. This is loaded with buck n' ball."

Hanks' hands went up automatically.

"Now you jes' turn this barge and go on over to that Yankee boat. We're goin' to have a little talk with 'em."

"Nigger, you are plumb crazy; they'll blow us out of the water." Hanks turned partially around and their eyes met.

"You call me that once more, and I'll—" Josiah pressed the gun into Hanks' neck till he squirmed. "Turn the boat."

* * *

There was a flurry of activity aboard the *Onondaga*. Its forward turret groaned and swung ominously toward the approaching boat. Decks cleared for action, all stations waited for orders from the armored pilot house atop the forward turret.

"They're flying a white flag, sir," Lieutenant Rossiter squinted through the narrow observation slit.

"It could be a trick, Rossiter. I wouldn't put it past those desperate Rebels to load up a boat with gunpowder and try to ram us." Commander Dwight leaned down to the speaking tube. "Engine room, one-half ahead . . . Helmsman, hard to starboard." Then he called down to the turret below: "Maxwell, ready on number two. . . ."

"Ready on two, sir."

"Put one across her bow."

"Aye, sir." The bottle-shaped Dahlgren lowered its 11-inch muzzle and belched fire and acrid black smoke which blew back into the turret, setting off a chain of coughs among the gunlayers.

A geyser of white erupted in *Malvern Hill's* path.

"Stop the boat," shouted Josiah.

"I tol' you so," Hanks pulled a bell cord twice and the vessel's vibration suddenly stopped as the fireman pulled a lever, disengaging the propellor shaft from the power take-off wheel of the 15-horsepower "steam kettle" engine.

"Now get on out there and wave nice to the Yankees," Josiah prodded Hanks in the back. Hanks pried himself out of his seat and hopped out on deck, holding on with one hand and waving his straw hat in the other.

Seeing this, one of the Onondaga's two cutters was put over the side, manned by four oarsmen and carrying a detail of marines. Six muskets were leveled at the *Malvern Hill* as the cutter approached.

"What is your business?" called Lieutenant Rossiter from the tiller station.

"This is the prisoner exchange boat, *Malvern Hill,*" shouted Hanks, one eye on Josiah, "bound for City Point."

"Then why did you make for the monitor?" Rossiter challenged the one-legged pilot.

Suddenly Josiah jumped up and flung his revolver overboard, screaming "Hurrah, hurrah for Jefferson Davis." Before the astounded Federals could react, Josiah had disappeared below.

"Corporal," Rossiter addressed the marine non-com. "Prepare to board. Search the vessel and bring that ungrateful scamp up on deck." The cutter came alongside and four marines clambered up on *Malvern Hill's* deck while two covered them.

Corporal Cooper drew his Navy colt and cautiously went below. "Come on out, you two," he leveled his revolver, "and no tricks." Cooper backed out of the hatch slowly.

"Are we glad to see you, Corporal," Josiah laughed. "I was only joking about Jeff Davis. I'm Corporal Josiah Holladay, Fifty-fourth Massachusetts, and this is—"

"You can tell that to the Lieutenant; now *git*—"

"You're absolutely right, Corporal," Nat struggled to his feet and rubbed some lampblack from his face with his sleeve.

"What is this," shouted Cooper. "A minstrel show?"

* * *

"This ain't the Yankee Lieutenant, sir." Private Stowers pulled the blanket from the curled-up figure and examined it. "Damn, it's a nigger, and I think he's dead." Stowers rolled the body over and found a book and a key.

After handing the key to the duty officer, he picked up the book and thumbed through the pages. Finding no pictures, he flung it into a pile of refuse in the corner of the cell, scattering a pack of rats.

The back cover of the book lay open and the last page caught a faint beam of morning light from a high, barred window, illuminating the final paragraphs:

> I see him, foremost of just judges and honoured men, bringing a boy of my name, with a forehead that I know and golden hair, to this place—then fair to look upon, with not a trace of this day's disfigurement—and I hear him tell the child my story, with a tender and faltering voice.
>
> "It is a far, far better thing that I do, than I have ever done; it is a far, far better rest that I go to, than I have ever known."